Dawn's Early Light

Don Candy

DAWN'S EARLY LIGHT

Dawn's Early Light

This novel is a work of fiction. Names, characters, places and incidents are either the product of the author's imagination or are used fictitiously. Any resemblance to actual events or locales or persons, living or dead is entirely coincidental.

No part of this material may be reproduced in any form without express written permission from the author and/or publisher.

No representation is expressed or implied, with regard to accuracy of the information contained in this work of fiction and no legal responsibility can be accepted for omissions and/or errors.

Copyright © 2018 by Donald W Candy
All Rights Reserved.
ISBN: 978-0-9964409-3-6

DAWN'S EARLY LIGHT

This work is dedicated to the men and women of the United States Armed Services world wide, especially to our Special Forces, who work tirelessly to protect us and our freedom 24/7/52, most often without our knowledge of their heroic deeds. God Bless Them All!

DON CANDY

ACKNOWLEDGMENTS

My heartfelt thanks to all my family and friends who gave me encouragement and ultimately enough time to complete this book. A special thanks to my best critics and editors: Paul Herrick for his knowledge, both technical and general, of just about every aspect of this book; military, aircraft, flying, aerodynamics, parachuting and myriad other related systems. Brad Collard for his willingness to drop everything he's doing to give me meaningful feedback every time I send him a manuscript. Rob Quintrell for his continued support and valuable feedback. Larry O'Dell for his undying encouragement. And finally my darling wife Karan, for her support, encouragement and willingness to carve periods of quiet writing time for me out of our busy schedule.

PROLOGUE

Three Hundred Miles Southwest of Taiwan
Tuesday, February 20, 1990 0520 hrs, Local Time

Commander Ashleigh McKensie glanced at her mach meter after nosing her F/A-18 Hornet into a shallow dive with her burners lit. She was only 2400 feet above the water, not much room to dive, but she had to run that missile out of fuel before it got to her. Two point zero on the mach meter – zero point two mach faster than her F/A-18C Hornet should do in low level flight but still a little slower than the Soviet missile on her tail.

"Commander that missile is a hundred yards behind you and slowly gaining – your last flares ignited behind it!" yelled Gator Two, McKensie's wingman. Her life had already begun flashing before her – there was nothing more she could do - other than eject and let that missile take her favorite Hornet into the deep blue. She heard Gator Two yell, "EJECT, EJECT, EJECT". She yanked the throttles and the stick back in an effort to slow down enough to eject. This caused the missile to swing wide and then overcorrect She looked over her shoulder and saw the heat seeking missile re-converging on her vertical track and then the exhaust expired – the missile was out of fuel – but it was too late. It was too close. Before she could accelerate the missile coasted into her starboard engine and exploded . . .

Three Hours Earlier

Night takeoff from an aircraft carrier has always been a hair-raising experience for all carrier pilots. On a Nimitz Class Carrier like the *USS Carl Vinson* in a fully loaded attack aircraft like the

DON CANDY

F/A-18C Hornet piloted tonight by Squadron Leader Ashleigh McKensie, the pucker factor, always present when operating from a carrier at night, was at least twice that of a normal training flight.

Commander McKensie was leading a flight of three Hornets on a face-off mission in response to the sinking of a Filipino fishing boat by a Chinese MiG-19 yesterday; fifteen miles off the coast of the Amphitrite Group of the Paracel Islands in the South China Sea. Almost every country bordering the South China Sea had at one time or another laid claim to these islands but China currently occupied them and had also recently laid claim through the United Nations to pretty much the entire South China Sea. The United States, a friend to most of the local countries involved, defended the international maritime law limiting the sovereign authority of any country to twelve miles off its shore and countered, once again, China's aggressive claims to international waters. Thus, this mission; to remind China that there was no international legal precedent or mechanism for claiming ownership of international waters. This was the third mission of a similar nature executed by *Carl Vinson* Hornets in the last month – the second for Squadron Leader Ashleigh McKensie.

"They need to make these damned helmets lighter," she thought to herself as her head was snapped backward against her headrest when the catapult shuttle was released and then again yanked forward 2.6 seconds later when the shuttle released the aircraft as it was just getting airborne doing a hundred fifty five knots. The flight formed up in a left echelon formation which they would hold loosely relying on exhaust light to maintain position until daybreak. No identifying lights on a combat mission. They had launched four hundred miles northeast of their target and were cruising at two hundred twenty five knots to preserve fuel while the *Carl Vinson* steamed toward them. The plan was to fly between two groups of tiny islands staying thirteen miles or more off shore. This would take them through a twenty eight mile wide channel between the Amphitrite Group and the Crescent Group of the Paracel Islands – something the Chinese didn't like very much. The crescent group lay to the southwest and the Amphitrite Group to the northeast. The entire Crescent Group and one Island in the Amphitrite Group were occupied by the Chinese but the Islands

DAWN'S EARLY LIGHT

were claimed by four other South China Sea nations as well as China. In 1974 China tried to lay claim to (control of) the entire South China Sea – an action soundly rejected by members of the UN including those bordering that body of water.

The moon, just a sliver tonight, hung a little off kilter about twenty degrees above the western horizon. The stars were brilliant at angels two zero – twenty thousand feet above the dark and peaceful sea below.

They expected a visit by two or more MiG-19s from an Air Base on Hainan Dao Island north of the Paracels. So far this latest set of face-off missions had resulted in close-in passes where opposing pilots made faces at each other and the MiGs tried to force the Hornets inside the twelve mile limit. Things might be a little more difficult if the chinks were flying a real airplane – the MiG-19 was no match for the Hornet.

As first light spread over the glassy sea from their rear left, Commander McKensie pressed the mike button on her stick, "Gator Flight this is Gator One, follow me down to angels six and close up to attack formation. Watch your GPS track carefully and let me know if anything looks wrong. We don't want to start a war out here because of a malfunction. Acknowledge. One out."

"Two."

"Three."

As the morning sunlight intensified to their rear left, the deep purple shadows in the eastern sky gave way to dark red, orange and pale yellow striations in the thin stratus cloud layers above them. Ashleigh couldn't avoid momentarily diverting her thoughts to probably the most beautiful sunrise she'd ever witnessed. *"Dawn's Early Light,"* she said aloud to herself as she wondered if the sunrise that inspired Francis Scott Key to pen our National Anthem could have been nearly as spectacular as the one before her eyes at this very moment.

"God made this beautiful planet, our home, among the billions of stars in the universe," she thought, "and humankind is intently focused on fucking it up.

"Father," she prayed aloud, "please let this world of ours last at least until I die of old age with lots of grandchildren. And Father, please keep watching my six while I hunt and kill the bad guys hear on Earth."

While flying their route along the northern edge of the archipelago things seemed peaceful. Ordinarily the Chinese would have intercepted them on the north side of the archipelago. Maybe they weren't going to waste the fuel today. Nothing north on the radar, but they could be hugging the waves below. Ashleigh began her wide turn south keeping the flight firmly glued to the pre-programmed GPS track. Still nothing. Then as she looked up from her Horizontal Situation Display (HSD) while rolling out onto a southeast course between the island groups she noticed what looked like a gunship about two thirds of the way down the channel and a few miles off to the south, probably inside the Chinese claimed territorial waters.

"Gator Flight, this is One, let's keep our eyes peeled. I don't like the looks of that gunship lying in wait down channel. Look's like he's not in what the Chinese consider international waters – this could be an ambush. Look for others boats or MiGs coming out low from one of the islands." Then she saw them . . . "MiGs, two of 'em eleven o'clock low – on the deck. Arm your flares. Let's stay calm; we don't want to be party to an incident here. You guys watch the MiGs – they might separate. I'll watch the boat."

"Flight, this is Three. The MiG to our port (left) is coming up, I'll take him".

"Roger Three, this is Two, I've got the starboard MiG".

"Flight, One. Arm your guns. Do NOT fire unless fired upon and target is clearly in international airspace. I'm going to move us to a parallel course three miles to the northeast." McKensie was doing everything she could to avoid an incident.

The F/A-18 sported a six barrel 20 mm Gatling cannon. Today they were each carrying four active radar guided air-to-air missiles; the Air Intercept Missile (AIM)-120, also known as the Advanced Medium Range Air-to-Air Missile (AMRAAM), two AIM-9 Sidewinder, infrared heat seeking, air-to-air missiles and two Air to Ground Missiles; the (AGM)-65D Maverick, air-to-ground (tank, ship, building, etc.) missiles, with imaging infrared seekers –

DAWN'S EARLY LIGHT

an excellent choice of weapons for the threats they were now facing.

"OK guys they're still coming up to us – don't let them get behind you. This looks like a full blown ambush. I'm going to break off and make a run at the gunboat on the deck until I get to their airspace. We need to know what we're dealing with here. Sure glad we brought the Mavericks. Turn your cameras on."

Commander McKensie rolled over and headed straight for the water, rolled another one hundred eighty degrees on the way down and pulled out of the dive just a hundred feet above the surface headed straight for the gunboat. As she approached the twelve mile boundary, about a mile from the boat she realized that it had no guns - then she saw three figures emerging from the forward cabin and taking positions on the bow, each holding a shoulder mounted weapon. One of the figures fired a missile at her!

"OH SHIT!" she yelled to the flight. "HSSMs (Heat Seeking Shoulder-mounted Missiles) – three of 'em. I'm gettin' the hell out of Dodge!"

She had three choices; she could launch a Maverick or two which she had armed on the way down and take out the boat which could cause an international incident because the gunboat was definitely inside the twelve mile limit. Or, she could execute an Immelmann (half vertical loop followed by a half roll. A maneuver used to gain altitude and reverse direction – the reverse of the split S maneuver she used to get to her current position), light her burners on the way up and run like hell. Or she could do both. She had to jettison her missiles if she was going to run. So she fired both her Mavericks at the gunboat, hauled her Hornet vertical and lit her burners as she jettisoned her sidewinders and AMRAAMs. The F/A-18 could reach mach 1.8 from sub-sonic flight in about four and a half seconds in low level flight. She was pretty sure she could outrun any shoulder fired missile the Chinese had but she was praying these guys didn't have the Soviet made 9K38 ILGA missile. She recalled it could do mach two plus a little versus her maximum (unclassified) speed of mach 1.8.

It was in fact, exactly that type of Soviet missile that they had fired at her. As she rolled out of the Immelmann, approaching mach 1.5, Gator Three called, "One, you've got a missile on your tail and it's gaining on you. We've been fired on! Cuffs off?"

Ashleigh replied, "Yeah, you guys take out the assholes in the MiGs – I got the boat already. We're not even gonna leave an oil slick out here. I'm gonna fire counter measures - call the hit for me; quickly please!."

The problem she faced was the second and then more likely the third missile. She was going to fire two thermite flares to fake out the first missile. These flares would fire slightly upward, ignite and then and spiral back toward the flight path of the F-18. Each would produce a tremendous heat signature. The missile processor would then have two converging primary heat signatures to choose from. To be sure the counter measures worked she would throttle her engines back out of after-burner briefly to reduce her heat signature and jink to the left to keep her hot engine off the boresight of the missile. The missile shooters had to wait a second or two between launches to keep the missiles from shooting each other down. So when Gator Three called the explosion of the first missile in the flare's heat signature it would be difficult to predict what the second missile would do. The slight loss of speed caused by retracting the throttles momentarily would put the second missile in fairly close proximity recovering from being called off course by the flares and maneuvers intended for the first missile s well as its resulting explosion. She decided to fire two more flares immediately when Three called the first hit, and then wait for the hit-call on the second one to fire a third set of flares.

Gator Three called, "First missile killed!"

She fired the second set of flares.

A second later Gator Three called, "Second missile killed!"

She immediately fired the third set of flares. Ashleigh couldn't believe it; the second missile went for the flares. Maybe the third... But her elation didn't last long – just a split second. The third set of flares had ignited behind the missile, which now, having only one target, flew directly into her starboard engine exhaust. Simultaneously she heard "EJECT, EJECT, EJECT" from Gator Two. She had already pulled the handle. Just as the rockets in her ejection seat fired the missile blew up inside the engine. The

DAWN'S EARLY LIGHT

explosion of the engine was horrific, sending her tumbling out of the cockpit head over heels in her ejection seat. She immediately felt severe pain in her right thigh and buttock. The ejection seat flight system stabilized her in mid air and her chute was able to open normally.

As McKensie floated toward the ocean after her chute opened she heard on her helmet VHF; "Two this is Three, your MiG is headed for the Commander! You see him?"

"This is Two, copy that Three, I've got a Sidewinder right behind him – hold one. . . Splash one MiG."

"Three, this is Two - I'm gonna follow the commander down and check out what's left of the boat. Go get the other MiG, climb to angels ten and call for help."

"Roger Two, I've got an AMRAAM after him already, hold one. . .Splash that second MiG! I'm going up for help as soon as I send one of my Mavericks to the chink's boat. It's listing but not down yet."

"Three, this is Two I'm also sending one now – that'll leave us with one more each. Four Mavericks will take that boat and who ever's in it to the bottom pretty quick. We'll go bingo in about thirty minutes (bingo meant just enough fuel to return to the carrier with minimum reserve). I'll give you a sitrep on the Commander. Have 'em send a couple of Hornets out here to guard her 'til the chopper can get here."

"Did you get everything on camera?" asked Gator Three.

"Roger that brother, got it all with GPS position and time tags. We'll probably never hear from the chinks about this little party. How'd your video look?"

"Same as you – I got everything and all the tags.

"Three, here's your sitrep; alert and waving. Blood in the water! Tell 'em to hurry!"

As Commander Ashleigh McKensie bobbed in the South China Sea under a beautiful crystal clear sky to the east, she realized she was bleeding badly from the eight inch gash in her right thigh. The shrapnel from her exploding engine had penetrated her ejection seat and she had been fortunate the ejection system had not malfunctioned. Now she had to find and disperse her shark repellant before her successful ejection became all for naught.

Chapter One

Forty Two Thousand Feet Above the Yellow Sea Saturday, May 5, 1990, 0015 Hrs, Local Mission Time

"Okay Commander. We're at Angels Four Two, ten minutes out, the ramp is yours," barked the pilot of the CAPV-727.

Thank God for small favors - in this case a pretty large one. We were at Angels Four Two - 42,000 feet above sea level on a night as dark as they come. A new moon. All of our equipment and all of our training is focused on nighttime operations. The darker the better. My uncle Bo Jameson and I, now made brothers by the yet to be written Navy SEAL creed, and Master Chief Petty Officer Rob Curtis were ten minutes from our IP (mission Initial Position) on our most dangerous mission yet. We had a fifty two nautical mile traverse to our target, the last seven to ten miles of which would be through dense clouds. We were depending on a very complex *Airborne SEAL Delivery System* (ASDS); a computer/GPS controlled High Altitude High Opening (HAHO) parachute system that our SEAL team helped developed during the mid eighties. It allowed multiple teams of up to six Special Operators each to traverse up to sixty nautical miles from an aircraft at an altitude of up to forty five thousand feet to a specific target; each operator landing within two feet of a pre-programmed spot. It did this using a built in Automatic Landing System (ALS). In addition to the ALS and the hi-tech parachute, the system consisted of a pressure suit with oxygen, a chest-pack computer, battery belt, a helmet with an integrated GPS receiver, classified infra-red (IR) night vision, a GPS driven visor system that displayed the relative location of each member of the team as well as the image from the night vision system, an intra-team secure communication system and a separate satellite communication system allowing secure communications to friendly forces anywhere in the world. Upon landing, the parachute and pressure suit could be discarded leaving the rest of the system completely operational with eighty hours of remaining battery life. If everything worked correctly we would arrive at our target a little less than two hours from now.

On a dark night like this we had some real advantages. First of all, stealth. Our delivery systems are essentially silent from the ground, whether the CIA's covert 727 or practically any military transport capable of flying above twenty thousand feet and able to dump special operators safely at night. Our parachute system makes only a small noise when opening and at high altitude can not be heard from the ground. On a cloudy night parachutes are very difficult to see after penetrating the cloud layer even when looking for them. Secondly, most of the world's military and police forces use an ancient light amplification technology which uses ambient light to generate a fuzzy green image in which it is difficult to pick out a stationary human target over ten yards away. These night vision systems are useless in total darkness. Our highly classified infrared systems, on the other hand, work best on cool nights in total darkness. Our night vision technology isn't limited by most atmospheric conditions such as fog, smoke and clouds – even rain. We learned a while back that by staying ahead of our enemies in night vision technology we *own the night*. In any enemy engagement, we do *not* believe in a fair fight.

Bo, Master Chief Rob Curtis, and I were already sealed up in our pressurized high altitude flight suits and communicating with the pilot through the ASDS (Airborne SEAL Delivery System) team network. The pilot had just given us control of the ramp on the Covert Air Penetration Vehicle (CAPV-727), a well equipped, highly modified Boeing 727 Airliner built for the CIA which was capable of passing for a commercial airline passenger or cargo plane in all phases of operation. It could land as a commercial

DAWN'S EARLY LIGHT

flight at Los Angeles International, or even Beijing China for that matter. As long as the paperwork was done properly no one would be the wiser. For those of you who missed the hay-day of the 727, it was the smaller three engine Boeing with stairs that retracted into the fuselage aft of the cabin.

We were members of a SEAL team called DEVGRU, the Naval Special Warfare DEVelopment GRoUp. From its inception in 1980 until 1987 this team was known as Seal Team Six. When formed there were only two other SEAL teams; one and two. Its founder, Richard Marcinko, wanted to keep the KGB guessing about SEAL Teams three, four and five, which, of course, didn't exist at that time.

We were the DEVGRU Black Angel Team (BAT), attached to the SEAL Black Assault Squadron. Our job was to introduce the latest technology into the development cycle of all Special Forces equipment, making it generations ahead of the current state-of-the-art. And then, to test those systems on combat missions before and during initial deployment to special ops units in all the services. So we were the development / test arm of DEVGRU located at El Centro NAF (Naval Air Facility, sort of like a junior Naval Air Station - NAS). The operational arm and headquarters of DEVGRU were located at Dam Neck Virginia. We joked that our primary job was trying to spend all the gold in Fort Knox. Bo joined the group as a three tour veteran A6 Intruder pilot in Vietnam with lots of post Vietnam HAHO/HALO experience. Rob was the previous temporary commander of SEAL Team Four. He and his team joined up with ours on several early missions using the new hi-tech equipment, after which he decided to move over to DEVGRU. I joined the team as a Lieutenant test pilot / engineer without the foggiest idea of what I was getting into. The BAT consisted of only twelve men, six SEAL operators and six very intelligent civilians.

Bo Jameson was pushing forty, about six two, lean, rugged, sandy hair, intense blue eyes. Didn't smile much. He was an accomplished pilot with over twelve thousand hours. Most of which was as a Navy pilot. He also had more than twenty one hundred HALO/HAHO jumps, possibly a record for all military forces. Bo owned an airport about thirty miles from downtown

Manhattan, Kansas – *Jameson Flight Service,* (JFS). I actually owned ten percent of JFS. Oh yeah, he's my uncle. More about that later.

Rob and I, each a little over six feet, could pass for brothers although he had nine years on me. We brought the humor and wise cracks to the team and we both kept short cropped brown hair and beards. Rob, A Master Chief Petty Officer with eighteen years experience in the Navy, eleven as a SEAL, came from a small farming community in central California. He had finished his degree in Language Arts at Cal State via Navy sponsored correspondence courses but decided he didn't want to do the officer thing. I bug him about that more often than I should. He's Fluent in English, Spanish, Arabic, Russian and Farsi. Smarter, more capable and much more experienced than most Navy Lieutenants I know.

I'm Sam McKensie; Aeronautical engineer, test pilot, hornet driver, Navy SEAL and the devoted husband to my wife Ashleigh, a former pursuit / instructor pilot flying disguised F-5Es and F/A-18 Hornets at the Navy's Fighter Weapons School known as 'Top Gun' at Miramar NAS, California.

Bo calmly asked, "ready?" over the ASDS network. Bo, Rob, Hal Nicholson and I were sealed in our pressure suits in the 'ready to pressurize' mode which the system automatically enters after passing all ready-to-fly self tests. After receiving a thumbs up from each of us he raised the safety shield and pressed the 'depressurize' button on the aircraft ramp control panel. As the ramp area of the aircraft depressurized our suits automatically pressurized keeping us at a comfortable ten thousand foot ambient pressure – no major ear popping. We were approaching a relatively small target on top of an eight story building so we timed our jumps at fifteen second intervals to allow the person in front to clear the area before the next person arrived.

Rob was first to go so he took his place at the top of the ramp as it lowered; waiting for the red blinking light on his right side to turn solid green. When it turned green, he walked down the 727's stairs and jumped. My turn. When my fifteen second timer flashed on my visor screen I jumped, then fifteen seconds later Bo jumped.

DAWN'S EARLY LIGHT

Then Lt. Commander Hal Nicholson, also a DEVGRU SEAL and BAT Team member, sprang into action. He was suited up but not jumping. His job was ramp management, which included the launch of a nine hundred pound cargo pack with all of our equipment in it twenty five seconds after Bo's exit. He pushed the button that collapsed the stairs on the 727 ramp, rolled the cargo pack to the top of the ramp, now actually a chute, attached the static-line ripcord to the ring provided on the left wall of the ramp area and waited for his timer to flash. When it did he pulled a lever on the left wall that opened a slot under the front wheels of the dolly supporting the cargo pack such that the surface of the dolly matched the slope of the cargo chute and the package slid gracefully down the chute into the dark void below.

Nicholson, who was wearing a full-up ASDS suit could immediately see the blue colored dot on his visor screen moving quickly rearward from the aircraft and he noted the three half second flashes of the blue dot that indicated a successful deployment. He announced over the net, "Good drop – Godspeed brothers."

The CAPV-727 maintained course, speed and altitude. After all, to the rest of the world it was a scheduled commercial aircraft on its way from Tokyo To Beijing. . .

As I swung gently beneath my chute my visor displayed a red dot (Rob) about three quarters of a mile ahead of my location (center screen), a green dot (Bo) about three quarters of a mile behind me and a blue dot (the cargo) a mile and a half behind Bo. So we were all out successfully and on our way. There was no moon but the starlight faintly illuminated the cloud deck, far below us at about fifteen thousand feet, providing a surreal, almost unimaginable feeling of being suspended in an alien environment. The feeling became more intense as time elapsed. The clouds looked like a bed of dimly lit fluffy cotton candy into which we would eventually be enveloped. I grew more familiar with this phenomenon with each mission and offset its weird effect by ignoring the fact that soon we would be landing in the bad guy's back yard without their knowledge and instead concentrating on thoughts that I seldom had time to ponder.

I had almost two hours and a lot to think about. First things first; the love of my life, my wife Ashleigh. When we met I was a test pilot at China Lake Navy Weapons Center near Ridgecrest California - in the Mohave Desert - testing High-speed Anti Radiation Missile (HARM) variants, mostly for foreign allied aircraft; British, German, NATO, etc. She was a basic jet instructor at San Diego NAS flying T-38s. For me it was love at first sight – a beautiful five foot four blue eyed blonde jet flight instructor – what else could a guy ask for? Less than a year later we were married on the beach at White Bay, Jost Van Dyke – the most beautiful beach in the British Virgin Islands.

Three months ago we finished our F/A-18 Hornet Squadron Commander tours aboard the USS *Carl Vinson* at the invitation of her Captain, Joe Garcia, the previous commander of the DEVGRU BAT – my Uncle Bo is the current commander. Ash and I had decided that we wanted to start a family. But things just didn't turn out that way while she was employed as a Top Gun pursuit pilot and I was still involved in ASDS production, deployment and training. So we decided to put off the family thing for a while and go be fighter pilots – and it had been fun. We could have done another tour, but while she was recovering from her little incident in the South China Sea we decided to take two weeks of the month's leave we'd accumulated to vacation in Tahiti and then take assignments back in the States. So we rented one of those little huts out over the water and had the first real vacation alone since sailing in the BVI on our honeymoon almost five years ago. We had two days left in paradise when I got a hand delivered message – no phone in our little hut – giving me a week to report to home base at El Centro NAF. At least we got to finish our vacation.

So I get back to my buddies at DEVGRU and we got all briefed up and trained for yet another trip down range to God knows where and she calls me day before yesterday from Miramar saying she just left the base doctor's office and she's pregnant! So at last I'm going to be a father – if I live through this mission *and* make it back to the real world.

DAWN'S EARLY LIGHT

Sometimes, when I have time to think - like now - I wonder what the hell I'm doing here. I left college with a degree in Aeronautical Engineering, a lot of flight time and a high level understanding of complex systems to become a test pilot for the Navy. I didn't even really know what a SEAL was, nor did I know that my uncle *was* one. I went to work for DEVGRU before I knew that it was previously SEAL Team VI, the tip of the special forces spear which became responsible for helping develop and test early high-tech weapon systems like ASDS for the Navy and then pushing them through the development cycle with defense companies like Texas Instruments, Lockheed and Boeing or government oriented organizations like DARPA, JPL and Aerospace Corporation for deployment to all special forces organizations. I became the lead design/development/test person on the ASDS program and helped TI, the lead contractor on the program, get the system into production. ASDS became very successful during its first few missions and caused a lot of visibility at the top of the command chain. I was then told what DEVGRU really was and asked if I would like to become a permanent member at a top secret meeting in front of a group of government dignitaries which included the President. How could I say no? I was just a lowly Lieutenant at that time caught up in circumstance that presented me with an awesome opportunity. All I really wanted to do was fly and have fun. But I jumped into the fire. Since then I've endured extensive water, jungle and arctic training, all part of the grueling Navy SEAL BUD/S training – a six month plus B*asic U*nderwater D*emolition / S*EAL training program designed to wash out all but the mentally and physically toughest trainees (damned near did me in). Down range I've been shot at a lot and hit a few times, wasted a bunch of bad guys and blown up myriad stuff – I think I'm getting to like this life as a SEAL – and folks, that's scary!

My problem was that 'this life' was beginning to define my being – I'm becoming addicted to the rush and excitement of the mission work and the camaraderie and brotherhood of my team. Part of my problem was my upbringing; growing up in a relatively safe and comfortable environment on a farm in Kansas. Never really seeing or knowing evil. Never understanding that there existed in this world radical elements that hide behind women and children to do their evil deeds or drug lords who routinely slaughtered innocent people as well as their enemies just to make a buck. The satisfaction of bringing these assholes to their own brand of justice grew with each down range assignment, as did my dedication to my brothers and love of my country and family. The average person just can't relate to the things we see and do and the resulting personal pride and honor we feel in doing what we do when we do it well. But then there's the personal sacrifice we endure from the reduced family time and social isolation associated with belonging to one of the world's most clandestine organizations.

*****

In the starlight, the cloud tops far below, I was cold but not uncomfortable. I seemed suspended in a time-warp. It was eerily quiet. Nothing was moving except a shroud puller occasionally making a minor course correction at the command of the ASDS' Automatic Landing System (ALS) which was programmed to land me within an imaginary two foot circle on top of a building somewhere in no mans land.

This would be my fourth ASDS mission through heavy thick clouds. You'd think I'd have enough faith in a system that I helped design to be completely relaxed. Not so. A fifteen second delay between jumps put us a little over three quarters of a mile apart so I couldn't see Rob's IR locator on his helmet in the thick cloud. All I could see was the little colored locator dots from the GPS system. If my system failed I might have no way of knowing for sure which part failed and whether or not I was still heading for the target. On this mission if I missed the target it literally meant a sure and very unpleasant death. This always caused a mild state of uneasiness until I broke through the clouds and once again acquired visual reference to the jumper in front of me – but tonight the uneasiness was a little more that mild. I think I know a little too much about how complex this system really is, I know where the hell we're headed and I'm about to become a father. Rob doesn't have the detailed technical understanding of ASDS that I do –

that's why I always honor his standing request to go first.

Then just before I broke out of the clouds, the little green x, representing the two foot landing circle pre-programmed into the ASDS, came into view at the top of my visor. I could see the target, or at least its location, on my facemask display. The tension evaporated, replaced with a feeling of mild elation, only to be gradually replaced by the apprehension which had subconsciously nagged me from the minute I was first briefed on the location of this mission – three days ago.

At the target everything went well. Rob was clear when I landed and I was clear when Bo touched down. I Watched the cargo pack, clearly visible with my IR night vision, s-turn and then turn into the light wind for a soft landing. It never ceased to amaze me even though I designed and tested that part of the system and had watched it work many times. The large nine hundred pound cushioned canvas equipment canister made just a slight thump as it settled on the roof of the Ministry of National Defense of The People's Republic of (North) Korea (PRK) in the center of Pyongsong, twenty two miles north of Pyongyang, North Korea's capital city - deep in Indian Territory. Enemy territory - completely surrounded by bad guys. . .

Chapter Two

CIA Headquarters, Langley, Virginia
Friday, May 4, 1330 hrs EST
Saturday, May 5, 1990, 0230 Hrs Mission Local Time

"They're down, situation nominal", said CIA Director Bill Conroy. A nominal situation report (sitrep) meant everything was going according to plan – so far. Because we were in hostile territory our satellite communications were necessarily brief. The system used the same very low power subcarrier-encoded, pseudo random code protected spread spectrum technology used by GPS, making detection extremely difficult if not impossible. Still, we couldn't be too careful. The stateside members of the secure network mission team included CIA Director Conroy; Wayne Hawkins, the CIA's nuclear weapons expert at Langley and prior manager of ORNL (Oak Ridge National Laboratory); President Bradley Stevens; Admiral George Bennington, JSOC Commander (Joint Special Operations Command); and the Chairman of the Joint Chiefs, Admiral Gerald Sterett. All, except Stevens were gathered in Conroy's secure situation room at CIA Headquarters, Langley, Virginia. The President had a secure video link in his secure situation room in the basement of the White House.

The fourth member of our down range mission team was an

DAWN'S EARLY LIGHT

in-country CIA agent named Chen Duong-ku. This in-country four man team and the four gathered at CIA, Langley plus the President were the only team members fully knowledgeable of the details of this mission. All others had only compartmental knowledge; only the information necessary for them to successfully accomplish their part of the mission; Top Secret - Sensitive Compartmental Information; TS/SCI. All information regarding the mission was classified Top Secret, Need-To-Know – TSNTK.

Since Duong was somehow pronounced sort of like Young, we called him Young-ku as did his fellow agents. Young-ku was a twenty six year old Olympic wrestler. His parents had inherited a nice restaurant just prior to the Korean War in the early fifties and were very well to do by North Korean standards. They had been subversively anti-communist before, during and after the conflict. After the communist take-over they helped their son develop an occupation that allowed world-wide travel. International athletic competition was a highly visible well compensated occupation in North Korea as it was in all communist countries.

As Young-ku gained athletic stature in the world circuit as a champion wrestler, he was approached by the PR(N)K (Peoples Republic of (North) Korea) government to take on a second job. He became an agent of North Korea's RGB (Reconnaissance General Bureau – the CIA of the PRK). On his third mission, a trip to Kazakhstan while competing in an international wrestling meet, he was approached by a local CIA agent and gladly signed up as a double agent for the U.S. His parents were delighted when he became an 'agent of the west', and they were, of course, sworn to secrecy by Young-ku. Abdu Kamali, the CIA agent who recruited Young-ku in Kazakhstan, was also an in-country double agent working for the Kazakhstan Intelligence Arm of the KGB (small world).

As the future of Kazakhstan was slowly turning toward independence while the Soviet Union crumbled as a result of the economic pressures from the cold war, it discovered that its inventory of 1,410 nuclear warheads actually totaled 1,416. After an exhaustive search through the documentation, the responsible agency discovered that they had received an undocumented shipment of six MIRV (Multiple Independently-targetable Reentry

Vehicle) nuclear warheads with serial numbers not matching any of the Russian documentation. These individual warheads, when disconnected from the MIRV guidance subsystem, weighed two hundred eighty eight pounds each. Each warhead had the destructive power of just over twenty five times that of *Fat Man*, the plutonium bomb dropped on Nagasaki Japan on August 9, 1945.

This discovery was made after reconciliation of inventories with mother Russia at the resumption of the Strategic Arms Reduction Treaty negotiations between the U.S. and the U.S.S.R. in 1987. As time went by Kazakhstan found itself facing a number of dilemmas. At the top of the list were how to economically survive their rapidly approaching independence from mother Russia and what to do with the six nuclear warheads that nobody knew they had. After much wringing of hands and gnashing of teeth they decided on the obvious solution; sell the nukes to the highest bidder and hide the money in their tax receipts. Their first potential customer was the North Korean RGB.

The PRK had barely enough money to maintain basic, fundamental governance. In fact, thousands (some say millions) of their citizens had starved to death and millions more were barely surviving. And yet their military budget held funds earmarked for 'buying technology' – like nuclear weapons. Their baseline strategic defense plan called for three nuclear warheads and the necessary delivery systems for retaliation to a South Korean or Japanese attack. This was their need and they would push hard in negotiations to buy the three warheads from Kazakhstan. After three months of negotiations they succeeded.

Fortunately for us, one of our CIA double agents acting as an intelligence agent for Iraq was able to buy a fourth warhead without the PRK's knowledge that the fourth unit even existed – after all, they were a very poor country and had need for only three in their defense planning. Kazakhstan negotiated with North Korea for the three units until they had reached their financial limit and then more than doubled their income by selling another unit to Iraq – they thought. The total sale netted Kazakhstan a little over the equivalent of nine hundred million dollars U.S., a nice financial shot in the arm for an emerging nation.

DAWN'S EARLY LIGHT

Using the single warhead procured by agent Kamali from Kazakhstan Wayne Hawkins and his team at Langley spent a month designing and building three fake nuclear cores – the central part of the warhead containing the radio active material that causes the nuclear explosion. These cores looked and weighed exactly the same as the real ones – about the size of a small grapefruit. They even gave off the same level of residual plutonium radiation. This mission was to covertly substitute the fake cores for the real ones in the three North Korean warheads thus rendering them nuclear duds – they would still explode but do minimal, non nuclear, damage.

After listening to the details of the infil (infiltration), Stephens said, "Ok gentlemen, let's stay close to our secure comms and we'll reconvene as necessary when we get updates. So far everything looks good . . . Stevens out." Which meant the meeting was over, for now.

Chapter Three

PRK Ministry of Defense Building, Pyongsong
Saturday, May 5, 1990, 0300, Mission Local Time

Master Chief Rob Curtis approached the roof access door and carefully knocked three times, waited two seconds and knocked once again. The door opened and a grinning Young-ku greeted him in near perfect English. "You must be Chief Curtis. I'm Chen Doung-Ku – just call me Young-ku," said the handsome five foot eight, muscle-bound young Korean. Rob handed him a pair of Infra-red goggles and after putting them on Young-ku looked all around the roof top in amazement. "Can I keep these?" he asked.

"No way, man. This technology is top secret – if we're compromised most of the tools we brought with us will have to be destroyed. Good to finally meet you Young-ku. We've heard a lot of good stuff about your service – some day we'll all have time to relax over a beer, but right now we need to get these nukes neutered. Lead the way," whispered Curtis.

The nuclear warheads were currently stored in one of four limited access storage rooms in the basement of the building. The Deputy Chief of PRK Armament was preparing an assembly building and launch pad at the Chong-Fal Missile Site to mate the warheads to the nose of three Soviet R-17 VTO (Scud-D) missiles. Young-ku was assigned temporary PRK leadership roles when not on a mission or wrestling in the world circuit. He was currently in charge of security at the PRK MOD Building.

Chong-Fal was located just north of the DMZ on the eastern

DAWN'S EARLY LIGHT

coast of North Korea, the PRK location closest to Tokyo. The assembly building would be complete within weeks, at which time the warheads would be transported to that site. The Scuds had the necessary range to cover all of South Korea and eighty percent of Japan. A later model missile was promised that would include the rest of Japan and Taiwan in the kill radius.

One of the rooms in the basement was currently not in use. Young-ku had reprogrammed the combination lock on that door so that our team could work nights in the warhead storage room and sleep days in the unused room with the reprogrammed lock. Master Chief Curtis had been to the CIA nuke school and was familiar with all Soviet and Chinese nuclear warheads. He also spent the last month working with Wayne Hawkins and his team creating and installing one of the fake nuclear cores into the identical warhead obtained by CIA agent Kamali as he was masquerading as an Iraqi agent. Replacing a core was a two man job using special equipment to disassemble, replace the core, and reassemble the warhead. The third man was necessary to assist with the timely movement of equipment from the roof down nine flights of stairs and between rooms in the basement twice a day to facilitate the swap and then to stand guard over the hallway, stairs and freight elevator during the swap. Also, the three SEALs planned to rotate in the close-up core swap activity to minimize exposure to radiation even though Hawkins had assured them that the protective gear they brought with them, a large part of the 900 pound payload, would be entirely adequate.

Young-ku would assist in the first night's transportation of equipment, recon of the warhead storage room and a dry run on the ingress, cleanup and egress operations to be executed for each core swap over the next three nights. After this first night the team wouldn't see him again until the last swap was complete – unless there were problems.

"Okay guys, it's been a long night already and we've still got a good four hours to go. First we've got to get everything into the home room then do a dry run into and out of the shop," whispered Captain Bo Jameson, "let's get a move on!" 'Home' and 'Shop' were the names they had chosen for the room they would live in and the room (laboratory) in which the warheads were stored,

27

respectively. After all the planned setup was completed sleep came quickly.

* * * *

Bo felt a gentle vibration from his watch. A quick look told him it was already 1830 hrs local time (6:30 p.m.) He felt as if he'd slept only twenty minutes when in fact they'd slept for a little over nine hours. He rolled over and shook my shoulder, "Up & at 'em Sam, it's 1830 already."

I'd had a restless sleep for about the last hour and was ready to get moving. Rob was already up getting things ready for the night's effort. The Chinese self-inflating mattresses we used were amazingly comfortable. Probably sold in U.S. department stores for ten times what they cost here.

Chapter Four

PRK Ministry of Defense Building, Pyongsong
Sunday, May 6, 1990, 0330 hrs, Local Mission Time

We successfully made the transfer of equipment from home to shop, had set up the disassembly holding fixture, placed the first warhead securely in the fixture, a three man job, and were ready to begin the core swap. The really important part of this operation was being sure the warhead didn't inadvertently fall. The Russians designed this warhead for an aerial detonation at twelve hundred feet for maximum area of destruction on the ground. They used an accelerometer to arm the warhead when the post-launch acceleration reached twelve g's and a barometric altimeter to detonate it when it reached twelve hundred feet directly above the target. The altitude had to be set prior to arming the warhead but the g setting was constant. Dropping the unit on a concrete floor could actually arm the warhead leaving only the altimeter to keep the city of Pyongsong, including us, from vaporizing.

Disassembly and reassembly were tedious but relatively easy from a mechanical perspective, but electronically it was quite complex. The procedure had to be followed very carefully. A wrong move in this area could cause problems ranging anywhere from making the bomb totally useless to generating a mushroom cloud much larger than the one at Hiroshima. Rob and I handled the first swap in five and a half hours. The total time for the swap including move-in, set-up, tear-down and move-out was seven hours and fifteen minutes. We made sure the room looked exactly like the pictures we had taken during the dry run earlier today. Rob and Bo were slated for the second core swap tonight - but for now food and sleep were the order of business.

So far all was well. . .

We had just finished dinner. Or was it breakfast? Didn't matter. Our Russian MRE's (Meals Ready to Eat) were all the same. We heard two loud raps on our little hideaway door, followed two seconds later by a single loud rap. I grabbed my Glock and approached the door. I knocked softly once and received two soft knocks two seconds later. I carefully opened the door and saw the smiling face of Young-ku. I let him in.

"A minor glitch in our plans has occurred," said Young-ku with a more serious smile on his face. "Two technicians will arrive from the Chong-Fal Missile Site this afternoon at around 1300. They will re-examine the warheads; weight, dimensions, etc. so the marriage with the Scud-D missiles will go without surprise. It should only take a few hours. The message we received indicated that if there were no foreseen mating problems the warheads would be shipped to Chong-Fal next weekend. The site preparation is almost two weeks ahead of schedule. I brought you a receiver for the infrared AV (Audio/Video) bug I just planted in the Lab The camera is in the ceiling vent near the far left corner of the room.. This afternoon you might choose to have the third man monitor their activity so you'll be sure when they leave and know what to expect. When they're gone and you re-enter the room, be sure to take a new set of pictures so you can restore the room to look exactly as they left it. I will report this to Home Base (Washington D.C.) tomorrow morning."

Well there you go – nothing ever goes as planned in la-la land. Hope to hell one of those PRK idiots doesn't drop a warhead. I'd hate to depend on a Russian made altimeter to keep me here on earth a while longer.

Chapter Five

PRK Ministry of Defense Building, Pyongsong
Sunday, May 6, 1990, 1300 hrs, Local Mission Time

Bo and Rob slept and since I was the third man tonight I woke at 1300 and watched the two commie technicians verify all the interface data they came to get using the warhead we "converted" last night. The A/V snooper Young-ku placed in the lab attached to the serial port of Bo's laptop worked great. I didn't speak Korean so I had no idea what they were talking about but they seemed to be doing what Young-ku said they would.

They had just finished what they had come for and were in the process of leaving when I noticed they had left an oblong black case of some sort on the corner of the work bench. Just peachy! Now we've got another anomaly. Was leaving the case an accident or a reason to return later in the evening to retrieve it? I felt like opening the door and yelling "Hey dumb-fucks, you left something behind." But that would make me dumber than them. Did they know or suspect we were here? Or was I just having an attack of stress induced paranoia? This meant my guard duty tonight was going to be tense, to say the least.

The alarm sounded on Bo's watch at 1630 and Bo and Rob woke up and joined me at the laptop.

"Are they done yet?" Rob asked.

Pointing at the case on the screen, I responded, "Yeah, they're gone – now we've got another fucking problem. They left something behind."

"Looks like a vernier caliper case. Can you zoom in on it?" asked Bo.

"I can zoom, but I have no angle control and it's not in the center of the field of view so th-i-i-i-s is about as close as I can get it. I think I can read the embossed label on the case, yeah . . . looks like 'Chicago'. They're the same Chinese made tools you can buy at discount tool stores in the States."

Bo stared at the screen deep in thought. This was the most dangerous and important mission of his career. Capture meant certain imprisonment and probable torture and death of his team, but the political implications could cause World War III. The North Koreans were not only hostile toward the U.S. and its allies, especially South Korea, Japan and Taiwan, they were totally unpredictable in their actions and reactions. The country's "Dear Father", Kim Il-Sung, was a narcissistic, megalomaniac hell bent on the PRK becoming a nuclear power and standing firmly against South Korea, Japan, the U.S. and most of the rest of the free world.

****

The team had spent a day and a half with Admiral George Bennington, Commander of JSOC, William Conroy, Director of the CIA and various experts and specialists in their respective organizations analyzing potential threats and developing a decision tree that best suited the implicit absence of the U.S. in any conceived outcome of this mission. We were disguised as Russians. Rob was fluent in Russian and Bo and I had a (slow) conversational grasp of it. After our arrival Young-ku incinerated all of our infil (infiltration) equipment including the expensive ASDS systems, parachutes and all. The gear we had left was made in either Russia or China. Our weapons were AK-47s, our clothes were Russian and even the air mattresses we slept on were made in China. We carried cyanide pills and hybrid high explosive thermite grenades with Russian made timers adjustable from one to five minutes – just enough time to take the edge off of life before the big-bang. If we made the wrong decision we would simply

DAWN'S EARLY LIGHT

disappear into the ashes of the PRK Ministry of Defense building. The Ruskies would take the fall.

After the two day session with Bennington and Conroy, et al, we met with President Stevens and Chairman of the Joint Chiefs, Admiral Sterett. Stevens, a past Navy SEAL, JSOC Commander, CIA Director and Senator from Texas and Sterett, also a past SEAL and JSOC Commander reviewed the mission plan and decision tree. With a few suggested changes the mission was approved and we were each asked separately if we wished to not participate.

"Master Chief Curtis?" the president asked.

"I'm in, sir," replied Rob Curtis.

"I'm in also, sir," I replied before the president had a chance to ask.

"We're all in, sir. We discussed this last night." Bo said, glaring at me sideways for interrupting the president.

"Very well then gentlemen, Godspeed and good hunting. And by the way, we have assets in the PRK other than Young-ku. They are not aware of this mission or any of the details leading to its requirement. But if needed we can rely on these assets to assist. CIA Agent Young-ku is aware of this possibility so keep him in the loop on all activity and any deviation to plan."

Admiral Sterett then reminded us of what of the mission's Top Secret Compartmentalized Need to Know classification meant. Basically it meant that there were only seven of us that knew all of the mission data and objectives. All the rest of the team members knew only the details necessary to get their part of the job done and absolutely nothing additional. Everyone one else knew nothing about the mission.

****

Every mission gets fucked up by Murphy's law, which in its short form states; 'if anything can go wrong, it will'. Well Murphy's here in his finest form. The implications of this piece of left behind equipment are not good. This was something obviously not envisioned in our pre-mission planning.

There were three possible outcomes to this little problem:

One; The guy who left the case could return to get it. He probably wouldn't have access to the building at night so he would most likely return in the morning. *Should we chance that?*

Two; If the case was empty or if he didn't need the caliper right away he might not bother to return at all. He could have someone here hold it for him until he returned to transfer the warheads to Chong-Fal next week. *Is it empty? Is he slated to return?*

Three; If, on the other hand the technician did have access to the building at night and returned to the lab (shop) to retrieve the caliper while we were working on the warhead – that was a big problem for us.

We'd have to play it safe and call off tonight's core swap - couldn't take the chance. This would put a crinkle in the exfil (exfiltration – covert egress) support plan and logistics which were set for a night execution this Thursday. This little problem would likely make us a day late.

The only capability we had to communicate with the outside world, including Young-Ku, was our satellite phone. Any other insitu type of communications would be too risky. Bo climbed the stairs and stepped out onto the roof every morning just before sunrise at 0500 local time which is 1900 (yesterday) Miramar time. Satellite phones don't work in large buildings. This was also the only way we could communicate with Young-ku. Young-ku checked in with Miramar at 0600 every day so any problems or changes in plans could be communicated to him then and vice-versa. His phone was kept in his 'office', a small cubicle behind a panel in a false rear wall of a closet in the basement of his family's restaurant behind the wine cellar. If he was caught with a CIA satellite phone he'd be shot within twenty four hours, world class athlete or not. One more day in this God-awful rat hole!

****

So we used the time to get our gear straightened out, compose a brief message for tomorrow morning's report and discuss our

DAWN'S EARLY LIGHT

egress plan, looking for contingencies we hadn't envisioned - like the one we had just encountered. After we'd gotten everything rearranged, sorted our gear into take and leave to be destroyed piles and spent a half hour refining our exfil plan, Bo woke up his lap top to look carefully at the shop for any other clues as to what was going on.

"Holy shit!" he muttered, "the fucking caliper's gone! What the hell's going on here?"

Sure enough the image on the laptop was zoomed in on the work bench just like it had been when we last looked at it four hours ago – no caliper case.

The micro miniature video bug was motion activated to conserve power and disc space on the recorder - Bo's laptop. It remained active for two minutes after its last detected motion. Bo didn't have to back up very far to find the culprit - Young-ku! He had snuck in, retrieved the case and left.

Just as Bo was scrutinizing the time-stamp frame by frame we heard two knocks on our door followed two seconds later by a single knock. Glock in hand, I knocked once and before Young-ku responded Bo said, "It's him, go ahead and open the door."

This young Korean CIA Agent who didn't look a day over eighteen years old and probably had one of the most dangerous jobs in the PRK, never quit smiling. At the other end of that spectrum Captain Bo Jameson, my uncle, never smiled until on his way home from a successful down range assignment. As Commander of Gold Team DEVGRU (the name given SEAL Team VI in 1987 to allow interface with the outside world with contractors, other military units, etc., without exposing the highly classified SEAL Team) he rarely took down range missions unless tagged by 'Higher' (up). 'Higher' meant Commander, JSOC or anyone above.

The smiling Korean double agent told us that at their dinner one of the technicians had mentioned that he'd left a tool in the lab and Young-ku had promised he'd retrieve it for him before he left for Chong-Fal in the morning. He had waited until he was sure the building was empty before retrieving the caliper.

Then he asked, "Do you think you have enough time to

complete tonight's core swap?

Bo replied, "yeah, I think so. Could you stay for a half hour and help us set up? I'm on guard duty tonight so we still have our nuclear expert involved in the swap. If Sam can follow directions we should finish on time. I think we'll be okay Young-ku. Thanks for handling this for us brother – that A/V bug is a lifesaver."

"Japanese technology – probably a copy of a U.S. unit. I brought a new one with a fresh battery. I'll swap it out and test it first thing," replied Young-ku with an even bigger smile. It occurred to me that maybe he was born with a built-in smile and I had just seen his real smile for the first time. Smile or no smile, for a CIA guy he was a damned good troop.

The second core swap went without a hitch. We got the swap completed before 0500 and Bo succeeded in not falling asleep while standing guard over our little soiree.

****

The next day was uneventful. We got a great day's sleep and Bo and I actually made the last core swap that night without having to rely on our resident nuclear warhead expert, Master Chief Robin Curtis. We did, however get him to look over the job after we'd finished. Bo made the 0500 call to home base at Langley, we ate the last of our Russian MREs (God-awful), and retired for a good day's sleep before the most dangerous part of this mission – getting the hell out of the PRK – alive!

DAWN'S EARLY LIGHT

Chapter Six

PRK Ministry of Defense Building, Pyongsong
Tuesday, May 8, 1990, 1900 hrs, Local Time

We had another good day's sleep. The primary mission objective of swapping the fake cores for the real ones had been met. We had returned the room to the configuration in which it was left by the two technicians from Chong-Fal, which was slightly different from that we had found when we first arrived. We packed the real cores, one each wrapped in a thin lead spherical shield, into three not identical Russian made suitcases which had been lined with a thin layer of lead. Each suitcase also contained a Russian built AK-47 with folding stock, three full thirty round magazines and two six ounce pucks of Russian C-4 with a Russian made combo timer / remote detonator. One suitcase also contained an IR scope mounted to the AK, another one held Bo's laptop, and the third held a handheld VHF radio and a GPS receiver, all Russian made except the Chinese IR scope and the GPS receiver which was U.S. made but 'Russianized' using Cyrillic characters on the case and display. We wore Russian clothes and carried Russian passports. All of our other remaining gear would be destroyed by Young-ku in the PRK Ministry of Defense incinerator located at the other end of the basement and used primarily for destroying classified documents and material..

Now all we had to do was make a successful escape from this God forsaken rat-hole called North Korea. Actually our exfil plan looked pretty good. As a North Korean world class athlete and a member of the PRK's RGB, Young-ku enjoyed a level of freedom unimagined by most North Koreans. The papers he carried gave him a fast-track visa access to most countries hosting United World Wrestling Organization events as well as Olympic and World Wrestling Championship events. He was recognized as a North Korean hero and treated like royalty by all of the world's communist countries. For these reasons the CIA was not willing to risk such a valuable asset on the exfil (exfiltration) element of this mission. Instead, his uncle Ki Jin-sung, a fisherman who operated a rather old but reliable fishing trawler based in the Bay of Sinju at the mouth of the Changchun River and spoke English almost as well as Young-ku, would take us on his boat out beyond the twelve mile limit into the international waters of the Korean Bay to rendezvous with an American submarine, *USS Providence*. The Korean bay is part of the Yellow Sea (both of which were claimed by China, along with the East and South China Seas. Ki Jin-sung, although not affiliated with the CIA or any other non-PRK organization, was an active participant in the North Korean underground resistance. It was important to protect him from any suspicion of wrong doing if we were discovered by either PRK or Chinese officials.

Just before 1830 hrs Young-ku knocked twice lightly and we responded appropriately and let him in. We took half an hour to review our plan. The good news was the weather was good; wind out of the southwest with a two foot chop decreasing to calm by midnight. We re-examined the 'home' and 'shop' rooms and Young-ku retrieved his A/V bug, secured both rooms, re-programmed the lock on the home room to its original combination and led us down the hallway to the stairs at the west end of the basement. At the top of the stairs we found ourselves in the receiving area of the building where supplies and equipment were received and stored for normal operation of the PRK's Ministry of Defense. Young- Ku had keys to every access door and gate in the complex. He explained that the evening guard was stationed in the guard shack at the front of the building and the perimeter fence was equipped with an alarm system that consisted of an uninsulated wire that ran along the top of the ten foot chain-link fence which alerts the guard if touched or otherwise disturbed.

He led us through the rear door and then relocked it from the outside and did the same at the seven foot chain-link gate through the ten foot perimeter fence (these guys are not security geniuses). His uncle met us half way down the block in a canvas covered truck that looked like a miniature two and a half ton WW II army truck. This was the North Korean version of a minivan or maybe an SUV. We drove north approximately fifty four miles to the little fishing village on the south side of Sinju Bay and stopped at the small marina where Jin-sung kept his trawler. The trawler, like the 'SUV', looked old and well used but, according to Jin-sung, it was in excellent mechanical condition. He left us in the vehicle while he went up to chat with the harbor-master, an old friend. He told the Harbor-master he was taking three Russian soldiers out to the fishing lodge on Sunchu Island and would probably return a little after midnight unless he was delayed and got caught by the low tide in which case he would sleep over at the lodge and return shortly before noon. The harbor-master wished him a good trip and asked that he check back with him upon return.

The four of us gathered our gear, climbed aboard *Chung-li* and idled out of the harbor. The tide swings were notoriously large in the Yellow Sea where tidal range occasionally exceeds thirty feet. The harbor, although deep, was only useable from about two hours before and after high tide twice each day due to shifting sand bars at its entrance. We had carefully planned our exfil around the tidal forecast for the area.

We motored at eight knots toward the island. When we had gotten about half way to the island, which was about eleven miles northwest of the harbor, Jin-sung turned his running lights off and took a new course, due west. Our rendezvous point was twenty miles west of the point at which we made the turn. We were just entering international waters at twelve miles out when Rob picked up a blue flashing light approaching from due north. I grabbed the suitcase containing the AK-47 with the scope and took a look. I saw a small patrol boat with a roof mounted machinegun and flashing lights approaching at what I guessed to be about twenty five knots.

Chapter Seven

Aboard *Chung-li,* Korean Bay, Yellow Sea
Forty Miles South of the Chinese Shoreline
Tuesday, May 8, 1990, 2307 hrs, Local Time

Our mission Rules Of Engagement (ROE) called for us to shoot to kill and scuttle any small craft interfering with the mission – so this approaching boat was going to be a problem we'd have to deal with accordingly.

"How fast can you push this boat?" Bo asked Jin-sung.

"She will do twelve knots at full throttle," replied Jin-sung as he pushed the throttles forward a little.

"Increase your speed slowly until you reach full throttle and then keep her due west at until the patrol boat is close. I'll tell you when to throttle back. Sam, you're the shooter – get on the roof behind the lifeboat canister without being seen." The further west we got the deeper the water. All good.

I climbed the port ladder leading to the roof of the cabin. I took a position with my body prone behind the lifeboat canister with my AK resting on the starboard railing about eight inches above the flat roof. I made sure the rifle was set to semiautomatic single shot. I slowly inched my head up to the IR scope not wanting to be seen by the gunner who was still standing with his elbows resting the port side of the forward deck where the port half of the windshield

DAWN'S EARLY LIGHT

had been folded down like the old WW II Willys Jeeps. He had a pair of starlight night vision binoculars. They were still a little more than a half mile away so I knew he couldn't see me – yet. But I could see him clearly. The AK's Chinese IR scope used first generation un-cooled IR focal plane array technology. Better than starlight but nowhere near our capability. I wanted them to get as close as possible before I started shooting.

"How many aboard?" yelled Bo.

"No forward deck hatch, so no one likely below. Two standing," I yelled back.

"Blue light – Chinese," yelled Jin-Sung.

"Okay Rob, that's one of your languages, you do the talking if we get that far. Jin-sung, you and I will say nothing."

The pursuer had closed to about a quarter mile and was about thirty degrees off our starboard stern, closing fast. The sea had calmed to a slight swell with a thirty to forty yard pitch creating a gentle rise and fall of the bow. I was close to amidships so the motion for me was almost negligible. The night was fairly dark. The sea resembled an undulating sheet of black velvet. The moon was just a sliver away from the new moon we had when we arrived and the clouds were high, thin cirrus. At this distance I could see their gun was covered – giving me more time to call my shot.

"Throttle back slowly Jin-sung – all the way to idle," yelled Bo, facing the patrol boat, waving his hands as if he'd just noticed it.

As the trawler pitched forward slowly, Bo and Rob had their full attention. Rob was yelling something in Chinese and Bo was preparing to bring the patrol boat alongside.

I inched forward around the canister and pointed my AK at the helmsman. Just as Bo had taken a line from the gunner the helmsman looked up. Using the iron sights just below the scope, I shot him between the eyes, then quickly traversed to the stunned gunner and gave him a center-of-mass shot followed by a head shot as he fell. I lowered the AK to Bo so he and Rob could board the patrol boat armed, search it and set a C-4 charge under the engine to scuttle the boat. The boat was all metal so there'd be few, if any, floating remains. There was no Styrofoam filler as required in U.S. boats to keep them afloat after an accident.

"Hey Bo, are you gonna set it timed or remote?" I asked.

"Why do you ask?"

"We're not in deep water yet – wouldn't it be better to tow it out to twenty two miles, release it and then blow it remotely?"

"I knew there was some reason we brought you along," Bo grinned.

"Smartass," I shot back.

At twenty two miles out Bo checked our GPS position and told Jin-sung to stop the boat. Using his handheld VHS, Bo made sure he was on the correct channel and spoke the following message;

"Roadrunner, Roadrunner, Roadrunner, this is Papa Kilo, Papa Kilo, break. Expect Sierra Delta (Small Detonation) near your position in two zero, break. Oscar Tango (On Target) in three five. Papa Kilo out."

The *USS Providence* (SSN 719) a fast attack nuclear submarine should be loitering sixty five feet below the surface about a mile west of our current position with a floating wire antenna deployed for radio communication. The SSNs (nuclear subs) could receive (but not transmit) voice or encoded messages via a 'floating wire' from depths up to 100 feet.

After reconnoitering the Chinese patrol boat Bo decided to place two C-4 charges; one next to the auxiliary diesel tank located aft next to the engine; the other along with the bodies inside the forward equipment locker which contained the larger of the two diesel tanks. Both charges would be wired to the same remote receiver which would ignite all the fuel tanks at the same time and leave less residual material on the surface. When he was finished and back aboard *Chung-li* we motored a couple of hundred yards west.

"I think we're ready for the fireworks," said Bo calmly as he glanced at us to see if we were ready and then pushed the button. C-4 never ceased to amaze me. How a couple of little chunks of clay-like stuff could cause such a huge explosion ... but then, of

DAWN'S EARLY LIGHT

course, this explosion had an additional two hundred or so gallons of diesel fuel to help it out.

Jin-sung fired up the trawler's twin diesels and Bo guided him, using the GPS, to the exact rendezvous point and left the engines running so *Providence* could hear us and surface nearby.

Watching the sea at night is mesmerizing. After a few minutes of rod and cone night vision adjustment a calm sea comes alive. I began to notice the reflection of the stars and the flashing of some fluorescent creatures from unknown depths. Turning my gaze skyward I could see more stars than I thought could possibly exist. After spending a while trying to pick some familiar constellations out of the mass, I was beginning to wonder if they had forgotten us. I was standing at the starboard rail of the trawler just aft of the wheelhouse staring at the sky. There was just enough star and moonlight to barely discern the horizon. When I looked down after taking too long to find the big and little dippers I suddenly could no longer see the horizon and the sea seemed to disappear about fifteen yards away. There was a huge dark patch in my vision. This momentarily scared the crap out of me – until I realized it was *Providence* surfacing and her sail was blocking most of my field of view – this thing was huge, and quiet. I looked up and saw a sailor waving down at me.

"Ahoy, Papa Kilo, prepare to board," yelled the sailor as he opened the forward gate on the sail, climbed down a built-in ladder, unlocked a hatch at the base of the sail and retrieved a rope ladder which he attached and kicked over the side. He also lowered a metal basket from a small crane which appeared to come out of nowhere into which we placed our Russian suitcases. We thanked Jin-sung, gave him all the Russian money we had and waved goodbye as he idled away.

Bo led the way up the ladders. Stopped at attention in front of the Officer Of the Deck (OOD) and said, "I request permission to come aboard, sir."

"Very well," replied the OOD. Neither saluted because Bo was in civilian (although Russian) clothes. I followed the same procedure and then Rob followed me.

As Bo stepped off the last rung and into the Conn a husky voice bellowed "Cap'n Jameson – we meet at last, I'm Cap'n Jason McNally. That was quite a 'small detonation'. What'd you do, blow up a cruise ship?"

"No, we just placed some charges under the fuel tanks of a Chinese patrol boat we had to scuttle."

"Not to worry, my SONAR guys had their headgear off – thanks for the heads up. Nobody busted any eardrums.

"We need to park these cases in your reactor room first thing," said Bo.

"Okay, we'll do that and then go to my quarters so we can talk."

The four of us squeezed into the Captain's surprisingly small cabin and Bo continued, "Captain McNally this is Commander McKensie and Master Chief Curtis, my partners in crime."

"McKensie! Commander, you wouldn't happen to be a Hornet driver would you?"

Somewhat surprised, I replied, "Uh, yeah, I've flown Hornets. Off the *Carl Vinson*."

"So you're the guy that helped start this little war we've got goin' on."

"What war? I don't remember starting any war."

"You didn't splash two MiGs and sink a decommissioned Chinese gunboat back in February?"

"Okay Captain, you've got the wrong McKensie – that would be Commander Ashleigh McKensie, my wife. She took first fire from the gunboat, got shot down by a triple HSSM attack and she and her team took out the MiGs and gunboat."

"What war?" asked Bo.

"Well, for a couple of months nothing much happened over that little incident except the Chinese whining to the UN the about the U.S. and our allies violating Chinese sovereign air and sea territory, and restating their claim to damn near the whole South China Sea. As usual the UN did nothing because there's nothing the UN can do except recite the current International Maritime twelve mile Law that the whole world, except China, lives by. We

DAWN'S EARLY LIGHT

continued to fly the slot in the Paracels with no further provocation by the chinks until day before yesterday when we shot down two MiG-21s and a MiG 29 in international airspace after being fired upon by them. Within hours, the U.S. issued a stern warning to China through the UN and also directly, that any additional firing upon U.S. or U.S. allied aircraft or watercraft in international airspace or waters would be considered an act of war and would be dealt with accordingly. Russia has remained surprisingly quiet offering no support through the U.N. or otherwise. China is slowly losing Russia's support because Russia is becoming economically impotent since the Soviet Union break-up. Then a Chinese Romeo sub (old Russian built diesel boat) goes missing last week in the deepest part of the South China Sea. Yesterday China pointed fingers at Taiwan and Japan and we've got half the U.S. Fleet over here trying to keep the peace, find that sub and direct traffic. It's a fucked up mess."

"Where are we going from here," Bo asked.

"You mean this boat or the world? 'Cause the world's going to hell in a hand basket and this boat's going to Yokosuka"

"Yeah, too bad about the world, I'm just interested in the boat. We've got orders to get these items back to Langley ASAP."

"I'm sorry to have to tell you this but your orders might have changed, read this."

Captain McNally handed Bo a sealed communiqué which read:

CONFIDENTIAL

TO: COMMANDER, DEVGRU GOLD TEAM
FROM: COMMANDER, JSOC

REPORT COMMANDER TASK FORCE 74 COMSUBPAC YOKOSUKA TO RECEIVE AMMENDED ORDERS

Bo looked up from the paper and asked, "When will we be there?"

"On the way up here we picked up an Akula class sub, the

Russian *Snow Leopard,* and he's shadowing us right now. We don't know who owns that sub. The Russians have been selling their older subs to India and recently to China. Problem is, eight knots is as fast as we can go, otherwise we could lose him in our own noise. Our standing protocol requires us to maintain contact with any suspected enemy vessel until clear. So even though it's a short distance as the crow flies – submarines don't. It'll take us two days to reach the southern tip of Japan. When we make our turn to east-northeast toward Yokosuka he'll head back to his own waters and we can increase to flank speed. That'll get us there in one more day if this monkey doesn't fuck with us.

"Meanwhile, gentlemen, we'll get you some clean clothes, hot showers, hot grub and a place to sleep. We just resupplied at Subic Bay less than two weeks ago – we've still got steak, fruit and ice cream. Until we get to Yokosuka you'll be our honored, off duty guests. I even snuck a bottle of Jack Daniels aboard for you."

I queried the Captain, "sir, how do you relax on a submarine? Do you have any books?"

"I've got some Tom Clancy and Stephen Coonts stuff and my exec has the complete twenty one book set of Patrick O'Brian's HMS Surprise series."

"That would be fantastic – I just finished *The Far Side Of The World.* That was book ten I believe. Probably the best set of sea adventures ever written – I've read the entire set once before."

Captain Jason McNally was what is known in the Navy as an 'Old Salt'. That moniker was applied with great respect to senior enlisted men and officers alike who had spent, what seemed to others, a lifetime at sea and had earned, along with myriad experience, the respect of all who knew them. A Bull Halsey class sailor.

Born and raised in Hampton, Tennessee, McNally had perfected his Tennessee drawl over the years. He joined the Navy at the bottom end as an E-1 Seaman Recruit. Along the way he managed to acquire enough college credit to be classified as a senior and he passed the OCS qualifiers. The Navy then paid for his last two semesters at San Diego State after which he passed

DAWN'S EARLY LIGHT

OCS near the top of his class and went to sea again. While at San Diego State he met and married a Navy Nurse, Mary Anne, who was finishing her degree in pre-med. They were happily married until she was fatally wounded in the last few days of the Vietnam War while helping move wounded soldiers out of a Saigon hospital. With nothing to keep him on land he turned to submarines. He made Captain in 1985 and took command of *Providence* a year later. His dreams of making flag grade melted away after he lost Mary Anne – but he was widely regarded as one of the best sub captains the Navy ever had.

"Sonar, conn," barked McNally into his sound-powered mike.

Conn, sonar," replied the Sonar Supervisor.

"Where's that Akula?"

"He's twenty thousand yards southwest, sir. Parallel course at four knots."

"Depth?"

"Four hundred feet."

"Control, conn.

"Conn, control."

"Make turns for eight knots, match the Akula's course, make your depth four hundred feet."

"Make turns for eight knots, match his course, make my depth four hundred feet, aye."

Chapter Eight

Aboard *Providence*, South Central Yellow Sea, Heading; South at Eight Knots

Wednesday, May 9, 1990, 0830 hrs, Local Time

Bo and I shared an officer's cabin for two that was identical to the Captain's cabin except for a pull down top bunk above the lower one. Rob bunked in an NCO cabin with three other Master / Senior Chiefs. Most crew slept in nine man cubby holes, three bunks on three walls. Can you imagine hearing eight sailors all snoring at once. Actually that doesn't happen because the sailors rotate shifts – but still, ear plugs are a necessity.

We got our clothes, showers and some great steaks with mashed potatoes, green beans, a bowl of fresh mixed fruit and apple pie alamode. I retired to my bunk and found my room mate, Lt. Commander Mark Lewis away on duty, so I grabbed about six hours of pretty good sleep.

Now it's breakfast time so I went back to the galley to get more chow and found Bo and Rob just finishing theirs. Bo said Captain McNally wanted to meet with us in the wardroom at 0900, so I'd better get my butt in gear.

I said "aye-aye sir," got my breakfast, ate it and headed for the wardroom. Where in the hell is the wardroom? I remembered seeing it just before I got here – hell, it's right next door.

Captain McNally was a large person to have been cooped up in

DAWN'S EARLY LIGHT

a submarine for a significant part of his life. He was about two inches taller than me so that'd put him at about six three. He looked to be a little over two hundred pounds, maybe 210, with a full head of grey hair some stress lines in his tanned face and steel grey eyes. He had a Tennessee drawl and a total disregard for proper English – in other words, a really likeable guy. I wouldn't want to get on his wrong side though.

He walked in, ducking slightly to get through the hatch. "Good morning gentlemen, hope you've had a good rest. Just to let you know, I've been read in to your mission by Admiral Bennington, here's the paperwork and I've got the documents in the ships TS container (safe). So I'm aware of the contents of your package and your need to get it to Langley quickly. If it weren't for this potential threat we'd be in Yokosuka by tomorrow noon. We are pretty sure this asshole's just dicking with us and ordinarily that would be the case. But due to the recent global events we're required to take all precautions to avoid losing this very expensive nuclear sub and one hundred twenty nine sailors, present company included."

Bo replied, "Not to worry Captain, we certainly understand. I assume COMSUBPAC (COMmander, SUBmarine Force, U.S. PACific Fleet) will keep the Admiral aware of our time line as best we know it."

"Admiral Bennington's aware of our situation and I've already requested that they keep him informed," replied McNally. "Now, if you'd like, I'll give you a brief tour of the boat before I take the conn at 1000. Have any of you ever been on a nuclear sub?"

We all said no and Bo accepted his offer so we toured the 'boat'. I thought it funny that most people in the Navy called anything bigger than a patrol boat a ship, but it turns out that if a boat carries other boats it's called a ship. Subs don't typically carry other boats so they're not ships. My initial impression was that the boat would feel very small and cramped – I was wrong, it felt huge and cramped. The sub was three hundred sixty feet long and thirty three feet in diameter. I've never seen so much hi-tech stuff engineered into such tight spaces. The 'boat' was truly amazing. The tour ended at the conn, where Captain McNally took the conn from his executive officer Robert (Bob) Nelson. He did this formally by saying, "Officer of the deck, I've got the conn."

To which the OOD replied, "The Captain has the conn, aye." The OOD was responsible for implementing the Captain's orders. He and the Captain were both normally positioned in the conn, but the Captain often visited the sonar room or communications room while dealing with other vessels or communications. They all wore sound powered communications gear when working threats like they were today. The OOD gave us each a headset with no microphone – a clear indication that we should keep our mouths shut. We listened for a while to the Captain and the Sonar Supervisor discussing the Akula that was shadowing us at about twenty three thousand yards, just at the edge of the Akula's passive sonar range. He was not behaving like a Russian and the conclusion had been reached that the Chinese were in possession of an Akula Class Submarine that the U.S. knew nothing about.

The rest of the day was relatively boring. I read about two hundred pages of *The Reverse of the Medal,* Patrick O'Brian's eleventh book in his HMS Surprise series, had a great game of chess with the Executive Officer, Commander David Winslow, which I lost. Chess is a game that I love to play – good thing I'm a good loser.

With nothing else to do I donned my mikeless headset and tried to figure out what was going on. After about ten minutes of silence and routine jabber I heard in my headset;

"Conn, sonar."

"Sonar, conn," replied McNally.

"Captain, this guy just firewalled his sub. Sounds like he's making turns for flank speed, cavitating like crazy. Bearing 260 and he's moving through twenty knots.

"OOD, make your depth one thousand feet; make turns for twenty knots."

"One thousand feet, twenty knots, aye."

McNally said, "we'll let him pull ahead a little and see what he's up to. We're entering the East China Sea so our depth just increased to three hundred fathoms. In about a half hour we'll start turning east to make our way around the Japanese mainland. I don't want that turkey on my tail."

DAWN'S EARLY LIGHT

"Conn, sonar."

"Sonar, conn."

"Captain, he's slowing and turning east."

"Speed?"

"He's down to ten knots heading 0100, bearing 10 degrees off our starboard bow. He looks like he coming around to face us."

"OOD, All stop, do not cavitate."

"All stop, do not cavitate, aye.

"Conn, sonar."

"Sonar, conn."

"He's dead on our bow, facing us, estimated speed two knots. Range eighteen thousand seven hundred yards."

"OOD, Battle Stations Torpedo, rig boat for depth charge."

"Battle Stations Torpedo, rig boat for depth charge, aye."

"Sonar, conn, status."

"Conn, sonar. He's dead in the water, sir. Uh, Captain, he's flooding his tubes."

"Sonar, conn, standby."

"Conn, sonar, standing by."

McNally turned to Bo covering his sound powered mike and said," I don't know what the fuck this turkey' doing – it looks like he's gonna fire on us, but it's probably just a feint."

"Conn, sonar,….he's opening his outer doors.

"Torpedo room and fire control, make tubes one and two ready and open outer doors."

"Make tubes one and two ready, open outer doors, aye."

"Conn, sonar, two torpedoes in the water."

The son-of-a-bitch fired!

"Sonar, conn, time to impact."

"Conn, sonar, thirteen minutes, forty five seconds."

"OOD, conn, match sonar bearings and shoot, tubes one and two.

"Match sonar bearings and shoot, tubes one and two, aye."

DON CANDY

The Mark 48 ADvanced CAPability (ADCAP) torpedo can be guided by a sonar operator through enemy Electronic Counter Measures (ECM) via a thin spooled out control wire until its powerful active sonar acquires the target. This gives *Providence* the options of guiding the torpedo all the way to its target for short to medium range shots or until the wire runs out and the torpedo closes and acquires the target on its own for longer range targets. A third option, called a snap shot is for very short range or when already fired upon. The snap shot allows the wire to be cut immediately and the outer doors closed so the sub can then turn onto course, accelerate to flank speed and employ its own ECM. The torpedo is then left to acquire the target with its own sonar and guide itself to the target as it was designed to do with deadly accuracy.

"Sonar, conn."

"Conn, sonar."

"Guide the torpedoes."

"Conn, sonar, guiding torpedoes."

"Sonar, conn, time to impact."

"Conn, sonar, eight minutes ten seconds, sir. Both Mk-48s have acquired the target and accelerated to homing speed

"OOD, conn, cut the wires and close the outer doors, report doors secure."

"Cut the wires and close the outer doors, report doors secure, aye."

"Conn, sonar, torpedoes one and two running hot, free and true, wires are cut, both have acquired the target and are homing.

"Conn, sonar, doors are secure."

"ECM, conn, noisemakers on my command."

"ECM standing by."

"ECM, conn, release noisemakers."

"Conn, ECM, noisemakers released."

"Come to one seven zero, make turns for flank speed, do not cavitate."

"Come to one seven zero, make turns for flank speed, do not

DAWN'S EARLY LIGHT

cavitate, aye."

SONAR (SOund Navigation And Ranging), RADAR (RAdio Detection And Ranging) and the human eye all work on the same principle. You walk into a dark room and turn on a light. What you see is the reflection of light waves off everything in the room. Now imagine that instead of turning on the light you take a flash picture with your camera. Now you see what the camera was able to illuminate in about one sixtieth of a second. Both RADAR and SONAR work the same way, only at lower frequencies than visible light. RADAR works in the radio frequency range (somewhat above your FM car radio) using an electromagnetic pulse in place of the camera's flash and SONAR works in the audio frequency range using an audio pulse (ping). The Mk-48 ADCAP torpedo is guided by its own very sophisticated sonar. The sonar uses what is called 'frequency agility' meaning that it randomly changes the frequency of each ping and then filters out all unexpected frequencies when receiving the sound 'image'. This makes enemy ECM devices that try to fool its sonar ineffective and the torpedo's accuracy very high. To the contrary, most enemy ECM devices use either a single frequency ping or noise similar to that of a submarine under way to try to fool an acoustic seeking torpedo (WW II technology) and are totally ineffective against the Mk-48 ADCAP. The term 'noise maker' is used for ECM against either the old-tech torpedoes that go after submarine noise or the modern torpedoes that home on what the torpedo 'sees' with its sonar.

"Noise makers released, aye," responded McNally.

Captain McNally knew that the *Snow Leopard* was one of the first six Akulas built and that it had probably not been refitted with the more modern torpedo capability. He would soon find out.

"Conn, sonar."

"Sonar, conn, whatcha got?"

"Captain, we've got two explosions on the target and the enemy fish are swallowing our noise makers."

"Aye, good job you guys – all of you."

"Sonar, report enemy condition."

DON CANDY

"Conn, sonar, enemy boat breaking up, she's gone."

A loud cacophony of war whoops exploded over the sound powered system – this was the crew's first combat action and the celebration was acknowledged by a wide grin on their skipper's face. After about two minutes everyone got back to their jobs.

"Sonar, conn."

"Conn, sonar."

"You guys were able to ID that sub with the current database on the SBY-1 computers, correct?"

"Yes Captain."

"COB (Chief Of the Boat), you've got the conn. Put us back on course for Yokosuka, maintain flank speed."

"Aye-aye, sir."

As we gathered in the ward room Captain McNally said, "this is the first submarine sunk by the U.S. Navy since World War Two. Sonar, did you check the recordings?"

"Yes sir, both recordings are complete and secure."

"I want two more copies made, actually three. Copy the primary sonar record from first acquisition of the Akula until silence after break-up to tape. Then copy that to the fire control computer and the ECM computer. Then give me the tape.

"We're reasonably confident that this is the *Snow Leopard,* the second of the first six Akulas built by the Russians. Five of the six have been accounted for, but number two – the second one, the *Snow Leopard*, commissioned in 1984 – went missing and was never found, supposedly with crew aboard. I think that never happened and this sub was as we determined, actually the *Snow Leopard* and they sold it to the Chinese. I've got the detailed signatures for those six boats somewhere on the ECM computer. It would be helpful if we could confirm this before land fall."

Every ship (boat) makes a unique noise as it powers through the water, above or below. This unique noise is its 'signature'.

"Now let's quickly review the action. First, any comments or questions?"

The ECM officer asked a question; "Sir didn't we keep him a

DAWN'S EARLY LIGHT

little too close?"

"Yes we did Lieutenant, but his maximum passive range is only twenty three thousand yards. At first encounter we picked him up at thirty five thousand yards. We were in the East China Sea Headed northeast to pick up our SEALS and about to leave their field of sonobuoys as we entered the Yellow Sea . He knew we were there, and his assignment was to find us and watch us as we journeyed into the Yellow Sea – something our subs rarely do. I'm sure Captain Jameson's little explosion in the Korean Bay followed by the sounds of a sinking boat gave him something to think about. So his tracking us at twenty thousand yards wasn't surprising. Note that when he came about he maintained twenty thousand yards because he knew we would go dead in the water and he didn't want to lose us. I believe he was ordered to faceoff with us but not to shoot. That is the big question; why did he shoot? Anybody got an idea?"

No one spoke. Nothing but shaking heads. . .

"I don't either, yet."

Chapter Nine

COMSUBPAC Headquarters
Yokosuka, Japan
Friday, May 11, 1990, 1930 hrs Local Time

Yokosuka, Japan has been the home of Commander Submarine Group Seven of the United States Commander, Submarine Pacific Fleet (COMSUBGRU 7, COMSUBPAC) since the early nineteen fifties. *Providence* was home based at New London, Connecticut. Nuclear submarines constitute a truly global force, and since she was visiting Pearl Harbor at the time of need, she was tasked to report to Group Seven at Yokosuka, the back yard of the world's current hot spot – the South China Sea. En route she received orders to pick up the SEALS in the Bay of Korea, Yellow Sea.

Captain McNally and several of his crew had served in Group Seven at some point during their careers. All were happy to take on an assignment based at Yokosuka, a very U. S. Navy friendly town with great food and lots to do. Or, so they thought. They had just sunk a Chinese sub. That meant nearly endless debriefings and paperwork to reconstruct and document the event - which took most of the planned four day refit to bring *Providence* up to battle ready status.

The three of us, however, were able to get a couple of days rest before boarding the next transport, an MC-130E Combat Talon in light cargo configuration, headed for San Diego. We left our three

DAWN'S EARLY LIGHT

nuclear cores, our AK-47s and Bo's laptop in the reactor room and arranged for a twenty four hour Marine guard to be posted at the bulkhead hatch which provided the only way in or out of that room. We got some decent civvies at the Naval Exchange on Captain McNally's credit card. He said he could expense the charge as long as we didn't go over $500 – we didn't. Then we went into town and ate at a highly recommended Chinese Restaurant. Only fitting – to eat Chinese food after sinking a Chinese sub. We had a few beers at a local Navy hangout. Ran into some of the guys we'd met on the sub and got back to the VOQ a little late but we slept in the next morning. We hung around the base all that day and took a base limousine (old navy car), with our Russian made suitcases with AK's and cores inside, to the Atsugi Naval Air Facility up the coast closer to Tokyo. We locked the cores up in a secure armory, found another cool bar, spent what was left of the night in their VOQ, slept in again the next day and boarded the C-130 at 1030 hrs for an overnight flight home. Although the Combat Talon was equipped with auxiliary fuel bladders and we could have made the trip non-stop, the C-130 had to deliver four jet engines to the repair center located at Whidbey Island NAS just east of the U.S. San Juan Islands, north of Seattle. Bo and I had spent a couple of weeks in the San Juans back in 1979 getting our American Sailing Association Advanced Coastal Cruising ratings. We almost wished we were overnighting at Whidbey Island so we could rent a boat and motor over to Outriggers Bar on Front Street, Friday Harbor, San Juan Island. Wishful thinking. We both needed to get home, but this was an awful long haul in a C-130. The break would have been welcomed.

Chapter Ten

San Diego Naval Air Station
Coronado Island, California
Monday, May 14, 1990, 1220 hrs PDT

We landed, secured the cores, ate lunch, argued about which meal it really was and then headed to the JSOC San Diego office to meet Admiral George Bennington, Commander, Joint Special Operations Command. The Admiral, now stationed at JSOC Headquarters, Fort Bragg, North Carolina, spent about a third of his time at other JSOC facilities including San Diego NAS. He had arranged transportation of the nuclear cores to the Trident Naval Base at Bangor Washington. The Langley folks were already there waiting for them and we were more than happy to get rid of them.

Admiral Bennington was more interested in the Chinese sub incident than our debriefing of the mission. We filled in the blanks where ever we could. He asked how sure McNally was that the sub was Chinese and not Russian.

Bo replied, "Captain McNally had a detailed signature file on his ECM computer of the second Akula ever, the *Snow Leopard*, launched in 1984. He had tracked and documented the signature for that sub in the Atlantic. Shortly after that it disappeared. The Ruskies said it was lost at sea with full crew in 1988. About that time or a little later we know through British intel that they leased

DAWN'S EARLY LIGHT

the third Akula to India. McNally believes the Russians sold number two to China and faked the loss. This was during the period when the Soviet Union, in its final days, was desperate for cash and China began its rise economically. Neither country would want the U.S. to know that China had bought or leased a nuclear attack sub from the USSR, hence the 'lost at sea' story. No Matter who it belonged to he is absolutely sure there wasn't a Russian Captain aboard. That sub acted very strangely. Nothing it did was in the submarine tactics doctrine of the Soviet Navy. To turn head-to and go dead in the water on a Los Angeles class sub and then open your outer doors at long range for the Akula and medium range for *Providence* is suicide – then to pull the trigger? "The guy's either insane or Chinese or more likely both," to quote McNally. As far as he's concerned there's nothing else he could do. He's got the whole thing on tape and backed up twice. He should be okay."

"What about you're Chinese patrol boat?"

"Well as we all know, we don't get issued cyanide pills, timed self destruct grenades and orders to shoot to kill unless what we're doing is fairly important," Bo replied – a little on the defensive side for Bo.

"We were in a trawler doing about ten knots and they're in a patrol boat on plane at about twenty two knots with a heavy gun on their roof. Sam was on our roof and took out both occupants just after the boat settled off plane and was slowing to board us. We grabbed all floatables laced them on the anchor chain and threw it overboard before we blew up the boat, occupants included. We put double charges under the fore and aft fuel tanks, wired them to the same remote receiver and stuffed the bodies into a forward locker right above the fuel tank. We had about thirty minutes before *Providence* surfaced. In that time there was very little evidence left on the surface. I don't think they'll ever find a big piece of anything."

"Okay gentlemen, this is Top Secret, eyes only; Cmdr *Providence,* Cmdr JSOC, Cmdr DEVGRU, Dir CIA, CJCS, POTUS and you three. When the report is complete, we'll sign the papers. Until then, discuss this with no one.

I'll carefully review your report on the PRK mission and get back to you if I need clarification on anything. The President, Jerry, Bill and I are all extremely pleased with the job your team did on this mission We'll have a post mission celebration with them as soon as we can get all the calendars aligned. But for now – Job Well Done Guys!

Now let me get to the more pertinent subject of this meeting; we've got a new mission. . ."

Chapter Eleven

Top Gun Operations Office
Miramar Naval Air Station, CA
Monday, May 14, 1990, 1605 hrs PDT

As I walked in to the operations lobby, Lieutenant JG Nancy Allen, the Captain's admin, saw me and picked up the phone to call Ashleigh, but I caught her in time.

"Shhh. I want to surprise her," I whispered.

"How'd your trip down range go? Nancy wanted to know.

"Smooth as silk," I lied, still whispering.

"Go on back, she's been going nuts with you gone – I think it's the pregnancy thing."

"So, what's a doll like you doing holed up in a dreary place like this on such a beautiful day in May?" I said over her shoulder after sneaking up behind her.

"Hey sailor, I'm pregnant! You're not supposed to scare the crap out of me anymore," she said as she jumped up, turned around, put her arms around me, kissed me and started crying all in one continuous motion,

"Hey, what's going on? You'd think I'd been gone a month or something."

"You've been gone nine days and that's too long when I'm pregnant. You're supposed to be right here at my side to help me."

"At your service madam. Whatcha been up to?" I asked, knowing full well that she wasn't happy doing anything on the ground.

"Just upgrading the training procedures to reflect the changes we've made in the last decade. Which means adding about ninety pages to an eighty page manual and making changes to the original eighty. I'm about three days ahead of schedule and due to be finished by the end of the month. Captain Erickson told me to take a few days off when you got back – Do you have any time off?"

"Yeah, I can take a week if I want to."

"Dirk (Captain Erickson) hinted that I might want to ask my doctor if I could take another PR flight in my old Blue Angel t-38. So I asked him. He asked me what was involved and I told him the conditions were similar to taking a trip on a commercial airline and then giving three ROTC cadets a one hour ride over a three day period. He asked if I could take someone with me and I said, I hoped so. He kind of made that a condition. Can you go – pleeeze?

"When is it?"

"Next week at K State! Can you believe that?"

"You sure it's okay?"

"Hey, I'm just pregnant, not terminally ill – I'll be fine. I'll let you do some of the flying. We could leave Saturday, spend two nights with your mom or Jim and buzz on over to Manhattan Monday morning."

"Can you get a T-38 off of a three thousand foot strip with two people and luggage?"

"I can do that in eighteen hundred feet."

"Then, by all means, let's do it."

"Different subject; The Doc says we can have 'gentle' sex, but not in the shower."

"Well fuck a duck, there goes our sex life!" I said smiling.

By now Ash had learned not to ask me about my missions because she knew I couldn't talk about them, so together we just

DAWN'S EARLY LIGHT

put that part of my life aside and made the best of all the good stuff that was left. So I guess the old saying that 'absence makes the heart grow fonder' is really true, at least it is for us. So far my longest trip down range has been two and a half weeks. For a couple of Navy pilots that's nothing. But the home-comings are really special. Back in 1985 Bo bought a Mooney M20J, a sweet, fast little four seat airplane that he used to get around in when he was working at El Centro. Over time I was using it more than he was and when he got promoted to BAT Commander and moved to San Diego he really didn't need it any more. DEVGRU Headquarters are in Dam Neck Virginia. Too far for a private plane – so I borrowed it from him. Now I use it to commute between Miramar where we live, El Centro NAF or Yuma Proving Ground, where I work and Coronado Island where I train for down range assignments - which can be pretty much anywhere in the world. Having our own plane simplifies our lives a lot. But getting a mini-vacation in a T-38 is just icing on the cake. We eat our cake when ever we can get it iced.

So Ash said she would let Captain Erickson know that the doctor said the trip would be okay and that I would go too.

"It's four thirty and the boss is away. I think I'll take the rest of the day off."

"Good idea," ahhh, back to a normal life.

Chapter Twelve

Angels Two Zero Over Central Kansas
Saturday, May, 19 1990, 1445 hrs CDT

"Jameson Tower this is Military Flight Oscar Two Four Seven at twenty thousand feet, thirty miles southwest, landing, over," Ash was still smiling. Looking at her latest chart she had just realized that Jameson Field had its own tower. We hadn't been here in almost five years.

"Oscar Two Four Seven, what type aircraft are you?

"U.S. Navy T-38."

"Uh Roger, report five miles southwest at three thousand, over."

"Five miles southwest at three thousand, roger that."

My uncle Bo built this airport from a family owned farm with a twelve hundred foot grass strip used for crop dusting and aerial advertising. Right after graduation from high school he extended the runway to two thousand feet of blacktop. When he was twenty two years old he owned eight airplanes and employed three pilots. He taught ROTC candidates how to fly while attending college at Kansas State University. But after his junior year he left the airport operation to his chief pilot, Jim Harrison, to go fly A-6 Intruders in Vietnam for the Navy. My father, Scott McKensie was an Air Force ROTC Candidate at Kansas State and Bo was his instructor. My dad met Bo's sister Lauren and married her. I was born before my dad shipped off to Vietnam to fly the F105 'Thud' against the North Vietnam Army anti-aircraft missile sites. He was killed by a

DAWN'S EARLY LIGHT

Soviet SA-2 Surface to Air Missile (SAM) while on his twenty eighth Wild Weasel mission before I even got to know him.

Bo stayed in Vietnam for three two year tours and when he came home he sort of became my father. Now we're SEALs on a team called DEVGRU, official name; Naval Special Warfare Development Group. When I joined it was SEAL Team Six.

Since I joined, eight years ago, the organization has quadrupled in size and spread it's home base across the country. The headquarters of the original organization are in Dam Neck Virginia but our little development group, known as the BAT, attached to the much larger Black Assault Squadron, is located at El Centro NAF in California. We're a small group tasked with co-developing advanced infil and exfil systems with defense contractors, and then deploying and field testing these systems on actual missions. These are systems that allow our Special Forces guys to show up un-announced in the bad guy's back yard, execute their mission with a very high probability of one hundred percent success and then exfil before the bad guys notice what happened. These missions are almost always conducted at night – *We Own the Night.* We train for missions with Delta Force and Force Recon Operators at the Army's Yuma Proving Ground and Coronado Island.

Three years ago the BAT Commander, Captain Joe Garcia was offered command of the USS Carl Vinson, which he took, and Commander Bo Jameson (uncle Bo) was promoted to Captain and became Commander, Black Angel Team. Bo and Colonel Jeff Morris, Commander, Delta Force Special Weapons Team, report directly to Commander, JSOC, Admiral George Bennington. All three are members of the super secret Presidential Special Operations Team (PSOT, pronounced p-sot) along with the Chairman of the Joint Chiefs, Admiral Gerald Sterett and Director, CIA, William Conroy.

Bo says 'Higher' (Higher Authority, which means anyone with authority higher than the commander of the group of the member speaking) may want him to move to Dam Neck and if that happens he wants his plane back. I told him to buy a new one – he can afford it. Jim Harrison had built the Jameson Flight Service (JFS) to ever increasing profits of nearly two hundred thousand dollars a

DON CANDY

year. Ownership is Bo – 55%, Jim – 35% and me – 10%. I got the 10% ownership as a reward for working my way through college as an ROTC flight instructor without taking a nickel out of JFS. Bo had promised my dad that if anything happened to him in Nam he would see to it that I got through college. Ash and I are both Commanders (same as Lieutenant Colonel in the Army) and I get flight pay plus combat pay because of what I do and Ash gets flight pay, plus we get around 20K a year from JFS and some additional income from some early investments I made, so we have a comfortable life. Condo in La Jolla, my seven year old Corvette, Ash's five year old Mercedes convertible all paid for. And, our Mooney M20J which I'll pay cash for when Bo gives in. . .

*****

"Jameson Tower, Oscar Two Four Seven, five miles southwest at three thousand."

"Oscar Two Four Seven, you're cleared to land, runway two four. Report left downwind."

"Roger that tower, report left downwind."

Ash greased the landing – as she should after more than two thousand hours in T-38 and F-5 aircraft.

We drew a crowd. As we taxied back to the main ramp about twenty people had gathered to gawk at the 'Blue Angel' configured T-38. Jim was standing behind the left wing as I dismounted.

"Sam, what a surprise – you should have called!"

"If I'd called, it wouldn't have been a surprise, right?"

"Does your mother know you're coming?"

"Ash has another ROTC gig at K State Monday – we didn't know we were coming 'til a couple of days ago so we didn't tell anybody. You guys free for dinner at Jake's tonight?"

"I can't think of anything better. I'll check with Janie."

"Wow, a new bigger hangar and ramp. I signed the papers on the two million dollar 'improvement' loan but I had no idea it would look this good. How long is that runway?"

"We got an extra five hundred feet out of the loan and cash on

DAWN'S EARLY LIGHT

hand. With a fifty five hundred by fifty foot runway we can handle all the corporate jets that come our way."

Ash had finished shutting down the electronics and filling out the aircraft log and was waiting in the cockpit for me to help her down. Six years now and I'm finally allowed to treat her like a lady – this pregnancy is good thing in more ways than one.

"Hey Jim, haven't seen you since our wedding on Jost Van Dyke," Ashleigh said as she hugged Jim.

"Yeah, why don't you guys come up here more often?"

I said, "It's a long story, we'll get caught up at dinner. Have you seen Mom lately?"

"We see her most every Sunday at church She's looking great."

"Good, I'll call her and see if she can join us."

Chapter Thirteen

Jake's Famous Barbeque
Highway 40, Two miles west of JFS
Saturday, May 19, 1990, 1830 hrs CDT

Jim wasn't the only one expanding his (our) business. Jake had nearly doubled the size of his restaurant, but he still had the big round table in the back room reserved for special guests. I called him earlier and asked him to hold it for us. Along with the expansion he now had a variety of fifteen beers on tap and five very nice wines, three reds and two whites. Mom told me not to stop and get her wine on the way because Jake had her favorite now. The place was busy for a Monday night but our table was waiting for us.

Jim got us up to speed on the physical and financial status of JFS while we were waiting for our food. Basically, the growth of Manhattan businesses and therefore business aircraft had driven more than our fair share of the aircraft to JFS. We had room for expansion where others didn't and we were very competitive in our pricing and services. In addition, the city limits were expanding toward us, mostly due to Interstate 70 (old U.S. 40) and our airport. We are just under thirty miles west of Manhattan Regional Airport, very close to I-70 with a better solution for growing businesses.

Jim's growth goal is to hold profits to two hundred thousand a year and reinvest everything else until we catch up with demand which he thinks will be about five years. This sounded pretty aggressive to me but without Bo present I didn't want to ask some of the questions I was forming in my mind. I made a mental note to talk to Bo and come back up here with him in the near future. Jim had done an exceptional job of growing JFS over the last ten years and Bo knows most of what he's done and is still doing so maybe I just need to keep my mouth shut and learn from Jim.

So I decided to pop the news.

"Mom, how would you like to become a grandmother?"

"Oh my God Sam, don't surprise me like that. I might have a heart attack or something. Are you kidding me? If you are, I'll never speak to you again." She could tell from the ear-to-ear smile on Ashleigh's face that I was serious.

"When am I going to be a Grandma?"

"The doctor thinks around the last week in November."

"Ashleigh, should you really be flying in airplanes?"

Ash grinned and said, "With my doctor's permission. He said I can fly for three more months or until I can't fit into the cockpit, which ever comes first. No tight turns or stressful flying and of course no aerobatics. Can I do my old job? Definitely not. But I can still fly around a little here and there when I want to, but not alone."

"Sam are you going to quit the Navy and do something less dangerous?"

"Mom, I've got some unique skills and my country needs me. I'd never be able to live with myself if I quit now. Bo and I are training others so we can take desk jobs as soon as possible," I lied. I've got a job that requires a skill set and a level of achievement I never dreamed I could accomplish. I've got to continue this work until I can find someone better than I am to take my place. Most of my work is developing systems in a lab at El Centro Naval Air Facility," another white lie.

"It's that other part that worries me and I'm sure it worries Ashleigh too." Mom was getting close to tears – time to change the subject.

"We might be able to tell whether it's a boy or girl at Ash's, next checkup but we don't really want to know. Do you want us to find out?"

"Of course not. That takes all the fun out of having children. Scott and I didn't know whether you were a boy or girl and back then all the doctor could do was make an educated guess. And, they weren't always right. We would have been just as happy if you were a girl." Then with a sideways look that I remembered from my childhood she said, "Maybe happier!"

"Okay mom, I got your message, but Ash and I agree with you, we're not going to find out."

"Oh Sam, don't just say you agree if you really don't. You are exactly like your father; you're going to do what you're going to do. I'm just happy that you've got Ashleigh to look after you and that I'm going to be a grandma."

"Mom, Jim, we're sorry we can't stay longer. This trip just came up last week so we jumped at it so we could spend at least two days with you all. We'll get Bo freed up next time and come up for a week or maybe more."

Ash spoke up, "Lauren, could we spend some time together while Jim and Sam do a tour of all that's happened around here in the last five years?"

"Ashleigh, I'd like nothing more. You can catch me up on what you and Sam have been up to since your beautiful wedding in the British Virgin Islands.

Chapter Fourteen

Pilot's lounge, Manhattan Regional Airport
Manhattan, Kansas
Monday, May 21, 1990, 1830 hrs CDT

We flew up to Manhattan Regional in less than thirty minutes most of which was flying vectors as instructed by Regional's Approach Control and tower. JFS is actually in the airspace controlled by Regional's approach control, so we were being vectored by Approach Control from the minute we left JFS until they turned us over to the Regional tower.

I elected to spend some time at an aeronautical museum near the airport while Ash did her presentation and flew the first two demo rides for the top six cadets in the Navy and Marine ROTC programs. She did ask me to come in to meet her six cadets before I left for the museum, which I did. Ash was delighted to see a young lady in the group – Navy, no less. Then she introduced me and talked a little about the pros and cons of being F-18 squadron commanders while married and on the same carrier seasoned by a few tales about the competition between our squadrons and havoc it caused the wing commander and the ship's captain. She also let them know that there would be no aerobatics or other 'wild flying' today because she was pregnant. She told them that if anyone broke that rule they would answer to me - a Navy SEAL. I blushed and left.

Ash continued with her spiel about life in the Navy as a pilot and a short slide presentation on Top Gun. Then she asked for and got a lot of questions. Wrapping up the session she said, "you guys scheduled your rides yourselves. So who's on for today?"

Two hands shot up, one was Jennifer O'Neill ("please call me Jen"), the other was a six foot two smiling, very polite young man, John Olsen. Ash asked, "who's first?" John replied, "ladies first."

Ashleigh never ceased to be amazed at the skills and knowledge these candidate pilots could pick up after flying only thirty five hours with only ten hours of ground school. She always let them handle the radios and communication as well as flying most of the trip. She usually took them twenty or thirty miles out over farmland at ten thousand feet to briefly fly supersonic (don't want to piss off the locals or their livestock). Then after letting them go through some basic maneuvers, ask the tower for a VOR approach, fly the approach and land the airplane (with Ash on the stick). Jen did really well and Ash let her know it.

Ashleigh had created what she called *The Blue Angel Club*. She had the Fixed Base Operator (airport manager) take a picture of the cadet and Ashleigh in their flight suits in front of her Blue Angel T-38. These photos were integrated into a very military looking certificate of membership in the club. The kids ate this stuff up. Ash actually worried that she was making the Air Force and Army cadets feel bad about their programs. I had to constantly remind her that that was her job.

Wednesday night after the last of her rides we returned to JFS and stayed one more night with mom in her condo, then back to the real world – well, our real world anyway.

Chapter Fifteen

Office of Li Peng, Premier of China
Beijing, China
Wednesday, May 23, 1990, 1000 hrs Local Time

The Chinese government found itself in a globally precarious position following student led democratic reform protests in Tiananmen Square in May of 1989 during which hundreds of protesters were killed. Led by the United States, much of the free world had imposed economic and/or trade sanctions on China for its brutal response to the protests remembered internationally by the iconic image of a young Chinese man facing down a column of Soviet T-34 tanks in Tiananmen Square. In an effort to regain its world economic stature and trade status the Chinese had made several recent concessions to its hard line position on human rights by releasing many of the imprisoned protesters. The U.S., Great Britain and several other countries were expected to remove many, but not all, of their punishing sanctions at the June meeting of the United Nations in New York City.

Jiang Zemin, General Secretary of the Chinese Communist Party (CCP) and Premier Li Peng met to discuss the issues at hand and examine the possible actions necessary to keep China on the road to prosperity.

"Comrade Li, we are at a critical point in our growth toward a position of world economic leadership. In our ancient past isolation was necessary to exist in a world of barbarism. We could provide whatever our people required for a life of reasonable prosperity. Despite our efforts to control our population it has expanded a thousand times since those days. Now it is imperative that we exist within a world of multiple ideologies, supporting our economy and benefiting from trade while resisting outside influence on our culture," explained Party Secretary Jiang Zemin.

Premier Peng replied, "Jiang, I am aware of our history and our needs and specifically our short term needs regarding the sanctions but we just lost seventy three sailors, our only Akula submarine, two Costal Officers and their patrol boat, not to mention five MiGs and their pilots, a gunboat and a diesel submarine still missing along with their crews; another forty seven sailors. And you wish me to just, as the American Christians say, 'turn the other cheek' and move on! I think Not.

"This whole mess revolves around our rights to the seas of our ancestors. We may not gain international sovereignty over the South and East China Seas but we will not reverse our claims thereto and I intend to extend that claim to the Yellow Sea. And do so without regard to our so called 'friend', North Korea."

Jiang responded, "Comrade Li, I don't disagree with your position, but I would suggest relaxing our resistance to these violations somewhat. At least until we can reestablish our economic and trade status with the Americans and British."

Peng shot back, "How can we relax when we are constantly threatened in our own back yard? Our military leaders are gun-shy. They risk their own lives as well as those of their crews because they are frustrated by the Americans and British. They feel they are being constantly bullied and have no recourse, so, bravely, they act alone. And we are embarrassed by their actions.

DAWN'S EARLY LIGHT

"The Americans stroll up and down our coastline with impunity in their Ohio class nuclear missile submarines and Los Angeles class nuclear attack submarines, like that *Providence* submarine that just sank our only Akula. Do you know what they carry? One Ohio version carries twenty four Trident intercontinental ballistic missiles. The other version carries one hundred fifty six Tomahawk Cruise missiles each with a range of one thousand to fifteen hundred miles depending on the model. Using just one of each type of Ohio class submarine they could completely disable our missile defense and then destroy all of our major cities. I'm just supposed to ignore this?"

Jiang continued, "Perhaps if we backed off our aggressive stance on human rights somewhat and resumed a more normal trade relationship with them we could negotiate an agreement to restrict traffic in our seas to free passage for commercial and private vessels involved in normal commerce. And with advanced notification, require a negotiated fee for non nuclear military vessels, disallowing nuclear missile bearing vessels all together. We could enjoy a significant trade advantage with the Americans and the Europeans due to their high cost of labor and materials versus our abundant resources of both.

"The Soviet Union has been dissolved and its remnants are rapidly destroying, disassembling, and mothballing its nuclear weapons and fleet. The Americans will have the only nuclear maritime super force on earth. That position might actually allow what I am proposing to become a reality. Maintaining that nuclear force will be a very expensive burden for them as it was for the Soviet Union. The American people don't want another cold war and they are tired of paying for their huge military presence in a world without the threat to warrant it. We have an opportunity to become a major economic power but we're being held back by sanctions and inadequate trade agreements. The Soviets couldn't afford the cold war and we can't either – maybe we could trade one for the other. Our economic opportunity for actions that reduce their military threats.

"If we combine a more docile human rights policy with a noticeable reduction in our aggressive stance toward our pesky neighbors regarding our fishing waters and our ancestral ownership of our bordering seas then we could expect a better relationship with the other world powers that could foster our advancement to a true world economic power. We have the infrastructure in place to be the world leader in trade."

Li mellowed, "Jiang, I have given these ideas some thought also. You have some valid points my friend; we do have some leverage with the Americans and it would be far wiser to test the peaceful solution before the alternative. I'll give you one hundred days of silence and suspend our aggressive posture toward the Americans and the British. You must take this 'period of peace' to negotiate an agreement that ends the economic sanctions we currently face and provides a solution that removes the threat to China imposed by nuclear capable ships, submarines or aircraft belonging to any NATO country. Then we'll review our options again. And then, perhaps, we will talk to the Americans and the British about our claims to the south and east China seas, the yellow sea and the Bohai Sea, before we renew our international claims."

Chapter Sixteen

McKensie Condo, La Jolla, CA
Saturday, May 26, 1990, 0830 hrs PDT

Ash made the coffee and while it was brewing she got her robe from her closet, retrieved the morning paper from the front porch, poured a steaming cup of the freshly made coffee and settled into her favorite chair.

LA JOLLA LIGHT NEWS

Saturday, May 26, 1990

Chinese Sub Sunk By U. S.

In a press release dated yesterday evening at 7:00 p.m. eastern daylight time, the Department of Defense reported that the submarine the Chinese reported missing in the South China Sea was in fact sunk by the USS *Providence*, a U.S. Los Angeles class nuclear fast attack submarine, in the East China Sea approximately ten nautical miles west of the southern tip of mainland Japan, near the island of Fukuoka, in

Japanese waters. A three day United Nations investigation regarding the incident included representatives from the United States, China and Japan. The Captain of the *USS Providence*, Captain Jason McNally, a highly decorated Naval Officer with twenty eight years of service, provided irrefutable proof that the Chinese sub had directly approached *Providence* head-to (head on) and prepared for attack by flooding its torpedo tubes and opening its outer torpedo doors. In a direct quote from Captain McNally; "You can't just sit there and let some idiot blow you out of the water. My responsibility was the preservation of my one hundred twenty nine member crew and the multi-billion dollar *Providence*. I did what any sane sub Captain would do in that situation. When he fired two torpedoes at us, I deployed counter measures and fired back. Our technology proved superior and he lost the battle he started." The SONAR recordings from *Providence* were validated by UN experts and showed clearly that the incident happened exactly as stated by Captain McNally.

The Chinese representatives tried to claim that the incident actually occurred in Chinese claimed waters in the South China Sea, over a hundred miles from the actual site. They also once again laid claim to practically all of the South and East China Seas, in total disregard for International Maritime Law. Unfortunately for them, immediately after the incident Captain McNally surfaced, documented his GPS position and applied his SONAR range and bearing equipment to pinpoint the location of the sunken Chinese sub. A Japanese salvage ship is onsite

DAWN'S EARLY LIGHT

in Japanese waters retrieving wreckage. It is being protected by Japanese and U. S. warships and submarines.

Since the release of the investigation's findings by the U.N. the Chinese government has remained silent regarding the incident.

As I walked into our living room with my morning coffee, Ash looked up at me puzzled and said, "read this." As she handed me the paper she asked, "You didn't have anything to do with this, did you?"

Eyeballing the headline, I lied, "Of course not," – not technically a lie - I was just an observer. I read the article. "so now we've wiped out five MiGs, a gunboat and two submarines, I wonder whether they're going to get really pissed and do something or just back off." Actually I also wondered why they didn't mention that the sub was a Soviet built Akula class nuclear sub – classified, probably.

"They *are* really pissed but they don't have the wherewithal to do anything about it," she opined. "Other than a trillion ground troops with obsolete weapons, a few modern MiGs and Soviet missiles, their military capability is woefully antique,"

"Don't belittle their nuclear capability, although ours moves up and down their coast daily in our nuclear subs and they don't have cruise missile technology, yet. The Chinese may be stupid, but they're not crazy – they don't want to do the cold war dance with us. I think for a few decades, at least, we will be able to force peace among the powers that be. It's the middle east and North Korea that I worry about – They *are* crazy. Or maybe just run by crazy people."

"Anyway," Ash added, "the Chinese just need to count their marbles and go home. They're never going to get control of any additional international water, much less the entire South and East China Seas or the Yellow Sea."

"How about diner at Harry's with Bo tonight. I'd like to ask him some questions about JFS that I didn't think appropriate to ask Jim?"

"You got a date sailor!"

"I'll call Bo."

Chapter Seventeen

Harry's Steak House, San Diego, CA
Saturday, May 26, 1990, 1845 hrs PDT

Ash called for reservations at seven and we were early so I announced our arrival to the Maître 'D and we slid into a two seat booth in the bar area. Bo got there before our drinks did so we moved to our table.

"Hey man, I owe you a beer. Go grab a taste of what I got, I think you'll like it - I'll go with you" I said to Bo – we needed to talk.

"If the waitress gets here before we get back tell her we'll just be a minute or two, okay babe?"

"Don't be long, I'm hungry."

"We won't," I said as we left for the bar.

I pointed to the new beer I liked and asked Bo, "Can you give me a heads up on the new mission?" I'd sort of implied to Ash that I would be home for a few weeks before having to leave again and just needed a little intel to help me manage her expectations.

"We start briefings and training at 0800 Monday at the at the Coronado snake pit, that's all I know"

The 'snake pit' was a small very secure building on Coronado Island that we and other Special Ops organizations used for classified briefings and mission planning.

"Grab a pint of this one, 'Old Glory', I guarantee you'll like it. I'll close out our bar tab and meet you back at the table." By the time I got back to the table Bo had already managed her expectations for me - badly.

"Bo says you guys will be working at Coronado next week. I hope this doesn't mean another mission," Ash whined.

"Ash, this is the Navy. You never know what's going down. Might be a briefing on some of the situations we're watching. Might be a higher briefing on our last trip. Might be the beginning of WW III, you just never know. The good news is I'll be home every night next week – couldn't do that from El Centro."

That put a smile on her face – time to change the subject. And as if on queue the waitress appeared and took our order.

"When was the last time you saw JFS?" I asked Bo

"I stopped by on my way back from D.C. when you were in Alaska – about four years ago, I guess."

"Things have changed."

"I know, did you take pictures?"

"Yeah but I don't have prints yet. I'll print you a set tomorrow and bring them down Monday. The runway's fifty five hundred instead of five thousand feet and he got another thousand foot overrun on the southwest end prepped for surfacing when needed. The ramp and hangar extensions are bigger than I imagined and business looks really good. I would like to look at the long range plan, specifically the cash flow and tax estimates over the duration of the new loan. Do you have these things? It's not that I know anything about business or that I'm nosey, it's just that Ash and I had not planned our future to include any income from JFS and I'd just like to see what Jim has in mind. It could have an impact on our future plans."

"Absolutely Sam, no problem. As I said You were in BUD/S when all this transpired and since then we've been so damned busy I never even thought about JFS – my apologies. I'll copy the papers and bring them Monday. We've got a ten year loan at a little over a hundred and fifty thousand a year in payments. We've already made the first four monthly payments. We've got the new hangar half full of business jets and Jim's got this year's payment covered already, so things are looking really good. Take a look at Jim's plan, current cash flow and the income and expenses for the last five years. Then make your best guesstimate for the next five years and see how it compares to Jim's and mine. I think he's being somewhat conservative."

We talked briefly about the Chinese sub that was sunk by a U.S. sub but since we 'didn't know anything about that', we just took turns bashing the Chinese until the food came. As usual Harry's didn't disappoint us. The steaks were off the chart and Ashleigh was smiling – all-in-all a great night. . .

Chapter Eighteen

Pyongyang, North Korea, Office of Kim IL-sung
Monday May 28, 1990 1015 hrs Local Time

The President of the Democratic People's Republic of Korea and Supreme Commander of the Korean People's Army, Kim Il-sung, welcomed his son Kim Jong-il as he entered the office, "Jong, my son, I trust you come with news of progress from Chong-Fal,?"

"Yes sir, we have successfully adapted the warheads to three of our five Hwasong-5/D missiles (a hybrid version combining the best performance specifications of the Soviet Scud-C and D missiles giving the missile both longer range and an increased payload). We have one each on hard pads programmed for Tokyo and Seoul. The third is integrated on a mobile launcher and located in a well camouflaged and heavily protected underground bunker fifteen kilometers southwest."

"Good work, my son. We are now a nuclear power. A power to be reckoned with. How well are the missiles on the hard pads camouflaged? We want them hidden until the time is right."

"Each missile pad was carefully placed in the tall pine forest to provide excellent cover from satellite observation. Each site will require removal of three large trees prior to completing operational

DAWN'S EARLY LIGHT

status. This will be done when the time is right."

With a grim smile Kim Il-sung said slowly, "We will be sure that America's spy satellites discover our little secret when the time comes, but not until we have all of our pieces in place.

"As you know, we have other looming problems. Our Iraqi friends are pressing us for an answer. They have increased their offer to four hundred million U.S. to include the missile and the launcher. We must respond soon, yes or no."

"Yes sir, I understand the need for recovering our investment in the warheads but is it not wise to retain the third warhead to complete our plan to target Taiwan as soon as our range enhancement modification to the remaining two Hwasong-7 ballistic missiles is complete?"

"Taiwan is a political target, Jong-il, not a strategic military target. Add that to the fact that we spent more than half of the funds we had earmarked for our nuclear development program for those three warheads and we now have an opportunity to keep two and increase our original funds by twenty five percent. This will allow us to accelerate the development of our own weapons. To become a true nuclear power we must have that capability. I intend to inform our friends that we will accept their generous offer."

"I will make the arrangements, my father, and also begin plans for accelerating our nuclear weapons development program."

"Oh," added the president, "and keep the threats against our oil thirsty friends to the south on the front burner until the exchange with Iraq is complete. Maybe a few flybys, some gunboats near the site, more threats to the UN, etc."

"Yes sir."

Chapter Nineteen

President Bradley Stevens' Briefing Room
White House Basement
Wednesday, May 30, 1990, 0735 hrs EDT

The morning's Presidential briefing was nearing completion when CIA director Bill Conroy took the podium to brief the president on two quick items on the agenda;

"First Mr. President, the PRK (Peoples Republic of (North) Korea) just filed a complaint with the ROK (Republic of (South) Korea) disputing the mineral and oil/gas rights in the waters north of the South Korean island of Yeonpyeong-Myeon," remarked Conroy pointing to a map of the area projected onto the huge eight by four and a half foot screen at the front of the room. "It seems the South Koreans have found a huge oil field there and are moving barges into the northern most area of the South Korean sovereign waters, just at the north edge of the field, to drill. The NSA says Kim Il-sung is going ballistic over this and threatening military action if the drilling proceeds."

"Sounds like the ROK picked this spot just to increase Kim's blood pressure – hoping he'll have a stroke – which might be a good thing," concluded Stevens.

DAWN'S EARLY LIGHT

"No sir, not really. The ROK says most of the field lies under and to the south of the island but the huge tides in the area preclude off-shore drilling anywhere else due to shallow water. And the island has been declared a wildlife sanctuary since before the Korean War. There is no basis for Kim's complaint. The drill site is clearly a half mile inside ROK territory."

"Well let's watch it but stay out of it, for now. Did the Chinese ever squawk about their patrol boat? "

"Actually that was my second item. Not a peep about either the Akula sub since the UN hearing - or the patrol boat at all."

"What bothers me Bill, is that Akula was less than fifteen thousand yards from *Providence* when our guys blew up the patrol boat and then *Providence* surfaced and the trawler headed back toward the PRK. If that Akula used a floating wire to communicate these strange events back to its base before we sunk it, the Chinese could start looking at this trying to figure out what was going on. Did George (Admiral Bennington) get the info we needed on that.

"Yes sir, that's the rest of my second item. George had his guys scrub the sonar and voice tapes on a matching time line. They are certain the Akula never got above four hundred feet, so unless that Akula has a floating wire technology better than ours there was no communications via a floating wire. *Providence* was dead in the water for only nine minutes. During that period the Akula did not go below four knots according to our sonar data. Not enough time for the Akula to deploy, use and retrieve a buoy-tethered antenna. *Providence* also monitors Very Low Frequency communications for all known types. There were no VLF communications in the area."

Bradley Stevens sat in deep thought with his hands clasped, forefingers steepled, tips at his mouth staring at the report on the table before him. "It would be very strange behavior for that Chinese Captain to react to his observations of *Providence* in the manor he did without communicating to higher authority. On the other hand, we regularly deal with air and sea face-offs and close approaches by their fighters to our carriers and subs. So perhaps irrational behavior is just part of their deep seated belief that the South China Sea belongs to them. But for an older Akula to fire on one of our nuclear attack subs – that's suicide. Or maybe a sacrificial move in a larger plan. . .

"I'll get back to George on all this. Those guys deserve a unit commendation for that PRK mission. Is that all?"

"Actually, no sir. Beyond the agenda, we've just gotten disturbing news from our Baghdad Station Chief, Olan James; Olan reports that Saddam has gained knowledge of the two remaining un-accounted for Kazakhstani nuclear MIRV warheads and may be considering the purchase of one or both. A quick look analysis last night by Meg and her guys says the likely use will be for strategic targets if the Kuwaiti conflict materializes. Primary would probably be Haifa, Israel. Tel Aviv is too close to Jerusalem and the Holy of Holies. Secondary would probably be Bahrain, home to the U.S. Navy's Administrative Support Unit (ASU) and the Fifth Fleet or the Saudi air base used by us near Riyadh. I have Olan's report with Meg's comments in a folder prepared for you. This will obviously require significant effort in the near future to figure out what is going on. One observation by Olan: If they buy both nukes we need to watch them carefully while they're en-route to their final destinations. If we're right the secondary target will put U.S. assets in harm's way. We'll need to ramp up our satellite surveillance significantly. I gave NSA a heads up."

"Good brief Bill, Let's call it a wrap."

As usual the briefing ended abruptly as Stevens rose and left the room.

Chapter Twenty

Snake Pit Ops Planning Office
Coronado Island, CA
Monday, June 4, 1990, 0800 hrs PDT

"Good morning gentlemen. I'm sure you're all eager to find out what this mission is all about. I have in my hand six briefing folders, each marked 'Top Secret-NTK'. As far as the need to know is concerned the people in this room are the *only people on this earth* with the need to know anything about the information in these folders. Is that clearly understood?" asked Captain Bo Jameson, Commander, Black Angel Team, DEVGRU.

With a positive response from all he continued, "for the past two weeks the NSA satellite intel and the CIA human intel (HUMINT) have noticed a gradual shift in the remaining military structure in Iraq to the south and east. Iraq has laid claim to Kuwait since it was given independence from Great Britain in 1961. As you know, the U.K. provided Kuwait military support for some time after that and eventually Kuwait became a recognized sovereign nation. But Iraq has had its eye on the Kuwaiti oil fields ever since. So it stands to reason that this shift in military power could very well indicate an Iraqi move on Kuwait. The intel we have so far is okay, but far from complete.

"Specifically, there are three underground emplacements near the border between Iraq and Kuwait that need looking at. They are spaced about fifty klicks apart on a line running parallel to and approximately twenty klicks northwest of the Kuwaiti border. They've been there since the early eighties when we first got orbital GPR (Ground Penetrating Radar) intel from that region. So, although we suspect they are mobile missile launchers (Probably Scud-2s) housed underground since the war with Iran, we have no real data and we need to know more than we do about what they are, how they are constructed, type of installation, contents, quantity of what ever's in there, etc.

"So you six operators will comprise three teams of two and go take a look. Infil will be via HAHO-Light (High Altitude High Opening-Light); the ASDS with only the helmet, chest-pack nav-com computer and external oxygen system) on the night of 16 June. For this mission you won't need a pressure suit, but you will need your small oxygen bottle and mask. Your navigation, communication and night vision will be standard ASDS using standard precision mode GPS. You will operate as three independent teams. Inter-team comm will be through your satcom link. Exfil will be on foot at night to Little Bird assist at the border.

"As you can see, this will be a multi-force mission. SEALS, Delta Force and, on loan to JSOC but fully trained with the equipment, and ready to go are Gunnery Sergeant Jeremy Tanner and Captain Todd Michaels from the Marine's Force Recon team. As you know, Force Recon and Delta HAHO teams train with our ASDS guys at Miramar NAS. Welcome aboard guys.

"From Delta Force we have Master Sergeant John Willard and Major Vince Harlow. The mission will be under direct JSOC command. Here's how we'll pair up; McKensie and Curtis, you'll take the northeast site; Harlow and Willard, you'll take the center site; Michaels and Tanner, you'll take the southwest site.

DAWN'S EARLY LIGHT

"Please take the rest of the day as a group to examine and discuss the content of these folders thoroughly. We'll regroup at 1600 and wrap up for the day. Tomorrow we'll develop a detailed plan and start on contingencies. I'll have lunches brought in. Any questions?

"Booby traps - explosives?" asked Rob.

"Don't know – in that stack of documents there on the table there is everything we know about Iraqi emplacements including these three. Figure out what you need and if you can carry it in your drop bags or on your back you will get it We don't envision ASDS cargo packs on this mission. If you disagree, I want to know right away. You will have to destroy and bury everything you bring in country that isn't needed or can't be carried during your exfil. Any more questions?"

Harlow asked, "since we won't know exactly what we're dealing with until we have eyes on the content of the targets, will we get real time orders on disposition?"

"That's affirmative Vince. You'll examine the content and report via satcom. Your orders in response could range anywhere from gather intel and exfil to complete but discreet disablement of content. You will carry tools for that purpose. As long as we know what's there we need to leave overt destruction until there's an actual conflict if at all possible. Anything else?"

Nothing.

Chapter Twenty One

McKensie Condo, La Jolla, CA
Tuesday, June 5, 1990, 1845 hrs PDT

"See, I'm home – and a little early at that," I said as I grabbed Ash and gave her a hug and a kiss. "Can't tell you much about our next trip down range, except that it's a simple recon mission and it should take no longer than three or four days – not a big deal. How're my babies – big one first."

"I had just a slight case of morning sickness this morning, after breakfast, but it only lasted a couple of minutes. The little one's fine, I guess. The doctor says it'll be several weeks before I feel any movement.

"Dirk said if I wanted to I could ride down to Coronado with you and work in the unclassified end of the same building you're in. The flight school has two offices there and one is unoccupied."

Captain Dirk Erickson was Commander of The United States Navy Fighter Weapons School known universally as Top Gun since the 1986 movie starring Tom Cruise. "We could eat lunch together when your schedule permits and have a little more time to talk. What do you think?"

"You got my vote – Dirk's been a great boss. Not many like him in the Navy. He treats people right and they perform with excellence. That's something you and I both need to remember as we get more responsibility.

"What're we doing for dinner – in or out?"

"I think I'm starting to crave my favorite foods. How about a pepperoni and onion pizza from Arnold's. We should go out – do some walking, I need the exercise! How about the beach after dinner – go down to our rock. That shouldn't be too hard, do you think?"

"As long as we don't chase each other around like we used to. Sounds like a great evening. Pizza, then walk."

The pizza was, as usual, really good. The walk was marginal though. For some reason Ash was having trouble with the sand. Center of gravity? No way – it's too early. Additional weight? – she'd only gained five pounds. Don't think so. Combination? Maybe. Over compensation – probably. . .

Chapter Twenty Two

Snake Pit Ops Planning Office
Coronado Island, CA
Thursday, June 7, 1990, 1200 hrs PDT

"Okay guys, your high level plan looks pretty good, what about contingencies?" queried Bo Jameson, BAT leader.

I responded, "We're working with limited intel here. Basically all we know for sure is the exact location of three anomalies in the southern Iraqi desert fifteen kilometers from the Kuwaiti border. We have a fair amount of knowledge about other Iraqi emplacements but while that's all well and good, we're still going in fairly blind on these three. Sites like these will have significant power coming in from somewhere - so there's a fairly high probability of electronic surveillance of some sort at each site. That said, it could take us more than one night to get in, get the required intel and get out. That means spending the next day inside, and egressing the following night - not much ability to hide outside in the open desert. We need a plan for that."

Rob added, "Right now the satellite drivers have three polar orbit birds set up over the area with twenty minute windows and ten minute gaps evenly spaced and a polar sweep bird to scan the whole country in daylight. If we could sneak a fourth IR bird in there it would cut the gaps to two and a half minutes. Our biggest contingency is the movement of Iraqi troops into the area. The latest satellite intel shows about two hundred Iraqi troops already digging in about two klicks from the border on the eastern edge of our target area in groups of about fifty. That means supplies and artillery will follow soon. On the northeast target we'll have to pick our way through that mire on the way out. That means real-time, low-gap IR guidance from above will be imperative. Obviously we'll have IR beacons on our helmets so friend/foe discrimination at night won't be a problem, but . . . "

Bo cut him off, "Something I forgot to mention in our initial briefing; While you, Sam and I were on leave and then off on our last down range party, Leroy and his techs back at El Centro implemented and tested the ASDS satellite target position concept we were talking about last month. On egress just set your visual range to ten kilometers or greater and you will see not only your team members represented by their respective colored dots but all enemy personnel within a twenty kilometer range represented by flashing white dots. The enemy positional data comes from satellites so it won't work during gaps in coverage. We'll request all the coverage we can get for this mission. I was surprised that they got that capability operational and fully tested in less than four weeks. Leroy said it was a simple straight forward software modification. Simple straight forward my ass! Those guys are becoming magicians. After next week we'll run the actual mission on the range at Yuma Proving Ground. It'll be as real as we can make it. We'll all get to see this new capability up close and personal.

"For right now, keep honing your contingency planning and include dependence on target content – anything you can think of.

"Let's eat. I'm buying the first round."

Chapter Twenty Three

Office of the Iraqi Prime Minister
Royal Palace, Baghdad, Iraq
Friday, June 8, 1990, 0900 hrs Local Time

The Iraqi President, Prime Minister, and Supreme Military Commander (i.e., Dictator), Saddam Hussein welcomed his Economic Advisor and friend, Alwar Ar-ruba'I, and his son, Honorable Supervisor (Commander) of the Republican Guard, Qusay Hussein.

"What news do you have for me?," asked Saddam. "All good, I presume."

Ar-ruba'i replied, "The gold brought about two and a half million U.S. more than we calculated using last weeks rates."

"And?"

Qusay continued, "Our agent in the DPRK supervised the loading of the disguised missile launcher, including missile and warhead, aboard the Nigerian freighter *Zaitgai*. Yesterday. The freighter left the port of Changjon this morning. We will transfer the funds when the freighter enters international waters."

"Very Well. Will this freighter be able to navigate to the port of Abu Flus southeast of Basrah?"

DAWN'S EARLY LIGHT

"Yes, it is a shallow water vessel as we requested," replied Qusay.

"Then the overland route will be entirely internal. That *is* good news. How well is it disguised?"

"The loaded launcher is covered with a shell that resembles a Russian MAZ-7911 large military transport. I believe it is a Soviet disguise designed expressly to hide R-17 (Scud) missiles mounted on a MAZ-543 mobile launcher en route."

"Find out where we can obtain these shells and buy a dozen."

"Yes sir."

"When will the freighter arrive?"

"The *Zaitgai's* top speed is twenty knots. It's most efficient cruising speed for this trip is sixteen knots to ensure arrival without having to refuel. Including delays for the Singapore Strait, the Persian Gulf and navigating the Shatt al-Arab river to the port of Abu Flus the estimate is thirty days."

"Has work on the silo south of the H-3 airstrip begun?" asked Hussein.

"Work is under way. The tunnel from the H-3 airstrip is forty percent complete; three and a half kilometers. This entire facility is being constructed while avoiding satellite surveillance. It has required a major effort and significant manpower. Fortunately, because the H-3 complex is in a remote desert area of the Syrian Desert there is only one American satellite passing with a twenty three minute window every thirty six hours. It's orbit is what their CIA calls a polar sweep. The problem is, of course, the sanitizing of the entire visible site every thirty six hours. We are very careful to track all spy satellites as their orbits can be easily changed.

"The entire complex will be complete and ready for operation in early November. We will need to coordinate its transport from Taji and insertion into the silo with the U.S spy satellites and accommodate any orbital changes the Americans might choose to make.. After the missile is inserted into the silo we will transfer the mobile launcher to one of the six empty launcher hides near the Jordanian border. We now have two hundred and twelve R-17 missiles, eleven Al-Hussein missiles and thirty seven mobile launchers."

Qusay handed his father a folder containing several charts and detailed lists and continued, "Here is the updated missile deployment document including the status of the missiles at the Taji facility."

Hussein smiled broadly, "You have performed admirably, my son. The Americans are signaling that they are loathe to interfere in Arab affairs – but as we know they are very unpredictable. If they secure the cooperation of some of our Arab brothers and attack us, the nuclear annihilation of Haifa will bring Israel into the war and we will gain the support of all Arabs. I do not believe this would provoke a nuclear war because Russia and China would intervene."

Qusay asked, "Haifa? Why not Tel Aviv?"

"Too close to Jerusalem. We can't endanger our Mosque with nuclear fall-out. Also, Haifa has one of the lowest populations of Muslims, only five percent. And one of the highest concentrations of Jews, eighty five percent.

"Do not place the Korean missile in the H-3 silo. Leave it on the launch vehicle and drive it from Taji to the to the underground launch bunker southwest of Ruwayshid. Do that immediately and have it targeted for Ramat David (Rah-maht Dah-veed) Air Base. Bring the new warhead to Taji and have it attached to one of our four latest model Al-Hussein missiles. Put that missile into the new silo when it is complete. It will have better range and accuracy and we won't have to separate the Korean missile from its launcher. Have it targeted for Haifa. We must stay on schedule. These UN deadlines are looming."

Chapter Twenty Four

Snake Pit Ops Planning Office
Coronado Island, CA
Tuesday, June 12, 1990, 1300 hrs Local Time

Bo Jameson brought the team to order; "Okay guys, you've got most of your intel needs and planning complete. This afternoon we'll begin the practice phase. Our Army friends have set up a mission simulation course over at YPG. We'll climb aboard our MC-130 at 2100 this evening, head over to YPG and make the first practice run at 2150 hrs. Your final exfil will be only two kilometers. During exfil we want you to become totally familiar with the new friend/foe display mode on the ASDS. One more time; switching to any of the three longest ranges - ten, twenty or thirty kilometers - will automatically put the system into the hostile identification mode if satellite IR surveillance is available. We've timed the mission tonight so that as you're gathering intel a modified bird will come over the range and your system will suddenly begin exposing the enemy. You will see all targets, moving or still, human or not. And tonight you will see plenty of both."

We had simulated the mission a half dozen times in the lab, so we knew what to expect. There were no questions.

"One more thing. This isn't just a run of the mill recon mission. It's just as dangerous as our last mission. You get caught, the U.S. is in a political nightmare, probably as bad as Eagle Claw, you might not come home. So your ROEs (Rules Of Engagement) are as follows; Shoot to kill – leave no visible evidence." Operation Eagle Claw was the infamous hostage rescue mission in 1980 where while attempting to rescue fifty two Americans being held hostage in Iran a RH-53 Sea Stallion Helicopter crashed into an EC-130 tanker airplane, killing eight American Servicemen and causing great embarrassment to the U.S. Special Operations Forces. "We'll do everything we can to get you out if you have problems but the entire exfil must remain covert. Sam, you're in charge of this mission. You are responsible for its success. Understood?"

"Understood."

"I'll be in Dam Neck when you get back."

What the hell did that mean – guess I'll find out when we get back. . .

****

We ran our first practice mission as a one tenth scale version of the planned mission. If everything went well we'd use one half scale for the next two practice runs with exfil shortened to two kilometers and then head for Kuwait.

Tonight's three drop points were five kilometers apart (1:10 scale) but the distance from the targets to the IP was full scale; thirty five kilometers, at the actual altitude of twenty four thousand feet.

The practice infil/exfil of the three two man teams all went well. A few minor issues were noted but nothing critical. We made a few changes in what we buried. By cramming the chutes into the drop backpack we could reduce the digging effort considerably.

DAWN'S EARLY LIGHT

Digging that hole was the toughest job of the mission. No reason to believe the Iraq desert would be any easier to dig in than YPG's.

At 2215 hrs each team auto landed twenty feet from its target. After landing they did a full-up test of all systems; IR gear, team communications, satellite communications, and other gear. Then they busied themselves with burying their 'not necessary for egress equipment', which involved digging the holes, insuring that the equipment would be at least three feet under the sand/dirt and then removing the equipment since this was, after all, a practice mission. Then each hole was refilled such that there was no remaining trace of the activity. Each man had programmed into his ASDS system the GPS coordinates of the access hatch to his respective bunker, the true locations of which had been accurately determined by satellite. When they found the exact location by walking to the little green x on their ASDS visor they knew that the hatch should be within ten feet of that point and using small telescoping metal detectors they started a patterned search of the twenty foot circle. Differential GPS would put them spot-on and they wouldn't need the metal detectors but it would be too difficult to set up in this tactical situation. Iraq had made significant recent changes in its deployment of forces. Two reserve divisions of the Iraqi Republican Guard – the Iraqi elite forces – had been activated to join two active divisions and all were heading southeast. It was becoming more obvious that if UN threats didn't work, there was certainly going to be an Iraqi invasion of Kuwait.

During the Iraq-Iran war (1980-1988) the United States, Saudi Arabia, the United Arab Emirates and Kuwait all supported Iraq. Arms and money from the U.S. and Saudi Arabia and money from the U.A.E. and Kuwait. Iraq had long laid claim to the Kuwaiti oil fields, particularly the fields along the common border where Iraq claimed the Kuwaitis were slant drilling into Iraqi oil fields. The mounting debt to Kuwait, the Saudis, the U.A.E, and the U.S. during its war with Iran and the unwillingness of the Arab countries to forgive that debt combined with the border disputes and the lack of support by the U.S. due to its desire to stay out of 'Arab issues' led Iraq to make the decision to annex Kuwait through force. Actually, the U.S. desire to remove its support from Iraq came more from the fact that less than a year ago NSA discovered that Saddam was sitting on more than fourteen and a half billion U.S. dollars in gold tucked away in a vault one hundred and twenty feet below his palace. More than triple Iraq's entire debt to the U.S. and its allies from the war with Iran. Although the U.S. preferred to stay out of 'Arab issues', Iraq was apparently taking a step too far and the U.S. and its allies began making preparations to counter this decision - if it became a reality. Warnings issued to Iraq through the United Nations were being ignored and it was looking like an invasion of Kuwait was becoming a sure bet. So the pressure was building to get as much intel as possible, quickly. The BAT was becoming the go-to team for quick covert operations.

After three successful dry runs we had the confidence to proceed and scheduled the mission for June 16th.

Chapter Twenty Five

McKensie Condo, La Jolla, CA
Wednesday, June 13, 1990, 1900 hrs PDT

"I don't want to know where the hell you're going but I'm not real happy about all this mission work you've been doing lately. You told me you were more of a developer/tester SEAL than a shoot-em-up cowboy SEAL. And the world's about to go to hell in a hand basket according to the news. So I have a pretty good idea where you're headed this time. Damn-it Sam, you're going to be a father in five months if I don't worry myself to death," Ashleigh said sternly, looking like she was about to cry. Then I realized she hadn't cried since I proposed to her at our private spot on La Jolla Shores Beach four years ago – or was it five?

"Babe, you know I can't talk about mission work." I responded, noticing that my response had generated the expected effect. She switched from almost crying to mad as hell in about three microseconds.

"You're not talking about your fucking mission work! I am! I have no idea where you go or what you do – I just know you keep coming home with new bullet holes in you. Doesn't sound like normal equipment designing and testing to me. Sounds like the fucking gunfight at the OK Corral!"

Not only does she never cry, she never swears either – we've gone from one emotional limit to the other inside of two seconds. This is probably only possible for a pregnant woman. I tried calming her down with my usual rhetoric.

"Ash, we talk about this every time a mission comes around. I wear the best armor in the world and we don't have very many armed conflicts. The BAT has never lost a man. Several of us have been wounded, but not seriously."

"What about Manny?"

"Manny Hernandez was the leader of SEAL Team IV – not DEVGRU, not the BAT. And he was hit with a spray and pray AK-47 lucky shot with the lights on. And he had none of the equipment we carry. You know pretty much about what we do and how we do it. When we fight, we fight at night with technology absolutely not available to the bad guys. Most of the missions are non-confrontational, but when we are confronted, we own the night. We're good at what we do, hell - we're the best in the world at what we do. I don't want you worrying about me. It's not like you. I love you and I will always come home, I promise.

"Okay, okay, I'm calm. Don't ask me how I know this, but I've got to ask; why isn't Bo going on this mission?"

"Bo's our Gold Team leader now. Above and beyond mission work he has a lot of other responsibilities. We don't need him on routine missions. I'm leading this mission but Bo went through the planning phase with us. Really, there's nothing to worry about."

Truth to tell, there were a lot of unknowns to deal with on this mission. More than any other down range gig we'd done. And I'm having more and more trouble with 'the truth' . . .

****

Captain Bo Jameson led the 'Gold Team', attached to the Black

DAWN'S EARLY LIGHT

Assault Squadron of DEVGRU (not related to the Gold Assault Squadron, one of four much larger combat organizations). As such he was responsible for four special weapons development and deployment teams; air, land, sea and common weapons systems. The ASDS was the only active advanced airborne weapon system in the deployment mode at this time and it looked like we might soon become an official operational unit.

From 1980 to 1987 the super-secret unconventional warfare team formed by Lieutenant Commander Richard Marcinko was known as Seal Team Six. In 1987 it was renamed the Naval Special Warfare DEVelopment GRoUp (NSWDG) and called DEVGRU. Also in 1987 the then existing Joint Special Operations Command (JSOC) became a major component of the newly formed US Special Operations Command (USSOCOM), stationed at MacDill Air Force Base near Tampa Florida. USSOCOM represented a more complete integration of Special Operations units from all US military organizations as well as a closer and more integrated connection to the US Intelligence organizations such as the CIA, NSA, DIA, DEA and FBI. At that time Seal Team Six, which no one knew about anyway, became DEVGRU.

Later as part of the ongoing USSOCOM integration Admiral George Bennington, the Commander of JSOC, approved Bo's recommendation to form the Black Angel Team, to be led by me. The BAT (that, of course, made us the BATs), was at that time focused primarily on ASDS, IR night vision and several other covert night-time infil and exfil system design, development and deployment programs. It then became responsible for all airborne infiltration systems, with design and development teams at El Centro NAF and a multi-force basic and operational training team at Miramar NAS near San Diego. Also as part of that integration the BAT became responsible for field and operational testing of several new hi-tech intel systems for other government agencies such as the new portable tactical drone systems being developed for the CIA. This left Bo to run the entire DEVGRU Gold Team, responsible for all Special Operations weapons development, from Dam Neck Virginia while I managed the BAT (advanced airborne infil and exfil weapon systems design, development and deployment) at El Centro NAF and Miramar NAS.

"Although nothing

"I've explained all the changes and you know what I do – we've talked about this several times. We good?"

"Yeah, I guess I'm trying to push too hard on this family thing, I love you and I don't want you hurt or dead, but I've got to remember we're both military, and since I've been grounded at Top Gun I guess I might have become just a tad jealous."

Wow, a rare confession! This needs documentation.

Chapter Twenty Six

CIA Gulfstream III, Enroute to Aviano Italy
Thursday, June 14, 1990, 1800 hrs Local Time

I drove Rob and me down to San Diego International and parked my Vette in the long term lot where a waiting silver Ford Taurus took us to the General Aviation terminal and we boarded one of the CIA's Gulfstream IIIs and flew non-stop to Langley Air Force Base, Virginia – nice ride, great food. A hell of a lot nicer than anything the Navy's got. Then we hopped up to Andrews AFB in Maryland in a Bell Huey II – the modern civilian version of the Vietnam era UH-1 "Huey" - where we jumped on a C141 Starlifter headed to Aviano AFB, Italy. The 141 was configured to carry both troops and equipment, both of which were being mustered in Italy, Turkey and Saudi Arabia should they be needed in the brewing Iraq / Kuwait crisis.

The long flight gave us time to get to know each other better. Rob, Vince and I had teamed together on several similar missions in Central and south America and Rob and I had done gigs together in North Korea, Panama, Libya and Kazakhstan. Rob and I knew John through training at Miramar, but Jeremy and Todd, the jarheads, were new to the rest of us. Turns out Gunnery Sergeant Jeremy Tanner (Gunny) is our senior member, both in age and length of service. In Special Ops rank plays a far smaller role than experience so the rest of us had met our match in war stories and wild tales of the past although Rob and I gave him a run for his money. All were married except Gunny who said he'd tried that one to many times.

"How many times is that?" Rob asked.

"One", Jeremy replied, then added, "she and the Corps didn't get along – the Corps and I made the right choice."

Gunny was a celebrated sniper in Vietnam who at the age of twenty two, according to Todd, had over thirty kills. He is six four, lean and muscular. Reminded me of Bo, body-wise. But his weathered face actually made him look older than his forty one years. He is our weapons specialist and sniper. He has two teen aged kids; a fifteen year old boy and a thirteen year old girl. He lives in San Diego. His ex-wife and kids live in Plano, Texas.

At thirty nine, Army Ranger Master Sergeant John Willard is our explosives and demolition expert. John's nickname is Owl.

"Nothin' to do with being a wise-ass, I just like doing my work at night," he drawled with a sheepish grin. Owl didn't talk much and he looked like the kind of guy you wouldn't want to run into in a dark alley, but he had the right attitude and when he spoke everyone listened. We didn't like 'Owl' so we called him Sarge He's career Army, married with no kids, Sarge had just moved to Chula Vista California.

Master Chief Robin Curtis is thirty eight, looks like a first round pick for linebacker in the NFL college draft, has a little three year old girl, Judy, and another child due in January. My wife Ashleigh is due in November. Rob and I joked about our kids being SEAL cousins since we were SEAL brothers. Rob and his wife Sara live near us in La Jolla California. We train together and run ten miles every morning before breakfast - when we aren't down range or on training exercises. Rob's early days in the Navy were spent as a Navy Corpsman (same as a Medic in the Army) and his nickname was Doc although he didn't like it used in his current job. So we re-named him bird (First name Robin), which he doesn't like much either. He's our corpsman, a senior SEAL, a trained sniper, fluent in five languages and previous second in command, and for a short time commander, of SEAL Team IV.

Major Vincent Harlow, like me, is an engineer. He came into the Army as a CW-2 (Chief Warrant Officer), managing contractor programs that developed weapons systems. He advanced to CWO - 3 and then became commissioned as a Captain after which he completed Delta Force training. He and I flew the second ever ASDS mission in Nicaragua in 1986. At twenty eight, he's a year younger than me. His nickname is Carbo. He won't tell us why. He has a wife and a four year old boy and lives in Phoenix.

Captain Todd Michaels doesn't have a nickname – yet. He's twenty seven, married with no children – yet. Lives in Oceanside, Near Camp Pendleton. He is one tough Marine. Trains hard, works hard and lives and plays hard. He's our communications expert, He's twenty nine, same as me.

The big Starlifter was a surprisingly comfortable ride. The six of us and twenty eight Delta guys plus a bunch of cargo and equipment had a relatively smooth nine hour trip – fourteen hours on the clock - straight to the U.S. Air Base at Aviano, Italy. We off-loaded our own equipment, stowed it in a secure room behind the operations area, got some food and headed for the transient barracks for some rest.

Chapter Twenty Seven

MC-130E Combat Talon, Twenty km southeast of the Iraq/Kuwait Border at Angels Two Four Saturday, June 16, 1990, 2100 hrs Local Time

After grabbing a few hours sleep, reviewing our plans and completing final preparations for the mission we left Aviano in a C-130, flew to King Salman Air Base in Saudi Arabia to refuel and check the weather. The current forecast for the target area was clear and visibility unlimited with winds from the south at twenty to twenty five knots at altitude reducing to ten to fifteen knots on the ground. Tomorrow's forecast was about the same with winds picking up tomorrow night and Monday. Not bad for the mission. Good that we weren't a day later.

We rechecked our gear, ran system tests and replayed the mission once again – each of us knew his assignment and was aware of the contingencies and appropriate counter actions. Piece of cake! Yeah, sure.

We took off on a northeastern route to fly twenty kilometers inside Kuwait parallel to the Iraqi border at twenty four thousand feet. As we entered Kuwaiti airspace we suited up and the Marine Force Recon guys, Jeremy and Todd, got ready to jump. When the pilot gave us the three minute warning we activated our oxygen masks, depressurized and lowered the ramp – no pressure suits at twenty four thousand feet, just the ASDS system and helmet and oxygen system. When the light turned green they jumped. We could see them move quickly away behind the aircraft as a pair of colored dots on our visors.

We repeated this process at the second IP for Vince and John and everything was proceeding as planned – until we got a sat-link call from Todd telling us that the wind speed at twenty one thousand feet was thirty five knots, not twenty five, and appeared to be increasing as they descended. And, the ASDS had them flying backwards and s-turning to lose as much altitude as possible, as quickly as possible. Our mission profile requires that we carry fifteen percent additional altitude above the perfect glide slope as a buffer against winds changing from forecast; in this case our buffer was three thousand six hundred feet. So our guys had a tail wind of ten knots above forecast and the system would need to bleed off much more altitude than planned. I had the pilot make a sixty degree turn to the south as he crossed our glide path, fly two minutes on that leg, then make a descending two hundred and ten degree turn back to the glide path at twenty thousand feet. This would put Rob and I close to the proper glide path for the higher than forecast winds.

We jumped when we got back to the glide path and immediately the ASDS put us into an s-turning dive. Our calculated wind speed was forty five knots – twenty knots above forecast. The system is designed to handle winds aloft, whatever they might be, as long as they are within fifteen percent of forecast. This wind was already over fifty percent above forecast and rising. And, we were descending into a fucking sand storm.

Just as I was trying to figure out how bad this was going to be Todd called on the sat-link saying they were s-turning into the wind at maximum dive angle, currently twenty two hundred feet above the glide slope, calculated wind speed forty five knots and climbing. They were picking up fine sand.

The arid regions of the middle east have dust storms, called *haboobs*, on a fairly regular basis. Sometimes these storms are unpredictable in the short term because they are beyond the meteorological knowledge of weather forecasting computer models in that area of the world.

Todd asked, "how far past the target will this put us?"

Vince chimed in, "Fuck the overshoot! How do we land backwards with a twenty five, maybe thirty knot ground speed?"

My hope was that as is normal the wind would lessen as we neared the ground but that wasn't happening. We were going to have to handle landing with a forty plus knot wind in a sand storm using a system with a design limit of twenty four knots and only tested to twenty.

Todd & Jeremy were approaching five thousand feet in a maximum decent mode and they needed advice before we descended into the blowing sand. This situation was not anticipated in our training program – I would have to fix that. I switched to the open satellite channel so everyone could hear me including Langley.

"Okay guys, as the system gives you the 'touchdown approaching' signal, switch the Automatic Landing System to manual, steer directly into the wind and reduce your vertical speed to 100 feet per minute. You'll be flying backwards at about thirty knots. When your equipment bag hits the ground the chute will go horizontal and drag you. When this happens hit your emergency release immediately. It shouldn't be any worse than falling off a motorcycle backwards and the bag should stabilize you and help you stop. Keep your helmets on and stay on oxygen until it runs out. That'll keep the sand out of your eyes and mouth and maybe give you VHF comms. In jump sequence respond!"

"Tanner, copy that."

"Michaels, copy."

DAWN'S EARLY LIGHT

"Willard, copy."

"Harlow, Roger that."

"Curtis, copy."

I added, "here's hoping there's no rocks in the sand down there. Report in as you recover if your comms are still working. If your ASDS is fucked up you've still got your hand held sat-phone, hand held VHF and GPS in your equipment bag. Probably the VHF hand held will be the only comms that will work in this sand storm and it might not work until it starts clearing. Use your VHF Automatic Direction Finder (ADF) to find each other. Click back in sequence. "

Five clicks.

"Good luck guys"

Chapter Twenty Eight

Iraqi Desert Fourteen Kilometers Northwest of the Kuwaiti Border – in the Air, Angels Eight
Saturday, June 16, 1990, 2117 hrs Local Time

Rob and I were at about eight thousand feet s-turning backwards at maximum decent rate when we got VHF a report from Gunny Tanner.

"We're down - damned rough landing. Best estimate is four klicks beyond target. Captain Michaels hasn't responded to my calls and I can't see his IR locator. He's probably two to three hundred yards northwest and west of our track. No GPS in this sand storm. I'm headed that way now. I've got everything I jumped with secured so my progress is going to be slow. Equipment appears to be okay. Call you back when I find Todd."

"Keep us posted Gunny. Are you injured?"

"Nothing I can't handle. I'll be okay."

Five minutes later Major Vince Harlow reported;

"I'm down, banged up but able. Visibility is practically zero. Sarge isn't responding to my calls. He was close on my locater until we lost GPS – should have been about a hundred yards behind me when I wiped out. Be advised; the fucking chute release is a bitch to operate with all that drag on the harness – be ready to

DAWN'S EARLY LIGHT

use both hands. I got drug over a hundred feet – and yeah, there are rocks in this sand. More like sand in these rocks. My back feels like hamburger. Back to you when I find Sarge.

*****

Just as my ground proximity sensor signaled "Approaching Surface," I saw a light below me in my helmet's rear-view mirror. As I continued toward the ground traveling backwards at about thirty knots the light, now in front of me, devolved into two lights before it was lost in the swirling sand – a friggin truck – and I was pretty close. This meant I was passing over the only road we'd tried to avoid in our mission planning. It was more than two kilometers north of my programmed landing spot. As I was pondering whether I had been visible to the truck I felt my equipment bag hit the ground. The chute started dragging the bag and I was pulled into a back down horizontal position. As my butt hit the ground I used both hands to pop the chute release and fell hard to the surface. I skidded to a stop in the rocks and sand with my bag just behind me. Felt like I'd spent ten minutes in a concrete mixer.

I got lucky. Got out of my chute harness, grabbed my bag, un-tethered the shoulder straps, got it on my back and headed north looking for my chute. In less than a hundred yards I found it lying flat on the surface as it was designed to do. Pulling the emergency chute release not only releases the jumper, it also disables the chute by opening the ram air cells on the outer two thirds of the airfoil. This causes the chute to roll up toward the center, destroying its lift. Until now this feature had only been wind tunnel tested at twenty four knots. Looks like it works pretty well at thirty. And if it worked for me it should have worked for the whole team. The chute release, however, needs to be modified for one hand easy release when dragging a body and a heavy drop bag over the ground – note to self.

I tried to communicate with my ASDS sat-phone and VHF

radio – nothing. The VHF worked fairly well all the way to Gunny and Todd while we had some altitude. But on the ground, not so much. The satellite comms and GPS wouldn't operate in a sand storm at ground level either, but I tried them anyway. Again nothing. The ASDS VHF comms were designed for local combat communications (up to ten or fifteen miles in the clear) to keep the battery drain as low as possible. The handheld VHF units would work well on a flat surface for up to forty to sixty miles in good conditions, depending on terrain. Conditions here were anything but good, so maybe a mile or so max. But, they ought to work well enough for each of us to find our partners. When the storm abated I expected the sat-phones and GPS to work – both the ASDS and handheld unit. Our handheld VHF radios had a built-in ADF (Automatic Direction Finder); a little round window on the top of the unit with a needle that pointed in the direction of an incoming signal with a connecting cord to the ASDS helmet display. This system was ideal for finding a partner in a sand storm.

I called Rob, "Blue Dog Alpha Two, this is Blue Dog Alpha One, over." No answer – he probably hadn't gotten his handheld VHF out of his bag yet. I busied myself bunching up my chute and stuffing it into my bag as best I could in the howling wind. It was now 2205 hrs (10:05 p.m.). We considered the unpredictable weather in our mission planning but not this bad or this early in the mission – the forecast was clear with moderate winds for two days.

On the ground the ASDS helmet was a lifesaver. The hybrid mini re-breather system with supplemental oxygen is good for five plus hours of normal breathing and it's isolated to the helmet even when the pressure suit is removed.

Murphy's Law in its finest form, *If anything can get fucked up – IT WILL, and it will do so at the most inopportune time!* And it almost always causes issues which are outside the mission contingency envelope.

Chapter Twenty Nine

Iraqi Desert, Twenty Five miles northwest of the Kuwaiti Border – on the ground
Sunday, June 17, 1990, 2145 hrs Local Time

Rob and I found each other using the ADF on our radios. He had also gotten his stuff buried – not easy. We walked a few kilometers south into the wind and sand, crossed the road where I'd seen the truck and found a small patch of large, smooth boulders that offered some relief from the sand blaster we were engulfed in. We decided to rest there until the wind abated enough to allow our comms to reach at least to John and Vince and then move forward only after John and Vince had established contact with Jeremy and Todd. This would allow us to communicate end to end with the center team as a relay.

We were in pretty good shape, considering. Not badly injured. All systems functioning, although we wouldn't have use of the ASDS satellite comms and GPS until the air cleared. We did know our VHF comms and ADF were working, albeit not much more than a couple of kilometers. We worked for about an hour on revising almost all of our contingency plans based on the weather changes, then tried to sleep a little and let the dust settle.

DON CANDY

*****

Major Vincent Harlow and Master Sergeant John Willard (Sarge) were not so lucky. Sarge had been dragged over a hundred yards into a group of large rocks after his chute release failed to work. He suffered a broken right clavicle and was forced to cut the right shrouds of his chute to reduce the possibility of being dislodged from the rocks and dragged farther northwest. He was unconscious and pinned against the rocks with his chute flapping in the storm when Harlow found him. Fortunately, he had the wherewithal to locate his handheld VHF and enable the ADF function before he passed out. Without the ADF beacon, Harlow couldn't have found him in the melee. Harlow secured and buried the chute and then cut away his chute harness.

Once he secured his chute and freed him of all his gear, Harlow administered a syrette of morphine and after shoving his broken bone ends into their proper position, he was able to apply a compression strap and sling to relieve the pain. Sarge regained consciousness after about a half hour and was able to hobble around to the leeward side of the rock formation and find a sitting position in which he could rest without major discomfort.

*****

Gunny Tanner and Captain Michaels had found each other, buried their stuff and were walking southeast toward their objective, RT (Recon Target) Charlie. Both were banged up but ambulatory. All of their required exfil equipment appeared to be fully functional.

Chapter Thirty

Iraqi Desert, Twenty Five miles northwest of the Kuwaiti Border – on the ground
Monday, June 18, 1990, 0515 hrs Local Time

As morning approached, the wind began to abate and the heavy sand was returning to its proper place while the fine stuff and true dust remained aloft obscuring horizontal visibility. Surprisingly, the first comm unit to work was the ASDS satellite link. We checked in with Langley and asked them to run a down-link check on our other two teams and set up a secure net between all four parties.

As we approached our target we saw the truck. Most certainly the one I had seen on my descent earlier. It was parked. No one in sight. The hatch to the bunker was open.

I advised Langley of the situation and asked if they had established communications with the other two teams yet. They said yes, the net was functional and under our control. I set the net to single comm channel and selected Langley. I asked the Admiral for direction.

Just as he was responding, "If possible do not engage. Bypass the target. If possible, hide and return when they leave. Otherwise abandon the objective," an Iraqi soldier climbed out of the hatch, turned toward me and raised his hands – probably because I had my MP5 aimed at his center of mass. He wore a black beret and the red triangle insignia of the Republican guard. Two stars on his shoulder. A Lieutenant. I told Rob to guard the hatch.

"Uh . . . Admiral, our situation just changed – possibly for the better. Give me a few minutes to get this resolved and I'll get back to you." And I hung up on Admiral George Bennington. Probably the first time that had ever happened.

I motioned for the Iraqi to step away from the hatch and place his sidearm on the ground. He replied softly in English, as good or better than mine;

"My name is Tariq Sa'id. I wish to defect to the United States. I will hand you my weapon, if that's okay."

Holding my MP5 squarely on his chest, I walked slowly toward him, held out my hand and retrieved his Sig Sauer P226, one of my favorite weapons, handgrip first. I asked him how many additional soldiers were in the bunker.

"Just one. He's a technician, not really a soldier, rank equivalent to your Spec-4 as a technician or a Corporal in a line company. He speaks only Arabic and a little Kurdish, no Pashtu, no English."

"Does he wish to defect also?"

"I don't think so. No, actually I'm certain he doesn't."

"Does your truck have a radio?"

"Yes, but it's over a hundred klicks out of range of any Iraqi installation."

"If you wish to come with us, what do we do with your tech?"

"That would be your decision. My decision would be to kill him and blow up the site with him in it. Make it look like an accident."

His use of the word klick, a slang term used in the military for

DAWN'S EARLY LIGHT

kilometer, and his suggested solution to the current situation indicated he had more than just a casual understanding of the American version of the English language, some knowledge of our military and a genuine interest in defecting to the United States.

"You talk and think like an American officer. Why?"

"I was raised from the age of three years in Morgantown, West Virginia where my father received his PhD in Electrical Engineering and taught a course in electrical power distribution at West Virginia University. I have a Masters Degree in Electrical Engineering in computer systems from WVU. My parents returned to Iraq during the Iran war because two of my seven cousins here had been drafted into Saddam's army. My Uncle had been killed in the war and my aunt (my father's sister) needed our help. I rejoined them after graduate school. It didn't take Saddam's people long to figure out I had an advanced degree in engineering and I got drafted into the missile defense organization. My family stands firmly against the Baathists and they are aware of my plans to disappear by faking my death. I was planning to do what I suggested to you before you showed up. My family and I will do what ever we can to help thwart the coming conflict with Kuwait. We have relatives there also. So, you see, to me the technician below is no more than collateral damage for a greater cause – the welfare of my family, the free world and me."

I took about thirty seconds to digest what the Iraqi had told me and about thirty more to analyze the fallout of his suggested solution to both problems at hand - his and mine.

"No gunfire. You must use a standing neck-break. Can you do that?"

"The Iraqi Army teaches its soldiers many ways to kill barehanded. The neck-break is the number one method."

"Are you prepared to proceed?"

"Of Course."

Tariq and I were standing about fifteen feet in front of the open hatch behind which Rob was standing with his MP5 at ready. We walked quietly up to Rob who turned his head toward us.

I whispered, "Stand down while our friend here goes into the bunker to kill his technician. I'll explain afterward."

Rob looked at me like I'd lost my mind, but stepped aside and let Tariq enter through the hatch. About two minutes later Tariq called through the open hatch. "You can come down now. Or shall I come up?"

I responded, "You come up."

He did so and we talked some more while we got Rob up to speed. Tariq retrieved a set of three folders from the truck which contained complete inventories and operational status of all weapons and systems contained in not only this bunker but the other two we'd been tasked to recon also. If we'd gotten to him first, this mission wouldn't have been necessary.

Then we took a tour of the bunker. There was a mobile missile launcher with a SCUD C missile mounted and ready to be erected and fired. There were six additional missiles in a hydraulic loading magazine designed to reload the launcher in a quick-fire sequence. There were massive camouflaged doors that open to allow the launcher to drive up a ramp to the launch position, fire the missile and then back down the ramp to reload. Tariq said the cycle time is less than twenty minutes. Impressive.

In addition to the SCUDS there was a weapons cache of two hundred Soviet RPG-7 Rocket Propelled anti-tank Grenades, one thousand hand grenades, three hundred AK-47 machine guns, thirty thousand rounds of 7.62 mm ammunition, fifty mortars with eight hundred fifty mortar shells and a variety of artillery shells.

Tariq continued, "My original plan was to blow up the identical bunker fifty klicks west of here. The second of three in a row. It is closer to the Ali AL Salem Kuwaiti Air Base which will likely be

DAWN'S EARLY LIGHT

targeted for destruction if this conflict happens. My plan was exactly what we're talking about doing here except for doing it at the other bunker."

"Give me the details of your plan for defection," I said, thinking so far it sounds like something we might want to assist him with if his plan had all of our bases covered.

"Place my tech's body on the launcher's maintenance platform right next to the SCUD programming panel access port with the access plate removed. This is required by a normal maintenance procedure in the routine inspection protocol and that procedure requires a series of sequential steps the order of which is critical to the safety of the personnel present at the time. Then place a timed explosive at a location in the missile most likely to hide its presence; behind the access port between the rocket engine and the fuel tank. The resulting explosion will practically vaporize the contents of the bunker. The roof of the bunker contains two feet of reinforced concrete and one foot of hardened steel interleaved in four layers. The walls are two feet of reinforced concrete. It's designed to resist penetration from the outside. While the internal explosion will blow the roof upward, the main force will blow the contents of the bunker through the opening caused by the upward movement of the roof. It will pulverize the bunker's contents as it does so. Lots of very small unidentifiable body parts spread over a very large area. We'll both be listed as casualties. My tech simply screwed up. The folders I got out of our truck are copies. The official folders are still in the truck. The truck needs to remain exactly where it is according to our inspection protocol."

I asked Tariq, "what if we closed this site up, documented its inspection, loaded the tech's body into the truck and traveled down the road to the next site as you had originally planned?"

"That would be my preference," replied Tariq.

"What kind of explosive do you have?"

"Just about everything we have here is Soviet made. I planned to use one of the fifty small mechanically timed devices listed on the bunker inventory you have in your hand. They are very reliable and will do the job nicely."

"Will it give us enough time to get to the Kuwaiti border on foot?"

"Variable from ten minutes to twelve hours. That ought to be sufficient. Don't you think?

"Rob, comments? See any holes?"

"It looks too damned good to be true. But I don't see any glaring problems. You gonna talk to the Admiral?"

"Yeah, but I've got to get the plan completely together before I do. We need to talk to Bravo and Charlie. Get them informed and integrated into the plan. Meanwhile, look at our plan modification relative to Admiral McRaven's Spec Ops Principles and give me your new assessed probability of success."

"Aye, Aye Skipper!"

I called Major Harlow on the sat-net and got the bad news on Sarge. I got him up to speed on our new plan and told him to stand down on the bunker inspection. He said they were still about three klicks from their target. Sarge's injuries were much more than just a broken clavicle and he figured they would be at the target in about an hour . I told him to take a short break when they got there, forget the target and then continue south to their exfil point on the border.

I called Michaels next. He and Gunny were almost done with their recon. I told them we had all the intel we needed on all the sites and to secure their site exactly as they had found it and head south. I'd be back with more info later.

"Okay Rob we've got a problem. Sarge has a broken clavicle and other injuries. His chute never released, drug him through a

DAWN'S EARLY LIGHT

field of rocks, then slammed him into a boulder doing about thirty knots. He's moving slow. Estimates their target in about an hour."

Rob looked up frowning and said, "Sans Murphy we've got an eighty seven percent plus probability of success at this point. The news on Willard's injuries will lower that some. I'll re-calculate. When you talk to the Admiral see if you can get a Huey or an additional Little Bird out of AL Salem Air Base. One Little Bird won't hold eight people and we need either the room in a Huey or an additional Little Bird with a litter attachment, if available."

"Copy that Rob. I'm calling the Admiral now."

I set the ASDS secure sat-net to one-on-one with Admiral Bennington and made the call. After a twenty one minute discussion I had given a realistic answer to every query he made about the altered plan and he agreed to let us figure out what to do with Tariq when we got to Kuwait.

The Admiral opined, "Sometimes a bucket of shit turns into a pot of gold. Beware of fools gold though, it smells just like shit."

"Okay guys, we're good to go. Let's stay alert and think on our feet. The sun's up. So that's a problem for us, except that we've now got the truck for cover. Get the tech out of sight under the canvas. We're taking him with us to site Bravo. We'll secure this site, document the inspection and maintenance tasks and head west. Then we'll blow the Bravo site. I'm sorry Rob but you'll need to ride in back under the canvas with the tech. Tariq, what's your normal position in the truck?"

"Shotgun, the tech always drives."

The truck was a well worn WWII Chevy one and a half ton canvas covered utility vehicle – a smaller version of the well known but little loved deuce and a half.

"He and I would look more alike if my hair and beard were black. Any ideas?"

None.

"Tariq, is it at all probable that anyone would come looking for you after that storm? Either in another land vehicle or an aircraft?"

"I would put that probability very low. I would be more worried about troop and equipment movement south toward Kuwait. Especially at this location. That probability will fall sharply as we move southwest. Another reason I had chosen the middle site. "

"Okay, so we need to get the hell out of Dodge. First, the three of us need to get the tech out of the bunker and into the truck. Tariq, Can you secure the bunker while Rob and I wipe the surface.

"Yes I can, ten minutes max," responded Tariq.

Damn! He actually sounds like a guy from the hills of West Virginia. But then, of course, he is. . .

Chapter Thirty One

Iraqi Desert, Twenty Kilometers Northwest of the Kuwaiti Border – Site Bravo Bunker
Monday, June 18, 1990, 0705 hrs Local Time

"They're not here yet. Rob, put your radio in ADF mode and see if they're emitting a signal. If not, call him on the sat-net and tell him to enable ADF."

Two minutes later Captain Todd Michaels groaned over the ASDS VHF channel "GPS says we're less than two klicks away but I can't see . . . never mind, I thought the truck was a rock. We've slowed down pretty much now so it'll take us a while to get there. I'm damn near carrying Sarge".

"Todd, find a place to get Sarge off his feet. I'm coming to get you in the truck."

"Rob, Tariq, can you guys grab the tech and start getting this place ready to blow while I Pick up Michaels and Sarge?"

"Sure Skipper."

"Rob, I'm going to take these guys straight to the border and drop them off at EP Bravo, then come back for you two. It'll take me about an hour. Don't set the timer until I'm back, okay?"

"Absolutely, we'll have this place all set up by the time you get back."

On the way to recover Captain Michaels and Sergeant Willard I called Langley, explained our casualty situation and asked the CIA to make three trips in a Little Bird with a litter and scratch the previous Huey request. The first extraction would be EP (Exfil Point) Bravo for one able and one injured in about forty five minutes. The second extraction would be at EP Charley as soon as the Little Bird can get there for two able and then EP Bravo again approximately one and a half hours later for three able. The CIA guy on the other end was confused.

"What about EP Alpha," he asked.

"Change in plans," I responded, "We found an old truck and a new friend."

"Why don't you use the truck to exfil?"

"We're going to blow it up."

"Never mind."

Tariq and Rob had Site Bravo ready for annihilation by the time I got back. We put the truck in its proper place, reviewed every detail of the remaining operation, set the timer for three and a half hours and started a twenty kilometer trek to EP Bravo. It was hot. The wind from last night was nowhere to be found. The sky was pale blue and totally cloudless. Our camel packs (water bags worn on the back with a tube to the mouth) were only about one quarter full, but Tariq had a half empty four liter bottle from his truck that he said he would share if one of us ran out.

Three Hours Later

From a kilometer away we could see the Little Bird sitting there waiting for us. I was hoping they'd brought us some water. We were totally out. The Little Bird pilot looked familiar to me as we approached.

DAWN'S EARLY LIGHT

"Jimmy Mac (McDaniel), I'll be damned. What the hell are you doing out here in the desert?" I yelled as soon as I was sure he was who I thought he was. Chief Warrant Officer, CIA/DEA Pilot, James McDaniel had rescued me three times before on down range assignments. Once from a Coast Guard cutter off the coast of Mexico after I'd been shot by a drug lord, once from Noriega's hideout in Panama last year and then again in Kazakhstan when we were ambushed by a squad of Kazi Republican Guard Special Forces while reconnoitering a nuclear weapon storage depot . Jimmy belonged to the Army's 160th Special Operations Aviation Regiment, known as SOAR. He was a CIA Little Bird pilot with exceptional skill and experience. His specialty was exfiltration (exfil) – getting whoever the hell out of wherever they were.

"I thought they only let intelligent SEALS operate in the desert. You get shot up again?" he grinned as Rob and I loaded our stuff in the back of his McDonnell Douglas MH-6 Little Bird.

"Nah, we just had ourselves a little party out in the rocks & sand. This here's Tariq. He saw us doing our thing out there and decided he'd better switch sides. Actually he's a resident American with an American Passport. We're takin' him home to Virginia to see his mother."

"Well, we better get movin' then. Don't want to put a dent in the Lieutenant's travel plans."

"Actually, Jimmy, I'd like to go up to about fifteen hundred feet and maybe creep northwest up to the border a bit so we can watch a little show that should start in about eight minutes. Did you get our beat up Master Sergeant taken care of."

"Yeah, they had a meat wagon waiting for him. The medic said he's going to be laid up for a while, but he'll live. What happened? Couldn't find his ripcord?"

"We landed in that haboob last night. His chute release didn't work. Drug him half way to Baghdad."

Jimmy leveled off at fifteen hundred feet and started drifting northwest slowly. After we had drifted maybe five hundred yards into Iraq we saw the huge explosion. It seemed to happen in phases. First, fire shot out sideways in all directions, followed by dense dark smoke and then about the time a secondary explosion happened we heard the first one and got rocked by the shock wave. After that there were several additional explosions and then so much smoke that it obscured any other explosions from sight but we could still hear them and we felt a couple of additional shock waves. Just as we turned south toward Kuwait City the smoke looked like it had risen to about five or six thousand feet. It was turning into a huge black roiling mushroom cloud and was still rising.

"What the fuck! Did you guys set off a nuke or something?" yelled Jimmy.

"No, just an Iraqi fireworks factory," replied Rob.

Jimmy flew us to the Al Ali Salem Air Base where we caught a ride in a staff car to the U.S. Embassy in downtown Kuwait City. Jimmy said they have a helipad at the embassy but they only want it used for emergencies, or important people, not peons like us. They did take Sarge there and they got him to the best hospital in Kuwait City right away.

When we got to the embassy the CIA Station Chief took Tariq off for 'a little talk'. Which in CIA-speak means a friendly interrogation. Said he'd be confined to the embassy until they got him checked out, probably a day or two. We got five individual rooms at a hotel across the street. Michaels, Harlow and I got together to generate some notes on the mission from which we would consolidate our efforts to write a mission report on the long haul home. We made plans to visit Sarge in the morning. They had taken him straight into surgery to correct some sort of internal bleeding. The doc said the surgery went well but it looks like he'll be hanging around the hospital for a few days maybe a week. Then

DAWN'S EARLY LIGHT

we joined Rob and Gunny in the hotel bar – one of only three bars in town. Probably because all three were across the street from the U.S. Embassy. We spent the evening trying to outdo Gunny with our war stories.

The next day we found an old USAFE (U.S.A.F. Europe) C-130 Hercules at Al Ali Salem Air Base bound for Zweibrücken AFB Germany. It was scheduled to take on a load of recon image interpretation equipment overnight and then proceed to Andrews the next morning. Zweibrücken was due to be shut down some time in the near future and its equipment was being moved to other locations as transportation became available. Since it was almost impossible to get a single airplane from Kuwait to Andrews we jumped on it. We ate and slept at the empty but very nice Zweibrücken VOQ while the equipment was being loaded and got airborne at daybreak next morning.

We caught an Air Force shuttle from Andrews to Langley, arriving at a little past 1300 hrs. The Admiral had a new black Tahoe waiting for the five of us. We spent the rest of a very long day in a secure CIA briefing room being debriefed by Admiral Bennington and Frank Horsley, the Deputy Director of the CIA. After I, with the help of the rest of the team, spent about two hours recounting details of the mission from when we entered Kuwaiti airspace to the big bang when the bunker blew up. The CIA guy focused the remainder of the meeting on Tariq, his story in detail and our impressions of his abilities and intent.

Chapter Thirty Two

McKensie Condo, La Jolla, California
Thursday, June 21, 1990, 1835 hrs Local Time

Getting from Langley AFB to San Diego NAS however, was not so easy. It was a Navy Air Force thing. The best military connection we could find was a three day two stop trip. Since two overnights would cost more than a vouchered flight on a scheduled airline, we booked a flight on American from Baltimore to Los Angeles with a commuter connection to San Diego. Six hours flying time but only a little more than four hours on the clock with the layover in LA and the three time zone changes considered. So we got to San Diego International a little after four – just in time for the five o'clock traffic on I-5 up to La Jolla. Murphy lives in southern California.

I dropped Rob off at his place, waved hello to Sara and headed on up the street to our condo. I had called Ash from the airport and she was out front waiting for me. I was stunned. Before me stood the most beautiful woman I'd ever seen – even more beautiful than the day we met at the O-Club at San Diego NAS almost five years ago. Sparkling baby-blue eyes, that killer smile and tousled blonde hair that made her persona timeless – which to me, she was. My mind flashed back to the day she traded in her F-5 pursuit fighter at Top Gun for a new FA-18 Hornet and landed at El Centro NAF to

DAWN'S EARLY LIGHT

show it to me. The same beautiful, timeless, love of my life. But now pregnant with our first child. We ran to each other and kissed like we had that day. The emotions we shared were exactly the same. I'd never been happier to be home.

"Hey sailor, get out of your BDUs. We've got reservations at Oscar's for seven thirty – that's fifty minutes", she smiled.

"Well, I guess our real party will have to wait," I complained as I winked at my girl. "What'd the doctor say?"

"We're still good – everything's normal. She said next time she'll be able to tell the sex – but she's officially sworn to secrecy. We don't want to know, right? Sam, are we being too old fashioned? Like, I mean, what color are we going to paint the baby's room? How will people know what to buy him/her? What about names?"

"Let's sleep on that for a few weeks – no need to decide now. If we're gonna make Oscar's by seven thirty I need to get moving. I really, really need a shower and shave."

*****

We got to our favorite fish house, *Oscar's Seafood Excelente*, three minutes early. The Maître 'D seated us at our favorite table next to the open area with an ocean view. The food was perfect. I had shrimp & scallops in garlic butter and Ash had salmon grilled with Thai basil and lemon juice over wild rice. We talked about all the good times we'd had over the last five years. Most revolved around our Navy friends and experiences. The Navy had become a way of life and for us it had been a pretty good life. We were both on a fast track to flag level officers by our early to mid forties if we didn't screw up. Ash would likely get their before me if she could figure out how to shuffle command life with motherhood. Her administrative (and flight) skills were well advanced of mine. It was very possible that she (and I) might decide that she should put motherhood ahead of her career. I was okay with either and made sure she was aware of that. This conversation and the fact that we were done eating led to our decision to make the trek down the beach to 'our rock', a large black outcropping about half way down the beach southward. We visited this rock several times before we were married and a few times since, albeit from the other direction. We used this getaway to discuss important things in a romantic setting, Ash's balance problems on our last visit seemed to have vanished. The walk down the beach gave her no problems. I had to help her a little when we reached the rock.

The moon was just edging over the mountains to the east, there was a cool on-shore breeze and the sea was fairly calm, much as it had been when we first found our rock almost exactly five years ago.

"So, what do you think?" I asked

"About what"

"Oh, I don't know, what we're gonna do with the rest of our lives, the price of bananas in Nicaragua, the fate of North Korea, whatever."

"I'd rather talk about bananas than North Korea, but it's us we need to talk about when we're here. This looks eerily like it did that first night – we hadn't even made love yet. You were way too much of a gentleman Sam McKensie – I would have jumped your bones right here on this rock if you hadn't been such a wuss,"

"Wuss hell! You fed me all that crap about the guys you dated only wanting to get into your pants – what was I supposed to do, walk in their shoes? Hell yes I was a gentleman, but no more than you were a lady!"

"Okay, touché, we both acted like prudes, but not for long. We've had a great life together Sam. I have zero regrets. I've never been happier – I just want it to last forever."

"'Til death do us part, remember?"

DAWN'S EARLY LIGHT

"That's okay as long as old age gets us together!" Ash smiled.

"The Admiral was at San Diego NAS yesterday – asked me to dinner. This women in the Navy thing is gaining steam. They're going to pay me half-pay for three months off when the baby comes. I can start it any time up to the day of delivery with the doctor's permission. He wants me back. Dirk says he would like to know if I'm going to fly again so if I decide not to he can start looking for another pilot. This is something I really want to do, but it's something that is for *us* to decide. We've talked about it but now the Navy's talking about it too. Dirk said his timeline for my return could stretch out to six months after I take leave. Admiral Bennington told me I could work at the NAS on the flight manual mods for the Super Hornet and the Marine Harrier upgrades after I finish the updates to the Top Gun and Advanced Flight Maneuver Manuals. That's three months of work minimum.

"So that's a month off before the baby's born, then three months off after, followed by another two months at the NAS finishing up the ground work – and, the baby can stay in the new on-base working moms nursery for those two months." We can afford a nanny after that. Sara has a friend who lives less than a mile away whose husband is an O-4 (Lt. Commander) at Miramar. Their only son is leaving for college this fall. They need the extra money and Sara says she's a great mom and would probably love a Nanny job, but she'll wait to ask her until we decide where we're headed. Sam I really want continue my career, but I don't want to screw up our chances at having a normal family life – what do you think?

"First of all – there's nothing 'normal' about military life. But we both survived growing up in a military environment. So it sounds like a good plan to me. There's no reason we can't both have our careers. Hell, everybody's doing it nowadays. We just need to be sure everything's under control while I'm down range. I need to know my family is safe and secure while I'm gone. Never had to worry about that before now – but a good nanny would probably solve that problem. Why don't you ask Sara to see if her friend might consider that sort of thing and we'll work it from there?

"You know why the Admiral's so accommodating don't you?

"Why do *you* think he is?"

"You're not only the best instructor and pursuit pilot Dirk's ever had; you're the best damned ROTC recruiter the *Navy's* ever had. That's probably what I'll worry about – all those good lookin' senior cadet studs with their tongues hanging out. When you get back on flight status I'll guarantee the Admiral will have Dirk sending you all over the country again – talk about a cushy job. . .

Chapter Thirty Three

Pyongyang, North Korea, Office of Kim il-sung
Monday, June 25, 1990, 1830 hrs PDT
Tuesday June 26, 1990 1000 hrs Local Time

"Yes, President Kim, we have the funds secured in equal parts in our five off-shore repositories. We now have an additional 280 million U.S. dollars with which to re-plan our nuclear weapons development program," announced Jin un-di, Kim's Director of Nuclear Technology. "I have developed an aggressive plan to accelerate the implementation of five 300 kiloton nuclear warheads designed to fit the Hwasong-7/F missiles we have already procured and which will be delivered next spring. The 2500 kilometer range of these missiles combined with the larger 300 kiloton warheads will give us our critical strategic position in three years, almost two years ahead of our previous plan. With your permission I will order the additional centrifuges and other necessary equipment to double our current production of U-235."

"This is very good news Jin. Go ahead and order your equipment and material that lie on the critical schedule path. Then come back for a meeting with the Strategic Arms Committee in two weeks to present your plan. Be ready for opposition from the nay-sayers, but fear not – I will have your back. Do not disappoint me with an unrealistic plan."

"The plan is solid, President Kim. The critical path is production of the U-235. But that element is scalable and we now have the resources to accelerate it even beyond the new plan. We actually have a twenty percent margin. You will be pleased."

Kim il-sung sat looking out of the large bullet-proof office window in his private down town twelve story headquarters building just north of the Taedong river in Pyongyang, capital of North Korea.. From his top floor suite he could see the Kim il-sung Square down river about a half mile and the Juche Tower just across the river from it. The tower, exactly one meter taller than the Washington Monument, was a 'gift' from the people of north Korea to him on his seventieth birthday. It symbolized Kim's brand of communist philosophy – If you are going to get anywhere in this country, i.e. survive, you must do it on your own with minimal help from the state; not exactly socialist and not exactly communist but certainly not capitalist. It was here, looking back at his favorite scene that Kim often reflected on his role as his people's beloved father. That millions had already starved to death and millions more were currently starving didn't rise to the level of conscious thought for Kim.

With this advanced strategic plan in place the PRK would be well on its way to being positioned firmly in the world's family of nuclear powers, adding yet another force to reckon with in the Communist bloc. Gaining a new and proper respect from his enemies (most of the world) as well as an elevated stature among his friends, Iran, Argentina and recently Iraq. And a new level of tolerance from the world's other communist and socialist countries; notably China and Russia.

As he surveyed the landscape of Pyongyang, 'his' beautiful city, he was filled with a new measure of optimism offsetting recent insults and incidents of aggression by his sworn enemies, the U.S., Japan, Taiwan, and the devils to the south on 'his own peninsula'. Kim said softly to himself, "In three years the DPRK

DAWN'S EARLY LIGHT

will have seven three hundred kiloton nuclear weapons. If Jin is correct about the effect of this cash infusion to the original plan, in five years we should have twenty, maybe twenty two.

"That is the level of power from which we shall gain respect from both our enemies and our allies. Until then we must put forth maximum effort to achieve this goal. All other priorities will be secondary."

Chapter Thirty Four

Secure Conference Room, CIA Headquarters
Langley Virginia
Monday, July 2, 1990, 0730 hrs EDT

Senior CIA Agent and Assistant Deputy Director Megan Donnelli closed her laptop after putting the finishing touches on a briefing she had started preparing yesterday afternoon. The steward had just delivered the coffee, fruit and Danish rolls and she was pleased at the thought of devouring a Danish and half a cup of coffee before the boss and his deputy were due to arrive - probably at about 7:45.

Meg had actually been performing as a senior analyst since recovering from a critical injury received when a safe house exploded in Saigon a week before the evacuation which occurred on April 29, 1975. She spent almost eight months at Walter Reed Hospital undergoing eleven surgical procedures to rebuild her right leg and foot and five procedures on other parts of her body including her right eye. She was the only survivor in the small safe house where the attack took place – four others were killed. At that time William Conroy was CIA Station Chief, Saigon. Conroy kept her on as a senior agent and promoted her to Assistant to the Deputy Director when he became CIA Director in 1984. She was highly respected and loved by Agents all over the world. A major

DAWN'S EARLY LIGHT

conduit between the top brass and field operations.

Meg was five foot seven or slightly shorter, depending upon which leg she was standing. She was Irish/Italian, dark complected and her demeanor covered the gamut. She was normally all business with straight forward and pleasant interactive skills. But in a heartbeat she could switch to her command persona that implied; "You know I'm right asshole, so shut up and listen." And she always was. She was very effective at whatever she did and however she did it.

Bill Conroy and Deputy Director Frank Horsley arrived, grabbed some coffee, a Danish and some fruit and found two opposing chairs about five seats back from the enormous high definition projection screen. While they were eating Meg linked the other attendees into the secure video conferencing network. Included were: CIA Station Chief Olan James, Baghdad; CIA Station Chief Oscar Rankin, Seoul; Admiral George Bennington, Commander, JSOC, Fort Bragg; and patched in from Sandia National Laboratories were Wayne Hawkins, CIA nuclear expert and Dr. Geoffrey Baggert, senior nuclear scientist, Weapons Development Section, Sandia National Laboratory.

"Okay, we're all here – or wherever," Meg announced with her authoritative voice. "Let's get started. Some of you have some of this information already. Bear with me; it'll only take a few minutes to get us all on the same page.

"We should all be up to date on the Nuclear Exchange Mission" – the name given the core swap mission in North Korea. "Be reminded of the security level of that mission and that this discussion today is a direct extension of that mission and consequently covered by your signed NDAs (Non Disclosure Agreements) specific to this subject. Are there any questions about that before we get into today's issues?"

There were none.

DON CANDY

"Good. We've got a new situation that we need to examine and develop a recommended solution to as quickly as possible.

"Our PRK operator gave us some interesting intel in last night's report; Kim has sold one of the nukes, launcher and all, to Saddam Hussein. The missile is enroute to Iraq as we speak. So this bestows myriad problems on us. Before I list the problems, I'll finish what Young-ku stated in his report.

"The missile was shipped on a standard Russian MAZ-543 mobile launcher disguised by a shell covering the launcher, resembling a MAZ-124 equipment transport vehicle. It left the Chong-fal missile complex in southeast PRK on June 10 and was loaded onto the Nigerian freighter *Zaitgai* on June 12 "NSA says the funds transfer was handled in five transfers of forty million U.S. dollars each from banks in Zurich. There could be more. NSA is looking deeper. This is what we know.

"Here's what we don't know and need to understand; Was there more money involved? What route is being taken to Iraq? What is the final destination? What is the intended use? What are the global implications of its intended use? What does the PRK intend to do with the funds? How does additional funding affect the southeast Asia situation? What do we do about any or all of this?

"Obviously as we dig into this mess we will discover many other questions and issues. I've taken the liberty with Bill's okay to get NSA started on confirming the money trail and finding the ship. As soon as we get that intel, you'll have it. Before this meeting concludes Director Conroy will set up a Team with security requirements and task IDs. We'll schedule regular but flexible meeting times using the meeting logistics set for this meeting.

"Does anyone have any other knowledge of events that might affect this situation?"

Olan James, Chief of Station, Baghdad spoke up, "let me

answer that question with a question; Has the CIA or NSA observed any recent emplacement construction in western Iraq that I'm not aware of? I get regular reports on satellite intel, but recently it looks like most of our efforts are focused on the eastern front and the brewing Kuwaiti problem; nothing in the western area."

Meg replied, "As a matter of fact Olan, we just re-targeted one of our wide angle variable longitude polar birds over western Iraq to do exactly that. At about four this afternoon another polar bird with the latest and greatest hi-res infrared capability will be placed into the same orbit offset by thirty degrees. These birds will be at different altitudes and precessed in opposite directions to confuse the Iraqis. Next week, Tuesday I think, NSA is scheduled to launch the first of four GPR (Ground Penetrating Radar) satellites. It has also been re-assigned to this cause. After a few days we should know if there's anything new going on in that area. And in a week or so we'll know if any of it's under ground."

Nobody talked about it much but the looming conflict between several Arab allies and Iraq was a real concern for the CIA and US Special Forces. If that conflict materialized, Iraq would stand alone against a group of very capable nations and very likely consider attacking Israel to firmly align Israel with the Allies and thereby gain the support of all the other Arab nations, save Kuwait and the minor nations on the Arab peninsula. James had included a statement of his concern about his limited resources in the mostly uninhabited western area of Iraq in several of his most recent reports. He had also requested more satellite surveillance than the single out-dated polar sweep unit currently in place could provide.

"Glad to hear that Meg. I'll see if we can get some HUMINT (HUMan INTelligence) out there also. This nuke could easily be, or rather, is likely to be, headed for somewhere near the Jordanian border."

"You're getting ahead of me Olan – hang on a minute."

"Copy that Meg, sorry."

"Don't be sorry. It's your station, you're responsibility – I'd be worried if you weren't worried."

"Roger that Meg." Olan was a member of SEAL Team Six in Vietnam. Still talked like a SEAL.

"So let's begin with the money. Olan, I just sent you a request to work with the NSA to find any transfers we don't yet know about from Iraq from or to major banks around the world. Many of these are closed right now so we'll give it twenty four hours.

"Nothing else on money from me – anyone else?"

No response.

"Now as far as the route is concerned, the only reasonable route between the PRK and Iraq is through the Singapore Strait, across the Indian Ocean and through the Persian Gulf. I expect *Zaitgai* is approaching the mouth of the gulf as we speak. We'll find it soon if we've got the right destination.

"Regarding final destination, our analysis here at Langley shows a ninety percent probability that they'll put it on or near the Jordanian border somewhere near their H1 extension of Highway Forty or near one of their H-3 airfields. Our guess is that they might place it on a fixed platform – probably a silo to hide it – to improve accuracy. Mobile launchers have two inherent problems for inertially guided missiles; stability and location. The stability problem can insert a two to five degree initial trajectory error in a mobile launch. Accurate knowledge of the location of a mobile launcher, on the other hand, can also cause significant delivery errors. Remember; our adversaries cannot rely on our Global Positioning System for guiding their weapons. All we have to do is introduce a temporary error into the satellite closest to the weapon to drive it to an unpopulated location. They know this because we've already demonstrated this to them multiple times. As far as location is concerned, without reliable GPS it is very difficult to know exactly where a mobile launcher is. Especially if you've recently moved it. Knowing where you are when you launch is just as important as knowing where your target is. So we believe they'll build a silo and next week we'll be looking for it with a satellite equipped with ground penetrating radar.

"Anyone have any other ideas on final destination?

Oscar Rankin asked, "Is there a possibility that they will take this nuke to a lab somewhere to reverse engineer it. There are rumors around the ranch that Saddam has already initiated a nuclear weapons program."

"That is a possibility Oscar. And it eats up the better part of the remaining ten percent in our analysis. We'll talk about that in a later meeting.

"Anything else on destination?"

No response.

"Intended use?"

"Tel Aviv?" Olan asked.

"We don't think so Olan. Reason being; too close to Jerusalem. If Saddam even scratched the Al-Aqsa Mosque in Jerusalem, let alone contaminated it with radio active fallout, he'd be hung by his own people. We're thinking Haifa or maybe mid Gaza Strip. This would, of course, be a ploy and a rather dangerous one at that, to pull Israel into the fray and move our Arab allies to Iraq's side.

"So from Saddam's perspective the global implications of that move include immediate retaliation by Israel, the US and some our allies in exchange for bringing Iran, the Saudis, Syria, Egypt and all other Muslim dominant countries over to his camp. He would be quite correct in believing the actual war would not go nuclear. The western allies would never allow that to happen. We don't believe he could garner a complete alliance reversal from our Arab allies but we think he would flip Iran and Syria and we would worry about Egypt and Saudi Arabia leaving our coalition and staying 'neutral' which would raise the possibility of losing significant air and ground access to Iraq. And although he has been searching for a shortcut to becoming a nuclear power we believe he's got a long way to go – right Olan?"

"Roger that ma'am."

"Olan, I don't sir you – you don't ma'am me, okay?"

"Sorry Meg," replied James grinning like a Cheshire cat. Olan James was a handsome forty six year old former Navy SEAL, six three about two twenty, black, with short cropped hair. He grew up in a seedy neighborhood in Los Angeles, joined the Navy at eighteen as a Seaman Recruit and retired from the Navy at forty as a Lieutenant Commander SEAL Team leader. To say that he was very intelligent and committed to the defense of his country is a significant understatement. He was awarded two bronze stars, a silver star and a purple heart among myriad other chest cabbage. The CIA made him an offer he couldn't, and didn't, refuse. He took only four years to rise to the level of Chief of Station, Iraq. Olan and Meg were actually very good friends – the banter was just part of their relationship.

"Actually, as you are all aware, none of this is actually going to happen because the weapon Saddam bought from the PRK has been neutered. But that leaves us in a peculiar situation. We need to figure out how to deal with Saddam's false threat without alerting Kim and his pirates in the PRK that they might also be in possession of nuclear duds. There are so many variables in this mess that the plan we come up will demand an extreme level of flexibility. The good news is we should have a modicum of time to consider all the consequences and generate a fairly complex plan – maybe a few weeks at least. Ironically the most serious consequence of whatever action Saddam takes may well be the potential acceleration of the PRK nuclear program. So let's discuss that next. Then we can return to Iraq."

DAWN'S EARLY LIGHT

The red light in the lower right corner of the conference room phone began flashing. Raising his hand to pause the conversation, Conroy picked it up, "Conroy here." He listened intently for about a minute, then said, "okay Martha, keep me posted on further developments.

"Well this is interesting," Conroy opined. "Yesterday A PRK MiG-15 (Korean War vintage Soviet Jet) strafed an ROK oil drilling operation in the Korean Bay barely south of the demarcation line. Killed two workers. The PRK just claimed the pilot accidently pulled the 23 mm cannon trigger instead of the camera trigger. The incident occurred at 1820 hrs over there. The camera story was announced at 2010 over there."

Conroy raised his index finger as he picked up the phone again, "Martha, see if you can get Captain Bo Jameson on the secure line, I'll hold.

"We need to get a reading on the validity of this event before we factor it into our discussion here. The PRK has recently executed several provocative actions toward its neighbors, the ROK, Japan and Taiwan. This quick response by them to an 'accident' at 0200 in the morning that otherwise would be clearly labeled blatant aggression smells a little fishy.

The red light on the phone flashed.

"I've got Captain Jameson on the secure line, sir."

"Thanks Martha. Uh Bo, I'm in a meeting concerning the PRK and we just got intel on the strafing of an ROK oil rig by a PRK MiG. Got a question for you; As I recall you studied the MiGs 15 through 19 while you were flying SAM suppression missions in Vietnam. On a MiG-15, is it possible to mistake the 23mm cannon trigger for the camera trigger?"

"I was just reading the intel on the PRK incident. My response to your query is *no way*! The MiG-15 has a 37mm and two 23 mm and cannons. On some Mig-15s the camera is operated by a button switch on top of the control stick right under the thumb, not a trigger. On older models it is activated by the master arming switch. The gun selector and arming switches are typically on the instrument panel, or as is the case on the newer MiG-15s slightly below and include a guard cover that has to be manually raised before the arming switch can be raised to the upward 'armed' position, also true on the older MiG-15s. So the camera is operated by the right thumb or a switch on the instrument panel, not the right index or 'trigger' finger. The master gun trigger is right behind the right index finger on the stick - where it should be. The weapons on any fighter from any country I am aware of are not armed unless there is a target in sight and the order to fire has been given or assumed. This can not be an accident."

"Thanks Bo. Appreciate your input. I've got a meeting going here – get back to you later."

"So here we have yet another blatant provocation, and this one deadly. No accident here. Keep that in mind.

"While I've got the floor I'd like to briefly add to what Meg said about security. Do I assume correctly that you have all read the briefing paper Meg put together for you?"

Positive response by all.

"Good; there are exactly seventeen individuals read in on this project. It is highly compartmentalized, meaning that individuals and teams within the project may not have the need to know and therefore will not know certain information or be briefed on certain Intelligence. Because we are dealing here with very sensitive intelligence and information on very sensitive global issues, only the President, his security advisor, the Chairman of the Joint Chiefs, the Commander JSOC, Frank and myself have full need to know. Some members of this project have never met – and may never meet for all I know.

"Frank will manage the disposition and compartmentalization

DAWN'S EARLY LIGHT

of all intel and sensitive information. Comments Frank?"

"You got it covered, Boss."

"Continue Meg."

"Thanks Director. Okay back to the PRK nuclear situation. With the help of Mr. Hawkins of CIA and Mr. Baggert of Sandia National Labs we have determined the following: Our initial assessment of the impact of current and predicted events on the PRK nuclear development status is affected by the distribution of incremental funds between Uranium enrichment and delivery vehicle enhancement. Both are necessary to achieve a viable PRK nuclear weapon strategy. Based on our current intel we believe the PRK will use a sixty / forty warhead to missile development cost ratio. Based on current intel, we are also of the opinion that they are using and will continue to use the less costly production process of U-235 as opposed to Pu-239 (Plutonium). The analysis concludes that the Iraqi cash infusion could accelerate their U-235 production to a quantity sufficient for construction of four five hundred kiloton weapons within eighteen months while in the same time period enhancing their missile capability such that it could cover South Korea and all of Japan and possibly Taiwan. Total time to this level of nuclear capability; three years."

The meeting lasted two days with a day of respite in between. The team decided the following:

Don't let the current situation affect decisions to be made regarding Iraq and Kuwait. However, if the conflict occurs and the US is involved, as it currently appears it will be, then the first order of business will be to take out the Iraqi nuclear missile site during the first few minutes of the conflict. This will require depositing enough nuclear material, i.e.; U-235, to convince Saddam's nuclear experts that the warhead destroyed was in fact a nuclear warhead. The U-235 used would necessarily need to be Russian since the source can be traced by analysis of the impurities in the manufacturing process. Of course that would not be a problem since our nuclear experts, Wayne Hawkins and Geoff Baggert had in their possession four real nuclear cores from identical Russian warheads. Admiral George Bennington opined that we should build a special version of our new GBU-28 bunker buster laser guided bomb to include a Russian core in a configuration that would guarantee that the nuclear core would not produce a nuclear explosion, just the nuclear material that was expected to be present when a conventional bomb destroyed a nuclear warhead. The silo would contain most of the radiation. If the US did not participate in the conflict, this weapon could be handed off to the UK, Israel or whoever. Afterward, be sure the details of the attack on the Iraqi missile site are leaked to the PRK and Iran. The message; 'You could be next – be careful.'

It was agreed that more intel was needed on the PRK nuclear program acceleration. A new analysis team was needed to work that problem. Bill Conroy took the action item to get that ball rolling in his south east Asia group. He promised a report in ten days.

Chapter Thirty Five

Nearing the Straight of Hormuz
Aboard the USS *Peleliu*
Tuesday, July 3, 1990, 1445 hrs Local Time

Captain Harry McKnight was reading a secure satellite communiqué from CIA Headquarters, Langley, Va. requesting a minor deviation in the course and speed of *Peleliu* as it approached the Strait of Hormuz. *Peleliu,* an amphibious assault ship (LHA-5) was enroute to Bahrain from its home base in Japan to support the brewing conflict in the Persian Gulf area. The request included the boarding of a CIA Little Bird (MH-6) helicopter and detailed instructions to maneuver in the proximity of the shallow water Nigerian freighter *Zaitgai* enroute to Basra Iraq via the river Shatt al-Arab. Then *peleliu* was to fully support the accomplishment of a classified photo reconnaissance mission. The mission priority was P1-P (Priority One POTUS). In other words the request had been approved by the Commander-in-Chief and therefore was actually an order for complete cooperation with the CIA. The Little Bird, based at Bahrain was to be prepositioned at Seeb Air Base, Oman, close to the passage of *Peleliu.*

Initial instructions were to reduce speed immediately to sixteen knots and to make a slight turn to port to a bearing of 280 degrees. This put *Peleliu* on a vector to rendezvous with the Little Bird.

The NSA had been tasked to find the *Zaitgai*, but it was sailing without papers. In other words it had not filed its intended route, port of departure, destination or even its intent to sail with the International Maritime Organization (IMO). While this action breaks no formal international laws, most reputable shipping companies use this service for the safety of their ships and crews. It's sort of like the FAA requiring commercial aircraft in the U.S. to file a flight plan – somebody needs to know where all the airplanes are. International maritime control isn't that easy and is often ignored by illicit operators or companies who don't want the whereabouts of their vessels known. The last IMO known position of the ship was a shipyard where she was fitted with new twin diesel engines in 1956. The bird watchers (satellite image analysts) thought they had the right vessel but the view from above had been well disguised. So the Admiral decided to make a recon photo run to be sure. The Little Bird was equipped with a gimbal-mounted high resolution 30X zoom digital camera that would allow detailed images from a two mile fly-by.

Peleliu was steaming northwest approaching the Straight of Hormuz bound for Bahrain Saudi Arabia. They were about ten nautical miles east of the suspected *Zaitgai,* also steaming northwest. Aboard the MH-6 was the pilot, none other than Jimmy McDaniel himself, whose current home was Bahrain, and CIA Chief of Station Saudi Arabia, Tommy Lee, the only available agent in Bahrain at the time. Bill Conroy had read them in on this small part of Operation Nuclear Exchange. He would ask for their opinion of what they saw on the ship as compared to pictures sent to them electronically. The data they took and the NSA images they had received were not to be printed locally but sent immediately by secure satellite relay to Conroy at CIA Headquarters, Langley. All relevant photo digital data at Bahrain were to be destroyed after transmission and confirmation of successful receipt.

DAWN'S EARLY LIGHT

The Saudi Arabia CIA Station Chief, Tommy Lee was a former SEAL from Team Four. He was the first CIA agent to be trained on the ASDS at Miramar. Now at forty four he didn't look a day over thirty five. Just after his second birthday he and his parents emigrated from Beijing just as World War Two came to an end. He graduated with a degree in physics from M.I.T. at the age of twenty one and joined the Navy, Completed OCS and entered BUD/S (SEAL training). A year after BUD/S he was accepted by SEAL Team Four and participated in several Joint Special Operations Command campaigns, the first of which was Granada and the last of which was Panama. Early (mid 1989) during the Panama Operation he was recruited by the CIA. He resigned his commission as an O-6 (Captain) and joined the CIA as second in command of the mission planning organization. As the conflict with Kuwait became likely he was named Chief of Station, Saudi Arabia (included the Arab peninsula at that time) with a team of seventeen agents. His team currently supported General Norman Schwarzkopf's planning staff on Operation Desert Shield.

Only in the middle east would you find a CIA Station Chief riding shotgun on a photo recon mission in a Little Bird. But they got the pictures. Jimmy flew on a forty five degree diagonal to the ship's stern at a distance of one mile at the closest point. The flight took them on a path directly toward the Strait of Hormuz on the south side of the ship so as not to arouse suspicion and keep the sun in a favorable position. Jimmy set the camera to one six megapixel frame per second with the tracking system set amidships. Lee used the twelve inch video display in the cockpit to compare what he saw to the pictures he was given. The picture he received from Langley was an actual photo of *Zaitgai* taken at the time of her registration at the Singapore ship yard where she was built with a to-scale picture of an actual MAZ-7911 large cargo transport mounted on her aft deck. So the comparison should be direct and properly scaled relative to the ship.

But sure enough something wasn't right. Both vehicles had eight wheels and the cabs were very similar, but the distance from the center of the wheels to the top of the covered load deck was consistently about a foot more for the truck on the actual ship than the one in the picture. In addition to that observation, Lee could barely make out the letters Z T   I and under that he saw "LAGOS", the name of a port city in Nigeria; *Zaitgai*'s home port. This was definitely the ship they were looking for although neither Jimmy Mac nor Lee knew why.

*****

"Chief Lee just called on the satcom – we do have the *Zaitgai* under surveillance and she appears to be headed where we thought she would – time will tell," announced Director Conroy over his secure link to President Stevens and CJCS Admiral Sterett. "I'll call Adam and give him his birds back." Adam Kivel was the Director of Space Management at NSA. He was responsible for the position of every U.S. Government satellite.

"At least we got something nailed down," groused Conroy.

"Good job Bill, give your guys some kudos. Stevens out."

Chapter Thirty Six

Seal Team III Training Facility
Coronado Island, California
Friday, July 6, 1990, 1700 hrs PDT

So Rob, Hal and I are down here at the hell hole by the sea, alias the Team Three sweat farm, seeing how much weight we can lose during a week of intense physical training after our little vacation in the desert. The Team Three guys are fairly tolerable as swabies go but they've got this illusion that they're the best there is SEAL-wise. Of course, Rob, Hal and I have to show them otherwise on a daily basis. The three of us are in the top five of the group of thirty we train with. Hal Nicholson is a Lieutenant Commander, two years younger than me. Rob is a Master Chief Petty Officer, nine years older. Hal is five nine, one 170 pounds, not really small for a SEAL. I am six one and weigh 185 and Rob is six feet and weighs 190. Who'd guess that the smallest guy would lead the pack, including the Team Three squad. The second spot is held by one of theirs, a Senior Chief P.O., name's Brian, nickname's Pusher, then me, then Rob. They call us 'tech pussies', we call them 'dickless frogs'. Rank-wise we're a little top heavy. They have one officer, a Lieutenant and their top enlisted man is a Senior Chief Petty Officer (Pusher).

DON CANDY

*****

Looks like I'm going to get my airplane. Bo did have to move to Dam Neck Virginia, although I just found out why. Three months ago when Rear Admiral George Bennington left DEVGRU to take command of JSOC (Joint Special Operations Command) at Fort Bragg North Carolina, no one stepped in to fill his slot. Actually Bo had been selected to run DEVGRU but wanted to keep it quiet until he got some critical loose ends tied up in San Diego, one of which was the PRK Nuclear Exchange Mission and the other was the mission in the Iraqi desert we just returned from. He'd known about his new job since the Admiral had moved to Fort Bragg and that's when he told me he 'might' have to move to Dam Neck. Well, he's gone and now I'm the Black Angel commander. I've got seven multi-force special operators reporting to me as of now. Rob, Hal and another Team four defector, Danny Labow make up the SEAL component of my little group, and we've got Master Sergeant John Willard and Major Vince Harlow from Delta Force and Gunny Tanner and Captain Michaels from Force Recon (jarheads). Right now I don't even know who I'm reporting to – but I might find out Monday morning. I've got a meeting with Admiral Bennington at 0730 – I have no idea what it's about.

Anyway Bo wanted $50K for his Mooney M20J. A steal – it was a beautiful airplane inside and out, still had six hundred hours until major overhaul and absolutely no maintenance problems. He bought the Cessna 310 from JFS which was also in top notch condition and authorized Jim to buy a used Gulfstream III and hire a pilot to fly it. Jim already had three large companies in the Manhattan area needing regular use of a corporate jet and he had submitted a business plan to Bo for setting up that service. This JFS thing was already netting Ash and I $20K+ a year and that could be $50K or more in less than five years. Maybe we could retire early. . .

Chapter Thirty Seven

West Coast Office, Joint Special Operations Command
Coronado Island, California
Monday, July 9, 1990, 0715 hrs PDT

IH-5 was crowded as usual, but it wasn't as bad as it might have been, so I got to the Admiral's Office about when I'd planned, fifteen minutes early. His office was the third on the left on the second floor. The name on the door said simply "George Bennington" nothing else, no stars, no title, no nothing. And there was no where to sit in the narrow hallway. So I walked back and forth for about five minutes, not wanting to be early. The Admiral heard me walking. The floor squeaked. He stuck his head out. "Come on in Sam, we need to talk and I've got a plane to catch."

"Sorry Admiral, I wasn't sure you were in there." 'There' was a small office. About 10X10. With an American flag in the corner and a picture of a Texas prairie in the spring time on the wall behind an old wooden desk with an old, maybe WWII vintage, guest chair in front and an identical one behind.

"Sit down Sam, we've got a lot to talk about."

Just as I was about to sit I noticed he had two black stars on the left shoulder of his BDU. So I checked the right one to be sure and sure enough there were two black stars there as well. I said, "Sir, I was unaware that you'd been promoted", as I took my seat. "Congratulations Sir, It's long over due from where I sit."

"Thanks Sam. It's not a big thing. When you get to my age it's all you can do to just focus on your job and pick good people to run your command."

"Sir, might I ask how old you are – you don't look a day over forty five."

"Actually I'm fifty five. Now shut up and let me talk for a while. First of all when we're alone I'm George and You're Sam. We're friends, you and I. We've been through a lot of shit together. You out in harms way and me watching you perform over a satellite link. We're all proud of you Sam. You've performed well beyond the call of duty and I, and others, want you to know that we know. You're a special ops guy and only a few people on this earth know that. As such you guys aren't supposed to, and most don't, look for or want glory or any other kind of recognition. And much of that anonymity as you are well aware is for your own safety and the safety of your families due to the kind of work you do. You've been wounded four times and haven't received a purple heart yet. Well, your classified file says you've been awarded all four. We're going to change that. I put you Bo and Rob in for the Silver Star for service to the United States at great risk to your lives accomplishing a very difficult mission of critical need in the heart of enemy territory. I got the "amen brother" from the president last week. The Congressional Medal of Honor would have been more appropriate except for that word 'congressional' and the inability of most any person in congress to keep any secret.

"So, we'll have a little private ceremony in the oval office per the president's request in a couple of weeks. And before that occasion I've got some other bits of information for you. First, as of now you will report to me – do you have any reservations about that?"

"No sir – I mean, no I don't."

"Good – I like how quickly you squelched that 'sir'. You'll get used to it.

"During your last mission you called me to advise you on a potential ROE (Rules Of Engagement) situation. Then when confronted by an enemy soldier you acted quickly and correctly without any help from me. I will not expect any more calls from the field regarding advice. I have a very high level of confidence in you, your judgment, and your actions. Is that clear?"

"Yes Admiral."

"George."

"Yes George."

"You're gettin' the hang of it.

"Okay, it turns out the CIA has vetted Tariq Sa'id to the point that they are offering him a position. Bill and I had a little talk about where best to place Mr. Sa'id and we ended up thinking that your team was a perfect first job for him. Also, Bill agreed to let you have a certain Little Bird driver you might know on loan to CIA from SOAR, CWO Jim McDaniel. That brings me to the real reason for this meeting. What you guys have done with ASDS is a big part of what we've been missing – getting into tango territory quickly and covertly, executing your mission and then getting the hell out before the they even figure out what really happened. We've been pretty good at that in the past using Little Birds and sometimes larger aircraft, water or ground vehicles. ASDS has added a whole new dimension. I want you to form a top secret quick response squadron, four teams of six operators. Each team should be led by an officer and if possible the other five special operators should be very senior enlisted experts. Expertise required

DAWN'S EARLY LIGHT

for each team should include: a leader, at least O-4, a medic or corpsman, a communications expert, an explosives expert, a SEAL with high BUD/S rank for water training and a linguist with at least four non English languages. Two members of the team should be cross trained as snipers and two as weapons experts. All personnel should have as an absolute minimum, two tours of duty and two combat engagements with exemplary performance. Then I want you to figure out how to get each of these teams to cross train themselves to the maximum extent possible. If necessary, in the beginning, no single team operator should be responsible for more that two of the expertise requirements and the goal is to have one man – one expertise, with each man highly cross trained in all areas. I want you to tune these teams to accommodate the middle east, Africa, South America, North Korea, China, Russia and Indonesia. "These teams will perform in situations requiring quick response and action – in and out as quickly and covertly as possible. The President suggested a nebulous administrative name like Advanced Systems Deployment Group (ASDG), in keeping with Richard Marcinko's DEVGRU idea.

You can call it what ever you want – I like 'Black Angels', but I'm not to sure about the BAT thing. But then I don't give a rat's ass what you call it. This is not unlike the requirements given to Dick Marcinko when he formed SEAL Team Six. The major difference is that you're using the ASDS technology and you get to select SEALS and other special operators who have already met equivalent requirements. We do not expect to grow this unit beyond twenty four operators and four MH-6 pilots. You will keep the R&D element at El Centro working on new infil/exfil systems at or below ten civilians with one retired engineer type special operator in charge. You will also keep the ASDS training command at Miramar. I would suggest putting Lt. Commander Nicholson in charge.

"You will report to Captain Bo Jameson at Dam Neck only for

administrative purposes and to me operationally. Is that clear?"

"Yes," I replied, not sure that it really was.

"Your billet calls for O-6 so when you reach time in grade, if you don't fuck up, you'll get your captains eagles.

"We Good?"

"Aye, Aye, George."

"Go do it Sailor! By the way, your budget is pretty much unlimited – I expect five Little Birds with four pilots as good as Jimmy Mac asap. Tariq Sa'id will report to you Wednesday Morning – This is your new office.

"One more thing – meet me on the Miramar flight line Thursday morning at 0730 hrs. I'll have you back at your place by 2000 hrs that night."

I was more than a little concerned about Tariq joining us on a mission after only a week at the CIA Farm in Virginia and three weeks (instead of the standard five) ASDS training at Miramar. Murphy was known to prey on newbie's.

And what the hell are we doing Thursday morning?

DAWN'S EARLY LIGHT

Chapter Thirty Eight

Miramar Naval Air Station
Miramar, California
Thursday July 12, 1990, 0735 hrs PDT

"You're driving. I had your wife's recruiting plane made ready for us. I brought my flight suit from San Diego, let's suit up," the Admiral quipped as we fast-walked to the locker room.

Ashleigh's F/A-18B was a standard two place training model except for the paint job which was Blue Angels with 'Cmdr Ashleigh McKensie' painted beneath the pilot's canopy and 'Future Blue Angel' painted below the rear canopy. She used it as her practice plane and for ROTC recruiting trips to universities around the country. She flew one of the four 'MiG-29 aggressor disguised' F/A-18Cs used for Top Gun training when instructing seasoned Navy pilots in the art of advanced combat maneuvers.

We're taxiing out to the runway and I still don't know where we're going. "Where to, Boss?"

"Due north."

"Okay"

An hour later I'm taking instructions on a classified frequency from Groom Lake Tower. The Admiral had given me a slip of paper with 'Clearance cipher: Oscar Bravo 739 Zulu' written on it.

163

When asked for the cipher I repeated it and received a vector to the runway and was told to report five miles out on a straight in approach to runway 35. We're going to Groom Lake. I've never been there – most people don't even know it exists. It's better known to the general public as Area 51. You know, it's where the living creatures from outer space and their spacecraft are hidden.

"I've got a little surprise for you," the Admiral said through the intercom as we taxied behind a gray well worn government pickup.

After clearing security as we approached the side door to hangar 17, the Admiral continued, "you know Sam, using that CIA CAPV-727 over North Korea worked pretty well. Problem is, how do you fly that plane over hostel countries in the middle east? Disguised as a commercial aircraft you wouldn't have any place you could fly to and only limited places to fly from. So Brad, Jerry and I were discussing the issue of how to covertly get your guys further into enemy territory without detection. I think we've solved the problem."

Just as I was trying to recall who Jerry was (Admiral Gerald Sterett, Chairman of the Joint Chiefs), he opened the hangar door and said, "here it is," pointing at an F-117 stealth bomber that looked like it was undergoing a major overhaul. The landing gear were elevated off the floor on some sort of pedestal jacks under the wings and aft fuselage that lifted the belly of the aircraft about six feet off the ground. The bomb-bay doors had been removed and there were assorted parts on carts that appeared to be waiting to be installed.

I was curious. "What're they doing to it?"

"This is your new ride Sam. Look over here," he said pointing to the hangar wall near the tail.

I saw what looked like a six seat giant ski lift chair.

"Two of those will replace the bomb racks in this Nighthawk

giving you a capacity of eleven operators and one dog. Combat range of a 117 is eight hundred miles. A loaded Little Bird has a range of two hundred fifty miles. We're developing auxiliary drop tanks for your four Little Birds to extend the combat range to six hundred miles. What do you think?"

I was aware of the Nighthawk – we used them in Panama (Operation Just Cause) last year – but I'd never seen one. This bird was both awesome and ugly. Looking at it nose-on one would swear there's no way this thing could fly – but fly it does. "Wow man, I don't know what to say. The bomb-bay is obviously not pressurized. What limitations does that create?"

"Initially, it will limit our missions to angels two zero. But when you think about it, with a stealth aircraft twenty thousand feet is plenty. You still have a twenty five mile ASDS glide range. Truth to tell, you don't even need 20K. Later if we need more altitude, our design will allow us to include a pressurization system for pressure suits. As is you will have heated flight suits and boots and oxygen. The time in flight should be about an hour and a half, plus or minus a half hour, depending on how close to the target we can take off. I think eliminating pressure suites will greatly enhance your overall mission effectiveness."

"I couldn't agree more. They are an unnecessary nuisance in this new scenario. I'm sure the guys will be happy to scrap them. How many 117s will be modified?"

"Well Sam, we're looking at forty million dollars plus per copy. We'll go with this one until we get the mission profile perfected. Then maybe we'll need more – I hope not."

"When can we use it?"

"Flight tests are due to be complete on one August. Operational testing with one of your teams should take a month. Then by mid September you should be ready for the next mission."

DON CANDY

Chapter Thirty Nine

Ministro Pistarini International Airport
Buenos Aires, Argentina
Monday July 16, 1990, 1635 hrs PDT

Sunday as we were on our way home from church the Admiral called and requested my presence at the San Diego Naval Air Station Officer's Club at 1800 sharp. It was important. Tell Ashleigh that he will take her to lunch tomorrow as an amends – I should have told him that wouldn't be enough, and it wasn't, she was pissed. But I didn't.

Anyway I got there and we repaired to his table in the back corner where no one else ever sits and we ordered drinks and dinner on a split tab.

He filled me in on our latest dilemma. Seems as though one of the Chicoms in the patrol boat we sank in the Yellow Sea last May had actually made a call to his base asking about a boat with '*Chung-li* Sinju, PRK' stenciled on the stern - the vessel's registered name per international maritime law. As the patrol boat approached Bo, Rob and I had been watching for any communication activity, but I guess we missed it - or they used hi-power binoculars on us before we got ours on them. On the Day before yesterday Jin-sung received a call from the Sinju Bay

166

DAWN'S EARLY LIGHT

Harbormaster saying that the Chinese authorities had queried him about *Chung-li* and that he had responded that *Chung-li* was in fact based in his harbor but was currently out at sea and not expected back for three to five days. Young-ku was in Buenos Aires at a week long Olympic Rules Committee meeting as the designated Olympian from the PRK. He would return on Wednesday. There was no secure way of contacting him. Jin-sung immediately packed his belongings, tossed them into *Chung-li*, locked it up and headed for the family's restaurant in Pyongsong to apprize Young-ku's father of the situation.

Jin-sung had never developed a formal plan of escape, but he had thought about it many times. His sister, Young-ku's mother, was the oldest of four siblings and as the youngest of five he was only five years older than Young-ku. Jin-sung and Young-ku were more like brothers than uncle and nephew. Similar to the relationship I have with my uncle Bo. Young-ku's parents and Jin-sung were well aware and supportive of Young-ku's job with the CIA. They knew of his office hidden behind the wine-cellar in the restaurant's basement and they knew of the CIA sat-phone hidden in a false compartment of the lower right drawer as well as the daily contact time, the speed-dial number and the identification code 'Suribachi'. They decided that Jin-sung must contact Young-ku's supervisor the next morning.

At his Saturday 0500 sat-phone check-in time Jin-sung identified himself and apprized Young-ku's CIA supervisor of the situation. By 0830 hrs (PRK time) CIA Director Bill Conroy was on a secure phone with Admiral George Bennington, Commander JSOC, making plans to extricate Young-ku and his family.

Later that morning Jin-sung drove back up to Sinju Harbor, boarded *Chung-li* and motored out to a point about thirty five miles southwest. Away from shipping lanes and fishing grounds, he could see nothing but water in all directions. He stopped *Chung-li*, opened the starboard maintenance locker and removed a can of mineral spirits, a crate of clean rags, two paint brushes and one can each of white and black paint. From the stern swim platform he quickly cleaned and repainted the white stern. Then, after the paint dried, in his best freehand style he painted in black block letters, 'Karan-ka', the name of an old girl friend, with 'Nampo, PRK just below. The location of the new harbor he was headed for.

It was now late afternoon so Jin-sung pointed *Karan-ka* southeast toward the mouth of the Taedong river and a dock he knew of near his engine mechanic's shop in Nampo. A perfect place to hide the boat, get fuel and depart for South Korea. He just needed the details of the defection which Young-ku's supervisor had promised he'd get on his next 0500 call.

Soon after he had secured *Karan-ka* his brother-in-law arrived to drive him back to their Pyongsong restaurant/home. The next morning he made the contact at 0500 local time and was immediately transferred to a Mr. Conroy. The Director explained that the best solution to the needs of both the U.S. government and Young-ku was to move the whole family to the U.S. and provide a relocation package that would give the family an equal to or better than lifestyle when compared to that they currently have. A midwestern town, new home or homes, new cars, etc. The family would be given a no-interest long-term loan to purchase a restaurant if they were so inclined. Did Jin-sung think the family would approve of his proposition?

Jin-sung hoped Mr. Conroy could not detect the excitement in his voice. His family had dreamed of a life in America. This offer was well beyond their dreams. He calmly replied that he would ask the other family members if they would agree but he was certain that Young-ku would agree and he himself would also agree. He asked for ten minutes while he explained the offer to his sister and brother in-law and get their approval. He returned with an emphatic statement that yes, the whole family approves.

DAWN'S EARLY LIGHT

The Director asked if Jin-Sung could gather his family and their belongings limited to two large suitcases each – they would have to pack two suitcases for Young-ku – and sail tomorrow to a point thirty kilometers due west of Hong Do Island off the tip of South Korea. He agreed that he could. If you can cruise at twelve knots the trip should take you slightly less than twenty four hours. So, if you leave tomorrow evening at midnight you should have no trouble arriving at your rendezvous point at exactly midnight Tuesday. Jin-sung said that would work fine. The director told him that the fast attack submarine *Providence* would find them as they had before if they left their engine running. It would be necessary to scuttle *Chung-li*. Was that a problem? – you'll get a new boat of comparable value. No problem. The plan is set.

So here I am on Monday evening at 1625hrs local approaching a Buenos Aires airport bar called *Fidel's Bistro* – I wonder – no, couldn't be. Oh yes it was. As I got closer I saw a three foot square picture of a young Fidel Castro in OD fatigues and cigar in mouth centered behind the bar. I heard a voice to my left,

"Looking for me?"

It was Young-ku with his signature grin holding a pint of Cristal - a popular Cuban beer. I recognized the logo on the glass.

"Why are we meeting?" Young-ku had received a cryptic message from a local CIA agent,

"Meet an old friend at *Fidel's Bistro*, airport, 1630. Important."

So you don't have any idea why I'm here, do you?

"Negatory Amigo."

When I'd finished he was dumfounded. He sat there staring at his beer.

"I'm totally fucked. They'll hunt me and my family down like dogs."

"I don't think so. Jin-sung paid a visit to his harbormaster friend and they worked up a feasible story of your demise or defection – take your pick. A week from Thursday morning he will report *Chung-li* missing along with all aboard. Your family had planned a week at the fishing lodge on Sinmi-do (an island fifty kilometers from Sinju Bay Harbor) – he made reservations yesterday. You will leave tomorrow morning. You will not arrive. Your mother made a sign for the restaurant saying 'Closed for a week - on vacation'. As I said, *Chung-li* will be scuttled thirty miles west of Red Island (Hong-do) in very deep water – it will not be looked for there and it will never be found."

"How do we live in the U.S. as citizens of the PRK?"

I handed him a brown envelope. Inside was his new U.S. Passport and citizenship papers. He looked at me with disbelief.

"You are an employee of the CIA, remember? They can do stuff like this. Your family will have to go through a fast-track citizenship program – shouldn't be too tough. Shouldn't take too long."

The other item in the envelope was his one way coach ticket to San Diego International leaving tomorrow morning at 0945hrs local time. I'd be on that flight too.

Chapter Forty

ASDG Secure Conference Room
Coronado Island, California
Tuesday, August 7, 1990, 0900 hrs PDT

Including our five ASDS instructors at Miramar we had twenty seven Special operators from three military branches squeezed into the tiny ASDG conference room which was designed to comfortably accommodate thirteen, twelve sitting, one standing. The news was expected, we just needed the details. Iraq had invaded Kuwait on August second and things were going badly for the Kuwaitis; rape, pillage, murder, oil fields on fire – general mayhem. The next day the UN Security Council issued a resolution demanding that Iraq immediately withdraw from Kuwait and three days later imposed a world wide ban on trade with Iraq. This morning our President announced a significant increase in coalition (NATO and Arab Peninsula countries) troops as well as a massive movement of equipment to Saudi Arabia to force Saddam Hussein to back out of Kuwait or face the military might of a thirty two country coalition in a war that he could not win.

Obviously, since we were already involved through multiple recon missions into Iraq, including our great haboob (sand storm) mission where Tariq Sa'id got his nickname, we were very interested in the future of this situation. Admiral Bennington was addressing all available members of JSOC through our secure video net. He was amazingly brief. He gave us everything he knew in thirty minutes. Basically he commented on the strength and commitment of the coalition, the horrific actions of the Iraqis in Kuwait and he reiterated JSOC's role in the overall profile of the U.S. military mission and expounded on how that might play out in this conflict; depending, of course, on future events. He raised our readiness to level two (not related to DEFCON – this is a JSOC thing). Level two meant no future scheduling of leave and our normal response time was now lowered from four to two hours – until further notice, of course.

At least the two weeks I'd already scheduled in November for our new baby's arrival had not, at this time been canceled – until further notice.

*****

The next day, August 8th, Saddam Hussein thumbed his nose at the world by formally annexing Kuwait. The world *was* going to hell in a hand basket!

Chapter Forty One

Office, Commander, ASDG
Coronado Island, California
Friday, August 31, 1990, 0930 hrs PDT

The Admiral sent me a classified message this morning concerning the status of our Nighthawk Delivery System (NDS) test program at Groom Lake. The integration flight tests were completed on time with minimal problems. The Project Manager has cleared the project to advance to Operational Testing (OT) commencing Monday, September tenth. They needed five ASDS Operators and one ASDS dog on site at 0800 hrs that morning. I had already completed the classified paperwork to get this team into Groom Lake, so everything was go at this point. The dog was a Special Operations Forces service dog reject that we used for jump training at Miramar. He couldn't roll over or shake hands but he liked to jump out of airplanes with students.

This is probably a good place to bloviate a little about how we fit into JSOC. As the name implies it's all about joint operations of special forces operators. These operations can be organized as separate service units working together or as integrated units with operators from diverse SOF organizations. The integrated units, like ASDG, are typically formed around new and advanced technology like IRNV (Infra Red Night Vision), ASDS and NDS. As such they are often tasked with developing operational strategies and tactics that enhance the effectiveness of that (those) technology (s). With the advent of USSOCOM (United States Special Operations Command) which includes JSOC and all the support organizations necessary to make integration of special operations forces work, it was imperative that the resulting organizational structure allow joint organizational flexibility. So an organization like ASDG, needing resources from and providing support to all Special Forces units could recruit operatives from all military SOF organizations and yet report to JSOC as part of USSOCOM. Those military SOF organizations include the Army's Delta Force, the Navy's SEALs, the Army's 160th Special Operations Aviation Regiment (SOAR) and soon the Marine's Force Recon. So ASDG would have resources from and provide support to all SOF organizations and other offshore government organizations (CIA, DEA, etc.). A small covert quick hitting organization like an ASDG squad of six operators would be useful in covert rescue, recon, capture, demo and other types of support operations for JSOC, the CIA, the DIA, the DEA and other offshore organizations. The one limitation on units like ASDG is of course the unique mission profile; ASDS infil and MH-6 exfil. Now with the Nighthawk Delivery System that limitation has been significantly reduced.

So here we were, September already and we'd recruited fourteen spec-ops 'experts' which when added to the seven we already had made twenty one of the needed twenty eight – twenty four for teams and four for MH-6 pilots not counting non-combat operations at Miramar and El Centro. I had to recruit two more officers as team leaders and the new enlisted operators needed to fill the remaining expertise requirements. The process was tough because we wanted the best. Fortunately we knew many of the folks we were after from their participation in the ASDS training program. That also provided an incentive to come aboard – almost every ASDS trainee wanted to be part of the teams that would eventually be deployed to use the system. Most were senior noncoms and officers. We now have five "homes" humble though they may be. One at Fort Bragg, one at Virginia Beach, one at El Centro, one at Miramar and one at Coronado Island. Two teams would be located at each facility except El Centro and Miramar. The ASDS training operation at Miramar would be administratively supported by Captain Dirk Erickson's 'Top Gun' training command and commanded by Lieutenant Commander Hal Nicholson.

Training had become the tall pole in our operational tent. We faced a very complex training schedule designed to get each operator properly trained in both group and individual skills. Of course training never ends, but right now our front-end loading was heavy and complex.

Friday Afternoon ASDG Meeting

For two weeks now we'd finally gotten our secure video conferencing satellite link working so we could meet via v-comm when necessary to communicate information to all personnel. I had finished a recap of the NDS status and the mundane interchange regarding daily operations and was about to close off the meeting.

"I saved this little note for last. The Admiral informed me this morning that we need to have a single team ready in two to three weeks for our first trip down range as ASDG. That's all he could give me right now. He'll know more in a few days, maybe mid next week.

"Comments?"

Tariq asked, "Any idea where?"

"Not yet. Anything else?"

Nothing.

"Okay, Let's double up on the PT and spend at least two hours a day at the range. Start thinking about how ready each of your teams is for a down range gig. If we have to we'll move some folks around to meet this first need – whatever it might be.

"That's all. Work hard. Stay healthy."

I had been working on more than building the teams we would need to meet the Admiral's requirements. We were going to need more high tech equipment too. So I put Leroy in charge of the El Centro operation with a plan to find a YPG (Army) Captain or even a senior Lieutenant to run the place administratively while Leroy ran the R&D. We now needed the CIA drones as badly as the CIA did. Leroy said the attachment problem had been solved but they still had occasional release problems on the 'moth drone' – a highly miniaturized drone resembling a large moth that could be flown remotely and attach and release itself from any surface, vertical through horizontal, including wet glass. Proper release was important because these drones would often need to be placed in inaccessible locations. Like the narc darts their highly classified status required that they not be left behind. And they weren't cheap. Closer, but I knew he would get it figured out.

He and I had also discussed ways to make MH-6/AH-6 helicopters more stealthy. All of our missions would benefit greatly from better stealth during mission exfil - after the tangos were dead or captured. There were an increasing number of situations where exfil would be a lot safer if we didn't make all that racket on the way to or leaving from the exfil point (EP). Plus it'd make things a lot easier on our pilots if fewer people knew they were coming. The tallest pole in our stealth tent was noise. We had talked with McDonnell Douglas about how to quiet the

DAWN'S EARLY LIGHT

rotors, both main and tail. They were already designed to be subsonic at the tips which eliminates most of the noise. Leroy and one of the McDonnell Douglas guys had some ideas about new composite blades with a twist and a vertical flare at the tips to greatly reduce or even maybe eliminate vortices, improve fuel efficiency, reduce noise and reduce adverse ground effect in tight spaces, but of course probably triple the cost of the rotors. The other noise was turbine generated. The airline industry had spent millions of dollars on research in this area to improve noise abatement during takeoff of turbine powered aircraft near residential areas. As far as we knew none of the results of this research had been applied to the MH-6, so there were probably major gains to be had in this area. Leroy had submitted an RFP (Request For Proposal) for an accelerated development program in these two areas containing a preliminary specification to fix these problems and make our Little Birds as quiet as church mice. We were pleased to find out that they had already solved the turbine noise problem and would have to make only minor mods to the existing design to adapt that solution to our MH/AH-6 Little Birds. And the existing turbine engines could be removed and modified. The rotors were a bigger and more expensive problem. The good news here was that MDAC (McDonnell Douglas Aircraft Corporation – often shortened to just MD) was in the final development stage of a quiet rotor system for the AH-64 Apache attack helicopter that could (and would) be adapted to other military helicopters as required. Of course the government units with the most money would get quiet rotors quickest.

We were also talking to the Defense Systems and Electronics Group (DSEG) of Texas Instruments about integrating their world class super-secret un-cooled Infra Red (IR) night vision technology into the MH-6 flight systems. They were currently developing an infrared driver for the TADS/PNVS, Target Acquisition and Designation System / Pilot Night Vision System being developed by McDonnell Douglas for the AH-64 Apache attack helicopter. We believed part of this design could be extracted and applied to the MH-6 integrated night vision requirement. We sent them (TI) an RFP for adapting their already developed IR Night Vision system. The guys at both MD and TI were excited about enhancing the capability of the AH/MH-6. Hopefully they or others would fund part of the development.

Chapter Forty Two

Office of Li Peng, Premier of China
Beijing, China
Wednesday, September 10, 1990, 0900 hrs Local Time

"Comrade Jiang, welcome my friend. Tell me about your progress. I'm hearing good things."

Jiang Zemin is the General Secretary of the Chinese Communist Party.

"Yes comrade Li we are making progress although nothing is in concrete yet. When I contacted the American Secretary of State, Mr. Robinson, indicating that we might be interested in talking about our differences with the U.S. and U.K., he suggested that it might be better for the U.S. and China to informally explore common ground first to avoid the difficulty sometimes found in three way negotiations. I agreed. Actually I was going suggest just that if he didn't. I suggested we set up a secure single-port communication system that would allow us to dialog at our leisure. We both agreed that we would work toward creating a strawman agreement and try to explain it to our leaders with no guarantee that a solution would be found. We started by defining our respective issues.

Primary issues for us:

- Human rights in China are a Chinese Issue only.
- U.S. military actions that threaten China.
- Our sovereign rights to our waterways.
- Unfair trade regulations with the U.S..
- U.S. nuclear weapons in close proximity to China.

"Mr. Robinson indicated that those exact issues from the opposite perspective defined their concerns:

- Human rights are an international problem
- China military actions that threaten the United States.
- China claims to international waterways.
- Unfair trade regulations with China
- China's nuclear weapon development

"On the human rights issue we agreed to disagree with the hope that by finding grounds for cooperation in other areas could lead to a resolution in that area.

"We came to the same understanding regarding our sovereign waterways, military interactions and bi-lateral nuclear threats.

"As I hoped, the resolution of most of the China – U.S. issues appears to lie in successful negotiations in the area of trade relations. Both Mr. Robinson and I believe that as our cooperation evolves in that area the other issues can be addressed with a better feeling of mutual trust and a new will for cooperation.

"We left our meetings with agreement that we would put forward to our respective governments a plan to move forward toward comprehensive trade agreements to be enabled by good will reductions in military aggression and further exploration of mutual ground for bi-lateral cooperation on the remaining issues.

"Comrade Li, there is no quick solution to our relational issues. But this beginning dialogue and its resulting possibility for us to focus in an area of our high interest does allow us a foot in

DAWN'S EARLY LIGHT

the door toward becoming a world economic power. As that happens I believe our global position on other issues will improve significantly."

"This news is encouraging, Jiang. You and Secretary Robinson have chosen a path in negotiations that provides initial focus on an area that I believe could be fruitful, especially for China. Successful trade negotiations would certainly foster better relations between China and the United States that could lead to our continued economical growth and expand our trade opportunities with other western nations. But I must warn you; as discussions lead to agreement and better relations in the area of trade you must not address what the Americans refer to as human relations or anything that deals with our legacy rights to our waterways. These issues deal with our national rights and are *not* negotiable. These issues are not to be in any way 'negotiated' relative to any other issue. I'm sure you are in complete concurrence with this mandate. Yes?"

"yes Comrade Li."

Chapter Forty Three

Oval Office, White House
Washington, DC
Wednesday, September 12, 1990, 1015 hrs EDT

We got word a little past noon on Monday that we would receive our medals on Wednesday at the White House. Bo and I had been there several times during the drug wars of the mid eighties, but this was new to Rob – I think he was a little nervous.

Bradley Stevens (POTUS), Bill Conroy (Director CIA), Jerry Sterett, Chairman of the Joint Chiefs (CJCS), and our boss George Bennington (Commander, JSOC), were present. The gathering of this group to honor us three peons was much more impressive than the medal itself. Surely they had more important stuff on their calendars. Anyway the presentation was short and sweet as I hoped it would be, but I was blown away by the fact that only the president, not usually present for Silver Star awards, spoke all the words and pinned all the medals – this had to be a breech of some obscure protocol somewhere, but what the hell, it was something I would remember the rest of my life and I was sure Bo and Rob would too. Brad Stevens, as far as we were concerned was a special president who like President John F. Kennedy held the special forces, including the CIA and NSA in very high regard. During his first term as a senator form Texas he drafted and pushed

DAWN'S EARLY LIGHT

a bill through Congress to preserve the honor of the U.S. special, clandestine, and intelligence forces through a special process administered by the president then and all presidents to follow. The preservation process included the retention of all items of recognition of said special forces and intelligence personnel, up to and including the Congressional Medal of Honor and any ceremonial photographs taken at Top Secret awards ceremonies. The physical evidence of which would be held in a properly installed safe (officially included in the inventory of GSA Top Secret secure containers) overseen by the Information Security Oversight Office (ISOO), the administration of which was the sole responsibility of the presiding POTUS. Said instruments of recognition were to remain secured as Top Secret until the recipient of said instruments of recognition was separated from the U.S. government and was a signatory to the attached release and hold harmless document releasing the U.S. government from responsibility for the signee.

In other words this Silver Star would be locked up here in the white House and if I ever wanted to see it again I would need to retire and sign a piece of paper. No big deal. SEALs don't give a rat's ass about medals or hooyas from anyone other than their Spec-Ops brothers. This particular award, on the other hand, was a little more special than most since all of the dignitaries present were in fact brothers – all had been SEALS. So I, for one, will return to get my star when the time comes. And it will mean a hell of a lot more to me than something from some run-of-the-mil asshole politician.

"Commander McKensie, Master Chief Curtis, I need ten minutes before you leave," said Admiral Bennington after the ceremony.

Huddling us off to a back corner of the room, he held his comments until the room had cleared.

"Regarding the mission I spoke to you about Monday morning,", he said as he handed me an 'Eyes Only' classified folder. "We've been successful at classifying a certain Somalian war lord as an international terrorist – which he is, and we need him dispatched. The intel is in this folder. This is why I planned your return tomorrow afternoon. It will give you time to review the mission data and make recommendations to me tomorrow morning before you leave. As you know Somalia is currently very close to anarchy. If left to be, this tango would have a better than even chance of executing a successful coup and becoming its leader. And our intel says that's where he's headed. Without ASDS the job would be very difficult. I want your assessment of how you could complete the mission requirements using ASDS infil with MH-6 (Little Bird) exfil. Let's meet in the President's briefing room downstairs after his morning security briefing – say 0815 or so. He might want to sit in. That okay?"

"Sure Admiral."

*****

So, after spending the afternoon and a significant part of the evening pouring over the mission objective, the intel and the physical layout concerning the mission, a few beers and a good night's sleep, we ambled down to the president's briefing room at 0805. Don't want to be late for this meeting. As we approached the security desk the Secret Service guy, nameplate 'Smith', informed us that the President and the CIA Director were already present and it would just take a few moments for him to check our ID's, verify our visitor passes and sign in – which we did. He then opened the door, announced our arrival and closed the door behind us.

President Stevens greeted us and said, "Gentlemen, grab some coffee and munchies and gather at the business end of the conference table. While you're doing that I want to, in person,

DAWN'S EARLY LIGHT

congratulate you on the successful Nuclear Exchange mission you guys completed in the PRK. Because stuff like this is highly classified your country is incapable of showing you, in a public venue, an appropriate measure of appreciation for your bravery and accomplishments during this recent action. As a special operations warrior, please remember that your classified anonymity is not only critical to the country you serve, it is also vitally important to the safety and welfare of you and your families," as he passed through the short coffee line after the others.

"I read and reread your mission report. Excellent document. When you see Captain Jameson, please pass my comments on to him."

"Aye, Aye, Sir."

"Well gents, (Stevens was anti-formal in small meetings) you've been selected for another operation. You've had just a few hours to review the CIA sitrep. I'm going to ask Bill and George to recap the history, importance, who, when and whys of the operation. Bill?"

"Thanks Brad.

"Here's a quick history of the country beginning in 1950. After a hundred year history of British, French and Italian occupation, border wars and internal disputes, in 1960 Italian and British Somali joined and gained independence as the Republic of Somalia. Aden Abdullah Osman Daar was elected president. Over the next few years Somalia had border disputes, first with Kenya and then with Ethiopia. In 1967 President Daar lost the election to Abdi Rashid Ali Shermarke who was assassinated in 1969 after which General Muhammad Siad Barre assumed power in a bloodless military coup forming the Democratic Republic of Somalia governed by the Supreme Revolutionary Council (SRC). Socialism - nationalizing much of the economy. He was supported by the Soviet Union. In 1974-75 Somalia endured a severe drought which significantly weakened the country and in 1976 Barre disbanded the SRC and formed the Somali Revolutionary Socialist Party (SRSP), a single party government based on 'scientific socialism'. In 1977 the SRSP invaded the Ogaden Region of Ethiopia in an attempt to consolidate the Somali people - sounds like Hitler, right? In just a few months the SRSP controlled ninety percent of the region after which the Soviet Union sent twenty thousand Cuban troops to push the SRSP back out of the Ogaden Region – which they did. The SRSP then expelled Soviet advisers and essentially broke relations with the USSR. This led to the demise of the Somali Navy and other military organizations, out of which independent militias began to grow. So who was left to become the SRSP's new best friend – you guessed it the good ole' U.S.A. As the 80's came to a close and the Soviet Union began to crumble, the Somali people became more and more dissatisfied with "Scientific Socialism" and multiple rebel factions emerged. One of these factions grew out of the Somali Navy and was led by strongman Abdul Rahmud Patish. Patish professed anarchy. With the help of disgruntled fishermen due to the collapsed fishing industry, which was caused by lack of government oversight, he initiated the Somali piracy industry. He soon developed close relationships with several Islamic Fundamentalist leaders, and a recently discovered alliance with Al-Qaeda.

"So here we are once again faced with the problem of who do we support; the failing government or one of the rebel factions. The only clear choice here is, we know who we don't want to survive. Don't think for a minute that this is some kind of political assassination – this guy and his close associates are first class terrorists and we need to stop them before they lead a country worth saving down the road to destruction – another North Korea. Somalia, like Afghanistan, has suffered enough from the radical elements in the area."

Admiral Bennington picked up the program from a planning

DAWN'S EARLY LIGHT

perspective saying, "So there's the history. Now on to the *What're we gonna do?* session. You are probably wondering why ASDS? Why not a SEAL Team on a CRRC (Combat Rubber Raiding Craft)? And, truth to tell, that's the first type of infil we considered. There are, however, problems with anything but ASDS. Patish's home base is a complex of four concrete bunkers spread over a little less than two miles at the base of and on the southern side of a mountain range about thirty miles southwest of the Horn of Africa coast. These bunkers are connected by tunnels cut into the mountain. Three months ago one of Bill's guys successfully penetrated Patish's inner circle – about fifty people. Our guy is in a position to know where Patish is and when he is or is not present at the complex. Our job is to infil while he's there, receive real time intel on Patish's exact position and call in a high altitude air strike using GBU-28 "Bunker Buster" bombs and the AN/PEQ-0 SOFLAM (Special Operations Forces Laser Acquisition Marker – a ground portable laser designator used to guide precision laser guided bombs to a target). Notice I said bomb<u>s</u>. We could use four of these babies to seal off the four known entrances to the tunnel complex. Problem is, there are probably other entrances we don't know about and he might not be inside the mountain when we need to get him. So for now we are targeting Patish, wherever he is, along with any of his buddies who are unfortunate enough to be close by. The operation is set for the night of September twenty second, Saturday week I think that is.

"Commander McKensie, you will lead the operation. You will use two three man SOFLAM teams. You and Chief Curtis will have a CIA agent with you, Tariq Sa'id – I believe you know him. He speaks Arabic fluently and is adequately conversational in several dialects of Somali. You need to choose three of your best qualified operators to fill out the teams.

"Bottom line, drop what you're doing and get up to speed on this mission. First thing; select your three additional members, get everyone down to Fort Bragg and get updated training on the latest model SOFLAM. You can come back with me tonight and spend tomorrow with the Delta SOFLAM expert. The production unit is much easier to use than the prototype you're familiar with. You'll carry three, one for each team and a spare. Take the weekend to get squared away at home and report back to Bragg Monday. Plan your mission with the most recent intel. You'll ship out to Salalah Air Base, Oman Thursday morning on the same C-130 you'll fly the mission with. The U.S.S. Tarawa will loiter off the Horn and dispatch Little Bird's to pick you up."

Picking the other three operators was a no brainer. I took Gunny with me. He's a world class sniper and he was the Marine's choice for the T&E (Test and Evaluation) team during the development of the SOFLAM system and he knows the specs on the operational model – although he's never seen one. I also took Tariq with me. We nicknamed him Haboob – means 'desert sand storm' - where we met. Although I like the guy and I believe he could be a spec-ops guy, he ain't one yet - so I need to watch him and I need him as a translator. Besides, I know the CIA likes him. I've seen guys take up to six months to get a clearance a notch lower than he got in two weeks – ahh, the rewards for clean living. Vince Harlow (Carbo), Delta Force Major, will lead Bravo Team. He'll have Rob (Now Doc – he didn't like Bird), also an ace sniper, and former corpsman (Navy medic) and Senior Chief Jeff Russell (Tracer), formally one of my ASDS instructors at Miramar.

The Little Birds – MH-6 and AH-6 – are the go to choppers for spec ops missions. The MH-6 is the people hauler, often armed only with the occupants' personal weapons. The AH-6 is the gunship version and carries a variety of weapons including rockets, hellfire and stinger missiles, a chain gun and mini Gatling guns. The two versions are often used together for covert missions by the Army Rangers and Delta guys. We use the MH-6 troop hauler for exfil on covert missions requiring small teams. Like the current

DAWN'S EARLY LIGHT

mission where we will use one to exfil our team of six at night. The Little Bird carries a pilot and six SOF operators and weighs only a little less than sixteen hundred pounds. It can carry more than it's empty weight in people, equipment and fuel. Usually when we exfil from a coastal operation the Little Bird coming to get us only has a hundred or two of the four hundred pounds of fuel it can carry. This works for us because we're typically no more than seventy five miles away from our target yielding a one hundred fifty mile round trip and the MH-6 has a two hundred and fifty mile range. So it can trade some fuel for over weight SEALS (no such thing) or equipment and captured intel. When I talk about miles I'm talking about nautical miles and speed is in knots which is nautical miles per hour – nothing else is important to a sailor. Statute miles and kilometers are unnecessary clutter in a sailor's mind. One nautical mile equals 1.15 statute miles.

This schedule is a little tight, although the operation doesn't appear to be terribly complex (yet). My concern is that when I call Ash and tell her I'm headed to Ft. Bragg with the Admiral tomorrow instead of heading back home – she's going to be pissed. But lately she's been a little less emotional than earlier in her pregnancy. I thought I had gotten to understand the female mind until the one I married got pregnant. The first trimester of her pregnancy was very emotional with just a tinge of morning sickness and a lot of unusual food cravings. Now she's transitioned into some sort of nesting mode. I've never seen a fat woman move so fast and eat so much.

Chapter Forty Four

Salalah Royal Air Force Base
Near Salalah, Oman
Thursday, September 20, 1990, 1015 hrs Local Time

We landed at Salalah Royal Air Force Base beneath the most beautiful deep blue and cloudless sky I had ever seen. The approach was over the dark blue water of the Arabian Sea and the city of Salalah shone like a white and golden jewel ringed by a crescent of hills and small mountains and the brilliant blue sea – not what I expected. The jewel thing and a lot of the beauty disappeared as we landed.

Until recently the Air Base had been a UK Royal Air Force Base equipped with British and American military aircraft bought with Omani oil money. The same planes were there, just the UK part was missing. The Britts and the Yanks still had a meaningful relationship with Oman, as they did with all the countries on the Arab peninsula; Agree to disagree on human rights and western morals and agree on the things that really mattered – oil, weapons and money. Oman was still a Sultanate (monarchy ruled by a sultan). As we'd noticed in all these countries, Arabs become real friendly when you make them rich.

DAWN'S EARLY LIGHT

We'd barely had adequate time to get this gig polished up, the way we like to, before we left to take down the bad guys. The C-130 is a noisy beast; especially the old ones. One of which we had thankfully just departed. So we got our ride to the embassy where we could get a little quiet rest, pick up the latest intel and get this mission nailed. When dealing with an asshole like Patish it's especially important to have all your bases covered. We were looking for the latest aerial shots of the complex, taken just this morning by an SR-71 almost in orbit. The new digitally stabilized, higher resolution cameras combined with the fact the Blackbird was flying above one of the driest places on earth promised excellent enlargements of the areas we had chosen from which we would 'shoot' the targets with our laser markers.

Our on-site agent reported that Patish would be present in the concrete bunker located between the two center entrances to the tunnel complex. The tunnel complex had areas where meetings could be held but the bunker had the only decent living and sleeping accommodations. To his knowledge no one had ever spent the night in the tunnels. He also said that other than ventilation shafts there were no other access points to the tunnel complex. This I took with a grain of salt – maybe a bucket. These guys would certainly have an escape route toward the sea. Probably an upward slanting tunnel with a well hidden opening on the seaward side. I also believed that the bunker was connected to the tunnels via an underground escape tunnel. Patish and four of his leaders were currently arriving for a three day meeting in the bunker complex. The meeting involved planning for the Arabian Peninsula portion of the first coordinated multi-continent Al Qaeda operation to date, known at the complex by only it's name, "Satan's Demise." The details of the meeting had been closely guarded, but there was a high probability that in addition to Patish there would be at least one high level Al Qaeda tango present. Maybe two.

This situation pushed 'higher' (JSOC, CIA, CJCS or maybe even the president) to go all out to 'send a message' by ordering complete destruction of the complex and as many terrorists as possible – to hell with collateral damage. So we were going for all four known tunnel entrances and the bunker. This would complicate things somewhat because we would need to illuminate multiple targets with each SOFLAM and it would increase the risk of partial mission failure if one of the SOFLAMs failed. It was also imperative to hit the central bunker first to eliminate the possibility of escape. Fortunately, one of the improvements in the SOFLAM operational model was timed illumination of multiple targets. This meant that the firing order we planned to use; Center bunker, entrance 1 (west), entrance 4 (east), entrance 2 (west), entrance 3 (east) and a final shot on the center bunker, could be pre-programmed into the units with seventy five second intervals between hits to ensure each laser guided bomb had only one target illuminated during its flight. Airborne target illumination with stabilized IR designators worked great for single easily definable targets like tanks, trucks and buildings on reasonably flat ground. But camouflaged tunnel entrances and other complex targets of that sort did not enjoy a high level of probability in the area of success. Thus the need for SOFLAM and yet another requirement for ASDS covert missions.

This mission required three F/A-18 Hornets, each with two GBU-28s, to be launched from *USS Nimitz* eighty miles north of the target area at 0320 hrs local time, flying properly spaced in tandem at angels four zero, ninety seconds apart. Five miles from the targets the lead Hornet releases his two GBU-28s at a fifteen second interval followed by the next Hornet releasing his first GBU seventy five seconds after the last GBU from the previous Hornet with following releases at similar fifteen and seventy five second intervals. When the lead Hornet calls "first weapon away" SOFLAM #1 illuminates the center bunker. When that bomb

DAWN'S EARLY LIGHT

explodes SOFLAM #1 hides its beam and traverses to the preprogrammed target, tunnel entrance four, for the third GBU. At the same time SOFLAM #2 illuminates its first target, west tunnel entrance one for the second GBU from the lead F/A-18 and the process repeats until all six GBU-28s have done their jobs. Interleaving the targets like this avoids double illuminations and gives the SOFLAM operators more time to double check proper alignment of the laser prior to impact. It also simplifies the process to the point where even a Jarhead F/A-18 pilot could handle the job.

I requested – and got – Jimmy McDaniel (Mac), the best damned chopper pilot I know, for our exfil. I've seen him do things with an MH-6 that defy the concept of rational thought. I would, and will, fly anywhere with this dude. Saved my bacon more than once! He's a CIA pilot on loan from the Army Special Operations Aviation Regiment (SOAR), hangs out at the Sakhir Air Base on Bahrain Island and flies what ever is needed to wherever it's needed whenever it's needed in the middle east. He was able to hook up with *USS Tarawa* as it steamed toward the Straight of Hormuz on its way to support our mission – a good thing too. All they had aboard were the two AH-6 Little Birds, the attack version of the MH-6 but loaded up with guns and rockets and missiles – makes the chopper too heavy to get all six of us out in one trip and still have room for gas and equipment.

We hoped all the complex infrared targeting on this mission would work – it had never been attempted before.

Chapter Forty Five

Salalah Royal Air Force Base
Near Salalah, Oman
Friday, September 21, 1990, 1500 hrs Local Time

We slept in the visitor's room of the small but adequate U.S. leased facility at the base. I was beat and slept until around 1400. We had a good plan, now we had to make it work. We checked, double checked and re-packed our gear. The SOFLAM equipment was fragile so Vince, Rob and I carried the units in padded drop bags that we would pull up just before landing. Another great feature of the automatic landing system on ASDS; You didn't need your hands in flight or while landing, leaving you free to shoot tangos on the way down, use your IR night vision to get the lay of the land while approaching the target or pull up your drop bag if it contained something fragile. Tonight we would jump with our MP-5s on our chest. The Admiral sent us a dog – a Belgian Malinois, along with his handler, Ritchie. When we arrived and I met Richie, we talked a little about canine jumping and I told him I had jumped with dogs during BUD/S training and we trained ASDS jumpers to jump with dogs but never I had never actually taken one on a mission and I didn't think starting now would be a very good idea. He told me that the Admiral said if I didn't want to, so be it, but I should at least listen to what this dog could do.

DAWN'S EARLY LIGHT

The dog's name was Amos. Amos was trained to work at night. One of the most useful jobs he performed was perimeter or outpost sentry. He wore a bullet proof vest equipped with a VHF receiver-scanner that silently scans all VHF frequencies that we use in combat. The receiver was terminated in earpieces fitted and adjusted so that only he could hear the transmission and the volume was tuned to his ears. Tonight, should I decide to take him along, he would be wearing two noise canceling earpieces to allow him to hear low volume external sounds while blocking Rifle fire and compression waves when the bombs explode.

He responds to all twenty nine required canine combat commands plus eight 'night' commands. He wore canine night goggles, one lens clear and one lens uncooled Infra Red using vanadium oxide microbolometric technology (you don't need to remember that). The IR lens was dimmed because a dog's eyes are more sensitive than humans at night and night vision needs to be preserved in both eyes. Some of the additional commands he responds to are:

Home - Amos can be assigned to guard and protect a location designated as 'home'. He will do everything within his canine ability to protect his home location and its human occupants, including patrolling and watching any station designated as *home*.

Watch – Amos will sequentially patrol and keep a three hundred sixty degree watch for any activity at any of up to five locations shown to him and designated as a *watch* station. If he detects activity by sight, sound or smell he will alert using a VHF signal to his handler's comm unit and three IR beacons positioned lengthwise on the top of his vest. The beacons will sequence once every two seconds, flashing in the direction of the threat. The alert is activated and deactivated by nudging a button on the right edge of his vest with his nose.

Retreat – If Amos is given the command 'Retreat' over the

VHF radio he will look for the rapidly flashing IR beacon at his home location and cautiously approach that home position until given a hand signal after which he will proceed post-haste. If he detects foul play and receives no hand signal at the home site he will maneuver to the best position for attack.

These are only three of the eight night commands in addition to the other twenty nine combat commands Amos can execute – damn dog's smarter than I am.

I had never considered using a dog at night but I got a quick sell on Amos. Ritchie said that this particular breed was very unit oriented – they don't get attached to one individual and will treat all good guys with respect and bad guys with disdain (including death if you don't get there fast enough or used the command **Kill**).

Done deal! Amos will fly with us tonight. Now I just have to tell Gunny he's going to be jumping with a dog. I approached Gunny. "Go talk to this dog's handler. Name's Amos. That's the dog, Amos. Handler's name is Ritchie. You're jumping together tonight. You and the dog - Amos. Richie's right over there," I growled at Gunny without eye contact, expecting some backlash but getting none.

An hour later Gunny came over to my bunk with a shit-eatin' grin on his face, "Hey Skipper, do you know all the shit this dog can do? We need one of these. Can we keep him?"

I had no idea he would react this way. I thought I'd get a ration of shit. I warned him, "this ain't no pet Gunny."

"I know that Skip, but this dog's probably a better friggin SEAL than you are!" he spat back. Then added, "no offence," with a sheepish grin.

"None taken, I'm just happy you're happy. You do remember how to jump ASDS with a dog, don't you"

DAWN'S EARLY LIGHT

"Never had any problems at Miramar. Me and Amos are gonna get along fine."

This team had really begun to gel. Back in the early eighties Richard Marcinko had created SEAL Team Six to be a totally unconventional unit. Long hair, beards, leather or denim jackets, jeans. He recognized the value of each man in the unit and wouldn't tolerate an officer who didn't respect and wouldn't learn from his enlisted team mates. In fact, he believed most of the knowledge necessary for success in a SEAL unit was to be found in the senior enlisted men. Like Senior and Master Chief Petty Officers in the SEALs and Sergeants First Class and Master Sergeants in the Army and Marines. And I'm here to tell you he was and is absolutely correct. During the early days of the development of ASDS (Airborne SEAL Delivery System) we had the mandate from JSOC – Joint Special Operations Command - to make the system available to all Special Operations Forces, across the military, to include Navy, Army, Air Force and Marine Corps – no mention of Coast Guard – yet. The genesis of the Black Angels occurred during the drug wars of the mid eighties. These early units evolved into three man squads and two squad teams. The small size and footprint of a Black Angel Team is due to our unique mission profile. We fight only at night, seldom seeing daylight during a mission. Typically we infiltrate (infil) using ASDS and other highly classified equipment such as IRNV (uncooled Infrared Night Vision – practically turns night into day) and exfiltrate (exfil) using one or two MH-6 Little Bird helicopters. Lately we've begun using AH-6 gunships on exfil to protect the MH-6 hauling men and equipment. A mission could be anything requiring our stealthy quick-hit capabilities with a HAHO stand-off of up to fifty five nautical miles (from forty two thousand feet) such as demolition, tango (terrorist) kill or capture, intel (gathering intelligence) or hostage rescue. Tonight we were doing all of the above except the last. We are now a multi force team of teams. Two six man teams operational and two teams in training. It is unlikely that we will ever grow larger than twenty four mission operators plus four pilots.

*****

We selected three locations for the teams. All were on small hills facing north toward the wall in the Ogo mountains containing the tunnel complex and bunker with the Gulf of Aden beyond. Each hill provided for adequate observation and illumination of the tunnel entrances and the bunker and a good three hundred sixty degree field of fire. Looking north toward the targets, our positions approximated a semicircle with the endpoints directly in front of entrance two (Team Bravo) on the west side and directly in front of entrance three (Team Alpha) on the east side. Both about a mile and a half from the targets. In the center, directly in front of the bunker and about a quarter mile farther from the mountain was Amos (Team Dog) on a hill slightly above Alpha and Bravo – a very good field of view.

We reviewed our mission plan one last time exploring in depth all known contingencies and accounting for every mission screw up Murphy could throw our way. Hope for the best – plan for the worst.

At 1830 hrs we headed out to our ancient C-130AX. Earlier, I had asked the admiral on my sat-phone shortly after we landed why he had sent us over here in a stripped down model A rattle trap. He told me that just before our 'Nuclear Exchange' mission he had acquired two C130-As (original C-130 model – Vietnam vintage) with run out engines that weren't needed (he really meant weren't wanted) anywhere else. He had them strip all the cargo loading and retention hardware out of the planes as well as the insulation and inner lining (the parts that keep the aircraft from driving passengers crazy with noise and cold) from the fuselage.

DAWN'S EARLY LIGHT

They added the new much more powerful Rolls-Royce fat bladed turboprop engines and removed everything else that wasn't necessary for our ASDS missions. (For those who might not remember, ASDS means Airborne SEAL Delivery System). All this to coax the aircraft with twelve SF Operators plus a dog and a crew of two with necessary mission fuel up to forty two thousand feet (angels four two), our latest maximum altitude in the ASDS Specification. So now that we've got the F-117 Nighthawk Delivery System being developed, I wonder what they'll do with these clunkers. I could use them back at Miramar for ASDS training. Note to self.

Now that we were getting ready to load up for the mission I thought about calling him back and telling him we couldn't take the dog because we'd be overweight. Then I remembered Bo's advice when I took this job; "don't fuck with the admiral" – so I didn't. Actually we were only going to angels three two tonight because our infil flight was only forty one miles. The X in the Hercules model number meant that there would never be another modification to these two planes. The A model was originally built in the mid fifties - slightly after Korea and before Vietnam.

We lifted off at 2100 hrs for the six hundred mile flight to our infil IP (Initial Position – the exact location from which a mission begins). Except for noise and cold the trip there was unremarkable. We suited up, checked all systems, depressurized the ramp and stepped into the night. We'd gotten somewhat paranoid about the weather in these parts since our little soiree with the haboob in southern Iraq. My computer was telling me I was moving over the ground, on course at twenty two knots, with a quartering tailwind of six knots. Four knots less than forecast. I could see forever. A bright moon waning to the west would be over the horizon when we landed a little more than an hour and a half from now. I set the timer for an hour on my sat-phone to take a nap. After about twenty minutes of deep slumber I was awoken by Gunny on the sub-team net saying;

"Hey Skip, I think Amos is asleep."

"I was too, dickhead, 'til you woke me up. Talk to somebody else." You just can't get decent help any more.

DAWN'S EARLY LIGHT

Chapter Forty Six

Northern Somalia
African Horn
Saturday, September 22, 1990, 0110 hrs Local

One of the most difficult things for trainees to deal with when landing the ASDS is to let the system do its job. Everybody wants to help. There are four lines, or shrouds in parachute-talk, running up to the canopy to control the descent of the payload – person, dog, equipment, whatever. In the early days the shroud pullers had a travel of only eight inches, which for normal flight is just fine. For landing, though, a little more travel was needed to adequately break the forward motion and cause a full stall of the airfoil. So we changed the pullers to sixteen inches and modified the software in the ALS (Automatic Landing System) to give the payload a soft, almost motionless landing in most wind conditions. The system always lands directly into the wind. But it does this with rather quick turns and sudden braking – like a skilled jumper would do when landing in a confined area. Many experienced jumpers just can't seem to give up control to a computer for landing. There's a difference between skilled and experienced. To solve this little issue in training we require that the jumper land with his hands behind his back. We tell him/her if he/she can't do that we'll tie their hands behind their back and push them out – works every time. My guys are all experienced ASDS jumpers. Their hands never go anywhere near the shrouds. We typically like to land at least twenty seconds apart when landing on a small target – small roof top, conning tower of a submarine, small boat, etc. to allow the jumper to clear the area before the next jumper arrives. Tonight we had plenty of room and we were jumping to two separate hills so we just programmed the ALS to park us ten feet apart at the same time. At Miramar NAS (Naval Air Station) I filmed five students landing simultaneously in a line five feet apart on the tarmac holding their hands behind their backs – impressive! It's one of the shots I use when I go before 'higher', usually CJSOC sometimes CUSSOCOM, to get funding for another SOF toy. (Commander, Joint Special Operations Command, Commander U.S. Special Operations Command and Special Operations Forces respectively).

Alpha Team made their usual splendific touchdowns at 0114 hrs local time. When Gunny released Amos he walked straight over to me and sat at doggie parade rest staring back at Gunny. Probably Gunny couldn't get anybody else to listen to him so he talked to the dog all the way down - and Amos has no way to disable his RF receiver. We may have a problem here, but I was pretty sure Gunny will forgive and forget – not so sure about Amos.

*****

We shed our pressure suits, keeping the helmets, video visors, chest computers and battery belts, got our gear unpacked and set up, then checked in with Bravo Team, no problems there. With the IR spotting scope we could clearly see our four targets We used the ASDS net to resynchronize clocks between Alpha and Bravo Teams. I had just been given the go message from Langley signifying that our inside man had confirmed that Patish was present and was over-nighting with his guest's in the bunker. At 0130 we would check in with Barracuda flight, three enroute F/A-

DAWN'S EARLY LIGHT

18 Hornets, each carrying two GBU-28 bunker-buster laser guided bombs. Everything looked good – too good. Where was Murphy? He hadn't raised his ugly head all night. Something had to be wrong. And there was Murphy, or the devil himself, staring me in the face. Tariq was using a sat-phone.

I raised my MP-5 and asked him to put the phone on the ground and raise his hands. He complied with a puzzled, surprised look on his face.

"Gunny, we've had a breech of mission protocol here. Please keep Mr. Sa'id guarded while I look into what's going on.

"Who were you talking to Tariq?"

"CIA."

"Who in CIA?"

"Steve Crossman, my supervisor."

As I picked the phone up I asked, "Why do you feel it necessary to speak to Mr. Crossman?"

"He asked me to keep him informed."

"You were present when I briefed the team on security, ROE (Rules Of Engagement) and communications protocol, were you not?"

"Yes."

"You knew then, that this mission has two and only two authorized sat-phones; mine and Major Harlow's."

"Steve said since I was CIA it was okay."

"NOT okay if I don't know about it and approve it."

I examined the phone. It was the same Motorola model as our military issue but it didn't have a government inventory control barcode sticker on it. Not Good.

"Tariq this is not a government issue phone. Where did you get it."

"From Steve."

I looked at the last number in the send/receive list. It had an asterisk by it indicating that it was an outgoing call – and the receiving number had a country code of 93 - Afghanistan. Extremely not good.

"We're fucked," I said to Gunny.

"Don't move a muscle, Sa'id. Gunny, cuff him." I was speed-dialing the admiral on my own sat-phone. We might be in serious trouble.

"Admiral, we've got a situation here – Sa'id called CIA on an unauthorized sat-phone with an Afghanistan country code. Can you dial in Director Conroy on a three way?"

"Doing that now. How do we know this?"

"Wait for Director Conroy - we don't have much time."

"Gunny, Call Amos back, then get on the net and let Vince know we've got a potential problem here."

"Okay Sam, I've got Bill on the line."

"Let me talk, then ask questions. I caught Sa'id talking on an unauthorized sat-phone. Not authorized on this mission and not government issue. Put my gun on him and had Gunny cuff him. Sa'id said that his supervisor had requested the unauthorized communication. Looked at the phone. It has an Afghan country code. We can't go forward without resolving this breech. Barracuda's inbound. I'll have them orbit to give us time to figure this out?"

Bill Conroy, Director of the CIA said, "Conroy here. Sam, did he name his supervisor?"

"Yes sir; Crossman, Steve Crossman."

"I'm on this. Keep this line open. I'll be back to you - asap."

DAWN'S EARLY LIGHT

"Bennington here, call Barracuda right away, ask for a delay. I believe they have a full load of fuel. Stand against the threat as best you can. Use the sky-net and keep us plugged in. If necessary, I'll dispatch more hornets from *Nimitz*, to help. Bill, I need help here. Stay on the line please."

This was the best shot Murphy had ever taken at me – I hoped it wasn't his last. I called Barracuda flight – told them we'd been possibly compromised and asked if they could orbit offshore for thirty minutes. Asked them to calculate their maximum delay based on their current bingo time and get back to me. Also I asked them to see if *Nimitz* had at least one, preferably three KA-6D tankers to get them past bingo if needed. These three Hornets were committed to dumping their GBUs. You can't land on a carrier with GBU-28s hanging on your wings.

Bingo is a pre-flight calculated fixed time, past which no pilot is allowed to continue (without refueling) before immediately returning to a specified air base with a minimum prescribed amount of reserve fuel. The KA-6D is the Navy's carrier based version of a tanker. A single KA-6D can re-fuel another aircraft with up to ten thousand six hundred pounds of jet fuel or service three F/A-18s increasing each bingo time by slightly more than an hour.

We were here. We had the equipment and plan in place to take this tango out and destroy a tango emplacement. If we failed now we may never get another chance. There were, on the other hand, some things that didn't add up. I only knew about a dozen CIA operators and Crossman was not one of them. Tariq Sa'id joined our team as a CIA operative. We normally like to have the CIA directly involved with a mission of this sort because we get better and fresher intel. But usually we have seasoned, proven agents who have either trained with us or other Special Forces units with similar capabilities. Why was he here? Was this real or just a Crossman fuck-up? We'd soon find out.

"Barracuda Lead, this is Python Lead, over"

"Python, Barracuda, go ahead"

"Give my your bingo status"

"Bingo plus forty five from IP" (time to head back with forty five minutes to spare, eight minutes from now when he passes the IP)

"Can you delay fifteen?"

"Roger that. New status, bingo plus thirty. Barracuda out."

"Gunny, call Vince on the VHF. Tell him Barracuda time at IP (Initial Position – the precise time and place where each mission begins) is now 0215 – fifteen minute delay."

"Copy that Skipper – New IP at 0215."

Damn! I just had my thirtieth birthday and already Murphy's determined to give me high blood pressure and ulcers – I hate that son-of-a-bitch!

Amos walked over to me and sat at doggie ease, looking at me with sad eyes, as if to ask; "what do you want me to do now, stupid human? I'm bored!"

"Gunny, we've got a little less than twenty three minutes to get this situation figured out. The more I think about it the more I think this is just a SNAFU (Situation Normal, All Fucked Up) on the CIA's part with Tariq as the victim. Go tell him we'll get a response from JSOC/CIA soon. Make sure he's comfortable – see if he needs water. Then put your dog back on guard duty."

"Roger that, Skip."

The sat-phone flashed it's IR signal – I answered.

"Python Lead"

It was the Director, "Sam, please accept my personal apology. Crossman screwed up. He knows better, I hope. We'll get this problem fixed and it'll never happen again while I'm still here.

DAWN'S EARLY LIGHT

Crossman is a training coordinator. He was a little unsure about releasing Sa'id for support on an SOF mission. He gave him a recently retired sat-phone and asked him to call with status before and after the mission. The phone previously belonged to the retired Chief of Station, Afghanistan. Crossman will be completely re-briefed on proper command and communications protocol when supporting Special Operations Force missions and I'll be sure it's emphasized in our training program for field operators. After the mission, please have Sa'id call me."

"Hey, Director, this is good news – no harm no foul. Thanks for getting it straightened out so quickly. We just took a fifteen minute delay. No problem, Sir. Python out."

"Gunny, cut Tariq loose and send him over here please. How'd you get back so quick?"

"I never left. One of the twenty nine commands he responds to is **Return**, same as **Retreat** except for the caution part. I just whisper that into his vhf command unit (he held up what looked like a normal vhf transceiver) and he's off like a rocket returning to the last position he was ordered to before the current command. Slip your NVGs down, look at his hill and watch this."

I did as Gunny requested and was amazed to see the flashing IR beacon on the back of Amos' vest moving quickly toward his watch post – maybe thirty yards to go. Super dog!

"Tariq, the CIA Director sends you an apology for Crossman's action. You're on my shit-list, however, for not informing me of this breech of security initiated by him. When we plan a mission we focus on safety and security. I am responsible for the safety, security and the ultimate success of this mission – NOT YOU, NOT CROSSMAN. Understood?!"

"Yes Commander. It won't happen again."

"Let's get this show on the road. Barracuda Lead will be at the IP in..uh…eight minutes. Gunny, double check the beam location on the SOFLAM and be ready to initiate the sequence."

"Roger Skip."

"Python Bravo, Python Lead, over"

"Bravo here."

"SNAFU resolved, eight minutes to IP. Sitrep."

"We're go here Skip."

"Let's do it then, Python out."

"Barracuda Lead, Python Lead, over."

"This is Barracuda."

"We are go for 0215."

"Roger that, Barracuda out."

"Hey Skip, I've got an alert from Amos. He's flashing toward the hill to our east at about sixty degrees from our position. I'll get my rifle and NVGs and see what's up."

"Okay Gunny. Is the SOFLAM all ready to go?"

"Affirmative, just push the button at IP confirmation."

I swapped places with Gunny and he got busy looking for the tangos Amos spotted (or heard or smelled). I called Carbo (Vince) to make him aware that we were go for 0215 and that Amos had found something.

"Hey Skip, I've got two tangos in camos with AK-47s at 067 degrees and two hundred and sixty yards. Looks like they're about a hundred or maybe a hundred and fifty feet below us. They're looking at Amos. They might have some sort of night vision. I turned his flashers off – which, incidentally puts him back in the watch mode. I'd like to take these guys out before they get Amos."

"Do it!"

He did. Two suppressed 'pfft' shots about a half second apart from Gunny's M91A2 rifle.

DAWN'S EARLY LIGHT

"Got 'em – head shots, down for sure. Amos still watching."

"Maybe you better start scanning with your wide angle binoculars – and keep your doggie comm close by."

"Hey Skip. Just a reminder – this ain't my first rodeo."

"Sorry Gunny."

We just got our bacon saved by a dog. Who'd a thunk it!? Two minutes to IP.

"Python Bravo, Python Lead."

"Bravo here."

"Vince, make sure Rob is watching Amos. We just took down two tangos on our right flank. Amos spotted 'em."

"Yeah, Rob saw the whole thing. He's scanning both flanks and our six right now. I'm watching Amos and Tracer is glued to the SOFLAM."

"Copy that. Python Lead out."

I looked around at the Alpha squad and then through the binoculars at the Bravo squad. Everyone was set – except, Tariq and Tracer Russell. "Python, Lead – ear protection now!" Each man had a fold-up head set type ear protector in his left breast pocket and we had exactly fifty seconds to get them in place. The compression wave from a GBU-28 can be brutal, even from more than a mile away.

The bunker explosion was huge. Chunks of concrete landed uncomfortably close to our position. I glanced at Amos. He stood looking at the blast site and then resumed his watch. I glanced at Gunny. He was shooting at something.

"Whatcha got Gunny?" He still had his muffs on – couldn't hear me. After three more shots he pulled his muffs off and I asked again.

"Two more tangos. On our west flank this time. Running like

gazelle after the blast. Had to wing 'em, then kill 'em", he said as if talking about a couple of ducks.

"Thought I saw movement just before the bomb hit. Sure enough they were there. They know we're here and I'd like to know how. We've got better equipment and the high ground. And Amos, of course, although I saw these guys before he did."

"Yeah, Gunny – you're as good as the dog," I thought but I didn't dare say it.

The next three GBUs performed as well as the first, completely sealing the two west (#1 & #2) and the outer east (#4) tunnel entrances to the complex. The fifth GBU-28 didn't release. This was a contingency we'd planned for (gotcha covered Murphy – you son of a bitch). GBU-28s are brand new weapons built by the Texas Instruments' Defense Systems organization. They were built from eight inch artillery barrels, weighed four thousand seven hundred pounds each and were eighteen and a half feet long. These six bombs were actually taken from a group of twelve prototypes to be used for concept validation tests. The only carrier based fighter/bombers equipped to drop them were the Marine F/A-18 Hornets. Because the Marines based their Hornets on both land and sea they were chosen to be the first to have the necessary heavy weapon pylons and drop systems installed and "tested" for several squadrons of their aircraft. One bomb on each wing. This mission was the first time carrier Hornets armed with GBU-28s had ever been launched. One of the three Marine pilots on this mission participated in the pre-concept validation air drop at Tonopah Test Range, Nevada, using bombs with sand replacing the high explosives. He warned us that the pylon release mechanism had had problems that had been "fixed". But if one got hung, the procedure was to shut down the electronic release system and use the manual system – which "always" works. So that aircraft simply re-cued itself to take out the near east tunnel (#3) after the second shot at the bunker, and I manned the SOFLAM to manually illuminate #3 tunnel at the proper time. Gunny and Tariq were busy scanning for tangos along with Amos and the Bravo Squad.

The last bomb sealed tunnel #3 and the active phase of our mission was successfully complete – five targets destroyed, four KIA tangos and no team casualties – yet. Now the exfil phase began. Our rendezvous point was the top of a small hill directly in front of and a little less than a mile from the now flattened bunker. Our rendezvous time was 0400. Our pilot of choice, SOAR / CIA Chief Warrant Officer Jimmy Mac, would appear flying east up the valley at the base of the cliffs into which the complex had been built. Flying solo with half fuel, he would climb about two hundred and fifty feet to our hill top and we'd load up quickly and be on our way. Loading a Little Bird with six SOF operators plus equipment (and don't forget our pilot, Mac and our dog, Amos) has to be carefully pre-planned or it won't work. We bury any non essential equipment such as batteries from all equipment after being replaced with fresh spares, empty drop bags and other expendable infil equipment and any expendable (not expensive or classified) mission specific equipment. The MH-6 standard configuration has four seats, pilot, co-pilot and two rear passengers. Mac flies with the rear portside seat removed so he can cram in equipment. He adds two strong but light weight benches on both sides of the exterior of the cabin which easily hold two men each. On an exfil operation like the one going down tonight each of the four, or at least the front two, operators strapped on to external benches would have either IR Night Vision Goggles (IRNVG) or a fully functional ASDS helmet with advanced IRNV and full satellite and VHF comms and his favorite sub-machinegun – ours is the MP5. If weight allowed, one might find a more powerful belt fed machinegun rigged up to the forward starboard position.

Chapter Forty Seven

Northern Somalia
African Horn – Homeward Bound
Saturday, September 22, 1990, 0310 hrs Local

Our plan was to gather at the junction of two streams that converged at the southern base of the exfil hill at 0330 hrs, climb the hill together, set perimeter posts and wait for Mac. At about 0310 both squads were well down the hills we had held and moving toward the meeting point when Amos froze, nudged his alert switch with his nose and shortly thereafter all hell broke loose. We were taking machinegun fire on both squads from a single point about a hundred yards north of our positions about thirty feet up the rock face of our exfil hill. Probably a well camouflaged bunker not picked up by the analysts from the intel photos – can't blame it on them we didn't see it either. Tariq went down right away with a hit to the shoulder. I laid down suppressing fire with my MP5 while Gunny grabbed Tariq and pulled him behind a rock outcropping. Two thirty round magazines later I managed to get back behind the cover with Gunny and Tariq. I hadn't noticed until I looked for him; Amos was no longer with me! Losing Amos would be almost as bad as losing one of the team – hell, he was one of the team. I left Gunny to patch up Tariq and worked my way to the other side of our covering rock

DAWN'S EARLY LIGHT

formation – about fifty feet. On that side there was some vegetation behind which I could observe the bunker. There were at least two tangos with AK-47s firing from a narrow horizontal slot in a solid rock wall about thirty feet above the confluent stream. I watched intently as one of the tangos exchanged fire with Bravo Squad while the other remained quiet – waiting for us to reappear. They definitely had night vision - but undoubtedly it was starlight. These were Vietnam vintage night vision goggles using light amplification. Fuzzy green picture, difficult to pick out stationary images, good to about one to two hundred feet. If they'd had what we have, we'd be dead already with no reason for me to give you all this extremely interesting information.

I moved back about fifteen yards to Gunny and Tariq at the other side of the rock outcropping. His wound was through and through in his upper left arm – about three inches down. The bullet might have nicked the bone. I couldn't tell. But it was on the outside of the upper arm – no major arteries and bleeding was not profuse. Gunny had packed the entrance and exit wounds and applied a compression bandage and a tourniquet just above the wound. Tariq was lucid and showed no signs of shock.

"You ready to climb a hill and head home?" I wanted to see a positive attitude and willingness to not be a burden.

"Aye, aye, Skipper. Gunny got me all fixed up – good to go."

"Okay young man. Take care of that arm. Keep it in the sling Gunny made for you. Keep Gunny informed of your status. We're headed home just as soon as we take out a few tangos in a bunker on our exfil hill. They're on our damned hill!"

Gunny whispered, "I gave him a morphine syrette. He'll be good for a couple of hours. I've got another and Doc's got some more. He'll be ok."

I sent Gunny and Tariq over to the side of the rock I'd just come from and told Gunny to keep the tango on our side of the bunker busy like Doc was keeping the one on the their side busy. I was going to move to their flank and look for a weak spot. After Gunny set up suppressing fire from his new position I poked my head out from behind the rock and got a pleasant surprise; fifty feet up our exfil hill Amos stood with his IR flashers pointing to a point twenty feet above the firing slot in the tango's bunker. How can a dog be this smart? The position had been carved out of the cliff face from an entrance in a cleft twenty feet above the firing cell. I carefully and slowly crawled thirty yards parallel to the cliff wall until I was beyond the tango's peripheral vision, then began to walk, crossed the stream and started climbing. When I got to Amos' altitude I turned toward him and moved on to the open vertical entrance to the bunker. I had two flash-bangs and two fragmentation grenades. I was thinking about what combination to use when it occurred to me that I may as well use them all – we were going to ditch our remaining ammo and explosives before we left to save weight. I dropped the two flash-bangs together and then listened for any activity. The gunfire stopped and I heard one tango screaming. He was having a bad day. I was going to make it worse. I tossed them two frags about a minute later. After the big double bang and everything had settled out of the debris cloud, absolute silence.

"Python Team, Python Lead. Tangos down. Proceed to exfil point with care. There could be more. Copy?"

"Gunny here. Copy that Skip"

"Bravo, copy"

We got up the hill, dug a pit into which we would dump any equipment we wouldn't need on the flight back to *Tarawa*. Mission accomplished with six EKIA and one minor casualty. We heard the Little Bird coming up the valley and Tracer, Doc and I tossed all the expendable weight into the pit and had it covered and camouflaged before he landed.

DAWN'S EARLY LIGHT

Mac jumped out of the Little Bird and looked around at his load, "Jeezus Christ guys. This ain't no Sky Crane I'm flyin' here. Who said anything about a dog?"

"Admiral Bennington," I replied

"Well, then, the dog can go, who's going to stay?"

"Shut the fuck up Mac – help us get this shit into your Little Toy and get the fuck out of here. I'm hungry," I had to keep Mac focused on issues other than weight.

"Some day you guys are gonna overload me and we're gonna crash and burn."

Mac was a small guy, about five foot six or seven. Weighed maybe a hundred and sixty pounds. Wore a camo T-shirt and light weight pants, no socks with Nike running shoes – claimed he didn't wear underwear or socks to save weight. Yeah, sure, the guy's a piece of work. He knows as well as I do that this bird would take another two hundred pound warrior if we needed it to. This particular aircraft was the best thing that ever happened to SOF infil/exfil operations. It's attack configured brother the AH-6 gunship was just as quick and agile and carried a full load of deadly weapons. We always brought in one, sometimes two, MH-6 Little Birds and an AH-6 when we had a probability of a hostile exfil. Two 7.62 mm mini Gatling guns will do wonders to keep the tangos at bay while the good guys get the hell out of Dodge.

On the way out we took a pass over the destroyed bunker to get some IR photos. No movement in the debris at all. If Patish was there as our intel said he was, he's explaining his evil life to Allah right now – and it's gonna him take a long time.

When we got settled on the ship I called the Admiral with a sitrep. He was obviously pleased with our success and said he would share the post mission intel with us as soon as he received it later that day. *Tarawa* steamed across the Gulf of Aden and Mac ferried us off the ship to Salalah Air Base in two loads. We got some sleep in a hot hangar office, climbed aboard our old rust-bucket C-140AX and headed to Bahrain. The re-purposed C-140 now had an inch thick gym type rubber mat on the floor, twelve shooting range quality ear muff headsets with built in stereo speakers and twelve sleeping bags like the ones we used during mountain training in Alaska. Which was good because at altitude these tin cans were colder than a well digger's ass. I was beginning to feel a little better about this "new" rattle-trap" aircraft of ours. Actually, they made four of these refurbs and this one was to remain stationed in Bahrain.

When we got to Bahrain, what do you know, the CIA Director had a Gulfstream III waiting for us there. An obvious mea maxima culpa for our little problem with Crossman. We flew the GS-3 all the way to San Diego, refueling at Ramstein AFB, Germany and Oceana NAS, Virginia – nice ride, great food and superb German beer and schnapps taken on at Ramstein. After landing at Oceana we shuffled Tariq off to the Naval Medical Center (Walter Reed Hospital) at Bethesda Maryland to get his arm fixed and spent the night at the Oceana VOQ. When we got to the CIA hangar at San Diego International Rob and I headed straight for the long term lot, jumped into my Corvette and headed home.

Chapter Forty Eight

McKensie Condo, La Jolla, California
Tuesday, September 25, 1990, 1805 hrs PDT

"Hey Babe, how're my girls?" I queried Ashleigh noting that she had put on some additional weight in the short time I'd been gone. Actually we didn't know if the baby was going to be a girl, but Ash kind of indicated she might want a girl first to take care of all the rest of the kids we wanted to have – so I played along; never mentioning my slight preference for a boy.

"I'm doin' great. We don't know it's a girl – yet. How's my XO?" Technically she outranked me by a couple of months time in grade and she never let me forget it. So I was relegated to the role of Executive Officer of the household while she held the coveted but much deserved position of CH (Commander, Household). While I was gone she'd painted the baby's room a light gender neutral yellow. Looked pretty good.

"How was your down range party."

"Everything went great – no bad casualties. Tariq got grazed on his upper arm – not too bad." Damn, I was getting better and better at lying. I just didn't want Ash to worry about me.

"Out to eat?" I hoped.

"Got reservations at Tony's; 7:30, get cleaned up."

DON CANDY

"Yes Ma'am, your highness!"

Tony's was a great little Italian place right on the beach where we could catch the sunset during dinner at this time of year – very romantic. I wondered what she had in mind. . .

Ash doesn't work for Admiral Bennington. She reports to Captain Dirk Ericson, Commander, U.S. Navy Fighter Weapons School at Miramar NAS, better known as 'Top Gun'. But while she's been grounded during her pregnancy and working in the same building as the Admiral at San Diego NAS she and the Admiral frequently lunched together and that's how I find out what's really going on with the Navy. Her latest G2 (Intelligence) was that Bo was now officially the Commander of DEVGRU and permanently located at Dam Neck (Virginia Beach) Virginia.. The Black Angels, now known as ASDG, (no longer called the Black Angel Team – the Admiral didn't like the BAT thing) were now an official organization operating as the airborne arm of the DEVGRU Black Squadron. Actually, the color of all our equipment is a very deep (dark) blue – but that name was already taken. It was organized, as I had recommended, as four six man teams of two three man squads each. It was a multi-force organization reporting to JSOC. Meaning SEALs, Delta, Rangers, Green Beret, SOAR, Force Recon, etc. would be eligible to join the team. Team members would be senior, fully trained Special Operators with combat experience and five weeks of ASDS training. I was the Commander of that organization as well as the Airborne SPECOP Advanced Weapons Development Organization – I didn't know what we were going to call that – consisting of three Navy Technicians and six highly qualified civilian engineers at El Centro. Some of this was new to me. I reported administratively to Bo at Virginia Beach (Dam Neck) and operationally to Admiral Bennington at Fort Bragg. But the most important tidbit was that Bo was now an east-coaster for good and

DAWN'S EARLY LIGHT

I needed to send him a check for $50K and get the title to my new (relatively speaking) Mooney M20J (sweet little airplane) transferred into my name.

Five Days Later

Life became routine once again. Pay attention to my beautiful fat wife. Go to parties with our friends. Train eight to ten hours a day five days a week, church every Sunday. Life was good. Then October slipped into November and Ash began to feel a little uncomfortable. The time was near.

Then Murphy sent me another down range assignment, this one to Libya. About thirty five miles southeast of Tripoli and inland about twenty miles from the Mediterranean Sea – a single hostage rescue. Vince, Gunny and I looked over the requirements and intel. The job looked straight forward. The hostage was ambulatory and being held in a small poorly built single cell concrete block prison, guarded by two tangos at night. His daylight hours were spent in a lab twenty klicks south of his prison home watched by two different guards. He's a U.S. citizen - optical engineer with a PhD from MIT. He was also instrumental in matching optics to our top secret infrared focal plane array used in almost all of our special forces night vision systems. He had been abducted at the Benghazi Airport, held captive for a little less than a month and the CIA/NSA had just located him day before yesterday. Vince could handle this one. He was approaching time in grade as a Major in Delta Force and in need of more command opportunity to move up to lieutenant colonel. I wanted to do everything I could to help him. Damned fine officer. Head screwed on right. Outstanding leader. Yep, Vince could handle this just fine.

*****

Tariq and I spent last night in a bar discussing his future. He called the meeting, caught a CIA flight from Langley and came up to La Jolla to talk and he bought the beer so he had my attention.

He spent the first round apologizing for the SNAFU with Crossman and letting me know that he was not the CYA (Cover Your Ass) type, and that he had come to regard his boss, Steve Crossman, as a real horse's ass. The next round was spent telling me about his family in West Virginia and what was left of his family in Iraq. The next two rounds were spent trying to convince me that he would make a great SEAL and that he didn't believe the CIA was where he belonged. He told me he had looked in detail at what is expected of a SEAL candidate – BUD/S and all the other necessary training. He had spent three weeks at the ASDS training center at Miramar NAS, California and a month (a week before and three weeks after our last mission) at the Armed Forces Experimental Training Activity (AFETA), located at Camp Peary, Virginia and known as 'the Farm' by CIA and SOF operators. The Farm is where CIA Agents get enough training to act as intelligence support operators on Special Forces down range missions – theoretically they can take care of themselves, coordinate with CIA assets and follow instructions. Tariq had a little problem with the follow instructions part on our last mission. I didn't hold that against him because he hadn't had any real training at that point. I mentioned the upcoming mission and he pleaded with me to request his participation.

I had no reason to reject his request but I told him, "Major Harlow is lead on this mission I'll have to clear it with him and then inform Admiral Bennington and Director Conroy. If that all works you damn well better listen to the Major when he sets the rules of engagement, security and safety specific to the mission – understood?"

"Yeah Skipper, I learned my lesson – the Major will have no problems with me. If you can get me into your unit I'll work my butt off to become your best operator. I like your team, the guys, the way you do your respective jobs, what you do and why you do it. I'm not cut out to be a spook.""

DAWN'S EARLY LIGHT

"Okay Tariq – we'll see what we can do. It ain't gonna a be easy."

Tariq smiled and said, "The only easy day was yesterday."

I said to myself, "Amen, Tariq. You're gonna find out what that really means!"

I said to Tariq, "We'll see."

*****

A week later Major Vince Harlow did handle the hostage extraction, rather well in fact. He, Rob, Gunny and Amos returned yesterday. Director Conroy nixed Tariq's participation in the mission, which was exactly the right thing to do. There was no reason to include a CIA liaison on this particular mission and Tariq had a long way to go before he earned his SEAL Trident, if in fact he ever got accepted into the Navy. The mission was both routine and successful; two tangos KIA and no casualties for the good guys. Doctor Peter Ballwin, Optical Engineer, graduate of MIT, previous Senior Member of the Technical Staff at Texas Instruments, Dallas, was extracted with no further intervention by Mr. Murphy. Amos got more kudos from all three operators. Looks like our dog is here to stay. Dr. Ballwin stated during the debriefing that he believes he set the Libyans back a decade in their understanding of infrared optics. I congratulated the team and warned them that no mission is routine. Routine is a dangerous state of mind. Don't ever forget Mr. Murphy - he hasn't forgotten you. . .

Chapter Forty Nine

Office of the Iraqi Prime Minister
Royal Palace, Baghdad, Iraq
Monday, November 12, 1990, 0835 hrs Local Time

Qusay Hussein knocked three times on the ornate cypress door to his father's office on the second floor of his royal palace overlooking the Olympic sized pool and grand gardens.

"Enter," Saddam was in a foul mood. His Minister of Defense had just finished briefing him on the status of the American fueled 'Coalition Force'. It seemed that countries as far away as Australia were pledging troops to stand against Iraq's annexation of Kuwait. What business did Australians have meddling in Iraqi affairs? And even worse than that; the United Nations was considering a 'Final Mandate' for removal of Iraqi troops from Kuwait by January 15th or face war with this 'coalition'.

"Please be quick, my son. I am extremely busy."

"Yes Father, I believe I may have some pleasing news."

"Well don't just stand there. What news could possibly be pleasing to me among all this ongoing saber rattling with the United States and its oil thirsty friends?"

DAWN'S EARLY LIGHT

"Abdul al-Rashid our IIS man in Kazakhstan has finally found and befriended the source of the nuclear weapons procured by the PRK. It seems the Kazakhstanis had a number of warheads that were not accounted for at the recent break-up of the Soviet Union. The number is not known to his source but he said there were at least six but maybe more. The PRK procured three of them, one of which is enroute to us at this very moment, and one was sold to a third party whose identity the Kazakhstanis will not reveal. None the less there are still at least two available. He has given us the Kazakhstani contact that we might query as to the terms for procurement of one or two of these remaining units. Al-Rashid is confident that an agreement can be reached quickly. He says Kazakhstan is becoming desperate for cash. This could be to our advantage."

"Qusay, I want you to begin making plans to liquidate more gold and generate a plan for the strategic placement of at least one additional nuclear missile. Let me think through this latest U.N. threat before we commit more of our precious resources to a third warhead."

Saddam arose from his desk and approached a large Lambert Conformal Projection wall map of the eastern hemisphere between ten and forty five degrees north that he used for reference during his eight year war with Iran. It was embellished with thirty four sets of colored concentric circles. Each set of circles had a radial line drawn from the forty five degree point measured from true north to the location of the missile bunker, silo or mobile launcher home position at the center. The circles were color coded, denoting the type and revision of each missile in the Iraqi inventory. There were five colors. At the center of each set of concentric circles was a push-pin denoting the type and revision of the missile currently in that bunker silo or mobile launcher. There was a legend in the upper right corner.

He studied the map for a couple of minutes and then addressed his son.

"Do not place the Korean missile in the H-3 silo. Leave it on the launch vehicle it arrived on and drive it from Taji to the to the underground launch bunker southwest of Ruwayshid on the Jordanian border. Do that immediately and have it targeted for the Israeli Ramat David Air Base. If all goes well in your negotiations with the Kazakhstanis, bring the new warhead to Taji and have it attached to one of our four latest model Al-Hussein missiles. The silo at H3 is ready, is it not?"

"Yes Father, all issues have been resolved. As you know from our continuing progress reports, the Americans have, over the last several months, increased their satellite surveillance of this and other areas leaving us fewer hours each day to complete the above ground work."

" Put that missile into our new silo. In the silo it will have better range and accuracy and we won't have to disconnect the Korean missile from its launcher. Have it targeted for Haifa. We must stay on schedule. These UN deadlines are looming."

Chapter Fifty

Scripps Green Hospital, La Jolla, California
Wednesday, November 21, 1990, 1805 hrs PST

Well there we were, the day before Thanksgiving at three a.m. plus a little; sound asleep.

"Uh, Sam," she said as she whacked me on the side of my head, "my water just broke. Dr. Sanders said to go ahead and head for the hospital when that happens."

The good news was that since the baby was a week late we'd already packed her suitcase and mapped out the shortest route to the hospital. Although, at this hour of the morning, that didn't really matter much. So we were off to the hospital – only a little more than seven miles away.

We were met at the curb by a nurse and a staff member (wheelchair pusher) to ask questions (the nurse) and push the wheelchair (staff member). Just as we entered the elevator headed for the fourth floor Ash experienced her first labor pain. It lasted about a minute. When it was over she smiled, "That wasn't so bad. This's going to be a piece of cake." Not a fortuitous statement, as she would realize later that afternoon when the real labor pains set in. Somewhere around eight o'clock that evening the pains let up a bit and she asked the nurse if something was wrong. She was told by the nurse that hers was a typical first time labor and by the time she got to the fourth child they'd just pop right out. Just what Ash wanted to hear. . .

So now it's actually Thanksgiving, 0115 hrs; a great day to have a baby. And then the pains got worse and it's time for the heavy breathing, pushing and yelling at me – turns out, this was all my fault. Okay, I accept the blame and get a smile back in-between pushes and the baby's here and it's screaming. The doctor whacks it on its back, turns it around and it's a boy! Secretly, I had suspected it was going to be a boy. Ashleigh is not a large woman; trim, fit and muscular – all in proportion. But this baby stretched her in every dimension except up – it had to be a boy. The nurse weighed him – eight pounds nine and a half ounces. No wonder it took so long. The nurse got the baby cleaned up and put him in Ashleigh's arms. She looked like she'd just finished the twelfth round of an eight round wrestling match – but she was smiling ear-to-ear.

"Handsome little guy," I observed.

"Not so little!" she snapped back.

Still smiling, she whispered "Scott Stephen McKensie," to the baby as she gently touched his nose.

We had agreed to name the baby Scott after my father, if it was a boy. My dad Scott died in a Wild Weasel attack on a North Vietnam Surface to Air Missile site in 1966. I was six years old. Stephen is Ashleigh's dad's name. He's a retired Navy Captain – lots of chest cabbage..

Life was good today!

Chapter Fifty One

McKensie Condo, La Jolla, California
Saturday, November 24, 1990, 1415 hrs PST

We got home a little after two in the afternoon. Our new son was the center of attention until he got hungry. The little guy could scream like a banshee – but he could shut it off immediately when he got what he wanted. Was this a sign of things to come? He was destined to grow up in a military family where you don't always get what you want when you want it - if you ever even get it at all. I could tell right away; we were going to have a challenge with Scott Stephen McKensie.

Thirty seconds after Scotty stopped yelling my phone rang. It was Bo.

"Hey Sam, got your voicemail. Congratulations to you guys, especially Ashleigh - since you had all the fun and she did all the work. Sounds like a world-class kid. Glad he looks like Ash – no offence.

"Seriously, I wish you guys all the best.

"Sorry to have to use this call to tell you we've got another DRM (Down Range Mission) coming up – half of the acronyms we use are for talking on un-secure lines. Monday morning there's a 141 (C-141 Starlifter jet cargo plane) leaving Miramar for Andrews. George and I would like you and Rob to be on it. Has

Ash got backup for Scotty?"

"Yeah, Helen's coming down Tuesday. She plans to stay a week or two – whatever Ash needs."

"If you can run out to Miramar tomorrow I can get you filled in on a secure video line."

"What time?"

"Say noonish. I'll be here all day."

"Yeah, I can do that – mind if I bring Rob with me?"

"Of course, the more the merrier. If there's a better time to get you both, call me back. We figure this is a three man job, but you and Rob will do the planning and we don't mind being wrong."

"Any other news - Uncle Asshole?"

"No, that's about it. I knew you'd be happy."

"Talk to you tomorrow."

"Tell Ash hi and congrats."

"Will do, bye."

I never thought I'd rue the day I let my only uncle into my chain of command. I mean I like Bo a lot, he was like my father until I joined the Navy. Then he became my boss, and there's a difference. A lot of our early ASDS missions were done by Bo, Rob and I. Hell, we helped develop the damned thing. But now there are ten or more other qualified officers or senior NCO's who could lead small team ASDS missions. And the Admiral's got this thing about always having an officer in command of ASDS missions. Not like it used to be. Christ, Master Chief Manny Hernandez led SEAL Team IV for two years while higher tried to find an officer more qualified than he was. Then we lost Manny on Joint Task Force drug bust and they still couldn't find an officer for ST4 so they promoted Rob to Master Chief and he led it for another year until he decided to come over to DEVGRU and help

DAWN'S EARLY LIGHT

us with ASDS. Any officer who thinks he knows more than his senior noncoms is full of crap.

I gotta get off my high horse here and figure out what to tell Ash. She's not your typical military wife. She's a career Navy pilot. The first ever female Top Gun Pursuit Pilot / Instructor – she's a better pilot than me and she knows it. She also out ranks me by a few months time-in-grade. But now she's a mother and I'm a father. If I'm not careful the family dynamics could take a nasty turn. This calls for a beer and some careful thought. . .

Chapter Fifty Two

Secure Conference Room
Miramar Naval Air Station, CA
Sunday, November 25, 1990, 1205 hrs PST

Rob and I were in the secure video conference room at Miramar NAS at noon sharp. It took the grumpy civilian technician a few minutes to get the room re-configured into it's secure state. When we got Bo on the screen, voice and all, I told the tech to go on back home. He immediately became un-grumpy, asked if I knew how to turn everything off and secure the room, thanked me smiling and left.

Bo filled us in on the mission. Basically, it was, in a way, a follow-up to our recent mission in Somalia. A month ago the crews and passengers of two fifty foot sailboats, sailing together, fifteen U.S. citizens in all, had been captured by Somali pirates and were being held hostage near the northern coast of Somalia. Not my favorite place to play.

They were being held by four tangos in an open desert area thirty klicks inland - just up the coast from our last mission. The ransom was set at two million dollars and communicated to the U.S. State Department two days after the abduction. It had taken the NSA almost two weeks to find them because they were not where anyone expected them to be and they were pretty well

DAWN'S EARLY LIGHT

camouflaged during the day. Of course Somali tangos weren't up to speed on infrared satellite imagery and the fact that at night warm blooded animals are easily spotted and identified due to the temperature differential between the cool air and a warm body.

NSA was in the process of understanding the tango support system; guard rotation, supplies, etc. At this point all they had seen is one large blacked out truck arriving just after dark with supplies. Their current satellite coverage window didn't allow following the truck back to it's origin. We would get additional intel on the support activity as it became available during the next twenty four hours.

The State Department had done a pretty good job of delaying the 'payoff' citing; 'congressional rules requiring hostage proof of life and proof of identification requirements that must be met before any funds can be issued for this purpose'. The NSA 'Negotiator' said this ought to work; blame it on Congress and never lose faith in the fundamental stupidity of most terrorists. Anyway, they found them night before last and they believe their delay tactics are good for a minimum of four and maximum of seven more days. The LHA-1, USS *Tarawa,* on standby for support of this mission for two weeks, left the U.S. CENTCOM Base at Bahrain immediately upon receiving intel from the NSA that the hostages had been found and headed for the north shore of Somalia. She won't arrive until day after tomorrow. She will provide exfil with a CH-53 Sea Stallion Helicopter accompanied by an AH-6 Little Bird gunship. Rob and I agreed that with Gunny and Amos we could handle the mission. We were given the mission file with the latest intel and general information and worked out a strawman mission plan. My team will depart tomorrow morning from San Diego Naval Air Station (NAS) on a Navy GS-3, refuel at Oceana NAS, Virginia and fly on to Bahrain via Ramstein AFB, Germany, arriving at noon on Wednesday. The mission will commence Wednesday evening and execution will commence at sometime between 0230 hrs and 0400hrs, local Thursday morning – depending on NSA satellite support availability. The Gulfstream III was equipped with satcom so we could get intel updates and make real-time requests as we did the detailed mission planning in-flight. I stepped out of the secure room and called Gunny to give him a heads up on our departure time so he could get Amos and all his equipment squared away. When I returned we decided we'd done all we could at this point and we adjourned the meeting. I secured the room and we headed home. On the way I called Helen (Ash's mom) to give her a heads up and see if she minded coming down a day early.

*****

So now all I had to do was tell Ash I was leaving for probably five days. Piece of cake, right? I didn't think so either. That's why I was stunned when in response to my telling her she said, "Let me call mom and see if she can come a little early."

"Done that already. She'll be here tomorrow around noon."

To which she smiled and said, "You're the best."

To which I smiled and said, "I know."

I thought to myself, "The girl I married is back!"

Chapter Fifty Three

Navy Gulfstream III
In-route to Bahrain Navy CENTCOM Base
Sunday, November 25, 1990, 1900 hrs EST

We requested a written intel update when we got to Oceana, so we didn't do any serious mission planning on our first leg. We did, however learn a lot more about Amos. Before we boarded the plane I asked Gunny how combat dogs relieve themselves on long flights.

He said, "wait and see."

After about three hours in flight Amos walked up to Gunny, stood still and placed one foot forward two inches.

"See this?" Gunny asked.

"He's gotta pee."

Gunny got a small package out of Amos' bag, unfolded it and strapped it around Amos' hind quarters. A clear plastic tube ran from the catcher pouch to a plastic bag, attached by a quick disconnect. When Amos was done the bag was detached and disposed of – nary a drop spilled.

"Different kit if he's gotta take a crap," Gunny said, "but it's just as slick."

Poor Amos actually looked embarrassed.

We landed at Oceana at about 2330 hrs to stretch our legs, replenish the plane with jet fuel, food and beer. We also got our intel update. For the third night since discovery the tangos had not changed anything. Same number of tangos and hostages, same sleeping positions, exact same location. The support system had been surveilled by an SR-71 Blackbird. The support depot was a cluster of small ramshackle buildings two hundred meters inland from a point on the coast directly north of the hostage position. It was supplied daily by a small trawler. It appeared that the truck brought a single tango for rotation each night. There would be follow-up intel on this when we arrived at Bahrain. Also we learned that *Tarawa* was scheduled to arrive on her initial station at 1630 hrs Monday afternoon. Her initial station was thirty five miles northeast of the final position which she would take under cover of darkness, arriving there at 0100 hrs Wednesday morning. Things were taking shape.

We left Oceana at 0030, Monday morning on our trans-Atlantic leg. The flight would only take about eight hours but we would cross six time zones; so we would move fourteen hours in our 24 hour time frame. We spent a couple of hours digesting our new intel; turning it into detailed mission plans. Then after a great meal and a couple of beers it was time for a nap. I know what you're thinking; eat a big meal, drink a couple of beers and then go right to sleep without exercise – that's not healthy! I gotta tell you; for people who exercise as much as we do, it's not a problem. This GS III had eight high-back seats that could be configured into four amazingly comfortable single berths, two on each side. We turned the cabin air down four degrees, passed out blankets and got ready for a four hour snooze. Before we turned down the lights Gunny got Amos squared away. He tapped the seat and snapped his fingers. Amos took a resting position on his new bed. Gunny said, "sleep." Amos rested his head between his legs and closed his

DAWN'S EARLY LIGHT

eyes. Wish I could do that.

We landed at Ramstein Air Force Base at 1430 hrs local time, Monday afternoon, November 26. Here we received two new pilots and the precise coordinates of the sleeping positions of the four tango guards. With this information we could program our ASDS computers to land 100 meters from each of the three guards on a line from the center of the site through each guard's position. Gunny will handle two guards by dropping off Amos to guard one of the tangos while he moves to dispatch the second. We would not be taking prisoners on this mission. Strong message to the tangos; do not fuck with the U.S. Navy.

This flight would take a little over six hours. But, we would cross two more time zones, pushing us two more hours into the future. We finalized the mission plan which included programming all three computers with precise landing coordinates and running a complete pre-op diagnostic on each system. At this time everything was go – no problems. I thought about the tango's support system and the opportunity it provided for Mr. Murphy but I gave him no public recognition – that creates bad juju.

Our ETA at Bahrain was oh dark thirty (0030 hrs – again? – didn't we just do that?) local time, Tuesday morning. So we took another four hour nap, after which we ate again. The good news was that the flight over the desert was at night. Even at forty thousand feet, flight over a desert during daylight can be rough. This one had been smooth as silk.

Chapter Fifty Four

Navy CENTCOM Base, Bahrain
Tuesday, November 27, 1990, Oh Dark Thirty, Local

When we finally touched down at CENTCOM, Bahrain. We'd been in the air for nineteen hours, had two one hour layovers and crossed eleven time zones. Our internal clocks had rolled forward one day plus eight hours. Maybe we should have gone the other way?

CENTCOM stands for the United States Navy's CENTral COMmand, headquartered at MacDill Air Force Base, Tampa Florida. The U. S. Special Operations COMmand (USSOCOM) is also based at MacDill. The official name of the facility at Bahrain is 'U. S. Naval Support Activity, Bahrain'. Maybe because it is also home to the Navy's 5th Fleet.

We retired to the Base Ops building lugging our equipment. While Rob and Gunny made another trip I got Amos some water in a bowl I found in the small kitchen behind the lounge. During our last hour of flight we had eaten our fourth meal; lemon glazed salmon over rice pilaf with buttered broccoli and garlic potatoes. AND, cherry pie ala mode for dessert. And you thought we were eating MREs didn't you? I guess my bitching to the Admiral about the first trip we made across the pond to Bahrain in the C-130AX rattle trap was bearing fruit. He made some improvements while

DAWN'S EARLY LIGHT

we were on the ground shooting tangos and now, not to be outdone by the CIA, the Admiral has blessed us with a GS III ride.

When the guys got back and we got the equipment secured (locked up), Gunny took Amos out to find some grass while Rob and I briefed the OOD (Officer Of the Deck – Navy talk for the guy who's in charge) on our current requirements for the mission – which were mainly a warm bed, plenty of food, beer, his pilots, our plane and access to the gym. He had a sealed envelop from Base Security for me. It was a little love note from NSA – they would provide us with some most excellent low altitude Infrared support with an audio link from the sand box at Langley. The open window would be for nineteen minutes beginning at 0223 hrs. Nineteen minutes was more than I expected from a low orbit bird. We were either looking at new technology or two birds in tandem.

We planned six hours of sleep beginning at 1330 hrs. At 2230 hrs we would load our gear onto the *Tin Can*, our nick name for the aged C-130AX refurb awaiting us on the CENTCOM tarmac. I mentally adjusted our take-off time to fit the IR window while we were on the ground leaving a five minute buffer to be sure we didn't waste any window time. The new departure time was 2353 hrs.

We then headed straight to the gym where we learned that Amos does a seven minute mile on the treadmill for four miles daily to stay in shape. We spent an hour and a half working off some of the calories we'd picked up on the way over and then retreated to the pilot's lounge to rest and read until the pilots showed up for lunch at 1200 hrs.

Our pilots showed up five minutes early; different guys than our last trip. We talked over lunch; mostly about the mission up until the point where we left the airplane, after which they didn't have a need to know and we could not divulge. The pilot was a scrawny little Lieutenant wearing sunglasses that almost covered his face. His name was Adrian Cox. I dated a girl in high school named Adrian - Hmmm. He seemed like a good kid but didn't look a day over nineteen. I hoped he could fly. The co-pilot was (or at least looked) a little older. His name was Tommy Anderson. After we'd finished our lunch we talked over coffee about the Navy, ROTC, Ashleigh's job, flight school, OCS and mission weather. We could talk a little about who we were and what we did but not who we are and what we do.

After a while we all got bored and left the cafeteria for parts unknown. I headed back to the pilots lounge as did Tommy. We both had brought good books along. I was reading *The Letter of Marque,* Patrick O'Brian's twelfth book in his HMS Surprise series; great books. He was reading a Clancy novel, the title of which I couldn't make out because the cover was overwhelmed by the author's name. At around 1315 we headed for the bunkhouse and some well deserved sleep.

We woke, had a light breakfast, reviewed the latest intel, got our stuff out of lock-up and rechecked everything, spent some time relaxing, reading or whatever. At 2115 hrs my watch vibrated on my arm telling me it was time to load up. While we were loading, Lieutenant Adrian Cox handed me an envelope he said he found in his seat. I opened it. From the Admiral, it read, "Sam, we've made a few more changes to your plane. The headsets now have an integrated local network and a new three position switch on the right earpiece; music, local net and off. The boom mikes have the latest noise cancelling technology. Amos' comm unit is on your net. No music, no off switch; so be aware, he hears all conversations. Be nice to him. Also new; the twelve vinyl beanbag pillows. Bon Voyage!

Chapter Fifty Five

Angels Two Six Aboard C130-AX "*Tin Can*"
Over Saudi Arabia, In-route to Mission IP
Wednesday, November 28, 1990, 0005 Local Time

We were set to reach our mission IP – the point at which we departed from our lovely aircraft and headed for tango-land – at 0045 hrs. Since we were landing separately we would jump together.

As we do on every ASDS mission, we reviewed our mission profile and time-line in minute detail. Having satisfied ourselves that everything was in order and that we had considered and planned around all imaginable contingencies we relaxed on our new pillows and tried to sleep. At 0015 hrs we donned our ASDS gear and ran the self-test programs. All was still good-to-go. So at 0045 hrs we went - together.

ASDS is a precision system tied tightly to the Navstar Global Positioning System (GPS). GPS keeps time accurate to less than a couple of nanoseconds and is accurate to within a few feet when aided by Airborne Differential GPS. This system uses LIDAR (same idea as RADAR only using a laser rangefinder) to simultaneously range on two known points on the ground plus the RADAR altitude to fix the position of the aircraft and then compare that position to the aircraft GPS position, generating a small systemic range error correction, due mostly to ionospheric refraction, which is fed to the user on a separate channel, in our case the comm link to our ASDS computers guiding us to the LP (Landing Point). There will not be a quiz on this subject at the end of the chapter, so just let me say that all this stuff happens continuously as we glide to earth and allows us to land on a pre-determined spot with better than two foot accuracy. The actual accuracy is classified. And you know the rub on that; I tell you, I gotta shoot you. And you're my friend. I think. This morning we don't even need that kind of accuracy because we're landing a hundred yards away from our targets; what's ten or fifteen feet?

Jumping at 0045 will put us on the ground 1.5 hours later at 0215 hrs; eight minutes before the satellite window opens for nineteen minutes. That should give us plenty of time.

*****

We started at Angels Two Six (twenty six thousand feet) and had exactly one and a half hours until we touched down. Plenty of time to think about things other than killing tangos. For me, thoughts went immediately to my week old baby boy, Scott Stephen McKensie, who I just barely got to know before being dragged off on this little down range party. Blonde hair and blue eyes; you wouldn't think I had any thing to do with the process. But then I'd rather he got his good looks genes from Ashleigh.

Then, briefly paying attention to my visor display, I noticed that Gunny's chute veering to the right and losing altitude. I called on the ASDS net, "Gunny, what's going on?"

"I don't know Skip, my nav system just quit. I'm trying to do diagnostics, but nothing's happening. At least I've still got comm."

"Go to manual flight asap, you're losing altitude."

In ALS mode (Automatic Landing System mode) the ASDS has control of four control lines (shrouds) allowing the computer

DAWN'S EARLY LIGHT

to optimize the glide slope. During development we tried to invent a manual system that would employ four control lines but settled for the two line system that parachutists had been using for years – because the four line manual system was primarily needed on final approach and during precision landings. We taught our students how to manually optimize the glide slope using the rate of descent meter and then using the laser altimeter for landing flare. This worked well for safely landing a jumper who had suffered loss of his nav system, but proved to be about 3 to 5% less efficient in glide performance causing him to be short of the target. My guess for Gunny's situation was that his landing would be about a quarter mile short – not too bad. But, he would be making a manual landing at night with a dog. There was still plenty of opportunity for our arch-enemy, Mr. Murphy, to jump in and screw up our mission.

"Okay Gunny, you're in front of and below me. Grab your manual lines and optimize your glide. Use your rate of descent meter to lower your descent rate to two hundred and ninety four feet per minute and turn left three degrees.

"Rob, let's go to manual and stick with Gunny. I'm going to guide him in. We'll be a little short, maybe a quarter mile or so. We have an eight minute buffer on satellite support so we'll only eat into the window by four or five minutes if all goes well. We can ditch our chutes and suites at the landing site and vector the AH-6 there for pickup on exfil."

"Sounds like a plan Skip. It's better we that stay together. Going manual," Rob replied.

The ASDS was designed to operate in a degraded mode in case of failure of the nav system or the Global Positioning System. Back in the mid eighties when we were developing the system my lead technician, Leroy Schmidt, insisted on isolating the degraded mode from the operational mode for safety. This required, among other things a separate power supply and lithium ion battery for each subsystem. I was worried about weight. On the final system design, Leroy came in only three and a half ounces over the spec. For the added safety of the isolated subsystem design the spec change was a piece of cake. Leroy now has a master's degree in electrical engineering and is leading the operational test phase of the development of a family of micro-drones for the CIA. We'll be using these little jewels in my next book.

"Okay, Gunny, you're looking good now. Keep that heading and rate of descent. We're right behind you."

In manual mode none of us had the colored 'location dots' on our screens telling us where we all were. But, we could see the IR beacon on Gunny's helmet and guide him from behind. When the auto-ranging on my visor switched to two miles the system placed a marker on my projected landing spot and I could easily see the distance to the original landing spot (the little green x). And, I could see that we were going to land about three eighths of a mile short. We'd lose probably six minutes or so. Not a critical problem.

As we approached the landing we all switched to enhanced IR vision. This allowed us to clearly see the ground and any obstacles that might be there. Fortunately, we were landing in a desert area without much in our way – just a few rocks, some occasional boulders and small desert vegetation. When we got to a hundred feet above the ground we turned forty five degrees directly into the light wind for landing and began our flare at twenty feet. At that altitude, with these chutes, you can slow your forward motion and your rate of descent such that your landing is much like stepping off a downward moving escalator.

We all landed safely in close proximity. I figured we had landed about seven hundred yards due north of the center of the target. It was now 0216 hrs – still seven minutes before satellite support. We piled our chutes and suites together and placed several large rocks on top in case the wind picked up. Then we headed for the target, making plans on the way. Gunny had Amos on a leash

DAWN'S EARLY LIGHT

leading the way.

We decided to take up our original planned positions. We knew one of the four tangos would be awake and on watch. But we didn't know which one. So we delayed our position assignments until we got satellite support.

"Scorpion lead, Scorpion lead, this is Overwatch, over."

I replied, "roger Overwatch this is Scorpion lead – Do you have eyes?"

"Affirmative, we show four tangos. One awake and walking around. Southeast, southwest and northwest are sleeping. Northeast tango is walking toward the southeast tango. Fifteen hostages appear to be sleeping in the area central to the tangos."

"Copy that Overwatch. Please advise active tango position, over."

"Active tango approximately ten yards north of southeast tango, over."

"How close are we to the northeast position, over."

"About a hundred and fifty yards. Look to your left. You should have visual shortly."

"Okay, I've got the walker. Keep us advised on any tango or hostage movement. Scorpion lead out."

On the ASDS net I said, "Rob, take your position on the southwest tango."

"Gunny, drop Amos here at the northeast tango's position and take your position on the northwest tango. I'm going to catch this guy on his way back from his walk if he doesn't wake the southeast tango up. If he does I'll have to take them both. We shoot on my command."

This is, of course not what we had planned – but it was close. The walking tango could cause a problem for me if the reason he was walking toward his compadre was to wake him for his watch.

That would require me to take them both out before they were separated by more than about twenty feet. These two would both have AK-47s.

Gunny reported, "northwest ready."

"Roger that Gunny."

" Rob, ETA?"

"About thirty seconds Skip."

"Copy."

I took a prone position about ten yards northeast of the southeast (sleeping) tango's position and watched the tango through the low power IR scope on my MP-5 submachine gun as he stood close to the southeast position. He was just standing there looking around. There was no indication that he was about to wake his sleeping buddy. But I had to wait until Rob got to his station and reported 'ready'. It was imperative that we all shoot together.

"Southeast ready," Rob whispered.

"On my command," I whispered.

The tango turned to face the northeast position.

I whispered, "execute!" And shot him in the nose.

The suppressed shots from our three MP-5s made just enough noise to awaken the remaining tango. When he stood looking around, I shot him just below his right ear. All four tangos were down. Barring Murphy, mission success was near.

I called *Tarawa* via satcom, "Seascape, Seascape, this is Scorpion lead, tangos down, send choppers, over."

"Roger that, Scorpion, choppers on the way, ETA 0252."

"Copy that, Scorpion lead out."

To those of you who are reading this account and wonder; "what kind of animal has this Sam McKensie become?" I would say to you; "you have not witnessed the evil that these terrorists

DAWN'S EARLY LIGHT

wield. They prey on innocent people in all walks of life, from infants to the elderly, with impunity and total disregard for life or human rights. And, they celebrate the demise of their victims. Neither I, nor my fellow special operators regret the elimination of this scum of the earth. If this operation had gone south, these fifteen hostages would have been immediately killed by the tangos. This ideology cannot be condoned. Here endeth my lesson.

Amazingly, only three or four of the hostages had been awakened. I grabbed a man who appeared to be a leader and explained the situation, asking him to keep the others calm and explain to them that we were American soldiers and they were being rescued. Their ordeal was over – almost.

The Admiral called on satcom and informed us that NSA had isolated the building on the coast housing the tango support team. They believed the building was currently occupied by four tangos and that he had dispatched the AH-6 Little Bird to eliminate the building on its way to us. I informed him that I needed the AH-6 to pick up our equipment on the way out and that we could recon the building if necessary. He affirmed, that would be nice, and reminded me that the AH-6 was flying cover for the CH-53. I assured him that we would keep the CH-53 in close proximity.

And we did just that. We loaded the CH-53 with the fifteen hostages, Rob, Gunny and Amos. I hopped over to our pile of equipment in the AH-6 Little Bird, crammed all our stuff into it, and returned while Rob and Gunny were getting the hostages loaded and comfortable in the CH-53. We hovered to one side as the huge helicopter spun up and lifted off. On the way back I asked the CH-53 pilot to follow us but maintain altitude while we took some IR pictures of the destroyed depot building. We saw no movement. Life was good today. Ours, that is. . .

Chapter Fifty Six

McKensie Condo, La Jolla, California
Saturday, December 1, 1990, 0900 hrs PST

"Look Ash, I can neither confirm nor deny that I had anything to do with that," I said, trying to stifle a smirk, responding to her query about our most recent mission..

My darlin' wife Ashleigh was holding a newspaper with a follow-up article on a pair of sailboats 'missing' in the Gulf of Aden just east of Djbouti. Seems like the charter company that owned the boats complained to the State Department, after a pair of EPIRBs (Emergency Position Indicating Radio Beacon)s were found floating in the water where the boats 'disappeared', that there might be foul play involved. Like maybe pirates or something? Anyway, since the State Department is better known for leaking secrets than keeping them, word got out about the missing boats and crews and it was reported by CNN that pirates were suspected in the disappearance shortly after we left for our latest soirée. So Ash pretty well knew where I had been and what I was doing while there. I hated lying to her. So after our little incident with the submarines I decided that I would act like a politician – which I hated even more than lying – and do the neither confirm nor deny thing.

"You guys are in the headlines now on just about every

DAWN'S EARLY LIGHT

mission. Don't you think you're getting just a little to much publicity? You're a father now, you might need to get a desk job!"

Aha, now I had her.

"Don't you ever want to fly again – you're a mother now.

Silence. . .

"Let's eat out with Rob and Sara tonight while mom's still here. We haven't gotten together with our best Navy friends in months," Ash said, changing the subject.

"Excellent idea. If they agree, you girls decide when and where." This was the first time I felt like the winner in one of our little confrontations over my job. I felt much better.

That Night

The ladies chose Harry's Steak House; one of San Diego's finest restaurants for steak and seafood. My favorite at Harry's was one of their four Surf and Turf selections; filet mignon wrapped with thick honey & pepper cured bacon, Alaskan king crab, lots of drawn butter, Italian green beans cooked with chunks of the same bacon and rosemary, mashed garlic potatoes with gravy, chives and bacon bits and perfectly seasoned asparagus roasted with olive oil and tarragon. Top that off with Harry's apple or blueberry strudel ala mode with almond butter ice cream, I would be thinking about dinner all day.

After completing my list of honey-dos and having skipped lunch in anticipation of Harry's, we finally got there and I was starved. We weren't disappointed. After dinner we decided to have a few drinks and adjourned to the bar.

Sara asked Ash if she still needed a nanny for Scotty. Her friend, Julie Morrison, told her she would like to meet us and get confirmation on the future for her as our nanny. Ash responded that she had just talked to Julie this afternoon. They agreed on salary and hours and set up a meeting for Sunday afternoon. Ash apologized for not calling Julie sooner – so busy, new mother, husband gone, yada, yada, yada.

It was great to have a chance to socialize with Rob and Sara for the first time in probably a year – maybe more. Our professional relationship was different; competitive in training and hierarchical in operations; but true friends on and off duty. SEALS and Delta Force operators are unconventional warriors. Most have long hair and beards. Rob and I keep our hair and beards close cropped – about a half to three quarters of an inch. Long hair and beards are a nuisance and not necessary when the bad guys never see our faces. We only wear BDUs (Battle Dress Uniforms) while on formal missions. Otherwise comfortable sports-ware and running shoes are generally preferred. Unlike the regular services, officers and enlisted men in special operations have an unusually high level of interaction and respect for each other. Officers tend to be younger, more educated and less experienced and knowledgeable in combat fundamentals with a propensity to lead. Enlisted special operators tend to be almost exactly complimentary; older, less educated and more experienced and knowledgeable in combat fundamentals with good following as well as leading instincts. I think these are all things that gave Rob and I the ability to exist as both complimentary warriors and best friends. This doesn't happen in regular service relationships.

We got up to date on Sara's pregnancy. Things were going well; her doctor pinned the date to the week of January 20th. They had a sonogram – it's a boy. Both said it's time to quit. "One boy one girl; that's it!"

We were all concerned about Iraq, Kuwait, and Desert Shield. Things didn't look good. Rob and I speculated on the usefulness of a system like the original ASDS, designed for standoff covert ingress across borders with a fifty five mile range, in a war like the one that was looming over there in the desert. We'd already done

DAWN'S EARLY LIGHT

all the recon we could think of that would be necessary in a situation like this one. DEVGRU and DELTA already had boots on the ground in northern IRAQ establishing a relationship with the Kurdish military leaders there - rebellious leaders at odds with the Baathists and Saddam Hussein. This was not the sort of deployment our unit was originally designed for. But now with the Nighthawk Delivery System (NDS) and our range essentially multiplied tenfold - or more - we could find ourselves delving much deeper into enemy territory. Maybe on our next mission. And, of course, I couldn't talk about any of that stuff with Ash. It was all classified Top Secret NTK (Need To Know). And Ash didn't need to know – for more reasons than just security.

Changing the subject, I mentioned the fact that Ash was starting to think about Top Gun and getting back to her previous career.

Sara remarked, "Seriously?"

Ash chimed in, "You bet seriously. Sam and I are both dedicated to our Navy jobs. I've already told my boss that I'll be returning full steam Thursday January second. Thankfully, my job is eight hours a day and Miramar is close. With Julie watching Scotty at our condo we should have no problems – even with Sam down range."

DON CANDY

Chapter Fifty Seven

Café Le Concordia
Champs Elysees, Paris France
Tuesday, December 4, 1990, 0830 hrs Local Time

A beautiful late autumn morning in gay Paree. Twenty two degrees Celsius. Unseasonably warm for this time of day and year. William Gregory Conroy, Director of the U.S. Central Intelligence Agency chose a sidewalk table from the row closest to the street and away from other patrons for his breakfast meeting. He was meeting with his Israeli counterpart, Ezekiel Sarvael. They were friends as far as friendship goes when trust is not considered a necessary ingredient. Zeke Sarvael was the embodiment of a tough and hardened Israeli ace, grown old. Not too old; he had just celebrated his sixty seventh birthday with family and friends in September. He was short but fit for his age with closely cropped salt and pepper hair that flowed neatly down to an identical beard. Intense blue eyes set in a slight perpetual frown. Zeke had become Israel's eighth ace, downing five Syrian and two Egyptian aircraft during the Yom Kippur War in 1973. He flew the McDonnell Douglas F4D armed with Sparrow and Sidewinder missiles and the pod-mounted M-61 20 mm Gatling cannon.

Conroy, on the other hand, was a sixty one year old, six foot three, two hundred pound ex Navy SEAL. He had grey-green eyes

DAWN'S EARLY LIGHT

that usually found themselves involved in some sort of smile. Bill Conroy and President Bradley Stevens, both career Navy officers, were classmates in the Navy's first Basic Underwater Demolition / SEAL (BUD/S) class at Coronado California just after President John F. Kennedy founded the SEALs in 1962. Both later retired from the Navy; Conroy joined the CIA and Stevens became the Commander of JSOC and then later was elected as a Senator from Texas. Stevens then became president in the close 1984 election. He immediately appointed Conroy as Director of the CIA.

Conroy spotted Sarvael about twenty yards away walking toward the café. As Sarvael approached he extended his hand and with a rare smile said, "I hope you had a pleasant trip William." Zeke never called Conroy by his nickname - always William.

"It was tolerable. I took a company plane, a Gulfstream Three. A little bumpy somewhere around Ireland. The pilots had to take her up to forty three thousand to find smooth air. By then I was wide awake – but I got six and a half hours of good sleep. How about your trip Zeke?"

"I took a Swissair up from Toulouse last night. I had other business there. The flight was pleasant. The Swiss know how it's done.

"So William, is this site suitable for our discussion?"

"Yes, I think so. As long as we're careful. If things here get too crowded we can take a walk along the river or head over to our embassy. Let's get some coffee, order and eat. Then perhaps we can walk or if you have no objection we have some very private and comfortable conference rooms at our embassy, just around the corner."

It was protocol courtesy to let his Israeli counterpart make the decision to meet at the U.S. embassy where both he and the Israeli knew that every syllable of their conversation would be recorded and forwarded on to Langley, probably before they were out of the building and on their way home.

The two men met in the embassy conference room for almost two hours. Most of the conversation involved recent Israeli intel on the planned sale of a MIRV nuclear warhead to Iraq by a covert Kazi (Kazakhstani) organization raising funds for the Kazi government while maintaining anonymity and creating plausible deniability for the government itself. Sarvael revealed detailed plans of the pending purchase of the weapon and its transport from Kurchatov Kazakhstan to Taji Iraq. The date of transfer was expected to be mid to late December. Sarvael and Conroy discussed and speculated on the regional and worldwide political impact of Iraq becoming a nuclear power albeit quite limited. They also discussed the known and yet to be discovered intelligence regarding the nuclear weapon development programs of Iraq, Iran and North Korea. Conroy was only mildly surprised at the detailed knowledge the Israelis had of the U.S. mission earlier this year to disable three identical MIRV warheads in the PRK.

Israel's Mossad intelligence organization was perhaps the best at what it did of all similar organizations worldwide. Mossad used technology more for communications and information storage and retrieval than for gathering intelligence. It's strength lay in it's HUMan INTellingence (HUMINT); feet on the ground gathering information everywhere. Having Mossad, a top notch intelligence organization, was imperative to Israel's survival. A small peace loving country surrounded by radical enemies couldn't last long if it wasn't much smarter than its neighbors.

After their meeting concluded and Zeke Sarvael had departed Conroy called Meg Donnelli and asked her to set up a secure conference in his situation room at Langley for 8:00 a.m. the next morning for his management team which consisted of himself, Deputy Director Frank Horsley and Assistant Deputy Director Meg

DAWN'S EARLY LIGHT

Donnelli. He also asked her to video in Admiral George Bennington, Commander JSOC and Baghdad Station Chief, Olan James via secure satellite link.

In Iraq, as in most countries in the middle east, CIA operatives were totally covert. In Baghdad Olan James was known as Abdul al-Hakim, proprietor of a small electronics shop in the northern suburbs of the city. His cell phone was physically and operationally identical to the most popular model used in city areas that had cell service. A coded keypad sequence, however, enabled a hidden mode allowing operation in the CIA satellite based communication network. This network used a highly secure spread spectrum technology where the signal itself was encoded with a 4096 state Pseudo-Random Code (PRC). The receiver had to replicate the exact code to lock onto the signal. If the particular code was not replicated the signal was of such low power it could not be detected above normal background noise. The PRC changed daily via a highly classified procedure using characters found in the King James version of the Holy Bible. James had two additional operatives in Iraq; one in Basrah, the other in Ramadi. The secure CIA comm link was used to communicate locally in Iraq or globally for meetings such as this one.

Director Conroy actually enjoyed sleeping on his GS-3. Over the years he'd grown quite used to it. Flying with the sun back to Langley, unwound some of the time lost as he flew into the future the day before. But that didn't really matter to Bill Conroy. His twenty years as a worldwide traveler had long ago inoculated him to the effects of jet lag. He slept eight of his eight and a half hour flight back to Langley.

Chapter Fifty Eight

CIA Headquarters, Situation Room
Langley, Virginia
Wednesday, December 5, 1990, 0800 hrs EST

Assistant Deputy Director Megan Donnelli got to her office a little before seven the next morning. She gave Darla, her executive assistant, instructions for the meeting setup; coffee, the Danish and croissants she should buy on the way to work and the audio and video requirements for the situation room. Then she put in a call to Olan James on the secure comm net. Sometimes it took Nolan as long as twenty minutes to respond to her call although she knew he would be more timely this morning since she had given him a quick heads-up yesterday afternoon; 11:00 p.m. his time. She called the Admiral's office to be sure everything was okay there. Shortly after she hung up from that call Olan checked in.

"Hi Meg. I talked briefly with Bill Conroy yesterday, so I'm somewhat up to speed. Do you want me to keep this call active or call back at 0800?"

"Hey Olan, keep it open and grab a drink. We'll start in twenty three minutes. Any questions?"

"Yeah, but I'll wait for the meeting."

"Hang on, we'll be back."

DAWN'S EARLY LIGHT

Meg left her office for the situation room just down the hall. The final bullet on her morning's checklist was to perform a security check on the situation room. She did this from a small equipment closet behind the restroom at the back of the meeting room. The comm panel in the closet had a master configuration switch which displayed the security status of all the electronic signals entering and leaving the situation room. In the up position a green light with the word 'SECURE' next to it would be lit when the comm systems had been electronically tested and determined to be in the secure mode. When the switch was in the down position a red light with 'NOT SECURE' next to it and below the green light would illuminate to indicate that one or more of the comm systems was in a non-secure state. Below the master switch and lights were a row of eleven buttons, each with a green light above it. These buttons confirmed that the security status system was functioning correctly. Meg pressed these buttons sequentially observing that each button she pushed caused the master status light to change to red as the button was depressed and return to green as the button was released. This human test sequence was added two years ago when a rather embarrassing electronic breach of security was caused by a defective relay in the status display system.

Director Conroy began the meeting. "Okay folks, we're all present and accounted for. We've got Frank, Meg and I here at Langley, George at Fort Bragg and Olan somewhere near Baghdad. Commander Sam McKensie will lead this mission. He's enroute to Fort Bragg on a plane with no secure comm – he'll get this briefing when he gets to Bragg. Brad (President Bradley Stevens) wanted to join us but couldn't miss his Wednesday morning Cabinet meeting without raising suspicion. So I told him we'd push the recording of this meeting to his secure ante-room so he could view it at lunch. Any objections?" Without waiting, he continued, "didn't think so.

"Meg, could you please get us up to speed on the issue before us?"

"Sure Bill."

Meg stood and continued. "As you are all aware Bill got a classified message over our private link with the Israelis yesterday and made an overnight trip to meet with Zeke Sarvael in Paris. And now, after yet another overnight flight he's back here with some pretty interesting intel.

"Seems the Kazis have decided to sell one of their two remaining MIRV warheads to Iraq. Just what we need as we get ready to dance with them over Kuwait. The warhead is one of the six that were 'lost' in the count precipitated by the resumption of the Strategic Arms Reduction Treaty negotiations between the U.S. and the U.S.S.R. in 1987. As you might recall the PRK bought three of the warheads and we bought one, leaving two remaining with the Kazis. Israeli intel shows a firm agreement between the Kazis and the Iraqis for one unit with only the logistics issues remaining. One of the issues being the fact that Iraq is having a hard time deciding where they want it shipped, citing security issues. As an option to the agreement the Kazis agreed to hold the second unit for 100 days at the same price. Also, as I'm sure you will recall, a team of special operators dropped out of a CAPV-727 onto the roof of the PRK's Ministry of Defense building in Pyongsong North Korea and proceeded to neutralize the three PRK nukes being held in the basement of that building by swapping the nuclear cores with fake ones.

"While that was a mission Ian Fleming would be envious of, we might be looking at act two in Iraq, and very soon. First order of business; Admiral, I believe Tariq Sa'id is at Miramar finishing his ASDS training. We need him at Bragg tonight and on the ground in Baghdad by Saturday noon. We have completed his extensive identity change and he will be our advanced party on this next mission. Olan, Tariq will arrive Saturday on Iraqi Air flight

DAWN'S EARLY LIGHT

194 from Amman Jordan arriving at about 1845hrs. You will receive a highly sensitive dossier on him this evening at your regular comm session. Sa'id has specific knowledge of the Iraqi missile capability including facilities, inventory and deployment. We will use his knowledge to plan and execute this mission. You will need his assistance in acquiring intel during the planning phase of this mission. He will be the in-country member of the mission team reporting to you. "We will need the new NDS, George. Any problems with that?"

"No Meg. Based on the successful operational test program and in anticipation of need in the near future I have requested an additional Nighthawk (F-117 Stealth Bomber) conversion to have a backup capability for this mission profile. We got the approval through the Joint Chiefs and took delivery at Groom Lake last week. The conversion and test will take an additional week. In the process of executing this new conversion the engineers at Groom Lake have developed a conversion kit. We now have the ability to convert a standard Nighthawk to an NDS and vice-versa in two days. So, with an operational backup NDS, the team is ready for a deep penetration covert infil anywhere the CAPV-727 option won't work."

"Thanks George. I had heard this already. Just wanted to be sure I had heard the correct info and for everyone here to hear it from you. It's looking like NDS will be a necessity for our mission requirements. Our CAPV-727 would be hard to sell there in the middle east with the tense political situation such as it is. I guess we'll find out how stealthy the F-117 really is, huh?"

"Yeah Meg, no worries. I've seen it work. If it can fool our best radars, the Iraqui's soviet made radars won't have a chance. This is going to be a totally new type of operation for us. We'll need very careful planning, top notch intel and careful contingency analysis. We'll need Sa'ids full attention at Bragg until at least Friday night. He's our best source of current local knowledge and we need to mine that knowledge before he goes over to gather fresh intel."

Meg continued, "Thanks George. Our guys here at Langley have put some brackets around some of the critical parameters:

"First, the infil; NDS at twenty thousand feet seems appropriate. For sure between eighteen thousand and twenty three thousand, depending on weather conditions. Eleven operators, one dog, drop bags, no cargo. For exfil we're thinking an HH-60 Pave Hawk with an AH-6 Little Bird escort, but we're second guessing Commander McKensie here so I'll move on.

"Second, Ground support; we'll need some sort of vehicle or group of vehicles to get ten operators, a dog and the warhead out of the populated area we expect it to be in. If they decide to ship it to a site like the main H-3 airstrip we can just jump over the Jordanian border and exfil with a Pave Hawk or Chinook. If on the other hand they decide to move it to Taji where they are known to have the tools and personnel plus a variety of available medium-range rockets then the egress/exfil is going to be more difficult. Tariq is 90% sure they will stage the marriage at Taji and then truck the complete missile to a site like K-3 or possibly Ruwayshid. We've observed them completing what appears to be a silo about eight klicks south of the H-3 Highway Strip Air Base. The base appears to be sparsely occupied and there is no visible road structure between the silo and the base or the highway . The Iraqis could have - probably have - tunneled from the highway to the silo. We're using NSA's new Ground Penetrating Radar (GPR) satellite to locate several underground missile storage bunkers like the ones your guys reconned last June near strategic border areas. There are eighteen such sites in close proximity to the Jordanian border, twelve of them near Ruwayshid. As we speak, Adam Kivel is re-tasking one of our two GPR assets to explore the silo area and map the tunnel we all believe is there. The optimal snatch might be to grab it on its way from Taji to the silo after it has passed through Ramadi. The problem with doing that is that the warhead will

DAWN'S EARLY LIGHT

already be attached to the rocket, which would require detaching it on the road to the silo. Even though it will be significantly more difficult to grab the warhead at Taji, the general feeling is that we don't want to chance them getting that missile into the silo before we can nab it; and the expected level of security along Highway 10 near the H-3 complex and the silo will be higher than that in the missile factory in Taji. We're relying on the false security of having the warhead in a populated area – like the situation last May in Pyongsong, PRK

"The destination depends completely on the Iraqis and Kazis and their logistics and security problems. This is one reason we needed to get Sa'id over there asap to help Olan's team develop the intel.

"An early decision will have to be made on whether to do a core swap or a warhead swap. This decision will have significant impact on logistics. The special equipment needed to do the core swap in the field versus the special container and transport equipment to manhandle the warhead on both infil and exfil. Master Chief Curtis and Commander McKensie are in the air as we speak headed for JSOC at Fort Bragg. They, along with Captain Bo Jameson are the experts on swapping cores and transporting two hundred and eighty eight pound warheads. Sam and Rob will make the decision and then run it by Bo.

"Third, exfil; as I indicated before, the closer to the border we can acquire the warhead the less complex the exfil but the more complex the warhead acquisition. So our key to exfil planning is location, location, location. At this point we are planning for Taji, easier warhead acquisition and more difficult exfil, but the exfil would not be as bad as it could be. There are several other possible, but much less likely and more difficult locations.

"Exfil from Taji will be a multi stage operation and it might require more boots on the ground. George, you've taken delivery on the second NDS. The mission is likely to be at least ten days out. Can it be ready for this mission?"

"I don't have a firm answer on the ten days", replied the Admiral, "but I'll say very likely and get back to you by the end of the day. Also Meg, I'd like to get Commander McKensie and a couple of his operators up here to do the detailed planning – is that what you guys had in mind?"

"That is going to be Director Conroy's request at the close of this meeting."

"Okay, they'll be there tomorrow."

Meg continued; "And last, for today, political implications. Do we execute a super-secret mission. In and out with no clue as to who-dunnit? Or, grab the nuke and announce the mission, sans NDS, to the world with a plea to the UN for enhanced sanctions on the Iraqis and strong cautions to our Arab allies and enemies. This, if handled properly could totally nix Saddam's desire to gain Arab Support by bringing Israel into the fray.

"This is, of course, a POTUS call. I brought it up just to give everyone something to ponder. I predict we'll have an answer to that pretty quick. But we need that answer before we do any detailed planning.

"Any questions?"

"Olan was first. "Meg, could you make sure everyone on the team has my secure link and ask Commander McKensie to please keep me in the loop and don't hesitate to give us intel go-dos?"

"Roger that Olan. We'd rather increase your daily comm times to two a day and limit off-comm-time access to George, Commander McKensie and myself. That okay with you?"

"Yeah, I'm good with that. Tell Sam to contact me right away. I have some info that will be important for mission planning."

"Will do Olan. I'm sure he'll be relying heavily on your guys, including Tariq, for ground support when mission night rolls

DAWN'S EARLY LIGHT

around. The net will remain at security level five. George and Sam both have comm gear to handle that.

"Anyone else?"

Admiral Bennington jumped in: "Uh Meg, I assume your guys will drive the NSA requirements. I'll need a direct command link to Adam Kivel. Can you take care of that?"

"Of course Admiral. As usual, Sam will have full access to the NSA Satellite Resource Group. Adam has already been briefed. Also, please ask Sam to provide twice daily summary reports on the net.

"Real quick everyone; we've got a short fuse on this mission so it's doubtful that we could increase any lower level comm sites to level five in time to do any good. Right now sites that are owned by level five operators associated with this need include Station Chief Olan James, Admiral George Bennington, Commander Sam McKensie, Director Bill Conroy, Deputy Director Frank Horsley, CJCS Admiral Jerry Sterett, POTUS Brad Stevens and myself. Jerry and Brad will be monitoring only. Any mission comm necessary outside that subnet will necessarily have to go through me. Everybody clear on that?"

Everyone was.

"We good here, for now? Any more discussion?"

No response.

"Okay folks, let's get with it!"

Chapter Fifty Nine

Aboard a CIA G - III Enroute to Fort Bragg, NC
Slightly West of the Mississippi River
Wednesday, December 5, 1990, 0830 hrs CST

Well, this is surely not what I was hoping for. I knew this Iraq – Kuwait mess was going to mean trouble for us but the latest UN deadline of January 16th gave me hope that we'd make it through Christmas without a major snafu requiring our deployment. Not to be. Murphy rides again!

Rob and Gunny are with me. Vince's home is actually Fort Bragg, he being a Delta guy. He hangs out on the west coast a lot because when we're not down range we each rotate through the instructor role at the Miramar ASDS school and we train with ST3 down at Coronado Island. The Admiral said to leave Amos at home which is a good thing. It might mean that we get to go home before leaving for Iraq.

It never ceases to amaze me how the CIA wants us to plan every mission before we even know half of the requirements We're operating on about ten percent intel right now. All we currently know is what and maybe why. We don't know how, when or where. And we're not going to find out how, when or where in a damned conference room at Fort Bragg.

DAWN'S EARLY LIGHT

I guess the good news is Tariq's at Bragg right now and we're going to need all the local knowledge he's got before we start planning this mission. He was an officer in Saddam's Republican Guard Missile Regiment for three years. He actually worked in the Al-Hussein missile factory at Taji for two years prior to last June. He has made regular visits to all Iraqi mobile missile bunkers. There's over forty of them.

Gunny Tanner looked up from a folder he was reading, "Hey Skipper, I thought Saddam used Soviet made Scud missiles. It says in this here overview paper that he's manufacturing his own missiles. Calls 'em the Al-Hussein. What's with that?"

"He *is* building his own – from Scud parts. It takes three Scuds to make two Al-Husseins. In his war with his neighbor Iran, which started in 1981 and only ended a couple of years ago, he found he was at a disadvantage. The Iranians and the Iraqis were both using Soviet Scuds. Iran could reach Baghdad with their 300 mile Scuds but Iraq needed 500 plus to get to Tehran. So Saddam's missile men re-engineered the Scud to fly almost 600 miles with a smaller warhead, more fuel and a better guidance system and called it, of course, the Al-Hussein. So the missiles we blew up last June were Al-Husseins. I wondered then why they were white. Scuds are olive drab, like most military equipment."

"Rob chimed in, "Do you think he's found out that the Scud he bought from the PRK has a fake core?"

"No Rob, I don't know. Wish I did. There's a lot of things we don't know that we should. Could be we *do* know, it's just that I don't. There's too many pieces to this puzzle. Remember that core info is NTK (Need To Know) – and Gunny doesn't, yet. Just you me, Bo and some highers. Don't forget that in the meetings coming up at Bragg. That's something we'll have to ping the Admiral on right away. Gunny, Vince and whoever else we bring onto this mission are going to have to get read in on the PRK Nuclear Exchange mission."

We had brunch on the plane, landed and headed straight for JSOC Headquarters. The Admiral had his secure conference room all set up for us. He and Tariq were sipping coffee when we arrived a little after noon. We would spend the next few days requesting, receiving and analyzing intelligence from the CIA, NSA, in-country agents and Special Forces operations. When I heard that Tariq would be headed to Iraq on Saturday I asked the Admiral to get that delayed until mid week. We needed his local knowledge right now more than any new intel he could possibly generate over the next few days in Iraq. One of our first requests was going to be to Adam Kivel, the NSA Director of Satellite Resources. We'd be stretching their capabilities on this one.

By Saturday evening we had a pretty good lay of the land. Tariq had been an invaluable source of operational knowledge on the Republican Guard led Scud missile enhancement effort during the Iraq/Iran war. He knew the site at Taji very well. Of course we didn't know for sure if Taji would even be a part of our plan – yet.

Also, our old friend Young-Ku had joined our team Thursday morning. His family had been successfully relocated from Pyongsong North Korea to a small farm near Rosewell Maryland on the north side of the York River, between Williamsburg and Gloucester Maryland. His Uncle Jin-sung bought a fishing boat that he keeps at a marina on the river which affords easy access to Chesapeake Bay and the Atlantic. His parents bought a restaurant in a small village close to the farm. Young-ku's smile was bigger than ever. He was a friend of our CIA agent in Kazakhstan who actually delivered the intel on the three MIRV warheads purchased by the PRK. So those connections were going to be extremely valuable in gathering intel on the Kazi end of this operation. We've got to get Young-Ku all trained up for the CIA so he can support us down range if Tariq ever manages to get into the Navy and become a SEAL. Not holding my breath on that one.

Chapter Sixty

JSOC Headquarters, Fort Bragg, NC
Tuesday, December 11, 1990, 1130 hrs EST

I asked Admiral Bennington to invite Captain Bo Jameson, Commander, DEVGRU (My mother's brother – uncle Bo) to come down to Fort Bragg and look over our progress to date. We were in the midst of the afternoon's interchange with Bo when he asked, "What do we know about the serial number of this warhead we're expecting from the Kazis?"

I reminded him that we knew the serial numbers of the four warheads we had touched and then referred the intel issue presented by the uncertainty of the serial number of the warhead of current concern to Young-Ku.

Young-Ku's smile seemed to increase as he began to speak, "After the PRK Ambassador to Kazakhstan made arrangements to purchase the original three warheads I became involved with the purchase process during two successive wrestling events in the dissolving Soviet Bloc; one in Kazakhstan and the other in Ukraine. Both meetings were with a 'government materials' merchant by the name of Vladimir Zholik. He was not an employee of any government, but a dealer in unclaimed and or undocumented Soviet Bloc equipment and supplies. The funds he acquired for 'surplus or unneeded' material minus his fee actually did go to whichever government he was representing.

"We dined and drank together after our meetings on several occasions and we developed a business level of trust. Provided he has not become aware of my parting with the PRK, which I believe is extremely unlikely, I should have no problem getting the serial numbers of the other two warheads and information on which one he still has for sale. It will be necessary for me to travel to Astana to achieve this. Traveling on a U.S. Passport should not be a problem if I am careful. But I will leave that up to my new employer. We have a covert CIA agent in Kazakhstan who might also be able to acquire the serial number information. But I don't believe he actually knows the merchant. That's the first stone we need to look under. But do not worry. We shall get the number."

Gunny butted in, "whoa, whoa, what the hell are you guys talking about?"

I filled him in; "Remember the other day when we read you in on the PRK mission. We mentioned that the CIA had obtained a fourth warhead which they used to fashion four fake cores that are identical in appearance and residual radiation characteristics. We still have the fourth warhead, fake core and all. The four real cores are locked in a lead lined vault somewhere in Hanford Washington. Our warhead with a fake core is locked in a secure vault at Langley. If we could be sure of the serial number on the warhead the Kazis are sending to Iraq we could simply match it on our warhead and make a covert swap of the warheads. That might or might not make the mission simpler or easier; but we sure need to look at the possibility. I checked with our CIA nuclear expert, Wayne Hawkins, and he says his guys will have no problem altering the serial number on our neutered warhead "

As if Admiral Bennington knew he was needed, he stuck his head in the room to let us know lunch had arrived and he wished to join us.

DAWN'S EARLY LIGHT

I responded privately, "Before we eat, Admiral, I would like to give you a request and a recommendation. The request is to ask Bill to check with his agent in Kazakhstan on how we might go about acquiring the serial numbers on the remaining two MIRV warheads and flag the number going to Iraq. Remind him that Young-Ku is trusted by the merchant involved in the PRK transaction. The recommendation is to suggest to Bill that he might want Wayne Hawkins to fabricate two more fake cores as a hedge on possible future missions. What's for lunch?"

"Hot sandwiches across the hall. She's got pastrami, Virginia ham, turkey and roast beef. Swiss, cheddar, provolone, and Asiago cheese. Rye, wheat and white bread. Mayo, brown or yellow, mustard, sauerkraut, thousand island and ketchup. Potato salad and cole slaw." He was reading from a menu.

"We'll get right on the serial number thing and I'll ask Hawkins to look at building the new cores – good idea. I'm gonna have a pastrami Rueben on rye."

We finished the day working on two viable scenarios for swapping warheads. Gunny's idea actually sounded best to me; pack the warhead in a specially built 55 gallon drum engineered to fully protect it with a lid secured by an electronically controlled internal release. Surround it with a mixture of some yet to be defined substance such that the weights of the warhead (288 pounds) and the other filler add up to the gross weight expected. Label it with something the Iraqis use and then deliver it to the building where the missile and warhead are to be married. It sounded kind of hokey to me until Tariq said he might know just the person to make the delivery. But then Rob mentioned that the bomb-bay of the nighthawk could surely be quickly adapted to drop a six hundred pound drum with a dolly strapped to it – after all it easily handled two thousand pound bombs. And then it occurred to me that we could drop the drum, retract the static line and then jump right behind it. So we could infil all together, make the swap and then exfil together. No need to depend on ground support. Also, we weren't going to need eleven men and a dog. We did the PRK with three operators. I figured we could do this with five. The static line issue was important. When using the NDS for infil the F-117 loses a significant part of its stealth when the bomb bay doors are opened. So egress is necessarily done as quickly as possible. In training at Groom Lake we got the time down to eight seconds. That would be impossible using static lines since there would be no way to gracefully retrieve the lines once the operators had jumped other than designating one poor soul to make the round trip in the unpressurized bomb bay so he could retrieve the static lines after the others had left. But with only five operators we could dump the warhead on a static line that could be retracted by the last man out while the others were jumping. I figured we could do this in under eleven seconds. Still a reasonable time to be unstealthy since the Soviet radars Saddam was using had a scan rate of fifteen seconds. A radar operator would observe a faint single blip on his radar screen if he happened to be looking at it. Not enough to be concerned about.

There were still plenty of concerns. Decisions on ROE (Rules Of Engagement) are usually political and on a mission like this would likely be a POTUS call and could range from shoot to kill on sight to using the CIA's narc darts. We'd used these darts before on a few missions. The 'sleeping darts' are dimensionally identical to the 9X19 mm parabellum rounds used by regular and special forces and police forces around the world. That's where the similarity ends. The cartridge holds a smaller and slower burning charge than a normal round and the projectile extends three millimeters further into the casing. The projectile is made of a special plastic alloy that changes from rigid to flexible shortly after being fired. Upon impact a titanium alloy needle attached to an eight millimeter disk encased in the plastic projectile is thrust

DAWN'S EARLY LIGHT

forward penetrating the nose of the projectile and injecting the target as the projectile flattens with 0.43 milliliters of a high power narcotic that disables a 200 pound victim in three to five seconds for a period of at least four hours. The dart has a small set of barbs at the tip allowing the shooter to remove the flat and deflated projectile without leaving more damage than an aggressive mosquito. In fact, the narcotic in the projectile contains an irritant that produces an itching effect very similar to that of a mosquito bite. Effective range is two hundred feet; we try to get within one hundred feet because we don't want to miss the target. The primary problem with using the narc darts is that the top secret status of both the round and the narcotic requires that we retrieve each dart used on every mission. Failure to do so is considered a security breech and the affected operator is then blessed with all the resulting paperwork and then his or her possible court marshal proceedings for negligence. This is not a problem unless you miss your target and can't find the dart. So far we haven't lost anyone to Fort Leavenworth. To the person every operator I know would rather shoot to kill than use the narc dart – unless they're using them on friendlies – and you can forget that I said that. Our DEVGRU advanced weapons development group at El Centro NAF perfected the narc round after the CIA fiddled with them for two years without success.

So we were off to a good start. Not nearly ready to go yet. But al least we had identified the critical intel requirements, basic infil and exfil strategy and tactics and personnel and most equipment requirements.

Chapter Sixty One

President's Secure Briefing Room
Whitehouse, Washington D.C.
Sunday, December 16, 1990, 1845 hrs EST

Admiral George Bennington, Commander of JSOC (my boss), Admiral Gerald Sterett, CJCS (his Boss) and President Bradley Stevens (his boss) and I met to review progress and set the ROE for the upcoming mission. I was definitely more than a little out ranked in this meeting and George had asked me to provide an overview of our progress based on current intel and to recommend infil, execution and exfil profiles for the mission.

I was actually fairly nervous until I got the middle east map projected on the large screen at the end of the room and started to speak and field some questions. "The Soviet MIRV (Multiple Independently-targetable Re-entry Vehicle) we're dealing with here is part of the group of six identical undocumented warheads the Kazis put on the black market a little over a year ago. Of the six three were picked up by the PRK and one by our CIA through one of our double agents. The remaining two are currently available from the Kazis to the highest bidder. The PRK sold one of theirs to Iraq mounted on a Scud-B missile with mobile launcher included. These MIRV warheads came without the independent targeting guidance system making them easily adaptable to the

DAWN'S EARLY LIGHT

Scud variety of short and medium range Soviet missiles, which just about all our evil friends have in their inventory. We executed a successful mission last June to neuter the three warheads at the PRK MOD in Pyongsong. Recall that our CIA and DOE nuclear experts fashioned the dummy cores that allowed us to swap them for the real ones. They fabricated four fake cores in all; three for the PRK nukes and one for ours. Now it appears that Saddam wants another warhead and a deal has been brokered with the Kazis to procure one of the remaining two. We propose swapping our complete neutered warhead for Saddam's real one."

The president waved his hand and asked a question, "Sam, remind me please, how much do these warheads weigh?"

"Two hundred and eighty eight pounds."

"Won't that be a problem?"

"Yes sir, it will. But not nearly as big a problem as swapping cores in the environment in which we expect to find ourselves on this mission. Swapping whole warheads will be much easier "

"Hmmm... Continue."

"We don't yet know exactly where the intercept will take place so we're preparing plans for three possibilities. We are reasonably certain, more than 80% plus, that the warhead will pass through the Taji Republican Guard Missile Repair Facility, their only facility with the personnel, tools and equipment to match the warhead to a missile. The Taji airport is less than a half mile from the facility. They will likely use their latest Al-Hussein missile which is built from Scud parts. It has a greater range, better accuracy, a little more payload and it's assembled and ground tested at that facility.

"The final destination is probably the H-3 area in far west Iraq near the Jordanian border. This area has four air strips, many missile bunkers and one new silo. Everything there is aimed at some point in Israel. We believe the nuclear warhead Saddam bought from the PRK is aimed at Haifa. Haifa is less than five percent Muslim and far enough away from Jerusalem to make contamination of the Al-Aqsa Mosque unlikely. A second possible destination is one of the two remaining Kuwait/Iraq border bunkers with Bahrain or Qatar as the target. Recall that we destroyed the third bunker last June. We believe this borders on insanity for Saddam. Instead of gaining support from Arab countries in the region, other than Iran, our experts believe he would lose it. Based on our current knowledge of Iraqi operations inside Kuwait we don't believe he will launch on Kuwait al all, but he could strike at something stupid like Riyadh, Manama, Dubai, Abu Dhabi or Doha.

"So, at this point in time it looks like the likely play is this; the Kazis will ship the warhead to Iraq, most likely by air to the Al-Taji Airport where it will be taken by some motor vehicle to the Republican Guard Missile Repair Facility less than a half mile northwest of the airport. At the facility the warhead will be attached to an Al-Hussein missile by designing and fabricating an adapter. The Iraqi's already have an identical warhead – one of the three we neutered in Pyongsong which was mated to a Scud B by the North Koreans. To mate this new warhead to an Al-Hussein missile they will have to design and fabricate a new adapter. This will give us a window of two days or maybe three or more to make the swap. The swap will necessarily occur during the night. The PRK technicians took a week to fabricate the Scud B adapter to their warheads. But that warhead was over two hundred kilometers from their missile so they had to be extra careful during the design phase. They had three warheads and we assume they built only three adapters.

"The other two possibilities are one; to swap the warheads at the airport prior to their moving it to the repair facility, two; take it out of the repair facility while they are mating it to the missile or three; waiting until the attachment is complete and the missile is enroute to its destination. After careful study based on current intel

DAWN'S EARLY LIGHT

we have determined that the first and third of these scenarios are fraught with problems that make them significantly more difficult and therefore less likely to succeed. So, barring additional intel that might change our situational awareness we are concentrating on the repair facility at Taji while continuing to request and review intel on the other two possibilities.

Changing slides, I continued, "On the northwest side of the long facility building there is a small parking lot next to the shipping docks and well away from the personnel entrance on the opposite side and end of the building. This lot affords an excellent landing area for three to five Black Angels and a nuclear weapon. We're getting new and better intel every day. NSA has already picked up chatter discussing plans for the move but the Iraqis must liquefy their gold discretely on foreign markets to avoid alerting us, Mossad or MI6 that they're up to something – that will take a couple of weeks at least and we know from the PRK deal that the Kazis will not ship until they have cash in their bank. We might be looking at early next year, Christmas at the earliest and maybe February at the latest; depending on world affairs.

"Infil is reasonably straight forward. Although Amman Jordan would be the closest base from which to launch and retrieve our assets, Ramat David Airbase, Israel is our choice due to security issues with the F-117 Nighthawk. These aircraft haven't been seen by most of the world and will draw attention wherever we send them. Our best chance of retaining secrecy is with the Israelis. We still need to fly over Jordan but nobody needs to know about that. Exfil will be, as always, the challenge. Our Quiet Knight Little Bird flight tests completed three weeks ago. The noise levels were suppressed twelve percent better than specification. We've run the QNLBs on mock low altitude missions in the Mohave desert at night. The results are impressive. They can be heard, but not from very far away and they don't sound like helicopters any more. They sound more like cooling tower fans. We've got two QNLBs;

one in attack configuration, the QNAH-6G, and the other in multi-use configuration, the QNMH-6H. We'll have to refuel at Jordan's H4 Airbase and stage a refueling station somewhere in northwestern Iraq for refueling in both directions. A CH-53 with fuel bladders will work nicely in the desert..

"Please don't compare this to Operation Eagle Claw. We're taking in two helicopters and less than a dozen men. And we're rescuing a 288 pound bomb, not 53 hostages. Our weather forecasting in the area is far superior to that in the 80's, and we now rule the night – both QN configurations have our latest omni-directional high resolution night vision systems integrated into the pilot flight control system. Kudos to TI for the night vision and McDonnell Douglas and our DEVGRU advanced design group at El Centro; together they've pretty much silenced our Little Birds.

"NSA and CIA are now working to get intel on all forms of transportation originating in Kurchatov and/or Semipalatinsk Kazakhstan and terminating in Taji Iraq, just so we'll know every possible mode of transport they could use to move the warhead. We're pretty sure it will ship by air. Probably a private shipping company since this shipment needs to be plausibly deniable by both governments if something goes south. We have agents in Kazakhstan working hard to get weapon serial numbers and shipping information. We're starting to get detailed intel on the Taji target. There are now three satellites giving us a zero, forty five and seventy five degree angular perspective from the north and south on the repair facility. Using our best infrared and Ground Penetrating Radar (GPR) data we're getting a very good understanding of the interior of the building. We're also getting a good understanding of their security protocol, although we expect this to change somewhat after the warhead arrives.

"I know part of the purpose for this meeting is to set the mission ROE. Our recommendation, as much as we hate to make it, is to use narc darts with extreme care to disable as few as

DAWN'S EARLY LIGHT

necessary and shoot to kill only if mission failure is at stake. If a kill is necessary the body will disappear, unless, God forbid, it's ours.

"Things are coming together nicely but there's still significant additional intel and some commitments that we'll need in order to pull this mission off," I commented as I fumbled with the AV remote to advance the frame,

" Here are the big pieces:"

- Confirmation on Taji and swap window
- Help from Israel and Jordan
- Warhead serial number & shipping information
- Any contrary intel

"Most important is absolute confirmation on the Taji repair facility site and at least a 48 hour window for the swap. This will require corroborating intel from our guys in Kazakhstan and Olan and his guys in Iraq.

"Israeli and Jordanian support on the mission. There are political implications here that extend beyond military logistics.

"The CIA needs the correct serial number on the warhead being shipped. Our double agent in Kazakhstan with Young-Ku's help should have no problem with this. But it *is* critical.

"Also very important: Immediate disclosure of any intel that indicates a necessary change to our current thinking – even the smallest detail.

"We'll keep looking at the other less likely scenarios while gathering intel and refining our plans for the mission I've outlined here. Are there any questions?

Admiral Sterett replied, "Sam it looks to me that you might be a little under-manned. Care to comment?"

"Yes sir. If you look at what we've been able to do on our nineteen ASDS missions to date, we have had excellent success with no more than six men and a dog when necessary – on this mission we'll leave our dog Amos at home. Actually the number of operators on this mission will be dictated by the number of handles on the warhead container being designed by our guys at Miramar and the CIA guys at Langley. We think four is the correct number of handles. So five would be the number of operators we're working with if requirements don't change. This is the maximum number for a single MH-6 extraction with a 350 pound warhead and container. When we exfil with a single Little Bird we always position a back up AH-6 (the attack version of the Little Bird) as close to the site as possible. Usually we are able to exfil with more than a combat useful load since the Little Bird gas tank is only half full at the beginning of the return flight."

Admiral Sterett continued: "Your stellar record over the past four years speaks for itself Sam. Stealth is your friend. You own the night. The addition of the Nighthawks to your infil capabilities allows you to penetrate much deeper into enemy territory. The deeper you go the more difficult your exfil will be and the more you depend on technology to get you out. We must be sure you can get your team out unscathed, every time. I worry about your lean footprint. God forbid, what happens if you lose a man. Now you're down to four. Can four men carry the weapon and the body?"

"Sir, believe me I share your concern for manpower. During exfil we always have an MH-6 pilot to help us and an AH-6 pilot close by. These pilots are SOAR combat trained – the best of the best. They've had to pitch in on several missions where things didn't go as planned and we've certainly had our share of problems. But we always consider every contingency we feel is real and modify the mission plan accordingly. We use Admiral McRaven's mission analysis tools to check our planning at every stage. We feel that we are at about the 25% stage of planning given

DAWN'S EARLY LIGHT

that we are planning this mission based on current intel and that the intel is correct. As the intel hardens we could be facing significant changes in the plan and the necessary resources. I'll keep the entire team posted on our planning progress over the complete cycle. We welcome advice and suggestions. And, sir, your comment is noted."

Admiral Sterett continued, "Thank you Sam. It's good to hear that the Little Birds have been adequately silenced. I assume there will be an upgrade kit available for other spec ops units needing stealth."

"Yes sir. Our charter is to make whatever we develop available to all Spec-Op organizations. My guys are working on it as we speak.. I'll be sure it happens."

Smiling, President Stevens said, "The ROE will be as you recommended Sam. In this business we've got to do whatever it takes to preserve mission profile integrity. I like what I see here. Keep me posted and tell your guys to keep up the good work."

Chapter Sixty Two

Harry's Steak House
San Diego, California
Tuesday, December 18, 1990, 1805 hrs PST

We spent Monday at CIA Langley refining and adding to what we knew about the Iraqi nuclear warhead situation. We received intel from Olan James in Baghdad that raised our probability that the warhead would pass through Taji to be fitted to an Al-Hussein missile to 95%. So I secured seats for Rob and I on an American Airlines non-stop flight from Dulles to San Diego International that left at 1205 hrs this morning and had us home in Miramar by 1600 hrs. We had to break the news to Ashleigh and Sara that there was a very real probably that we would be down range this Christmas. And Sara was due to deliver Judy's baby brother on January twelfth. Not a discussion we were anxious to have. I had called Harry's from Langley last night and reserved Admiral Bennington's favorite table: the one with a spectacular view of San Diego Bay and Coronado Island. I would just tell them the Admiral got called away at the last minute. I don't think they save tables for commanders.

I dropped Rob off at his house and headed for home to play with my new month old baby boy. I'd been gone two weeks and he had visibly grown. Ash said he'd gained two and a half pounds

DAWN'S EARLY LIGHT

already.

We got there about fifteen minutes early and paused by the bar to decide if we should order a drink and take it to the table when it was ready or just wait. No sooner had we pondered this, Alice, the Maître D approached and asked if we would like to go ahead and be seated or wait for George. Sheepishly I said, "We really thought George could make it, Alice, but he got tied up - again."

"Commander McKensie, you know you can reserve his table any time you want to. He asked me to do that for you."

"Yeah, but the lady who answers the phone and takes reservations doesn't know that – does she?"

" Of course she does. What ever the Admiral wants, he gets."

"So if I give her my name she'll treat me like an Admiral?"

"We've been treating you and Ashleigh like Admirals for years. Why would we stop now?"

That's what I liked about this place, other than the outstanding food and libations, they really did treat you well."

Alice took us to our table and Lisa, our favorite waitress, came right behind her. We ordered drinks and talked about babies. The new Curtis boy would be Rob and Sara's second. That gave them bragging rights on parental knowledge and experience, so Ash and I played the less informed student role. We learned a lot. Ash was particularly interested in how to survive as a career mom while married to a Navy SEAL. Sara was a Senior Trauma Nurse at the Navy Medical Center, San Diego. Unlike Ash, she wasn't actually in the Navy. But that didn't change the challenges facing career mothers with SEAL husbands.

"It's not really as bad as I sometimes make it sound," Sara smiled. "I can't let Superman here think he's got all the tough jobs in this journey. Got to keep him on his toes."

Ash shot back, "Yeah Sara, I can sympathize with you. Sam

gives me the same rub; 'waah,, waah, waah, I work my butt off while you get all the perks and that cushy training job.'"

I laughed and popped Rob on the shoulder. "It's true! I *do* do all the work – but I *never* complain.

"Ash, you're such a damned prima donna. You pull rank on me every day – and all you've got is three months time in grade. That's why I do all the dishes and most of the other housework when I'm home. And you *do* have a cushy job – compared to mine."

Silence. . .

Rob and I had known each other for going on five years now. We met during a campaign that took down some of the Central and South American kingpins of the cocaine industry. He was second in command of SEAL Team Four when its commander was killed by the cartels. He took command of the team for about a year and then decided to come over to DEVGRU as second in command of our advanced system development Black Angel group. Rob was a natural leader. Had all the necessary tools. Very intelligent. Respected from above and below. There wasn't a better Master Chief Petty Officer in the Navy. He just didn't like the command position; being responsible for the lives and possible deaths of operators in his command. I respected this. I didn't much care for it either, but, you know – somebody had to do it.

Chapter Sixty Three
CHRISTMAS DAY

McKensie Condo, La Jolla, California
Tuesday, December 25, 1990, 1230 hrs PST

I'm blessed! Not only with a wonderful, beautiful wife and baby boy but also with a mother, uncle and extended family on Ashleigh's side. And, going on seven years in the Navy and I've been home every single Christmas, except of course, 1985 when Ash and I got married on White Bay Beach, Jost Van Dyke, BVI. On that day, that beach was our home because our combined family members were all there.

We decided to ask Stephen and Helen, Ash's parents, and her brother Mark to celebrate Christmas with us. Stephen and Helen drove down from Pasadena yesterday and we had dinner with them at Harry's. Afterward we attended the 8:00 Christmas Service at Saint Matthew's Episcopal Church in La Jolla – the church Ash and I had been attending for the last three years. Bo arrived and was waiting at our condo when we got home from church. Mark drove over this morning from his new home in El Cajon. Bo and I discussed asking Mom, Jim and Janie down from Kansas to celebrate with us but our schedules got in the way. Maybe next year.

DON CANDY

Mark Garrison is the Director of DEA, Southwest. Even though of all our relatives Mark lives closest, we seldom see him. Matching up DEA and Navy schedules is harder than you might think. So when we gathered at our place Bo and I took a few minutes to catch up with Mark's perspective on the drug issues facing the United States. In the mid 1980's Bo and I worked with Mark to eliminate a large cooperative group of cocaine oriented drug cartels operating out of Columbia, Nicaragua and Mexico. This group had smuggled thousands of tons of cocaine into the U.S. using chemical hosts like naphthalene and later sophisticated submarines. They had amassed a twenty plus year supply of cocaine stored in public warehouses throughout the continental U.S., Hawaii, Alaska and Puerto Rico. In a single twenty four hour operation the FBI, DEA, CIA and our Black Angel SEALS took down the entire group of organizations. We lost one SEAL. The cartels lost hundreds.

During the latter half of the 80's significant progress was made in the push to completely eliminate illicit drugs in the U.S. But as the new decade rolled around we began to hear about new problems and the possibility of using a SEAL Team IV ASDS squad in another raid on a growing drug threat in Central America.

Bo pinged Mark as the three of us retired to our lanai with beers, "So Mark, please get us current on the status of the U.S. drug thing."

"Well we had a good run at becoming 'drug free'. But the reality is, that's never going to happen – and we weren't kidding ourselves, we never believed it would. But it was important to create a country-wide drug free goal both from a public perspective and from a funding perspective. We made positive progress for about three and a half years but the combination of money hungry thugs outside the U.S., too much money inside and a government

DAWN'S EARLY LIGHT

not willing to stay the course leaves us – the DEA – unable to hold our gains. Yes, we're slipping. It takes continuous effort to accomplish our ultimate goal and our government just isn't willing to fund the level of effort necessary. That being said, we *are* still in the best shape we've been in since the early sixties. Our combined team made a big and lasting dent in the country's drug problem. It'll be years before we slide back to where we were – if we ever do."

We talked over several beers in the cool evening out on the lanai about drugs, the looming war with Iraq, new technology that might help the DEA, and myriad other guy things until Ash stuck her head outside and accused us of being anti-social.

Chapter Sixty Four

Ramat David Airbase, North Central Israel
Thursday, December 27, 1990, 2205 hrs GMT

Major Alan Robertson of the US Army 160th Special Operations Aviation Regiment (SOAR) watched as the Galaxy C5-B turned onto final approach for landing on Ramat David's ten thousand foot runway. The huge aircraft looked like a ghost silently sliding beneath the lumbering clouds in the Israeli night. Its navigation lights barely visible in the distance. He was beginning to wonder if the pilot was going to land without lights when at about a hundred feet off the ground the landing lights were flicked on and the big plane lowered itself onto the runway.

C-5s were currently over worked, in short supply and difficult to schedule due to the ongoing Desert Shield material transport activity. The Air Force's Air Mobility Command at Scott Air Force Base, Illinois was coordinating the shipment of megatons of military equipment and supplies to various staging areas in the middle east in preparation for a war most people were praying would never happen. Robertson accompanied by his Priority One POTUS documentation was able to short cycle a C-5 to haul a CH-53D Sea Stallion, two Little Bird helicopters and a variety of other equipment, weapons and supplies to Ramat David Air Base, Israel.

DAWN'S EARLY LIGHT

The Israelis had been kind enough to lend us an entire hangar for up to a month. Major Robertson's only knowledge of the mission dealt with logistics and security. He would be read in to more of the mission when we arrived three days later. Meanwhile part of Robertson's crew would be busy reassembling the Sea Stallion. As huge as the Galaxy was the Sea Stallion was also a huge bird, for a helicopter. And as such it was a challenge to transport. The rotors and the main rotor hub had to be removed as well as the tail rotor, its hub and part of the tail assembly. Reassembly was a two day, three man job, one of which had to be a master aircraft mechanic. The Little Birds; no assembly required.

The Major supervised the unloading operation using hangar doors and security personnel to obstruct outside visibility. Security would be tightened over the next two days to accommodate the arrival of the F-117 Nighthawks Early Sunday morning. As a SOAR officer, the Major was familiar with and in charge of the security requirements for the F-117.

*****

Meanwhile, it's 1405 hrs here in La Jolla, California and I'm getting my personal gear ready to head down range. Rob and I returned from Fort Bragg last Sunday evening. Ash and I had a great visit with parents and her brother over the Christmas holiday. Ash had taken care of all the details so all I had to do was show up, smile and act like everything was normal. Actually, I did a pretty good job – it was great spending some time with Helen, Stephen and her brother Mark, but I really savored the time I had to play with my son – and my wife.

So now I've got to go steal a nuclear warhead from a badass dictator without getting killed or wounded. This is the boldest operation we've ever contemplated. Murphy is loitering in the shadows. The good news is that we've gotten some pretty good and trustworthy intel. Our CIA double agent spook in Kazakhstan, assisted by our own team mate Young-Ku, got us the guaranteed correct serial number for the nuke and the guys at Langley have already altered the single digit on the dud we'll swap for the real one. We got corroborating intel from our Kazi and Iraqi agents that Taji is the firm destination and the warhead will arrive there via private air cargo tomorrow at 1330 hrs. Adam Kivel at NSA has got us fixed up with really good optical and IR surveillance at the Taji site with no less than eight satellites. The Israelis and Jordanians are set to do their part and we're building operational behavior intel on the ground personnel at the Taji repair facility. The refueling site has been reconned, the choppers have arrived in Israel and the Nighthawks will be on their way tomorrow. I'm getting a warm fuzzy feeling. Not sure that's good. . .

Chapter Sixty Five

Langley Air Force Base,
Langley, Virginia
Friday, December 28, 1990, 2105 hrs EST

Chief Warrant Officer Charles Pitman mentally readied himself for yet another ferry flight to the middle east. At least this flight terminated in Israel, not Riyadh, Saudi Arabia. That shaved almost two hours off the total trip of twelve and a half hours. Pitman and fellow ferry pilot Major James Bergman were part of the Thirty Seventh Tactical Fighter Wing's effort to move twenty two F-117s from Langley Air Force Base, Virginia to Riyadh during the Desert Shield force buildup. Pitman, Bergman and six other ferry pilots were almost finished with the task when somebody stuck two more Nighthawks in the cue and caused them to make an additional trip. Oh well, it all paid the same low rate.

The only problem with moving the 117s was that takeoffs and landings and therefore the entire flight had to be made at night due to security issues. Night flights were extremely boring unless the weather was bad in which case they became somewhere between exciting and terrifying. On boring nights, although their wing commander strictly forbade it, the pilot pairs would frequently separate themselves by a thousand feet vertically and take a two hour nap on auto pilot. But not at the same time.

The leg from Langley to Ramstein Air Force Base, Germany took a little over seven hours and required a refueling over the Atlantic in addition to the five thousand pounds of fuel in the bomb bay ferry tanks. Night time refueling was not particularly more difficult than day time, unless, of course, bad weather prevailed. In which case the difficulty could easily escalate to the afore-mentioned state of terror.

Pitman and Bergman were lucky on this leg. The weather was good and the refueling routine. At Ramstein they would get a good breakfast and a restful day's sleep followed by a great supper at an off base German restaurant frequented by most of the ferry pilots on every trip. The flight path they would take over the ground would be only slightly north of the path to Riyadh. They didn't bother contacting air traffic control in the various countries they overflew because nobody knew they were there and they had very good omni-directional radar to watch for any traffic that might be at their above normal forty thousand foot altitude.

Sunday, December 30th, 1990, 0345 hrs GMT

The Nighthawks landed safely at Ramat David Air Base in north central Israel. The pilots were met by a Humvee with Israeli markings driven by Lt. Colonel Bertal Coppedge of the Israeli Security Force and accompanied by Chief Warrant Officer Jimmy McDaniel, our Little Bird pilot and Olan James, CIA Chief of Station, Saudi Arabia. Olan was there to sign for the two Nighthawks, the CH-53 and the two Little Birds. Somebody's always got to be responsible for everything. Olan would sign off responsibility for the F-117s to the mission pilots and the CH-53, MH-6 and AH-6 helicopters to Jimmy and the other mission pilots when they arrived later that day and mid afternoon the next day.

DAWN'S EARLY LIGHT

Sunday, December 30, 1990, 1400 hrs PST

Our Black Angel Team gathered at Miramar NAS for a 1400 hrs departure on the same Gulfstream III we used last time. Present were Rob, Gunny, Hal, Vince, and me. The GS-3 ride was a surprise to all but Rob whom I had already told after one too many beers last night. Bill Conroy sure knows how to travel right. After wheels-up at 1400 we refueled at Oceana, where we picked up the two Nighthawk mission pilots, and Ramstein where we restocked on food and beer. Then settled in for a long but uneventful flight to Ramat David AB, Israel.

The mission was set for 0100 hrs New Years Day. Olan James with his laptop was our link into the CIA network where mission intel was being concentrated. The quantity and quality of intel was almost overwhelming. We had eight satellites positioned to give optimum twenty four hour surveillance of the repair facility using high definition optical, infrared, synthetic aperture radar (SAR), Laser Imaging Data And Ranging (LIDAR – Laser radar) and Side Looking Airborne Radar (SLAR). We also had data and images from two SR-71 Blackbird over-flights. Currently, Adam Kivel's guys were moving the satellites to give us continuous coverage during the mission. We would also get another SR-71 fly-over just prior to t_0 (t = 0, mission start time at the IP). We had all day tomorrow to figure out what all this information meant.

Chapter Sixty Six

Ramat David Air Base,
North Central Israel
Monday, December 31, 1990, 1100 hrs IST

We're now in the Israel Standard Time zone (IST), which is Greenwich Mean Time plus three hours, and we'll remain there for the duration of the mission. Major Vince Harlow and I are in a small semi-secure office at the rear of our Israeli ops hangar. The hangar now contains our two F-117s, one huge CH-53D Sea Stallion helicopter, one unarmed QNMH-6Q Little Bird and one armed to the teeth QNAH-6Q Little Bird configured with one M134 7.62 mm six barrel Gatling-minigun, one seven tube LAU-68D/A rocket pod with seven Hydra 70 mm rockets, two AGM-114 Hellfire anti-tank missiles and one AIM-9 air to air Sidewinder missile. All three helicopters were equipped with AN/ALQ-144 infrared heat-seeking missile guidance system jammers. The attack configured Little Bird will quietly land in a vacant lot less than a half mile from the repair facility and only be used if things go to hell in a hand-basket and a forced exfil is required. Jimmy Mac will fly the QNMH-6Q and his friend CWO Larry Morris will fly the QNAH-6Q The Sea Stallion will be crewed by two pilots and two crew chiefs manning fifty caliber door machine guns and operating the stationary refueling system.

DAWN'S EARLY LIGHT

Vince, Olan and I are preparing a mission ready briefing we'll present to all mission operators at 1500 hrs this afternoon. At this meeting we will review the detailed mission profile which begins and ends here at Ramat David Air Base. Each mission operator will receive and recite his detailed role in the overall mission profile. Any perceived potential problems will be discussed and the impact analyzed and changes made if necessary. Then after supper at 1900 hrs we will make a final pass through the mission to be sure every operator understands every element of the mission including contingencies and possible reactions.

Monday, December 31, 1990, 2100 hrs IST

The big Sea Stallion lifted off the ramp at Ramat David Air Base at exactly 2100 hrs flying almost due east toward its destination in a remote area of the Syrian desert one hundred and fifty miles west of Taji. After landing two and a half hours later the pilots stood watch while the crew chiefs made ready the refueling system. The two Little Birds would arrive for refueling in less than an hour.

At 2145 hrs the two Little Birds arrived almost unnoticed. One of the crew chiefs commented that the wind was picking up before looking over his shoulder to see the MH-6 Little Bird landing behind them not fifty feet away. With both Little Birds on the Ground Jimmy used his sat phone to report in to mission control in the President's Situation Room in the White House basement. Then all hands busied themselves refueling the Little Birds. The AH-6 got a full tank. The MH-6 got just enough fuel for the round trip to the repair facility plus a fifteen minute reserve. It would be doing the heavy lifting tonight.

At 2200 hrs the selected Nighthawk, loaded with five Black Angels and a neutered Russian built nuclear warhead, cradled in a sturdy yet light weight titanium custom container, taxied out to the

291

end of runway 10. The aircraft was barely visible due to its unexpected shape. It didn't look like an airplane so therefore at night it was difficult to associate it with anything that should be on an airport. The takeoff was very smooth, unlike the runway we used at Groom Lake when we were doing flight tests. We were plugged into the aircraft oxygen system and could communicate with each other through our ASDS network. It was also connected to the aircraft comm network so we could converse with literally anyone we wanted to, anywhere in the world. I had promised George a sitrep as soon as we got off the ground and finished our complete system and personal gear tests including a test I ran on the warhead's cargo ASDS. It passed its test and I got a thumbs up from my other four compadres, so I channeled in to the CIA world net and called the situation room.

I began, "Checkpoint Alpha, sitrep nominal." That's a single word report that says everything is working and all is going according to plan. Then I added; "Admiral we really need to get some cushions on these seats. I'm not sure my hind quarters are going to work after an hour in this thing."

"Well I can see everything's truly normal. McKensie's found something to bitch about," returned the Admiral.

I said, "We'll call you back when we're ten minutes out."

The president said, "Godspeed Sam. Stevens out."

DAWN'S EARLY LIGHT

Chapter Sixty Seven

Above the Syrian Desert at Angels Two Zero
Fifty Miles West of Taji, Iraq
Tuesday, January 1, 1991, 0005 hrs IST

We did call back at ten minutes out. Everything was still good. Now our red light was blinking meaning we were five minutes out.

"Okay guys, five minutes out. Disconnect oxygen, comm and aircraft power. Run your self-tests," I said over the ASDS net as I quickly initiated the tests on my system as well as the warhead's cargo system. I looked around after I got the 'good test' signal for me and the warhead. Four thumbs up – everything was go at two minutes and counting.

The CIA guys at Langley built a great shipping container out of titanium and dense synthetic foam. The warhead fit snugly inside. No rattling around. It was cylindrical with four handles and didn't add much weight to the package. I was, however, a little bit concerned about the release mechanism they used for turning it loose. It was a quick-release carabiner used for attaching halyards to sails on sailboats. These things work great on sailboats. I had just never used one with a three hundred pound load on it. They assured me that it would work and that they had tested it – we'll see.

The red flashing light turned green indicating one minute. Last check. I gave a thumbs up and got four back. The order in which we would jump was: Rob, Hal, Vince, Gunny, the warhead and then me. Somebody had to release the damned warhead, but nobody else wanted to. I don't know if it was the radiation thing or the release mechanism.

The light turned solid green, the bomb bay doors opened and Rob disappeared, followed in five second intervals by Hal, Vince and Gunny. I waited ten seconds and yanked on the pull-pin. They were right – it worked. As I retracted and stowed the cargo chute static line I watched my visor display looking for the cargo drop status signal. There it was. A blue position indicator flashed three times and then remained solid blue indicating a good drop. Then I jumped.

There was no moon. It was very clear and at twenty thousand feet it was very cold. We had appropriate clothing for the cold, so we were okay, but still cold. No pressure suit because at twenty thousand feet it wasn't necessary – just oxygen. The really nice thing about ASDS (Airborne SEAL Delivery System, in case you forgot.) is that it doesn't really matter when you jump as long as all jumpers have an adequate margin of altitude for adjusting the descent and proper preprogrammed time separation for landing. The Automatic Landing System (ALS) in the ASDS adjusts your descent in accordance with your programmed arrival time and automatically maintains proper vertical and horizontal separation on the trip down. So the choreography of the landing sequence; the clearing of jumpers, cargo, etc. can be practiced, perfected and then preprogrammed into the system. It didn't always work that way. Once in Nicaragua I programmed six of us to land on the same spot. Someone landed on top of me before I could get out of the way. Broke my little finger.

I could see the whole soirée out in front of me; colored dots all in a row. The ALS hadn't started maneuvering us yet. That usually doesn't start until you get below two or three thousand feet. Rob wasn't due to arrive before 0055 so I had some time to think – or not. I hate to over think things.

So, as usual I thought about Ash, Scotty and me. We needed some more time off. We were both back up to four weeks accumulated leave. I'd had eight down range gigs this year plus twenty two Hornet sorties while off the Carl Vinson in January and February. We took two weeks in the South Pacific but that was part of Ash's recovery time after getting shot down and wounded in the South China Sea. So here we are again with four weeks each and no plan. I'll change that when I get back!

My thoughts returned to the mission. This was by far the deepest penetration we'd ever made. Lots of stuff could go wrong. Mr. Murphy was hiding in the shadows waiting to pounce on us.

I could see Rob (white dot) being maneuvered toward the LP by the ALS. We were getting close.

I heard Rob on the net: "I've got a tango on a smoke break. Gonna take him down."

Then a minute later, "One tango down for the long count. Cobra Three down and clear."

Hal reported, "Cobra Five down and clear."

Vince reported, "Cobra Two down and clear."

Gunny reported "Cobra Four down, clear and ready for the package."

And then: "Package secure and in place."

Then I landed and sent a sitrep back to home base; "Five angels down safe, package secure, one tango out for the night. Little Bird on its way to his wait station." A vacant lot a half mile from the Taji Repair Depot.

Chapter Sixty Eight

On the Ground, Personnel Parking Lot
Missile Repair Depot, Taji, Iraq
Tuesday, January 1, 1991, 0102 hrs IST

Using hand signals I sent the guys after the remaining five guards which according to our satellite and ground surveillance we were expecting to encounter. Our plan was to use the low power darts already loaded in our handguns. We knew where the guards were likely to be and how to take them down unaware. Each man knew the importance of retrieving the expended darts. I found my guy just inside the building at a desk normally occupied during daylight hours by a security guard checking worker IDs on the way in and lunch pails and packages on the way out. I had entered through a side door that was built into the huge sliding/folding hangar door at the north end of the building. Iraqi locks were simple to pick. Security here was oriented more toward employee theft than sabotage or foreign intruders. We caught these guards totally unaware. All six were sent into lala land completely unaware of what had happened to them. A metal tray with damp towels and an empty bottle of an Iraqi brand of medicinal Halothane (a sleeping agent) was placed in both primary air handlers. Four ten liter kegs of hydrazine liquid rocket propellant and a carton of six warhead fuses were stolen to cover the intrusion

DAWN'S EARLY LIGHT

and place the blame on terrorist factions in the south.

We found the warhead in what looked like a model shop in the rear of the building. Marked it 'REAL' with a sharpie, checked that the serial numbers were identical and made the swap. We loaded the real warhead into the shipping container and I made a call to our three sentries to come help carry the container and a call to Jimmy to come in for exfil. Then I heard a five round burst from an AK-47.

Damnit, I knew this was going too easy. We had obviously not paid proper homage to the ghost of Mr. Murphy because things had just gotten TARFU (Totally And Royally Fucked Up). I grabbed my MP-5, which had real 9mm ammo in it, and headed for the door where the sound came from. I looked left and saw a uniformed Republican Guard soldier laying face up, eyes closed, on the concrete driveway that ran down the side of the building. I looked to the right and saw Rob rolling in pain on the same driveway. I checked the soldier and found he'd been darted and was out. Then I ran to Rob. He had a flesh wound in his left leg and a through and through bullet hole through his right shoulder. Above the lung and below the clavicle but probably through the scapula. I grabbed my med kit out of my jump suit, popped a morphine syrette and jabbed it into his right thigh. Unfortunately Rob is our medic. He joined the Navy as a Corpsman. The next in line from a medical knowledge standpoint was Gunny. I got him looking after Rob and herded the other guys, equipment, warhead, hydrazine, fuses and sleeping guard to the exfil point in the parking lot.

I called the situation room: "Have the AH-6 advance to our exfil point, immediately. We've got one wounded and one sleeping enemy to deal with. The MH will be over-loaded." There was room for both Little Birds in the parking lot and this was high on our list of contingency plans. So the only real problem now was what to do with the sleeping guard.

When Jimmy landed with his Little Bird we helped Rob into the co-pilot's seat, shoved the warhead canister into the area where the left rear seat usually resides, slid the hydrazine and fuses into the baggage area behind the rear seats and put Gunny in the right rear seat. I told Jimmy to take this load back to the refueling site and wait for us. As they lifted off I could see Gunny leaning over Rob's seat still packing his wounds. They had an hour flight back to the refueling point. I prayed that Rob would make it alright. I was worried. I didn't know what level of medical training the other operators had. The CH-53 pilots, the crew chiefs. I was certain the Sea Stallion had plenty of medical supplies and equipment, but Rob was three hours plus from any real medical attention. Ramat David AB did have a base hospital. Except for North Korea we'd never been this deep into enemy territory before. We (I) hadn't planned properly for this kind of problem. I called the sit-room and told them what had happened. I fully explained the current situation and asked them to tell Vince to put the warhead on the CH-53, bury the hydrazine and fuses and have Jimmy take Rob and Gunny on back to Ramat David if Gunny thought it necessary. We had the CH-53 to get the rest of the people and stuff back. I also asked them to enable our ASDS net through the satcom network so I could talk directly to Gunny. The communications had been restricted to direct comm with the sit-room to increase security. But the slight increase in comm security had been over-ruled by the current situation.

I looked through the personal effects of the Republican Guard soldier. His wallet, contents of his pockets, etc. The only things of interest were his radio, a folded A4 sized paper he was carrying in his shirt pocket and, of course, his AK-47. The radio was a six channel Motorola VHF with volume and squelch controls. Nothing fancy. The radio was on but nothing was being broadcast. I increased the sensitivity with the squelch control and left it just

DAWN'S EARLY LIGHT

below the squeal. And waited. Nothing. I turned the volume up a little and hooked it on my belt.

Then I examined his AK-47. It was the standard Russian model 4a. Millions produced. 7.62X39 mm cartridge, thirty round magazine. This rifle looked to be well maintained. It had been recently cleaned and oiled. He had two extra full magazines in a three magazine canvas holster.

We had about five minutes before the AH-6 would get here. Plenty of time for Murphy to plan and execute a full scale fuck-up.

Then I heard Gunny on my ASDS net, "What's up Skip?"

"How's Rob doing?"

"He'll be okay. The wound is through and through. The exit is a little ragged but I've got both sides packed tight. No significant blood loss. Probably nicked his scapula on the way out. We've got plenty of morphine. He hasn't asked for more yet. The Admiral passed on your message about sending Rob and I on back to the air base. Don't think that's necessary. In fact, I advise against it."

"Roger that Gunny. I agree. Cobra One Out." Now that we had opened up our ASDS net, we needed to start using call signs.

I looked at the piece of paper from the guard's shirt pocket. It looked like a shipping document or a bill of laden or something like that. Written in Arabic. Rob was our only operator who could actually read and write the stuff. Remind me to give that boy a raise.

Hal, Vince and I began gathering all remaining equipment and ASDS gear into a pile next to the spot where the AH-6 would land.

Then the radio came to life saying, "Ahmed, Ahmed, come in. Where are you? You should be back here by now. If you hear this, please reply." I can't read or write Arabic but I can speak and understand most of it. Well, a lot of it anyway. This was not good.

DON CANDY

Murphy was close by.

Chapter Sixty Nine

On the Ground, Refueling Point
One Hundred Fifty Miles West of Taji, Iraq
Tuesday, January 1, 1991, 0155 hrs IST

We got off the ground in the AH-6 before Murphy could strike. Things were looking better. We landed at the refueling site about ten minutes after the MH-6. Now all we had to do was gas up both Little Birds, stow the refueling equipment, climb aboard the Sea Stallion and get the hell out of Dodge.

Just as we were securing the refueling gear in a rear compartment of the CH-53 we got a warning from the sit-room that an aircraft was heading for our position at 400 knots, 50 miles out. Then a few minutes later an Iraqi MiG-21 made a low pass over our position and circled back toward Taji. Jimmy Mac had switched Little Birds since he was the more experienced pilot. He was sitting in the AH-6 waiting to play his role of protector in the three bird flight back to Ramat David. He immediately fired up the AH-6 and was airborne and on the radio.

"We've been compromised. I'm going to fly east low and fast. Try to get behind this guy and take him out with my Sidewinder before he gets the CH-53. Recommend all personnel get away from the CH. He'll go for the high value target first."

Lieutenant Commander Richard Malone, pilot in command of the CH-53 knew what he had to do. The warhead was already stowed in a secure position at the rear of the aircraft. He and his crew of three had to get it off and away from the aircraft. Destruction of the CH-53 with the warhead aboard might not cause a nuclear explosion but it would certainly cause a 'dirty bomb' explosion with radiation that would kill everything within a thirty mile radius. They were successful in getting the warhead off the CH-53 and secured behind a small berm over two hundred feet to the side of the aircraft and close to the MH-6. Commander Malone sent his crew away from the site to the relative safety of the open desert while he returned to the giant helicopter to retrieve the medical kit in case it was needed.

Meanwhile, Jimmy Mac had covered about ten miles of empty desert when he spotted the MiG at about five hundred feet and ten degrees to his starboard side. Since he had the low altitude and night vision advantage it was unlikely that the MiG pilot had seen or would see him. He banked the Little Bird hard to starboard coming back hard on the stick in a climbing turn that put him into a firing position as the MiG passed. As soon as he stabilized his aircraft he armed and fired his only Sidewinder missile.

The Black Angel Team had been authorized two AH-6 and two MH-6 helicopters for BAT operations. All four had been substantially modified. Auxiliary fuel tanks had been installed and made permanent, increasing the range from two hundred fifty to five hundred miles. New 'quiet' rotors had been designed to greatly increase the aircraft's stealth and fuel efficiency. And, the starboard rail had been modified to carry a single AIM-9 Sidewinder air-to-air missile, or a single AGM-65 Maverick radar guided air-to-ground missile, or one of the original weapons: the rocket pod, two Hellfire missiles or a six barrel minigun, it was already able to support. The Sidewinder was a mach 2.7 proven missile, known among pilots as Fox-2 and responsible for over two

DAWN'S EARLY LIGHT

hundred and fifty kills with very high reliability.

Jimmy's Sidewinder did its job, but it was about one, maybe two, seconds late. Just before his Sidewinder flew into the MiG's exhaust and took out the rear half of the plane, Jimmy watched in horror as the MiG fired an air to ground missile toward the refueling site. He took his Little Bird to combat power and headed for the site. Then he saw the smoke from a large explosion. He knew the Sea Stallion had been destroyed.

I called the sit-room, "Admiral, I've got some really bad news. Jimmy got the MiG with his Sidewinder but not before the MiG fired an air to ground missile at the CH-53. Unfortunately Commander Malone had gone back to the CH to retrieve the medical kit. He was KIA. So we're now in deep shit. I saw three Apaches at Ramat David. Do you think they can help us?"

"Actually when we were cleared by the Israelis to use RDAB as our base of operations the base commander said they would stand ready to assist if necessary. Let me see if that still holds true. Hold on, I'll be right back to you."

I grabbed Hal and the CH-53 co-pilot and got them and the warhead back into the MH-6 with CWO Morris (the pilot), Gunny and Rob and sent them off to Ramat David Air Base. Five operators and a nuclear warhead headed for safety. I could breathe a little easier. But not much. I still had the two Ch-53 crew chiefs, Vince, Jimmy, myself, the sleeping guard and Commander Malone's body plus all the equipment we'd brought in and the aircraft mounted missiles, rockets and guns that we couldn't leave. The AH-6 couldn't haul it all and it was our only defense.

'Right back to you' became the longest twenty minutes of my life. While I was waiting I tried to view the situation from a world wide political perspective. The Iraqis very likely viewed this as an Israeli action, but to what means they couldn't be certain. In fact, they were surely confused. We had left no trace of American involvement in the covert raid on the Taji facility. The warhead had been secured in a locked model shop in the repair building. We didn't breech the lock – we picked it. Very carefully. No Marks. They surely checked on it. It was still there. Hadn't been moved. Questions abounded on both sides.

For the Iraqis; What was going on? Maybe the Israelis, or maybe the Americans coming through Israel, were looking for the warhead, got interrupted by Ahmed and fled taking him with them? Or maybe it was something else. But what? No, it had to be the warhead. But they still had it. Was it worth them risking any more assets on an aborted ploy? The MiG pilot had the answers. Did he radio back what he'd found? Was he actually shot down? Did he survive?

For us; Was the MiG pilot able to identify the large helicopter he reported flying over before he was shot down while launching a missile at the helicopter and radio back what he'd found? Did he survive? Will they send out another plane to find him? Will it be another MiG?

If he's still alive, both sides needed to find the pilot. I called Jimmy on the ASDS net. "Did the pilot bail?"

"If he did, I didn't see it. I watched carefully as the MiG went in. The rear half of the plane was totally blown apart. It was rotating like a boomerang. Not uncommon for a MiG-21. If a heat seeking missile gets in far enough into the exhaust to explode in the huge engine the resulting destruction from the engine flying apart will take the rear end completely off. Often not survivable. I'm ninety five percent certain our pilot is toast."

"Okay, thanks Jimmy. I can see you approaching our site. We'll talk when your down."

I didn't want to mention that Commander Malone was in the Sea Stallion when the missile hit. He's probably going to blame

DAWN'S EARLY LIGHT

himself. I wanted him safe on the ground when I told him.

*****

I looked at my watch. It had been twenty minutes. My comm unit buzzed. I answered, "Cobra One here."

The Admiral said, "Good News Sam. They're sending help. An Apache and a Blackhawk followed by a Strike Eagle (F-15). Will that help?"

"Damned right it will Admiral. I love allies you can count on in a pinch! I sent Hal, the other three Ch-53 guys and the warhead back to Ramat David in the MH. At least it looks like we'll get what we came after."

"The F-15 is coming from another base. ETA uncertain."

Then Jimmy landed. I walked over to his Little Bird.

"You're going down in the record books, man! The only Russian jet ever shot down by a Little Bird."

"Don't try to smooth it over Skip. We lost the CH," Jimmy said with his head down.

"Shit happens, Jimmy. You did the impossible. Don't apologize for it."

"We're in a pickle now because I fired too late."

"That's bullshit and you know it. I don't want to hear this crap! Settle down. I've got worse news. Malone went back to the CH to get the medical kit. He's KIA."

"Well, fuck me! Now I'm really pissed! If they come back, I'm gonna kill those bastards!"

Chapter Seventy

On the Ground in the Syrian Desert, Iraq
A hundred yards northwest of the Refueling Point
Tuesday, January 1, 1991, 0245 hrs IST

We fell back to a ravine we had tagged as the only decent cover on our straight line track across the desert between Ramat David Air Base, Israel and the Republican Guard Missile Repair Facility near Taji, Iraq during our planning activity. This spot was an important factor in the choice of the refueling site. A large flat alluvial plane drained into the ravine through hundreds of small rivulets. The ravine drained onto another large flat area about thirty feet lower and formed a small creek leading off to the southwest along the base of a rocky thirty foot cliff. The area reminded me of the Army's Yuma Proving Ground near Yuma Arizona where we often held ASDS training sessions. YPG was desolate with very little rain. But when it did rain it poured. We called them 'gully washers' and they caused features in the desert there that were very similar to those here. We placed the Little Bird a hundred yards down the creek below the cliff with Jimmy and I close by. The others gathered at the mouth of the ravine with all the remaining equipment and gear.

We didn't have to wait to long. They didn't send a MiG-21.

DAWN'S EARLY LIGHT

They sent two.

We got a heads up from the sit-room. "Two aircraft heading your position at four hundred knots. Seventy miles out. Likely more MiG-21s" Jimmy and I crawled up the rocky cliff and took up our observation position with binoculars. The only weapon we had left that had even a remote chance of fending off a MiG-21 was the M134D-H Minigun. Jimmy had loaded the AH-6 with three five thousand round belts of NATO 7.62mm Ammunition. He had it assembled at the armory with tracers on every other round. I would fly with him to change belts and operate the rocket pod. The Hydra rockets were un-guided and would likely not hit anything but Jimmy wanted me to fire one each time he yelled 'fire' to distract the Iraqi pilots just before he fired the minigun.

Jimmy scrambled down the cliff, jumped into the Little Bird and started it up, took off and hovered just high enough to see above the top of the cliff. About twenty feet above the ground below the cliff. Jimmy said the cliff would partially cover our radar image and present a confusing picture to the MiG pilots. After about five minutes I could see the jets coming in the starlight. I gave Jimmy a hand signal and he nudged the Little Bird up and over toward me so I could climb in. I did.

Jimmy yelled, "ready on the rockets." And then as he pulled the helicopter clear of the cliff edge he aimed the copter about twenty degrees up leading the first jet by thirty degrees and yelled, "Fire one!"

I flipped the #1 switch on the auxiliary rocket pod control box and a rocked zoomed across the nose of the lead MiG. They were flying in a tight left echelon, the wingman's nose almost even with the lead's tail. What happened next was hard for me to process. Jimmy steadied the nose at about twenty degrees up. Shot a short burst to gauge his aim on the lead plane. He then made a slight adjustment down and to the right and let loose with a five second strafing burst from the nose of the lead jet to the tail of the trailing jet covering both aircraft with a rapid saw-tooth pattern. The burst hit both jets many times. The lead plane rolled left as if running away but the roll continued until he was inverted and then nosed in. Scratch one MiG! The other jet flew on.

"Hot Dam!," he yelled. "Now it's a fair fight!

"Change belts on the gun," Jimmy yelled.

I did.

In the maneuvers that followed it became obvious to me that the MiG pilot had no idea how to handle an accomplished helicopter pilot. The MiG-21 had a single twenty three millimeter auto-cannon. One round from one of these guns could easily disable an AH-6 if the shot was placed correctly. But the combination of an extremely agile aircraft and a savvy quick thinking helicopter pilot made it fairly easy for Jimmy to stay out of the crosshairs of a jet pilot trained in conventional jet to jet dog fighting. This Iraqi pilot, frustrated by his inability to keep the little chopper centered in his gun-sight long enough to get away a decent shot decided to rely on his missiles to do the job. Unfortunately for the Iraqi, what he didn't know was that the little helicopter that was currently harassing him was equipped with an AN/ALQ-144 InfraRed CounterMeasures (IRCM) system. In fact he didn't even know what an IRCM was. What it was, was a highly effective infrared heat seeking missile jammer. Iraq's most recent foe, Iran, had no such countermeasure capability. So Iraq's Soviet supplied heat seeking missiles worked well on most of Iran's aircraft. If Saddam chooses to go to war with the U.S. and our allies over the annexation of Kuwait he will be dismayed by myriad advanced military technology. Stuff he is currently totally unaware of.

The Iraqi MiG-21 was carrying two radar guided air to ground missiles, two heat seeking air to air missiles and two radar guided air to air missiles. In an air to air situation he was trained to use the

DAWN'S EARLY LIGHT

heat seeking air to air missiles first because they were much less expensive than the radar guided missiles and often more effective. Not today. Thanks to the AN/ALQ-144 IRCM both of his heat seeking missiles missed. While he stared in disbelief at the second missile as it veered off to his left missing the little Bird by twenty feet Jimmy did what I would call a high g chandelle, a fairly violent maneuver where he pulled the nose up sharply while reversing our direction by one hundred eighty degrees. The net effect was that suddenly we were slammed into our seats, the rotors momentarily over-revved and then we sort of floated in mid air looking down on the approaching MiG-21 which a moment ago was a mile behind us. Jimmy had his finger on the trigger with the minigun still selected on the weapon selection switch. From our position above and in front of the MiG he began firing a short zigzagged pattern into the path of the approaching jet. The other pilot didn't have time to react. He flew straight through the hail of 7.62 mm bullets being fired at two thousand rounds a minute. It all happened in a flash and it was night. What I saw was what looked like a six inch pipe of red fire sweeping back and forth that was interrupted by a solid object, generating a momentary fiery blur maybe fifty feet below and a hundred feet in front of us. And then the pipe reconstructed itself for a half second and disappeared. Jimmy did another climbing one eighty in place and we watched the MiG destroy itself on the desert below.

"Jimmy McDaniel, you just saved our lives. Not just you and me. All of us. I didn't get a chance to tell you before we started dealing with this second round of MiGs; The Admiral got the Israelis to send us some help. An Apache and a Blackhawk are on their way from Ramat David and a Strike Eagle is coming from another air base."

"I'm glad you didn't tell me. I might have recommended waiting for the Eagle."

"The Eagle is coming from a different base. The Admiral said the Ramat David Base Commander was going to get an F-15 sent from another base but he didn't know which base or how long it would take. That's why I didn't tell you. Hell man, you're three fifths of the way to ace fighter pilot in less than an hour. And you did it all in our smallest helicopter! That's something to celebrate!"

Jimmy smiled for about two seconds, then lowered his head. The loss of Commander Lieutenant Malone and the Sea Stallion was going to be a major issue for Jimmy and I suspected it would take a while to fade.

I called in another sitrep to the White House Situation Room. Found a bunch of really happy people back there. President Stevens told me to give the team a big oorah from him. Job well done, etc. etc. George reminded me to bring the Black Angel team straight to Fort Bragg for debriefing. I told him we would be celebrating with a few Israelis tonight after a good day's sleep today. He reminded me of how highly classified this mission was. I asked him how come the Ramat David Air Base Commander already knew about the mission. He said the Base Commander and his immediate staff were necessarily read into the operation. I told him those were the exact same people we would be celebrating with tonight. He said, "Loose lips sink ships." I said, "I know that. Cobra One out" And hung up. I was tired and ready to call it a night or I guess, morning.

DAWN'S EARLY LIGHT

Chapter Seventy One

Ramat David Air Base,
North Central Israel
Tuesday, January 1, 1991, 0930 hrs IST

We got back to Ramat David in the twilight just before dawn. We were tired puppies ready for a hot meal and eight hours of sleep. I checked on Rob right away. They said he was at the base hospital. He had already had surgery on his right scapula and the doctors had cleaned out the wound and closed up his entry and exit holes. They grafted a chunk of skin from his lower back to close the exit hole. He should be ready to return with us tomorrow.

Our Israeli hosts were a gracious bunch of friendly warriors among whom about thirty percent were women. Israeli women were required to serve in the military and quite a few were choosing the Air Force. Something the U.S. was just now warming up to. The Base Commander, his three Wing Commanders and combat staff met with the four of us plus Jimmy briefly after we'd had a chance to clean up a little and eat. He wanted to let us know that Admiral Bennington had read his people in this meeting on The high level elements of Operation Nuclear Exchange. He handed me the executed paperwork and asked me to initial a note

311

at the bottom of the document regarding this meeting.

We gave him a brief overview of the mission. Its successes . It's failures. They were all already aware of the Loss of the Sea Stallion, the pilot killed in action and the destruction of three MiG-21s by an AH-6 Little Bird. One of the wing commanders asked Jimmy why he thought none of the Iraqi pilots were able to eject.

Jimmy responded, "The sidewinder got all the way into the engine before it exploded. As you guys probably know when that happens and the engine flies apart it pretty much cuts the plane in two. It also usually kills or badly injures the pilot. All we had for the last two MiGs was the 7.62mm mini Gatling gun. It's very difficult to take a MiG down with 7.62mm NATO ammunition. It's easier to disable the pilot. That's what I was evidently able to do."

The wing commanders began clapping and that was the start of a standing ovation. I'd never seen Jimmy Mac embarrassed. Three MiG-21s shot down by a Little Bird pilot. Who would ever believe that?

When the question and answer session was over the Base Commander asked me to express his country's gratitude to all the people involved in this mission. He said he hoped Israel would have an opportunity in the future to return the honor.

He cracked a bottle of expensive champagne, filled toasting flutes and we all toasted his hope for peace in the middle east. Then we adjourned to the VOQ where we slept the rest of the day. After a great evening meal we adjourned to the Officers Club where we were each given three drink tokens and one snack token. The bar closed at 2300 hrs. Our little gathering was held in a guest room at the back of the building.

I spent an hour with Wing Commander, Lt. Colonel Dan Kopin. Interesting man. His father was killed in the 1967 Six Day War. Shot down in his Mirage on the last day of the conflict. Six

DAWN'S EARLY LIGHT

years later his mother, an F4 Phantom rear seat Radar Intercept Officer (RIO), was shot down in the 1973 Yom Kippur War. Dan had almost seven thousand hours in the McDonnell-Douglas f-15 Strike Eagle. He had three kills in the limited actions from 1980 to 1990. He had high praise for American built fighters. He also had high praise for Jimmy Mac.

We checked Rob out of the hospital at 0800 hrs (Wednesday morning) and headed straight to the ramp outside the our 'loaner' hangar. We climbed aboard our GS-3 and headed home. Our first leg would be to Ramstein Air Force Base, Germany where we would leave Lieutenant Commander Malone's body for processing, to be followed by a proper flight home. From Ramstein we flew to Fort Bragg, North Carolina for a debriefing with the Admiral. Rob looked like a new man except for his right arm in a sling. The Israeli Medic gave me enough morphine to get Rob home comfortably. I asked him for a little more so I could get him through the debriefing and back to La Jolla. With the Admiral's blessings we left Ahmed with the Israelis until Olan and the CIA could figure out what to do with him.

Flying with the sun got us home in just a little over seven hours total clock time. Add in eight time zones and the flight time becomes a little over fourteen hours in the air plus an hour and a half on the ground. We were fed and settled into our somewhat comfortable beds in the Fort Bragg Visiting Officers Quarters by 2100 hrs. I was asleep five minutes later.

Chapter Seventy Two

JSOC Headquarters, Fort Bragg, NC
Thursday, January 3, 1991, 0900 hrs EST

Before beginning the debriefing the Admiral wanted our thoughts on the Iraqi's take on the events of the last fifty five hours.

I answered, "They had no idea we were coming. Our observations and our intel agree on that. We successfully disabled the six guards we were expecting. Our friend Ahmed was a surprise. Best we could figure he was one of the gate guards. Intel tells us the two gate guards never leave their posts. Maybe they had three gate guards and they rotated duty when our birds weren't overhead. We may never know. We think, based on what we do know, they bought our ploy. We were very careful making the swap. The shop was left in a totally undisturbed state. Door locked, no sign of entry, no finger prints, nothing moved. The store room, on the other hand, had a visibly breeched lock, disturbed cabinets and closets, missing hydrazine and fuses and a left behind well used Iraqi penlight. The two almost empty one liter Halothane bottles next to the open filter doors with damp towels spread over the filters and an Iraqi army gas mask near the breeched security fence. I think they bought this hook, line and sinker until that MiG radioed back his sighting of the CH-53. After that I don't know what they thought. Could be they thought someone – the Israelis, us, the Russians, whoever, had come for the warhead and had to abort when discovered. And they might still believe they have a working warhead. Could they know that we had a warhead from the same group that the Kazis sold to the PRK? The CIA did an excellent job on the serial number. Rob and I examined it very closely. I believe they think they still have the warhead they bought from the Kazis, regardless of any other conclusions they might come to over the recent events. I have no way to be the least bit certain what those 'other conclusions' might be."

Debriefings for a successful mission were usually not an unpleasant formality; to be dealt with as quickly and efficiently as the situation would allow. This mission was successful on paper. We got the nuke and the Iraqi's were still scratching their heads. They sent three modern fighters to intercept us and none returned. However, we were left with bitter memories of the ordeal. And a lot of what-ifing.

What if we had brought an extra man for better security during the operation? Rob might not have been blindsided by a guard that was obviously on site but unaccounted for. The extra man would have caused us to also use the AH-6 for exfil. But we ended up having to use it for exfil anyway. The Admiral thought we were short on operators for such a large facility. He was right. I have always favored the small footprint the Black Angels are able to achieve on the types of missions we are selected for. So I nixed expanding the force. But due to the refueling requirement this was a somewhat larger operation and in hindsight, which is always 20/20, we needed at least one, maybe two more men. This issue caused the problem that initiated the sequence of events leading to the destruction of the CH-53 and the death of Lieutenant Commander Malone. And that was on me. Malone had a wife and three kids. Two in college. He was forty nine.

DON CANDY

What if Rob had used his MP-5 to take down the guard instead of his Glock loaded with darts? How Rob acted was exactly what the mission plan called for. We each had an assigned tango to take down with a dart. We had our pistols at ready not our MP-5s. It was the fact that this guard had been able to suddenly and unexpectedly appear that caused the problem. Had we known there were seven, not six, we could have covered the extra guard easily. Incomplete intel? Obviously.

CWO Jimmy McDaniel insisted on having his own what-if, continuing to blame himself for the destruction of the CH-53 and the death of Commander Malone. Malone was a combat veteran. He knew better than to go near the Sea Stallion with an enemy fighter/bomber on its way.

"If I could have just sent the Sidewinder two seconds sooner," he said with his head down.

Admiral Bennington broke in, "How could you have possibly known that your timing was critical. Neither you nor the MiG were in visual range of the CH-53. The pilot could have fired his radar imaging air to ground missile a full thirty seconds either side of when he did. You waited until the off-boresight angle to the target was less than forty five degrees, as you were trained to do. Your timing is not a mission issue. As Sam told you then and I'm telling you now – shit happens, get over it!"

Jimmy looked stunned. He was an individual who took his job with extreme seriousness. And that probably had a lot to do with his tendency toward self-criticism. And the Admiral had just criticized him for exactly that. In my book Jimmy was not perfect. But close.

What if I had ordered Malone and his men to stay away from the CH-53 as I had ordered mine to? In retrospect, I should have. They were in a support role and I incorrectly expected Malone to look after his own men – and himself.

DAWN'S EARLY LIGHT

We all felt bad. It's a natural thing. I knew it would happen some day. Our casualty record – for a special ops unit always operating behind enemy lines – had been remarkable. Actually, I had taken the brunt of our casualties; shot in the arm, shoulder, leg and butt, and a broken finger. Nothing really serious.

We got past the what-if stage and spent two hours developing a lessons-learned document from a step by step re-hash of the entire mission. Basically our strategy and planning had been pretty good. This was our second covert mission deep into enemy territory and the first with the Nighthawk/Little Bird infil/exfil combination. We all agreed that we had a viable mission profile for our area of responsibility. Our strong point was stealth; the ASDS, the Nighthawk, the CAPV-727, the Quiet Little Birds, the highly suppressed MP-5 machine guns, the 9mm narc darts and our super-secret Infra Red Night Vision (IRNV) were our primary tools for stealthy operation. So fine tuning our base-line mission profile required honing our operations to both support and be supported by these tools. When we were done we had two type written pages of lessons-learned. Each leading to a modification, tweak, addition or complete rewrite of strategy and tactics elements of our Mission Planning Handbook. All this rolled into a Bottom line;

We own the night!

Chapter Seventy Three

Harry's Steak House, San Diego, CA
Saturday, January, 5th 1991, 1830 hrs PST

George Bennington had a west coast JSOC Officers conference on Joint Special Operations Logistics to facilitate on Monday and Tuesday so he saved some travel bucks by hitching a ride with us Friday afternoon on Bill Conroy's Gulfstream III. Tightwad though he was, he still kicked in a few extra dollars to upgrade our on-board cuisine from Navy standard to CIA executive. Steak and lobster two nights in a row. At least that was what I was planning to have tonight - again. Rob, Sara, Ash and I got there a little early so we got a booth in the bar area and ordered drinks. Rob and I ordered Harry's crab cake appetizers. The best crab cakes in the world!

Rob was doing really well. He was actually eating his crab cake with his right hand. Ash and Sara had joined us for the evening. Rob had told Sara that he'd had just a minor gunshot wound in his shoulder and didn't even mention his leg.

Since Jimmy Mac was going to be permanently attached to us for at least a year we both thought it was time for him to relocate out here on the west coast. His actual current home is Bahrain. Ash and I will help him look around the San Diego, Chula Vista, La Jolla and Miramar areas tomorrow. Scotty is putting on weight like

DAWN'S EARLY LIGHT

a summa wrestler. He's over ten pounds already. He'll spend the day with his aunt Sara and Uncle Rob tomorrow.

Gunny Tanner, our Marine San Diego resident, tried to get out of dinner with us tonight, but couldn't. We're going to humanize this guy some day. Doesn't look like soon though.

Vince stayed at Fort Bragg for a wedding. So he missed out on both Steak and Lobster dinners. During dinner on the plane the Admiral and I had quietly discussed letting Vince pull lead on the next few missions so I could spend more time stateside getting the ASDG fully staffed, equipped and organized. I haven't told Ash about this. I'm waiting for a high value opportunity.

When Gunny showed up, Alice, our favorite Maître D, showed us to George's table with a view.

The Admiral thanked us for coming and informed us:

"Eat up ladies and lads. I'm buying."

"It's that new star, I'll bet. It must be tough to have more money than you know what to do with," I shot back.

Admiral Bennington had been recently promoted from Rear Admiral Lower Half (one star) to Rear Admiral (Two star). There is no upper half – nobody knows why. The promotion came without any fanfare on his behalf. He just showed up one day wearing two stars. A lot of people didn't notice – but I did. That's the kind of guy he is. Once a daring young Lieutenant in Vietnam flying A-4's, A-6's and F-4's from aircraft carriers, married to Julie - the love of his life, George rose through the ranks to Captain as Air Wing Commander on the USS Enterprise (CVN-65). During that tour the Enterprise's Captain rotated out and the new ship's commander was actually out ranked by George. Both were Captains but George had time-in-rank seniority. It was during this final tour that Julie developed breast cancer of a particularly aggressive type. He took a desk job on Coronado Island until she passed away about a year later. A year after her death he was contemplating retirement when he was offered command of JSOC and a promotion to the lower half. This dinner tonight is an example of his style of leadership. He can make the tough calls required by his job but he leads from behind. Attracting the finest officers and enlisted men and women the Navy has to offer and enabling them to excel in their jobs by never ignoring their needs, giving them the same opportunity to grow and succeed that he was given. He always puts his people out in front for their own success. He doesn't care about a second star or a third. The sailors in his command will do anything he asks. And now, with his JSOC command, that leadership style is affecting the Army's Delta Force and Special Operations Air Regiment and the Marines Force Recon as well as us frogmen.

"James McDaniel," the Admiral almost shouted as he rose from his seat and approached Jimmy.

The Admiral continued in a much lower voice as he reached for Jimmy's hand for a hardy handshake, "You shot down three enemy aircraft in a Little Bird!"

Jimmy's eyes got big. He stammered, "Uh y-yes sir," as he rose to respond.

You are an Army Special Ops Chief Warrant Officer attached to a JSOC organization managed by the Navy, right?"

"Uh, yes sir."

"I would like to offer you a commission in the Navy. It would be an attractive offer. We can discuss the details later, say next week. Would you be receptive to looking at that opportunity?"

"Absolutely, sir," Jimmy responded with a broad smile creeping across his face.

The dinner was outstanding. No surprise. The Admiral announced that he and I would take our dessert in the bar. Which we did.

DAWN'S EARLY LIGHT

"Sam, Jimmy's action is in Medal of Honor territory. As you recall from a similar situation with Master Chief Manny Hernandez, due to security issues we did the Navy Cross instead."

"Yeah George, I recall the issues. The good news here is that Jimmy's still alive. And, he's not expecting any sort of recognition. He's one of the most unassuming individuals I've ever known. He probably doesn't even know what the Navy Cross is. Do you think he'll take your offer?"

"I don't know. I plan to offer him Lieutenant Commander with the Special Ops adder on top of his combat pilot adder. What do your think?"

"I think he'll take it. He's got a girl friend back in Macon, Georgia that he only gets to see two or three times a year. I think he's ready to settle down stateside and get married. He's mentioned to me several times that he wished he had a cushy job like mine."

"Tell you what. I'll work on the transfer and grease the skids on the Navy Cross. You write up the citation. Okay?"

"You got it boss!"

DON CANDY

Chapter Seventy Four

ASDG Headquarters, San Diego, CA
Monday, January 7, 1991, 1107 hrs.

I sent the citation to the Admiral last night and Jenny, my new Petty Officer First Class Group Administrator announced over the intercom that he was on my line now. Here's what I sent;

CITATION, NAVY CROSS

Lt CMDR JAMES McDANIEL

For conspicuous gallantry and intrepidity in action at the risk of his life above and beyond the call of duty. Lieutenant Commander James McDaniel, Naval Advanced Systems Development Group of the Joint Special Operations Command, distinguished himself while serving as pilot of an AH-6 helicopter. He unhesitatingly maneuvered his helicopter into close quarters with an enemy supersonic fighter/interceptor while defending nine comrades and one enemy prisoner during an

DAWN'S EARLY LIGHT

extraction refueling operation at night. Lt Cmdr McDaniel proceeded to destroy the enemy aircraft using a heat seeking air to air missile, but not before the enemy aircraft managed to fire a radar imaging air to ground missile destroying the friendly refueling vehicle and killing its operator. Stranded more than two hour's flight time from friendly forces, Lt Cmdr McDaniel and his AH-6 were the only remaining defense for the group. When two more identical enemy fighter/interceptor jets appeared, McDaniel took off in his Little Bird helicopter against overwhelming opposing forces to defend his grounded comrades. In an amazing display flying skill Lt Cmdr McDaniel, using his only remaining effective weapon, a 7.62 mm M-134 minigun (Gatling gun), twice maneuvered his aircraft such that he was able to disable each of the enemy pilots and subsequently their aircraft while not allowing the enemy pilots to attain a firing position on him or his comrades on the ground. Within a period of one hour Lt Cmdr McDaniel completely destroyed three supersonic enemy fighter/interceptors flying the smallest helicopter in the U.S. military inventory. As a direct result of his selfless conduct, the lives of eight comrades (and his own) were saved The extraordinary heroism displayed by Lt Cmdr McDaniel was an inspiration to his comrades in arms and reflect great credit on him, his unit, and the U.S. Navy.

I worded the citation to be effective after Jimmy accepted his commission as a Navy Lieutenant Commander We needed to be sure Jimmy was actually in the Navy before we awarded him the Navy Cross. The Admiral liked the citation as I had written it. No changes.

The Admiral had just gotten off the phone with Jimmy and let me know that Jimmy was pleased to accept his offer. He also said he was already working to push the paperwork through as quickly as possible. Earlier this morning he had gone straight to the top with a conference call to CNO Admiral Stinson; Chief of Naval Operations, the head of the Navy, a member of the Joint Chiefs of Staff, four stars; and CJCS Admiral Sterett, Chairman of the Joint Chiefs of Staff, reporting to the president. A position that could held by a four star general officer from the Army, Navy, Air Force or Marines. Both admirals were amazed that such a feat could have actually been accomplished. All three agreed that this young man should be in the Navy and that there should be no problem with the citation and resulting honors.

Chapter Seventy Five

ASDG Headquarters, San Diego, CA
Wednesday, January 9, 1991, 1420 hrs.

Secure message:

To: CMDR ASDG

From: CMDR JSOC

Subj: Status elevation; DEFCON 3

All U.S. Military forces will move to Defense Readiness
Condition (DEFCON) 3 this day at 1800 hrs. Meeting with
Iraqi Foreign Minister Tariq Aziz failed…

Not really a surprise. I called Jenny in to review the process of
contacting my staff and having each of them report back when
action on the notification was complete for their respective units.
We were already at DEFCON 4 so this process shouldn't take
more than a few hours for notification and conformation and then a
week for us to implement.

We expected Saddam to use missiles on Israel and we had a
pretty good idea of when and where.

When would be early in the conflict. Bringing Israel into the
conflict would no doubt alienate some Arab opponents starting

with Syria, Lebanon and Iran. But it was obvious that Saddam thought it would go much farther than that. It appeared that he expected all Arab Nations to fall in with him against the coalition. Of course the more aggressive the Israelis became the quicker the other Arab nations would join a rising Arab force. I guess he was expecting this to roll up to world war three. Nuclear weapons would definitely raise the probability of a major conflict but not unlimited nuclear war. It would take Chinese and/or Russian intervention to cause that level of escalation. At least that was the U.S. thinking at this point. Especially since we knew Saddam had no nuclear weapons.

Where would likely be Haifa and/or Tel Aviv. Not Jerusalem.

There was also growing concern that later in the looming conflict Saddam might launch missiles toward Saudi Arabia, Bahrain, Qatar, the United Arab Emirates or even Turkey. In which case Riyadh, Manama, Abu Dhabi and Ankara would be, respectively, the most likely targets, although western intelligence was not aware of any military infrastructure close enough to Ankara to allow an Iraqi missile strike.

In the late eighties the U.S. defensive strategy for destroying in-flight Soviet Inter Continental Ballistic Missiles with space-borne laser beams, called the *Strategic Defense Initiative* (SDI) or "Star Wars" by the press, did its job of unsettling the Soviet Union to the point of collapse. Star Wars was never completed or tested but it caused the Soviet Union to increase it's defense budget to the exclusion of a sustainable government infrastructure resulting in an economic collapse in 1989/90. It's certain that the nuclear meltdown at Chernobyl in 1986 also plaid a part in the fiscal collapse of the USSR. That being said, shooting down a ballistic missile whether it be inter-continental or a medium range SCUD is not an easy thing to do. With the onset of the desert wars of the nineties the United States was seriously trying to solve the

DAWN'S EARLY LIGHT

problems associated with hitting a medium range supersonic ballistic missile whose rocket motor had been shut down long enough to eliminate any heat signature strong enough to home on. This was not a job that current missile radar technology could handle. So the system was designed using a ground based phased array radar as the heart of its guidance system. Shooting down a ballistic missile traveling at mach five with another missile traveling near mach three with a system containing a ground based radar, computer and radio link in the control loop isn't easy either. It took a while to perfect.

In war, deception is a tool not to be overlooked. Deception certainly played an important role in the successful execution of Operation Overlord (D-Day) in world War Two. And certainly it was critical in the 1953 Argo mission (also known as the 'Canadian Caper') to spirit six U.S. diplomats out of Iran in early 1980, three months before the fateful disaster known as 'Operation Eagle Claw' where eight U.S service men were killed when an RH-53D helicopter collided with an EC-130 transport aircraft being used as a refueling station in a dust storm. And it would play a very important role in the coming war – if we did in fact go to war with Iraq.

That the United States would allow, or maybe even encourage, the touting of a weapon system that was privately known to be short of its specified design goals and untested in its anti-ballistic missile role to be considered as the 'solution to the SCUD threat', is certainly understandable given the potential global exposure to a SCUD enabled nuclear war.

So it came to pass. . .

Chapter Seventy Six

Later in January, 1991
Various Locations

United States Congress, Joint Session January 12, 1991

The United States Congress passed a joint resolution authorizing military force in Iraq and Kuwait. The resolution passed fifty two to forty seven in the Senate and two hundred fifty to one hundred eighty three in the House. Certainly not a mandate. In fact it was the closest margin in any similar authorization since the War of Eighteen Twelve.

January 15, 1991

The United States announces Operation Desert Storm.

Iraq continues to ignore U.N. resolutions and U.S. warnings.

January 16, 1991

Coalition forces begin deployment into Kuwait to support a massive forty two day air campaign to destroy the Iraqi anti-

DAWN'S EARLY LIGHT

aircraft command and control military infrastructure throughout the country.

January 17, 1991

Operation Desert Storm is launched. The initial air strikes are launched in Iraq and Kuwait. The U.S. deploys Patriot Missiles to Kuwait, Israel and Saudi Arabia.

January 18, 1991

Iraq launches twelve SCUD missiles at Haifa and Tel Aviv. Twelve people are killed. These twelve missiles all hit the ground. The Kazi warheads would have produced a non nuclear explosion at twelve hundred feet. Probably breaking some windows and minor destruction. Maybe nothing more serious. The Kazakhstani warheads were *not* launched. The United States convinces the Israelis to remain calm and not enter the fray.

January 19, 1991

Iraq launches a single SCUD missile at Haifa, Israel. The missile explodes at twelve hundred feet. The United States, backed by Israeli 'eye witnesses', claims success with a high altitude intercept by the first Patriot missile to be fired from the newly operational installation at Haifa causing minor damage on the ground with no nuclear traces. The United States is quick to make a public apology to Israel for the delay in bringing the Israeli Patriot installations on line at Haifa and Tel Aviv. A six month old film clip from the only successful night time Patriot missile test to date was shown to the world as the actual destruction of the Iraqi SCUD missile. The U.S. publicly assures Israel, Saudi Arabia and Kuwait that they are now fully protected. Only a few trusted leaders from each country are aware of the real facts.

January 21, 1991

Iraq launches six SCUD missiles. Two at Haifa, two at Tel Aviv and two at Ramat David Air Base. The missiles fired at Haifa cause minor damage; one person killed and two suffered minor wounds. One missile struck harmlessly in the Mediterranean Sea a half mile offshore; the other struck a date farm on the southern outskirts of Haifa with aforementioned casualties. The missiles fired at Tel Aviv also missed the densely populated central area of the city claiming two lives and two wounded. The missiles fired at Ramat David Air Base claim eight lives with eleven wounded.

Israel and the United States immediately claim Patriot success in Haifa and Tel Aviv – missiles disabled in flight, no casualties. Unfortunately, the Ramat David Air Base Patriot installation was not yet complete.

The United States announces that the twelve additional Patriot Missile installations under way in Israel, the eight additional installations in Saudi Arabia and the two installations in Bahrain and Qatar, all currently under way, are being accelerated and should be complete in less than three days.

January 23, 1991

Iraq launches twelve more SCUD missiles at smaller Israeli cites. The missiles miss the smaller cities causing only two deaths and minor damage.

With large cities believed to be protected and the apparent low casualty effectiveness on smaller cities Saddam Hussein abandon's his missile strategy.

No more SCUD missiles are launched by Iraq.

DAWN'S EARLY LIGHT

January 26, 1991

In a small ceremony held in the Oval Office of the White House on this Saturday afternoon James Richard McDaniel received his Navy Cross immediately after accepting a commission in the United Stated Navy as a Lieutenant Commander. The presentation was made by President Bradley Stevens and attended by Chief of Naval Operations, Admiral Robert Stinson; Chairman of the Joint Chiefs of Staff, Admiral Gerald Sterett and Commander, Joint Special Operations Command, Rear Admiral George Bennington *and* yours truly.

January 31, 1991

The United States announces that the installation of a total of twenty seven Patriot missile sites in the major cities of South Korea, Japan and Taiwan is complete and the systems are operational.

In Iraq sanity prevailed, praise the Lord!- - -North Korea?

After the Gulf War, reports on the analysis of unclassified video footage captured by various news cameramen during the Desert Storm conflict shows the effectiveness of the Patriot missile defense system to be somewhere between zero and ten percent.[1] These reports were suppressed for over a year.

---

[1] *Optical Evidence Indicating Patriot High Miss Rates During the Gulf War* Theodore A. Postol, Professor of Science, Technology, and National Security Policy, Massachusetts Institute of Technology. Committee on Government Operations, U.S. House of Representatives, April 7th 1992.

Epilogue

McKensie Condo, La Jolla, CA
Halloween, 1998, 1730 hrs.

Life had been good to us this year. A little hectic at times with Ashleigh and I both still very active in our respective Navy careers. But all things considered, good. Very good! After Scotty's birth Ash reclaimed her position of second in command at Top Gun, but her command advancement opportunity remained very limited due to the narrow command structure at the Navy Fighter Weapons School. There's Captain Dirk Erickson, Commander and then there's Commander Ashleigh McKensie, XO. And Dirk's not ready to retire just yet. So a couple years ago when I got my eagles for my ASDG command I also captured the much coveted position of 'Commander, Household'. And I'm still having to remind her almost daily of who's in charge – you'd think she'd learn!

We had settled into a life that was probably becoming a little too routine. While most SEALs my age – I'm only thirty seven now -- were spending the majority of their professional lives either down range or training with their teams, I found myself spending too much of my time planning operations and dealing with logistics, development programs, budgets and funding of all of this. Not a tough job but I really miss the adrenaline induced action of night time ASDS missions. It has become ingrained in my self

DAWN'S EARLY LIGHT

image. I had never imagined myself in a "desk job" this early in life. I'm worried that I will lose my fighting edge. From an income and career path perspective, I couldn't ask for more. I just need to figure out how to get my self involved in a little down range action. Keep my dogs in the fight. Hmmm, maybe delegate logistics and planning to Rob and Vince

It had been a tough week. Ash had spent Monday through Wednesday on her fourth - this year - ROTC 'Blue Angel Tour' as they had come to be known by Naval ROTC organizations all over the country. This trip was to Texas A&M University, College Station, Texas. For the first time since Scotty was born we experienced a schedule conflict that required intervention. Lieutenant Colonel Vincent Harlow, Delta Operator and Executive Officer of the Advanced System Development Group (ASDG) known as the Black Angel Squadron to the President, the CIA, the Joint Chiefs and the President's National Security Council, came down with the flu. The only other team leader I had with the knowledge and experience to handle the delicate extraction mission at hand was already down range. So it looked like I was going to going to get some of the action I was craving – and I did. I left a week ago Friday morning to lead the mission and returned last night. It was a touchy but benign extraction mission, no shots fired, way too routine when compared to a lot of my missions as a Black Angel. Probably a good thing. So Ash asked her mom to come over for three days to watch the kids while she did her ROTC thing. Ash's father, retired Navy captain Stephen Garrison passed away two years ago from a heart attack while running his daily five miles. So her mother, Helen, had moved down to El Cajon to be near us and Ash's brother Mark who lives there.

Oh, almost forgot; you are correct, I said kid<u>s</u>. Scotty's little sister, Kaylie, is almost five now. She's going to be (already is) just as beautiful as her mom. Anyway we were getting ready to take the kids out trick-or-treating on this beautiful Saturday evening and Ash is calling me from the living room;

"Sam, come in here just a minute."

She was in the living room watching the five o'clock news.

She had rewound the DVR and said, "Listen to this."

The news anchor repeated himself; ". . . Dubbed *The Iraq Liberation Act of 1998,* the bill was introduced as H.R. 4655 on September 29. The House of Representatives passed the bill 360 - 38 on October 5, and the Senate passed it by unanimous consent on October 7. The President signed the Iraq Liberation Act into law this morning. The Act reads;

"It should be the policy of the United States to support efforts to remove the regime headed by Saddam Hussein from power in Iraq. . . ."

"What the hell does that mean?," Ash wondered out loud.

I threw in my two cents. "Sounds like more nation building to me. It probably means we're not done with our time in the desert."

Maybe I'll get some of the action I've been craving. . .

December 16, 1998

The Fox News *Morning Report* anchor; "This morning, in Iraq, the United States and the United Kingdom commenced *Operation Desert Fox,* a four day bombing campaign intended to destroy much of Saddam Hussein's cache of weapons of mass destruction along with the infrastructure he has amassed to produce them. Justification for the strikes was Iraq's failure to comply with United Nations Security Council resolutions and its interference with United Nations Special Commission inspectors."

And the beat goes on. . .

DAWN'S EARLY LIGHT

A Word About Acronyms

I find it almost impossible to operate within the Military Thriller Genre without acronyms. The United States (US) military is fraught with them. They have acronyms within acronyms. So, what to do? After muddling through this issue in my first book *Angels Three Five,* where necessary, I decided to treat acronyms like this:

First use	Air to Ground Missile (AGM)
Second use	AGM (Air to Ground Missile)
Third and subsequent use	AGM

This gives the reader two commonly used representations of the acronym's definition and a higher probability of retention. Of course, although the genre regulars probably don't need this extra representation, my hope is they won't take offense. During my market research I have engaged several book clubs and gotten some interesting feedback. From the in-genre clubs; positive feedback on the story-line and realism with no comments on acronyms. From the out-of-genre clubs; praise for the handling of acronyms and explanation of weapons systems.

Ann Andrews, founder of *Support for Indie Authors* wrote on *Goodreads:*

"I often find that military thrillers are written for people in the military. The lingo, abbreviations, codes, etc. often go over my head and leave me feeling like I'm missing out on a huge aspect of the plot. Fortunately, Don Candy has written Angels Three Five with easy to read prose that answered all of my questions regarding lingo and other military terminology before I even had a chance to mentally ask the question!"

My goal is to attempt to satisfy both groups.

DAWN'S EARLY LIGHT

Acronyms

AAA	Anti Aircraft Artillery
ADCAP	ADvanced CAPability Mark 48 torpedo
ADF	Automatic Direction Finder
AGL	Above Ground Level
AGM	Air to Ground Missile
AIM	Air Intercept Missile
ALS	Automatic Landing System
AMRAAM	Advanced Medium Range Air to Air Missile
ASDG	Advanced Systems Development Group
ASDS	Airborne SEAL Delivery System
BAT	Black Angels Team
CAG	Commander Air Group
CAPV	Covert Air Penetration Vehicle
CDT	Central Daylight Time
CH	Commander, Household
CIA	Central Intelligence Agency
COB	Chief Of the Boat
COMSUBGRU	COMmander SUBmarine GRoUp
COMSUBPAC	COMmander SUBmarine PACific Fleet
CRRC	Combat Rubber Raiding Craft
CST	Central Standard Time
CJCS	Chairman, Joint Chiefs of Staff
ECM	Electronic Counter Measures
EDT	Eastern Daylight Time
EST	Eastern Standard Time
EWO	Electronic Warfare Officer
DEVGRU	Special Forces DEVelopment GRoUp (SEAL Team 6)
DGPS	Differential Global Positioning System
ETA	Estimated Time of Arrival
EP	Exfil Point
F/A	Fighter / Attack Aircraft
GMT	Greenwich Mean Time (also ZULU)
GPS	Global Positioning System
HAHO	High Altitude High Opening
HALO	High Altitude Low Opening
HARM	High speed Anti Radiation Missile
HSD	Horizontal Situation Display
HSSM	Heat Seeking Shoulder-mounted Missile
IFR	Instrument Flight Rules
IP	Initial Position from which each mission is executed
IR	Infra Red
JFS	Jameson Flight Service
JSOC	Joint Special Operations Command
LADAR/LIDAR	LAser Detection And Ranging / Laser Imaging Detection And Ranging

DAWN'S EARLY LIGHT

LF	Low Frequency
MDT	Mountain Daylight Time
MiG	Mikoyan Gurevich aircraft (Russian)
MRE	Meal Ready to Eat
MST	Mountain Standard Time
NAF	Naval Air Facility
NAS	Naval Air Station
NATO	North Atlantic Treaty Organization
NDA	Non Disclosure Agreement
NDS	Nighthawk Delivery System
NFWS	Navy Fighter Weapons School (Top Gun)
NSA	National Security Agency
NSWDG	Naval Special Warfare Development Group (DEVGRU)
NTK	Need To Know
NVA	North Vietnam Army
NWC	Naval Weapons Center, China Lake
OCS	Officer Candidate School
ORNL	Oak Ridge National Laboratory
PDT	Pacific Daylight Time
POTUS	President of The United States
PST	Pacific Standard Time
RADAR	RAdio Detection And Ranging
ROTC	Reserve Officers Training Corps
RT	Recon Target
SAM	Surface to Air Missile
SATCOM	SATellite COMmunications network
SEAL	Navy SEa Air and Land Special Forces
SECDEF	SECtary of DEFense
SF / SOF	Special Forces / Special Operations Forces
SOAR	Special Operations Airborne Regiment (Army)
SOFLAM	Special Operations Forces Laser Acquisition Marker
SONAR	SOund Navigation And Ranging
SSN	Nuclear powered submarine
TI	Texas Instruments, Inc
TS	Top Secret
TSNTK	Top Secret, Need To Know (Compartmentalized)
UHF	Ultra High Frequency
ULF	Ultra Low Frequency
USECDEF	Under SECretaty of DEFense
USS	United States Ship
UTM	Universal Transverse Mercator
VFR	Visual Flight Rules
VHF	Very High Frequency
VLF	Very Low Frequency
VOQ	Visiting Officers Quarters
YPG	Yuma Proving Ground
ZULU	Greenwich Mean Time (also GMT)

Made in the USA
Columbia, SC
27 February 2019